William M

Fankwei

SALZWASSER VERLAG

William Maxwell Wood

Fankwei

Reprint of the original, first published in 1859.

1st Edition 2022 | ISBN: 978-3-37512-856-2

Verlag (Publisher): Salzwasser Verlag GmbH, Zeilweg 44, 60439 Frankfurt, Deutschland
Vertretungsberechtigt (Authorized to represent): E. Roepke, Zeilweg 44, 60439 Frankfurt, Deutschland
Druck (Print): Books on Demand GmbH, In de Tarpen 42, 22848 Norderstedt, Deutschland

FANKWEI;

OR,

THE SAN JACINTO IN THE SEAS

OF

INDIA, CHINA AND JAPAN.

BY

WILLIAM MAXWELL WOOD, M. D., U. S. N.,

LATE SURGEON OF THE FLEET TO THE UNITED STATES EAST INDIA SQUADRON;
AUTHOR OF "WANDERING SKETCHES IN SOUTH AMERICA, POLYNESIA,"
ETC.; "A SHOULDER TO THE WHEEL OF PROGRESS," ETC.

NEW YORK:
HARPER & BROTHERS,
FRANKLIN SQUARE.

1859.

TO

THE HON. THOMAS CARSON,

OF MERCERSBURGH, PENNSYLVANIA,

This book was dedicated in life, as an offering of respect for one of whom the following has been publicly said:

"His sterling integrity and uniform fidelity to all official duties intrusted to him, stamp him as one of the few public men in our commonwealth who are proof against all the seductive influences of public life.

"One whose large abilities and clear perceptions are overshadowed by his modest demeanor and freedom from the arts of the popular politician."

Under that more noble title which he won amongst men, and which will serve him better in the world "of the hereafter" to which he has passed, it is now inscribed to the memory of

"HONEST TOM CARSON."

A FEW FIRST WORDS WITH THE READER.

THE sunsets on our great lakes are peculiarly beautiful, and scarcely a bright day closes into evening without attracting admiration by its varied pictures of colored and gilded cloud-scenes. As I have looked upon them with a group of friends, each one beholds scenes unnoticed or unrecognized by others. Some see human figures in forms which are to others those of grotesque animals; and what to one may be burning cities or embattled armies, is to another but a confused and unmeaning cloud mass.

Thus do we all see differently what has the same external form, and hence a reason for writing many books upon even frequently-described countries and peoples. It is not the ground over which the traveler goes which alone appears in his book, but the individuality of him who observes it. Each prismatic observer presents his own colored ray to make up the clear beam of truth; and no aggregate description of multiplied observers will make foreign nations accurately acquainted with each other, even when in close proximity, or derived from the same stock.

There is, then, room for my gatherings from the remote regions respecting which I write, and I am conscious they will not be missed from the vast mass left for other observers and future years.

In addition to this justification for presenting the public with the present volume, I have been for thirty years by necessity of position an observer in an important national institution, with its own peculiar usages and internal politics. It has been my conviction, from an early period, that this institution, in its organic structure, was not in harmony with our national character; not a natural emanation from it, but a graft from a morbid outgrowth of systems we have rejected as wrong in themselves or inapplicable to us. The only reform which has yet taken place in the

Navy has been the spasmodic relief of a temporary and pressing necessity. No active principle of a self-acting and permanent character has yet been introduced. Conservatism, which in general society is but a healthy regulator of progress, becomes, in a limited military institution, an institution of rules and precedents, an immovable and enormous mass of dead weight; and it is not surprising that the individual representatives of this quality should think that reform was sending the whole Navy to that being who was so early and so effectively busy in Eden, and who may perhaps be found in our establishment, especially if he is correctly described as one

> "On whose nature
> Nurture can never stick; on whom all pains
> Humanely taken, all, all quite lost;
> And as with age his body uglier grows,
> So his mind cankers."

As one party is so desirous of keeping the Navy from going to him, and the other of getting him out of it, there is hope that so wholesome a rivalry, shared equally by each, will secure his final discomfiture.

Most of the time of these travels was among that people who, claiming to be Celestial themselves, regard every Western as a Fankwei, or "foreign devil."

As Fankwei and Celestial we saw each other, and as Fankwei I tell the story.

CONTENTS.

THE VOYAGE OUT.

SIAM AND THE SIAMESE.

IN CHINA.

FANKWEI.

I.

THE VOYAGE OUT.

THE VOYAGE OUT.

I.

ON BOARD AND OFF.

It was a murky October evening as my friend and I stood at the foot of that great thoroughfare, which is at once the pride and the nuisance of New York. Our parting words were spoken to the sulky dashing of the waves against the shores of the "Battery."

"A pleasant cruise—an interesting cruise—you are going to have," were his words as we shook hands and said "Good-bye."

A pleasant cruise! an interesting cruise! They were soft-sounding words, but it was the vinegar upon niter—the singing of songs to a heavy heart.

He might well have music upon his tongue, for he turned to walk up that broad, bright avenue, whose myriad lights were just beginning to blaze upon the increasing darkness, and his day would close amid the endearments of home. But I, with a number of small parcels, the last gatherings of conveniences for shipboard existence, stepped into a small boat, and with a few strokes of the boatman's oars, we shot out upon the dark waters, and I had left the shores of my country at best for years. We glided through the ships, heaving and rolling at their moorings, and in a few minutes I and my bundles were passed up the sides of a clumsy, black-looking vessel, with a smoke stack protruding from the deck, and guns projecting from her sides.

It was once more a shivering plunge into the ceremonies, the restrictions, the petty formalities, and mole-hill mountain jealousies and privileges—to say nothing of the physical privations — of man-of-war life. If I tell the reader what these are, it is not to weary him with unhappy complaints; but to deal justly by him, and to present him, in this narrative, not only with the scenes before my eyes, but also with the spirit which looked out upon them, and to show, I hope, for the good of those who come after me, how many gratuitous annoyances are added to those necessarily incident to a naval life.

To appreciate to the full this unnatural existence, one must have a nature which leads him from even the splendid trammels of city life, must have formed many of his habits in the freedom of a frontier residence, and learned to love his country, not alone because it was his country, but because of his close communion with its inmost nature. He must have courted that nature's varying forms, and true to its beauty alone, have been won by the attractions of each new season from any regrets for the enjoyments of that passing away. Welcoming the bursting life and budding blossoms of spring, he yields their fresh fragrance, to wander, with riper affections, amid summer heats, by babbling brooks, in deep forest shades, or over fields golden in the setting sun;—and wished no change until his eye caught the first crimsoning of autumn's gorgeous garment, fluttering on the forest's edge. Satiated with rich luxuriance and brilliant hues, he reposes in the soft languor of an Indian summer's haze, until, in the bracing air of a northern sky, brightly arching over the snow-clad earth, in the sleep of nature, human energies and activities spring into new life and vigor. The crashing forest falls beneath the woodman's ax; the full contents of barns and granaries glide on smooth runners, cumbrously silent, over the frozen roads; while the jingling bells of sleighs dashing over the crisping snow are in harmony with all this life and motion.

With evening comes the gathering from the sports and labors of the short day; the social union of friend and neighbor, with all those heart-interests and affections which cluster around the winter evening's fireside.

> "What should gild the wheat in harvest,
> If the spring endured forever?
> How should apples in the garden
> Ripen were it always summer?
> How should wheat sheaf be up-gathered
> If there were no time but autumn?"

From these memories, vividly recalled, the transition was to oakum and bilge water; to *my* room, dark, cramped and dreary; six feet square, broken upon by crooked ship-knees and heavy beams. Permissions to go and orders to come, given by strange men younger than myself, whom I never saw before; my light at mid-day an allowanced candle, and that blown out at ten o'clock at night by an humble ship official, whether I would or no. A booming gun and the reveille of a rolling drum awake me at daylight, and the same sounds tattoo the closing day.

The day lowered in congenial gloom, the wind moaned and sighed through the rigging; a cold, drizzling rain of October 24, 1855, baptized my first day on board the United States steam frigate San Jacinto—the beginning of from two to three years of such an existence.

I sat in my *state-room.* It was the Surgeon's room—the fourth one—the last but one back on the port side.

The Chief Engineer, the Master, the Purser, were all ahead of me, although in age and service I was by much the oldest officer in that mess; and, except the commander-in-chief, the oldest in age in the ship. At this time I am in my thirtieth year of service; and twenty-nine years ago, as acting surgeon of a sloop-of-war, I inhabited the same relative cell. Time and service had brought no change of position, of privileges, of physical comfort in my shipboard life. I was worse off: then there were youth and hope to buoy me over annoyances, and my companions were of congenial years; now I was alone. Those of my original associates who were left—and they were but few—as captains and commodores were separated from me by duties, rank and distant stations. Of the occupants of the nine state-rooms besides my own, all, save one, were strangers to me. The difficulty of forming social intimacies increases with years; and I could not expect the tastes, sympathies or conversation of those so much younger than myself, to accord with my own. I had now the high sounding title of the "Surgeon of the Fleet," with its real duties and responsibilities, but this was simply a gilded cap upon my head, while I was left shivering in the tatters of the old garments of my youth and more humble position.

Our ship was filled with boxes of presents for the King of Siam. Immense mirrors, large chandeliers, clocks, and various other articles, show that we have some designs upon the good will of their Siamese majesties.

On the following morning the outside world brightened up a little; and it was a fine, cold, clear October morning, when we passed out to sea through all the beauties of the harbor of New York. Our first port is a dead secret; because, if we all knew that, the commanding officers would be no wiser than ourselves, and the profound humbug of mysteries would be lost to our wonder. This much we do know, that we are to go to Pulo Pinang, in the Straits of Malacca, and take on board the Hon. Townsend Harris, Consul General to Japan.

At our first Sunday morning muster we had read to us the articles of war in all their thundering terrors, and the ever recurring penalty which closes so many offenses: "Death, or such other punishment as a court martial shall adjudge"—the bullet and the halter.

There seems to be among us a strange overlooking, or inconsistent view of human nature, or Navy nature is not human nature. In the first place, there is an expectation that every one who goes on board of a man-of-war is to hold all sorts of death—hanging, shooting or drowning—in utter contempt. Indeed, he is to seek them as the natural end of existence, and to be hung or shot for avoiding them; and yet these are the official threats.

> "To haud the wretch in order."

And once a month, on sacred Sabbath mornings, they are ferociously shaken over our heads, begetting no other feelings than contempt or defiance.

The assembled wisdom of the nation, by slow and painful processes, got a kind of inkling that terror and threats were not the most expedient means of governing the American seaman; and they devised a code which, in pay, privileges and honorable testimonies, offers a reward for fidelity and obedience. But this ray of sunshine was not permitted to gleam through the cloud of the death penalty and the gloom of the articles of war. It was a mistake. How many besides Chinese are befogged by "ola custom!"

II.

CLOTH.

On two successive Sundays we had first an undress and then a full-dress uniform muster. Our costume has been inflicted upon us by some golden-fancied authority; and devised by a rule of wide departure from the fitness of things. It is to be hoped that imprecations, as well as prayers of better significance, have their efficiency at least modified by the source from which they emanate; otherwise I should fear much for those who perpetuate cocked hats and full-dress blue cloth coats lined with white silk and stiffened with embroidery.

It was a busy scene in all our apartments on the Sunday of that full-dress muster. Gold and glitter all about —hanging over the chairs and lying on the tables. Officers and their servants busy in tying epaulets upon the shoulders of these same white-silk-lined, blue cloth, embroidered coats; buckling on swords, and giving the right swing to sword-knots, the accurate range to the sharp corners of their cocked hats. An animated running commentary was kept up during these proceedings.

"Twenty dollars for this thing, case and all!" said one, as he looked in the glass and gave his cocked hat a little twist, bringing it obliquely across his face.

"And fifty dollars for this coat, to lie in my locker and blacken with bilge water. We wear them now to show that we have them; and shall not perhaps use them again during the whole cruise."

"Seventy dollars for hat and coat; yes you may say a hundred sunk in things we shall never want," said a third.

"It would lay in a whole outfit of shirts and stockings."

"It would school a young lady for a year," said a prudent father.

"It would buy an eighty acre lot," said a prospective farmer.

But, my friends, this time the folly may be excusable. We are going to Siam—we are paraded against barbaric pomp and must outshine the Orientals.

"All hands to muster, gentlemen," said a messenger boy; and we proceeded to the deck, where the crew were already assembled in dark blue cloth.

Guided by splendor of decoration, the eye, in marking our distinctions, would first light upon the Commander of the Marines. I can not undertake to analyze the elegant amalgamation and blending of dark blue, of brilliant crimson, and dazzling decorations which made up his costume. The officers of the line—the Captain and Lieutenants—were bound in golden bands around collar and cuffs; the seams of their pantaloons being broadly striped with glittering lace. We of the staff—Engineer, Purser, Medical Officers—symboled the vigor and enduring vitality of our country by modest wreaths of the acorn and leaves of the live oak. The olive-branch and paddle wheel on the collars of the Engineers designated their special vocation and spoke of the peaceful progress of art and science. There were smaller lights whose twinkle was scarcely noticed in this golden blaze.

"Stand in a line, gentlemen," said the First Lieutenant; "the Captain wants to see that you are all right;" and the Captain marched slowly down the line scrutinizing our costume closely. We were pronounced "right;" and the ceremony was over.

If all that which is now but tawdry decoration had a purpose of practical utility;—if epaulets were steel plates to defend the shoulders from sword cuts, and crimson sashes were for stanching blood and bearing off the wounded—they might be in accordance with common sense. However, there is yet hope, even for Uniform Boards. The time was when they cuffed and caped me in sable velvet, and tapered me off in white small-clothes, and silk stockings, and gold knee and shoe-buckles.

The inappropriate and expensive character of the uniform of officers is, however, a small matter compared with the infliction of an unsightly and distasteful garb upon the crew—adding another to the unnecessary disgusts of public service. There are few things in which seamen are more tenacious than in the fitness of their costume; and yet our authorities have imposed upon them a dress burlesque and unsightly, and so distasteful as to have excited general dissatisfaction. It consists in appending large white duck cuffs and collars to their blue flannel shirts.

We had been at sea some time, when another muster of costume was ordered, to see if these supplements were appended to the shirts.

Of a supply of green turtle we had on board, all had gone but one burly reptile of about five hundred pounds' weight, belonging to the Commodore. This fellow lay conspicuously on one side of the deck, back up and flippers spread out. Silent, solemn, and sombre as he was, the first proclamation of dissatisfaction with the order came from this turtle. He was found one morning with a broad muslin collar tied around his throat and folded back upon his warty shell, and a broad cuff folded back on each fore-flipper. Ridiculous as he looked, in a short time the crew of the San Jacinto looked just as ridiculous. The muster came, and as we stepped upon deck, where all the crew were assembled, it was difficult to suppress a smile at their appearance. The expanse of white collar and cuffs, contrasted with their dark blue clothes, made each weather-beaten, knotted, gnarled, bearded head seem to emerge from a child's pinafore pinned behind.

"Jack," said one, "you look like you had stolen a sheep and was carrying it home, with its legs tied round your neck."

"I feel just that way," replied Jack.

"Our men look," said one of the Lieutenants to me, as he passed, with a suppressed smile, on the quarter deck, "as though they had been robbing a washerwoman's hedge of napkins and towels."

It must be admitted that some of the men, to ridicule their unsightly dress, had enlarged the borders of their garments, and a few of these muslin mutineers were, after muster, arraigned for reproof; but the men had so much the sympathy of the officers that not much came of it. I never heard of any being punished.

It seems impossible for the Navy to forgive Doctors for being at once respectable men and part of the naval service. But it must be admitted they deserve all they get. Any man who is so wanting in common sense as to be a doctor, and then, being worth any thing anywhere else, to enter the naval service, is guilty of such a violation of common discretion that he should be ever paying the appropriate penalty. It is too amusing to excite one's anger to notice the tenacity with which the "Line" of the Navy adhere to any thing which they may imagine in any degree tends to humiliate their medical brethren.

There was once upon a time, under the "old discipline," a regulation which said: "The Surgeon, or his assistant, must daily inspect the boilers and cooking utensils, in order that they may be kept perfectly clean. Their condition will be reported to the First Lieutenant."

"When, in some by-gone days to which the memory of man does not reach, the cooking utensils may have been of copper, and supposed to generate poisons, which the eye of science only could discover, such a rule would have been justifiable. Even in such a case, ordinary household cleanliness, ascertainable by any one, would have been the remedy. But now that the whole apparatus is nothing but good wholesome iron, it with every propriety comes under the supervision of the police of the deck upon which the galley is placed; and the disposition to impose the supervision upon the medical officers, as a specialty, is only a manifestation of that illiberal spirit which would delight in degrading them to a scullion's duty."*

The regulation upon this subject, after much dissatisfaction, defiance, and ridicule, fell into disuse, and was formally repealed by the Department, on the 24th of April, 1848. A discreditable attempt was subsequently made to revive it. The effort of commanding officers to minutely detail the duties of medical officers has always been a ridiculous failure; because, in proportion to the detail, the commanding officer assumes the responsibility of the medical officer's conscience and sense of duty; and he still has to leave every thing essential in his department to the skill, ability, and honor of that officer; and if these are not sufficient to render him useful in his vocation, there is no power that can.

Soon after getting to sea, the code of internal regulations was sent down to me, and the First Lieutenant especially called my attention to the one of inspecting the ship's coppers. Of course it was expunged when I called attention to the fact that it had been repealed eight years before.

But the United States is the only social paradise of doctors, and those who follow kindred humble and useful pursuits. They should always stay at home. This fact is the secret of the intense opposition which the line of the Navy has for so many years manifested toward any respectable rank and privileges being conferred upon their medical brethren. It is a historical fact that our

* Editorial *New York Times.*

Navy is not an outgrowth of our institutions, but of the British Navy; and except in a few very modern instances of spasmodic originality, has servilely copied it. Even the very uniform which the last board hatched, after a long incubation, is a literal copy of that then existing in the British service; and, like Laban's goats, they stole their golden streaks from staring upon models before their eyes; and as the stripes carried the goats of his father to Jacob, they bring vital vices from our paternal British fold to us. It is well known that doctors are not, in England, no more than mechanics or farmers, "first class people." They may be very respectable men; but there are social grades into which they are not only not born, but to which as doctors they can never be elevated; with which they never associate on an equal footing. Who ever heard of an English peer, or an English peer's youngest son, turning doctor? The places in the naval service are kept for these men, who are excluded from humble, useful pursuits. The naval doctors come from another sphere, and consequently all the arrangements of the service are to perpetuate these established distinctions of civil life. As we have no such distinctions in our country, when we are all doing the best we can at home on our small pay—Doctors, Captains, and Commodores, living in quiet streets and country towns—the Doctor does not think that he is patronized, and the Captain may be willing to acknowledge him as a social equal. The atmosphere of his country is upon him, and is too healthy for the fungus of disgusting pretension. But when, removed from that, they meet in squadron upon a foreign station, a new influence is upon us. There our line officers find that their compeers—the midshipmen, and the lieutenants, and the captains—are Prince So-and So, the Honorable Mr. So-and-So, or the son of Lord John, while the doctors are only the doctors—"merely middle and lower class men, you know." Some of our folks get a vague idea that as English naval line officers are princes and lords, American naval line officers are something of the same kind, and now they are very nervous as to the presumption of their medical brethren, and anxious to serve out the English law and custom to them, and lament the democracy which forbids it, forgetting to ask where and what the sons of their fathers would be under the institutions which put medical men in an inferior class? I know I have been very ungrateful for the patronizing manner of these gentlemen. Those who have reached to any thing like rank, if they have had any doctor friends in the squadron to whom they have been committed by imprudent intimacies at home, look upon them as a sort of poor relations. There is a kind of obligation to invite them to dinner occasionally, but not when any first class foreigners are present—a special patronizing sub affair must be got up for the purpose. All this is very natural, and only shows human weakness more than human wickedness. Few men have strength of character sufficient to rise above surrounding influences, even to wear a hat not the fashion, much less a principle; and it is scarcely to be expected of a service of routine, usage, and precedent, that it can represent abroad the glorious sublimity and originality of the social structure of our country, which the foreign associates upon whom we model can neither respect nor comprehend—indeed look upon with contempt. I speak only of classes and general influence; our service is so fortunate as to have in it those broad-minded men who are more proud of being and acting the American citizen than the American naval officer, and who do not dwarf the broad principles they represent into a persevering opposition to brother officers, who, equally with themselves, serve their common country, nor do they waste their energies in contests respecting strips of gold lace.

An excitement about what appeared at first to be a boat full of men, but which proved to be an abandoned wreck drifting about the ocean solitudes; a gale of wind which sent the sea washing through the stern ports impetuously, crushed and deluged the ward-room—our apartment—prostrated several with sea-sickness, rolled the San Jacinto terribly, dipping up the sea into her suspended boats on each side, and carrying away boats and davits, with our stock of potatoes and other vegetables, were the principal external incidents in our run from New York to Madeira.

III.

"SLUSH."

Some years ago, during a visit to the West, I was in one of those growing, active, and prosperous cities, the sight of which is a source of patriotic exultation. Its commerce, social elegance, architectural splendor; its temples of religion, halls of literature, and museums of art, were all resting upon that humble and despised animal who literally lards the lean earth, whose brilliant light is now outshining that of the waning whale, and whose solid substance is one of the foundations of our naval existence.

With the natural curiosity to see something of the processes by which these animals are brought into a condition of practical utility, I visited one of the most extensive slaughter-houses. Immense droves of swine in a large inclosure were grunting impatiently to enter a narrow passage, at the farther end of which swung a gate, which was, to every hog who passed it, the gate of death.

On its inner side he met the fatal knife, and his life-blood flowed a steady current into the neighboring river. Tumbled into vast cauldrons of boiling water, around which were crowded busy laborers, he passed with many of his fellows down the steamy tide, was stripped of his bristles, robbed of his bowels, and soon hung with distended limbs, clean and white, in a large room, amid whole platoons of his predecessors.

I am almost glad I have forgotten, as I should fear to write, the incredibly small space of time occupied in this whole process. Not one of these hogs is owned by the proprietors of the establishment. Its great outlay of capital, its capacious buildings, its corps of laborers, steam-engines, cauldrons and lard-vats, are all kept up to do their slaughtering gratuitously for the owners of the swine—better than gratuitously: the establishment pays a small charge for the privilege of doing the work, and finds an ample reward in the possession of the lumps of fat whieh are found adhering to the (I do not wish to offend ears polite) animal's interior arrangements. Such is the profit of small things.

The "Slush Fund" of a man-of-war owes its valuable accumulation to a like economical savings of the oozings and drippings of the same animal.

The manner of serving the rations is as follows: the crew is generally divided into messes of ten or twelve persons, and one of this number is called the "cook of the mess." *Lucus a non lucendo.* He does not cook, but takes care of the mess chest, the pots and pans of his mess, receives from the purser's steward the daily ration allotted them, ties the various articles in separate and appropriate bags and bundles, marks them with a tally or stick on which is cut the number of the mess. The rations are served out by the purser's steward, by tap of drum, on the day preceding that to which they belong.

Each mess cook delivers his share to the ship's cook, who prepares it all in the large apparatus under his charge. Just before the hour of serving he brings a sample to the officer of the deck, to show that it is properly done. The mess cooks spread black painted cloths upon the deck, arrange the pots and pans, receive their "grub" again from the ship's cook, and the boatswain's mates pipe all hands to their meals.

It must be distinctly understood that all this refers exclusively to the men or crew, each division of officers having its own apartment, its own cooking apparatus and special cook, because upon this distinction rests the uncertainty of the "Slush Fund."

This fund is the product of the sale of the grease skimmed from the water in which the crew's rations are boiled, and during a cruise it amounts to several hundred dollars. Now, where rests the proprietorship of this fund? With the crew, with the officers and ship generally, or with the United States government? It is a mooted question, unsettled by statute law or by that ocean of naval reference for doubtful points, the "usage of the sea service"—which latter, like other oceans, varies its currents with the varying winds, or, in other words, according to the changing opinions of commanding officers. I believe the government, for the first time, became a claimant on this fund in the following circumstances. It seems to have asserted the arbiter's right to the oyster, leaving the shell to the litigants.

NAVY DEPARTMENT, September 29, 1855.

SIR:—Your letter of the 28th instant, requesting authority to ship a band, and for the purchase of musical instruments for the "San Jacinto" has been received.

The Commandant at New York has been directed to cause a band to be enlisted.

You will direct the purchase of the musical instruments, and the payment, for the present, out of "Contingent," to be replaced, in time, from the "Slush Fund."

I am respectfully,

Your obedient servant,

J. C. DOBBIN.

Commander H. H. BELL,

Commanding U. S. Steam Frigate "San Jacinto," New York.

This then led to various expressions of opinion. One party contended that the "Slush Fund" belonged exclusively to the crew out of whose flesh it came, and that it should be expended, for their benefit, for such ship indulgences, in which the crew could participate, as the government did not allow; or for salutary fruits for their use when in port. This party admitted that a band might be a legitimate claim upon the "Slush Fund," provided a band was not regularly allowed by the government, because the crew had the benefit of the music. But the band being a regular government allowance to a "flag ship," to tax the "Slush Fund" with it, this party contended, was the rich man's infringement upon Naboth's vineyard.

Another party, I think it might be called a minority opposition—but I may be prejudiced in my judgment, as I belong to the other side—contended that although the "slush" did ooze out of the crew's meat, yet, as they could not individually save and take care of it, but this had to be done by the ship, therefore it might be expended for decorations of the ship and of the boats, and such other things in which the crew had no special interest. This argument was replied to by saying that the ship was bound either to furnish the men with the means of taking care of their slush, or else to take care of it for them.

Sometimes, in the uncertainty of the matter, both parties agree to hand it over to some charity. I heard of no faction sustaining the claim of the government, which may have arisen from the tendency of human nature not to side with the strongest party, no matter how just its claims may be. This question, like many others, is still an unsettled one. It may ever remain such, as it involves principles of right, of interest, and of power. Thus far power has it, and as most of the questions which agitate the various able debating societies spread over our land have lost the interest of novelty, I recommend this to their notice, suggesting that they may favor the ends of justice by communicating their conclusions to the federal government.

IV.

MADEIRA.

But little over two weeks since we left New York—just sixteen days—but days of such shipboard tedium and discomfort, they seem as many weeks, and now on a bright Sunday morning, November 11th, we are running along the mountain shores of Madeira, with its white villages and cottages perched along, and, one above another, far up the mountain side.

Soft and balmy is the air; blue, and gently rippling, the sea stretches away on our right hand; while on the left—rocky, brown, red and purple—the mountain island rises from the ocean. At such time and in such a scene one may be excused a little poetical emotion—nay, would not one without it have that unmusical soul which the master of the human heart has told is "fit for treason, stratagem and spoil?" Islands, all islands, are poetical existences in themselves; their philosophy is poetry: growing gradually from the deep sea depths by the microscopic labors of the coral insect, or thrust at once into the upper air amid earthquake throes and volcanic convulsions shaking the earth to its center. Mysterious in their sea boundaries—cut off from the grave, solid, unchanging character of the main land—they are the abodes of Calypsos, of pirate heroes and goat-skin clad Crusoes. But Madeira has its own special story to tell—a story of its first discovery being one of a love whose roughened course was o'er the stormy sea. Somewhere about five hundred years ago, when Edward the Third was King of England, the beautiful and noble Anna D'Arfet was loved and approved the love of Robert Machim, a gentleman of low degree. After the natural series of mishaps, impediments and other family obstacles consequent upon so unequal an attachment, the pair attempted to fly to France, but were driven they knew not whither by a violent storm, and in ten days were cast ashore on this island. Here the unfortunate Anna died of grief and suffering soon after landing, and Robert, refusing all food, in a few days was laid by her side. His followers erected a cross over the graves, and a request that the first Christians might build a chapel on the spot, and then leaving the island, some of them communicated these facts to Gonçalves Tarco, and Tristam Vaz, who in 1420 took possession of the place for the King of Portugal. In memory of Robert Machim they called the bay in which he had landed Machico. The church has been built over the graves of the lovers, and a piece of the cross which marked the spot is still retained as a relic. This was however but a rediscovery. The islands were known before the Christian era, and were subsequently called the Purple islands, by Juba, who had a scheme for manufacturing the Gætulian purple; and the Desertas, as the barren and rocky islets near Madeira are called, at this day furnish the orchil, a beautiful purple dye, and hence the name. Zarco, from the forests covering the mountain sides, gave it the name it still retains—Madeira.

But Madeira, to the wide world, does not mean the island or its forests. Soon after the occupation of the island, Prince Henry, son of King John of Portugal, sent the colony seeds and the materials of agriculture. Among them were a few slips of vine from the isle of Cyprus. What a future was before those vine slips; and where have they not borne the word "Madeira," associated with the glowing liquid which had its origin in them, and upon which the fortunes of the island have flowed? In the northern palaces of the Muscovite and the castles of the German. Diffusing its blessings with that of constitutional government, it appears on the table of both cit and noble, dispelling the gloom of England's fogs. Adopted by the conquering Saxon, it has followed him in Africa and the Indies, amid the orange groves of Southern and the forests of Northern America, in the wastes of the ocean and the perils and privations of the camp. In all climes Madeira has been found, cheering social and festive communion. It has been heard in pledges of patriotic fervor, in those of love and friendship to present and absent. Entombed at the birth it appears at the bridal, and as the dusty and cobwebbed bottles come to light, they are regarded with a reverential awe due to the provident spirits of the departed ancestry who first deposited them in the vaults where they have ripened.

But whilst we are thus sentimentalizing under the shadow of Madeira upon days and usages which are falling beneath the onslaught of "Maine Laws" and teetotalism, our ship has run along the rocky shores until, just off a point, and standing out isolated in the sea, is the "Loo Rock," with a fortress upon its summit. From this point, for the distance of two or three miles, the rocky wall of the island sinks to a pebbly beach, along which is built the city of Funchal, white and brilliant, house above house and street above street, climbing up the mountain side; and outside the city, still on higher terraces, are the cottages and "quintas," or country residences; while yet further up, beyond all visible habitation, and overlooking all, is the church of "Nossa Senhora do Monte," Our Lady of the Mount, its white turrets contrasting with the dark background of the mountain which now sweeps away until its summit arrests the morning and evening clouds and mists, and is occasionally capped with snow.

We have anchored, and numerous small boats are hurrying off from the shore with washerwomen, and other persons desirous of our patronage, and of supplying us with the many comforts which we sea-worn people are likely to require. Among these boats is one bearing the Portuguese flag. It is that of the Captain of the Port, who, in the uniform of his station, comes aboard to inquire into our character, state of health, etc., and also to arrange for an interchange of salutes.

Before going ashore, and while they are drawing the shot and making other preparations for the salute, we can amuse ourselves in looking at these boats, and they are worth it, as they lie floating, all now dropped astern to be out of the way of the guns. They are prettily painted, are very deep, appear buoyant, and have at each end a slightly curved stick or handle, rising two or three feet above the boat. The salute of thirteen guns being fired and returned from the castle, we are now ready to put our feet on the shore. Several of us left the ship in one of our boats. But large and commodious as it was, we could not land in that boat. There was the smooth, regular beach before us; the sea was calm, but it so rolled and curled upon the beach, that we should have been cast away. Therefore, stopping our way, a native boat came alongside and received us; then, pulling in close to the beach, we turned about, keeping our bow to the sea and our stern to the shore, and waited until a sea came rolling in, when, by a nice management of the oars, keeping our position, we rose upon the sea, were swept onward, and as it returned we were left upon the beach, and before another sea could catch us a rope was passed around the handle at the stern of the boat, and we were run up, amid shouts and cries, upon the Madeiran shore; the boat having two side keels or runners to facilitate this movement. And now we have our first introduction to the humanity of the place—the beach combing, refuse humanity, it is true, but it is the first thing that arrests our attention, and I wish my readers to see every thing just as I saw it. Amiable, courteous, and respectful, off go their hats at our approach, for these people about the beach have generally caught foreign fashions and wear hats; but we are very much amused at the ridiculous appearance of one or two fellows who have the very summit of the head surmounted by a blue cloth funnel with its spike, three or four inches long, sticking stiff and straight up from the crown of the head. This is the caripuca, the national head-dress worn by both male and female. What could have originated such a head-dress is a matter of speculation, and equally to be wondered at is how the thing is retained on the summit of the head. It affords no protection of course from the rays of the sun, and being of double woolen cloth it must generate much unnecessary heat in the few inches of scalp covered by it. I have, however, my own theory, associating it with the national characteristic of courtesy. It is necessary to have some means of making their constant salutations, and this caripuça being grasped by its spike and carried in the hand as they are passing those to whom they wish to pay respect, is exactly the thing, and in all respects a *capital* appendage. But a less agreeable characteristic than courtesy is thrust upon us at the beginning—the want of energy and self-respect, which leads to a general demand for alms. "Pobre, pobre, pobre," salutes us on all hands as we continue our way to the Consul's. One poor old wretch, with a hideously distorted countenance, beseechingly thrusts herself and her hand in your way. Your are about to take out your purse when a lad runs before you with a mutilated arm. Your first movement of charity has drawn a crowd: hurrying on his crutches comes one without a leg—a woman with a baby—then little sparkling black-eyed boys and girls, with a sudden melancholy dropped over their countenances, and scarcely vailing the smile lurking on their lips, thrust forth their little hands, and in mingled English and Portuguese piteously ask our aid. Most of us have babies and little boys and girls at home, and there is no resisting them here. But some practical familiar of the place lays his hand upon your arm, and says, "Do n't give." He explains that the demand is interminable, that you will be beset wherever you move, on foot or on horseback, in town or in country; that you are now the victims of the tender-hearted indiscreet who have preceded you. If you do put up your purse, you will need some reasons to satisfy your conscience, and they will come upon you in this wise: "I could n't give to all." "I did n't know who needed most." "Did any really need?" Where there is so much begging there must be much charity, systematic as well as casual. They looked all in pretty good case, and the really needy must be provided for by some regular establishment. They are—and so we leave the pobres to beg on to-morrow and next year, as they have done in days and years that are past.

We will take a look at the streets—queer streets they are. You who walk on brick side-walks, with broad carriage ways intervening, would call them lanes and alleys, and, except where there are shops and stores, not lanes and alleys running between stores, but between dead walls, with here and there massive gate-ways and doors opening into the grounds and to the houses behind the walls. Your attention will soon be attracted to the pavement over which you are walking, and especially if you happen unfortunately to have on a pair of thin-soled shoes. It is all composed of small stones about the size of an egg, in many places set in regular figures, squares, diamond, etc., sometimes lined off by white stones. It looks very pretty, and the streets are neat and clean, for, being sharply inclined planes, they are thoroughly washed by every rain, and besides, through most of them a gutter of mountain spring water is rushing. In addition to these natural means of cleanliness, a police regulation requires each householder to sweep before his premises every Saturday. It will readily be seen that such toy looking streets as these would soon be torn up by carts and carriages. But there are no such things as wheeled vehicles used. They would be unmanageable on these steep ascents, and here we have before us the mode of carrying burdens. Two pleasant chubby little oxen, not taller than our six month calves, are harnessed to a thick plank, about two feet broad, which, resting upon two narrower thick pieces as runners, is the island sledge. This one we are now looking at is laden with a hogshead, and seems to glide easily enough over the smooth polished stones. Having seen these things in our short walk to the Consul's, we enter the great gate through the outer wall of his residence, and are immediately surrounded by the rich luxuriance of the climate. Our way is up the pebble paved walk, shaded with overhanging foliage, a banana grove on one hand, and on the other a garden of orange, fig, pomegranate and coffee trees, laden with fruit, with a profusion of bright colored flowers, among which glow conspicuously the large scarlet petals of the "Manhao de Pasco" or "Easter Morning," as the Portuguese call it, the Poinsetti Pulcherrima of the Euphorbiaceæ. Among the curious growths of the garden attracting our attention, conspicuous is the "Durante." We notice that a large space of the pebble-paved yard, from forty to fifty feet square, is completely and darkly shaded by foliage, the whole of which is the product of a single trunk, which, about eighteen inches thick, rises from the centre of the space to the height of five to six feet, and then spreads out as a vine, supported upon frame-work, and matting together for a thickness of two feet or more, covers the whole space as with an enormous umbrella of green leaves, small violet blossoms and bunches of bright yellow berries.

Amid all this luxuriant vegetation, fruits, bright flowers and clear skies, we take a sleigh ride. Having a visit to make to an acquaintance far up the steep, it is suggested to us that we take a "carro," and one being sent for, we are apprised of its approach by long-drawn cries of Bu–oy, Buo–oy, and going to the gate we find two of the patient-looking little oxen yoked to a regular sleigh —or, as the English will call it, a "sledge." This sleigh is heavily built of mahogany, has a top and curtains, two cushioned seats, back and front, and is mounted on springs and runners heavily shod with steel. Four of us taking our seats in this vehicle, with a man and goad alongside the oxen, a boy running ahead of them, and a troop of beggars, little and big, alongside and behind, off we go up the hill amid cries of Buo-o-oy, Bu-o-y, the man every now and then dropping a greased cloth under the runners to facilitate their gliding over the stones.

Neither do we want snow for a grand "coasting" ride. It would delight all those industrious juveniles who toil with their sleds up snowy hills to dash coasting down them, and it exceeds all which Russians can do by their artificial mountains of ice and snow.

There, far up the mountain side, you see the church of "Our Lady of the Mount." We ride up to it on horseback, ascending slowly from terrace to terrace, riding along the edge of vast gulfs, with rivulets groping through them like silver threads, overlooking quintas, valleys, Funchal, and seeing further and further out to sea with each step of our elevation. We are about three quarters of an hour reaching the church, about two thousand feet above the sea. From this point there is, however, a precipitous road nearly directly down the mountain into the city. Our horses were now given in charge of the borroqueros who had accompanied us, clinging to the tails of their horses as we trotted up the steeps, who drove them back, while we took our seats in a wicker or basket-sled for a coasting descent down the steep. Two men, by a jerk upon ropes at each side of the car in front, gave it the descending impetus, when away we dashed, with great velocity, down the hill. The men jumped back, and bearing their weight upon the arms of the car, as they ran panting by our side, controlled its motion, and skillfully directed it around the turns and curvatures of the road. Gliding and whirling, shouting to foot passengers to stand clear, in sixteen minutes we were in the city.

There are yet other modes of conveyance. The palanquin, shaded and curtained, and occupied by some lady in her silks and embroideries, is frequently met, suspended from a long pole borne on the shoulders of two men. Another more melancholy mode of conveyance is the hammock. Made of colored cord, red, yellow, blue and green, like the palanquin suspended from a pole and borne upon the shoulders of men, it is seldom met except when occupied by one of the pale emaciated beings, who, in consumption's hopeless doom, have yet hopefully sought the balmy breezes of this clime. Amid all the brilliancy, the verdure, the soft and genial atmosphere of this island, it is melancholy to know, and to be continually reminded by those you meet, how many of its visitors have sought it, clinging, with their feeble frames, to a few more months of life. How wide the circle of apprehensive and wakeful affections, passing through distant homes, finds its centre in this island. Husband for wife, wife for husband, brethren for brethren, and parent for child, are ever hoping its healing power over the absent loved one. And in many a Northern home, while snows are driving and storms howling without, some bereaved one sits by the fireside glowing within, but, sadly musing, has wandered in thought from the broken domestic circle, away from the hearth and over the storm, to some verdure and flower-clad grave in the stranger's cemetery of Madeira.

V.

WINE.

Now that the world has had its faith shaken in the generative principle of nobility, and doubts both the justice and the expediency of those institutions, which, as Pascal says, "give to the infant in the cradle an influence and consideration that could not be acquired by half a century's practice of every virtue," we hear of merchant princes, and it is to be hoped that in further progress we shall hear of engine, loom, and anvil princes.

Madeira has its wine princes, and where could one be supposed to taste the juice of the grape in higher table perfection than in the house of one of these noblemen, who live in a style justifying the title?

If I take any curious, inquiring reader with me to the table of one of these princes to which I am invited, he must not fear a wine debauch. This place of epicurean refinements and of delicate bouquets is not that in which a man puts pints and bottles under his belt, overwhelming all delicate perceptions. The wine drinkers of Madeira are true epicures. A highly-flavored glass or two during dinner, a lengthened coqueting with a glass of some choice vintage after the cloth is removed, and that is all. Indeed those of the most nicely discriminating tastes rarely *drink* wine at all. Of course this commendable moderation may be in some degree departed from when they have a set of strangers desirous of taking advantage of a chance visit to go through all the choice vintage at one sitting. Well, we have dined and taken a glass of the ordinary table wine, generally known abroad as "London Particular," or else a glass of a dark port looking and astringent-tasted Vino-Tinto. Both are pronounced to be extraordinarily good, of course. As we are now drinking for wine information, we inquire what these wines exactly are. But stop—we will say nothing about the matter until there is a greater variety under discussion. The dinner is over, the dessert finished, the cloth removed, and with the nuts—among which are plates of roast chestnuts—old Virgil's "castanea nuces" —enormous nuts, such as, according to Professor Owen, antediluvian megatheria may have sat upon their hind quarters and picked from the top of the tree—decanters are placed at each end of the table, and the silver necklaces suspended from their throats indicate them to be *Malmsey*—*Bual*—*Sercial*—the aristocracy of wines. In addition to these we have the *Verdeilho* and the *Tinta*. These five constitute the principal wines of the island of Madeira. They are all named from the kind of grape from which they are made. There are three others, but they make only a low order of wine seldom seen. The *Verdeilho* is that generally used and known as Madeira, London Particular, etc. It is deepened in color by a slight addition of Tinta, and flavored by the rich and aromatic Buol. Sercial is also a highly-flavored wine. Malmsey is generally known to be a sweet, luscious and cordial-like wine. These three last are the most costly. The Tinta is made by pressing the husks and seeds with the juice. According to Dr. Christison and others, the proportion of alcohol in these wines is as follows:—

Madeira (Verdeilho)	20.35
Sercial	18.50
Malmsey	15.60
Tinta	20.35

It may not, even with the most delicate and fastidious, detract from the flavor of the rosy fluid to know that it has washed the feet of not over cleanly Portuguese laborers, for it has all been trod out by bare feet in the wine-press. Having tasted gently of these choice wines, another element of quality was brought under discussion—the element of age. Our host told us that the bottle he was then having opened, was of the vintage of 1815—going on while Napoleon the Great was off the island on his way to St. Helena, and was, therefore, at the present drinking, forty years of age. But neither its age, nor its unhappy historic association, was the cause of its excellence; but at that period L'Este, a hot, dry wind, the Sirocco or Harmattan of Africa, was of more than usual prevalence, and the grapes ripened in superior richness. It was, to my, and I believe to the general taste, a finely-flavored wine. Next, with due ceremonies and honors, a bottle was opened which our host, an English gentleman, told us was their "Independence" wine, being of the vintage of '76. My companions all thought it very superior, but, to me, it had very much the taste of a vapid medicated ether, and I honestly pronounced it, to my taste, unmitigated trash, and I remembered to have tasted, eighteen years before, a wine at the same table which had made the same impression upon me. My associates earnestly opposed the correctness of my judgment, and I found myself in a minority of one. I ventured to sustain myself by quoting the opinion of Dr. Christison, which seems to be founded both on reason and experience, viz., that wines do not improve by great age. Like ourselves, they have their growth to their best condition and then deteriorate; but the period of deterioration is different for different wines, or under varying circumstances for the same wine. At this stage of the discussion our host directed a bottle to be brought with great care from a specially named corner of the garret, and when brought he took it carefully in his hand, drew, and decanted it himself, and handing a glass to me, he said, "Now taste that, and tell me what you think of it, and be careful do n't commit yourself." The wine was very clear, and of a pale amber color. I tasted it, mild, unspirituous, aromatic, and at once said, "It is the best on the table, and by far the best I ever tasted in my life." It was then handed to my companions, who all thought it very good, but by no means equal to the '76. Our host then said, with an earnestness and solemnity befitting the occasion, "It is a rare wine—a wonderful wine: there can be nothing superior to it, but it is one *hundred years old;*" and thereafter our host and myself took up with the centenarian; but the Seventy-sixers, with commendable consistency, and perhaps from patriotic motives, stuck to their first judgment. How much honest judgment, or that enemy to progress, pride of opinion, had to do with our pertinacity, none of us will ever know.

In even all this tasting there had been but little wine-drinking—none of that reeking debauchery unfortunately so often seen in our own country, which mars, blunts, and vitiates the palate, and makes wine really grateful only from the amount of alcohol it conveys, and brandy itself more grateful than wine. It is, however, somewhat to our credit that the best Madeira, and that the least brandied, is sent to the United States, and besides coming to us the best, our climate improves it more than that of Europe does.

I trust that honestly-observed facts in relation to the character of wines, and in reference to the social habits of an eminently wine-drinking country, will not be considered as a eulogium upon its use, but if those who use wine habitually in the United States all used it as I have seen it used in Madeira, temperance men might rejoice; but upon that "if" the propriety of its use may depend.

> "Bright are the blushes of the wine-wreathed bowl,
> Warm with the sunshine of Anacreon's soul;
> But dearer memories gild the tasteless wave
> That fainting Sidney perished as he gave.
> 'Tis the heart's current lends the cup its glow,
> What e'er the fountain whence the draught may flow."

It would really seem as if the hand of Providence was directing physical influences in favor of total abstinence by the blight which has come over the grapes in wine-producing countries. Upon a former visit to this island I rode to the Great Curral or Curral das Freiras, an enormous chasm, which seems, when it first bursts upon you, to open to the earth's centre, with its six thousand feet of depth inclosed by the red, rugged pinnacled rocks shooting away to the clear sky above you; but away down in the bottom of the depth you see miniature houses and a church, and they are two thousand feet above the sea.

It is a long up-hill ride of eighteen miles to the point which looks down into the Curral, and much of it is along the edge of frightful precipices, and much of it also, when I made the excursion, was through vineyards where vines arbored over the road, or trellis work, and hung their rich bunches just above your head and ready to your hand. But now such scenery no longer exists. The prophecy of Joel the son of Bethuel is in literal fulfillment. "Awake, ye drunkards, and weep and howl, all ye drinkers of wine, because of the new wine; for it is cut off from your mouth." For four years this wine-press has not been trodden, and the vine, fruit, leaf and stem, has disappeared. The annual product of the island was from fifteen to twenty thousand pipes, and this past year not two hundred were made in the whole island. The whole stock on hand is only about ten thousand pipes, not more than the half of one good year's product, and this will be exhausted in from five to ten years; even if the grape were to be recovered now, it would take several years before the new wine would be fit for exportation. The disease, a mould or fungoid growth, has so far resisted all methods of cure, and scarcely more than a lingering hope exists of the recovery of the vine; this hope would have the more encouragement if they could ascertain certainly that the disease had ever existed before and passed away, but although documents and records have been carefully searched, the only evidence of the kind is in some old leases which specify that the rent is to be paid unless a failure of the grape occur.

It is well known that in the first year of the present

failure great distress and famine prevailed in the island, which was relieved by contributions from various parts of the world, and especially from the United States, by the introduction of the sugar-cane, sweet potatoes and other roots and fruits, abundance of which, at low rates, are now found in the markets. The Irish potatoes are of very superior quality, equal to the best in any part of the world. Those which are of the first quality are the product of seed sent out from the United States during the famine.

I suppose it would not do to talk about Madeira and not say any thing of the extent of population, although any gazetteer would give the information. That of the island is a little over one hundred thousand, and that of Funchal about eighteen thousand. But there has been much emigration, diminishing the population. Famine drove away many. Demerara, offering a premium for laborers, drew off many; and a recent Protestant reformation has driven from their kindred and genial home, to the wilds of America, several hundred martyrs for conscience' sake. And as, like our own Pilgrim fathers, they sought

"Freedom to worship God,"

may their descendants be equally rewarded. Although the changed agriculture of the island has removed the apprehension of starvation, yet the destruction of trade and commerce caused by the wine blight has necessarily brought poverty to very many, and to some who have been in elevated and prosperous circumstances. The female members of such families, turning to account the exquisite skill in embroidery for which they are celebrated, devote themselves to the working of edgings, handkerchiefs, collars, sleeves, etc., which are sold by their servants to the strangers visiting the island. If the very low price at which this fine work is offered were not an inducement for those who can afford it, to buy, the reflection that one is at once gratifying his own taste and relieving a necessity, ought to be.

Among the light manufactures of the island a variety of beautifully manufactured baskets are industriously offered to strangers at very low rates, by street peddlers. Their mechanics also excel in the manufacture of inlaid wood work. Paper cutters, card cases, work boxes, writing desks and tables are beautifully made in varied colors. The ground is generally of the black Til wood, and that is preferred which has darkened by age in some old wine press. It is inlaid with red cedar, orange, and other bright-colored woods. Centre tables made in this way, with vine wreaths inlaid, are exceedingly beautiful, and cost about thirty dollars. According to the fitness of things, and the tendency of our ordinary experience, one expects to see a water-mill at the foot of a hill or on the edge of a stream passing through a valley. In one of my rides with a friend up a steep hill side, I saw before me two red painted wooden tubes, coopered up like barrels, but about fifteen or twenty feet high. They were at the extremity of a stone wall. The wall inclosed the little mountain stream which plunged in at the top of these tubes, turned a wheel at their bottom, and was the power of the mill which ground the corn and wheat of the neighborhood.

During this, my last ride in the island, we passed the large and elegant estate of a rich widow, whose history, illustrating, more than a little, island romance, may not unfitly close our visit to Madeira. The possessor of this estate and spacious mansion formerly came down from the mountain a barefooted peasant girl, laden with bundles or faggots of small wood, which she sold in the town. Tempted by a wealthy individual, somewhat advanced in life, she exchanged her hard and laborious existence for a more luxurious but less honorable position, but which finally terminated in her becoming the wife of her protector. After his death she married a lawyer of talents and rising fame. He finally became the governor of the island, and the once barefooted, faggot-burdened peasant girl filled her distinguished position with a courtly grace and elegance which my informant said none others had excelled, and this among a peculiarly courtly and formal people. What then becomes of the opinions of those who think that one must be "to the manner born" to fill such stations without the stamp of awkwardness and vulgarity?

VI.

CINDERS AND LAVA.

Get down the map, my good reader, and unless you have the whole world dotted and spotted geographically in your eye, look out the little island of Ascension, in mid-Atlantic ocean, between the coasts of Africa and South America, almost upon the equatorial division of this planet of ours, just a little south of the Line. Unless you not only understand but feel the wideness and wildness of its desolation, the tiny minuteness of its size, eight miles in its longest dimensions, and with one mountain peak, two thousand eight hundred and eighteen feet above the sea—unless you have all this before you, and at the same time the cindery, hard, dry, sterile character of the island, you can not feel the greatness of its interest.

It must be among the youngest of Pluto's volcanic children, for there stand all around it and through it black and red volcanic cones of pumice, cinders, and calcined iron ores, with ashy, dry, dusty plains between them. No moisture, no vegetation, no verdure, except on the summit of the "Green Mountain," which rises fresh and beautiful amid all this barrenness, and is the heart of all the usefulness of Ascension.

This is one of the tapping places for the drum of our great ancestral nation, whose "beat salutes the rising sun around the circumference of the globe."

When the world-sin of caging the great Napoleon in St. Helena was perpetrated, the English occupied Ascension as a military station, and out of the evil necessity, by the blessing of God, has sprung a great good. With characteristic energy they developed and created resources of inestimable value in that lonely ocean. The arable land that lies around the summit of "Green Mountain" has been brought under cultivation, seeds and plants imported, so that now the garrison not only has enough for itself, but sufficient to refresh those who come in from the surrounding ocean wastes. More than that, they have collected the drippings and moisture from the mountain, and brought them down, by thirty-three thousand feet of three and a half inch iron pipe, to tanks near the shore, from which ships of all nations in urgent necessity are supplied with this necessary of existence in its purest form. But water, the supply of which is dependent upon casual rains, and might be cut off by a drought, is too precious an article to be recklessly wasted, and therefore it is under almost as rigid a surveillance as it would be on board ship. The tanks, even the small ones of the officers' quarters, are under lock and key, and the allowance to each person on the island is limited for all purposes—one gallon a day for drinking, and four gallons a week for laundry purposes. Occasionally the island has been threatened with a fatal want of water, and upon one occasion water was brought from St. Helena, a distance of about six hundred miles. They have, however, a distilling apparatus, which would prevent any urgent suffering. To make most available the limited resources of the place, no one is permitted to settle on the island but those under the control and in the employ of the government, and every thing produced on the island, even the turtles which land upon its shores, is the property of the government. Among the public buildings is a good hospital, indeed two of them, one for convalescents in the cool air of the mountain summit, and a delicious resort in the healthy dry air of Ascension for all invalids, and especially for those broken down by the terrible fever of the African coast, or by the ravages of scurvy. During my stay of three days, several vessels passed in sight of the island. An American came in, was watered, and departed immediately. A French merchant ship came in in consequence of the illness of her commander, who was at once taken to the hospital.

At the death of Napoleon, the necesity which originated the occupation of Ascension ceased, but being so useful in relieving the distress incident to this mid ocean, it has been continued and made the depot for the British squadron on the coast of Africa. A large supply of coal is also kept here for the use of ocean steamers, and, like every thing else, furnished to strangers at only cost and charges. Our ship was thus supplied with what coal and provisions we needed, besides being gratuitously filled with water, and presents of milk and fish kindly sent off to our messes by the officers on shore.

The only aborigines known to the island are female green turtle, Testudo Mydas, and they are still held in high honor. Upon our arrival we were desirous of making the usual arrangements for saluting the British flag, but were told that it must not be done, and no firing of guns or pistols was permitted in the harbor, lest it should frighten the turtle which, from December to June, come up on the island beaches to lay their eggs. So that honor to aldermanic turtle, sunk into silence the cannon bellowings and air concussions which are wont to tell how much greater one man is than another. I wonder when the old native forest Indian nature will wear out of our civilized hearts and usages. This saluting business, at least so far as it is done in honor of individuals, seems to me one of the most silly and undignified Indianings, to make a word, which our higher cultivated nature retains. And a particularly ridiculous effect of the custom is the fact of two great and grave nations disputing, because they can not determine which of their captains ought to fire most guns for the other. Why not end the matter by saying, "We think our man ought to have so many guns, and you think your man ought to have so many; we will not take any offense at the difference of opinion —indeed it is fortunate, because we can compromise without firing at all, and save our powder for more useful purposes." The Ascension Turtle custom is by far the most sensible. The stars and stripes looked just as bright, the cross of St. George kept its place at the peak of the Tortoise, the harbor ship, Commodore Armstrong of the San Jacinto, and Captain Seymour, Governor of the island, were unshaken in their places or their dignity, and our magazines were the richer for so much powder. Revenons à nos tortues. In the season they come up on the sand beaches between the rocks, particularly on moonlight nights, and crawling high up on the sand, with their flippers dig a hole ten feet wide by two deep, and depositing their eggs, 70 or 80 in number, cover them and turn again to the sea. But on each of these beaches, of which there are five, look-outs are stationed, and these cutting off the turtle on her way to the sea, turn her on her back. In the morning, all so captured, are carted to ponds walled off from the sea. They are thus preserved for victualing the island and ships, and are rationed to the inhabitants twice a week. The average number taken each season, for many years past, is 513. In one year over 1200 were taken. In 1854 there were taken in January 101, in February 175, and in March 196—total, 472. The young ones as soon as hatched, which is in five weeks, take immediately to the sea, and it is remarkable that none ever return but the *females*, and these not until they have reached from 500 to 700 lbs. weight. No small ones are ever seen. How long are they in reaching this immense size? Where are they in the meantime and where are the males? I was told that a turtle marked on this island had been captured on the coast of California. It is also remarkable that although all or nearly all which come up are taken, yet about the same number comes up each year. These large turtles give about 150 lbs. of meat, and have one fixed price, about twelve and a half dollars each. An officer who has served his term of duty here, say three years, has the privilege of taking two turtles home with him. The inhabitants of Ascension, including those on board the harbor ship, the "Tortoise," number about four hundred, every one of whom is necessarily borne upon the books of the paymaster, as they are all victualed by him.

Among the inhabitants are a number of native Africans, Kroomen, who do all the hard labor, that which, in their absence, would be done by the common sailors and soldiers, so that still the children of Ham, though free, are the hewers of wood and the drawers of water, the servant of servants for Japhet. The worthy and excellent Chaplain of the island introduced me to a school in which some six or eight of these liberated Africans were being educated, and had learned to read and write tolerably well.

Whilst taking our walks round about and among the neat one story buildings, used as officers' quarters, in their midst we came to one in front of which sits a large portly negress, and the whole establishment, from parlor to kitchen, is evidently in possession of Africans. We enter. Bow your heads reverently, all ye disciples of Hume, Sir Walter Scott and Sir Archibald Alison, all ye venerators of divine right, for you are in the presence of royalty. This is the residence of the King of Bonny, in Africa, a state prisoner to the Queen of England, and the portly lady who received us so graciously is his queen, or one of them. In court language, he received us graciously, and asking us to be seated, he directed wine to be handed to us and to himself. Speaking English imperfectly, he asked us our names and occupations, and manifested much satisfaction that we had done him or ourselves the honor, whichever it was, of calling on him. He is said to be a man of wealth and influence in his own country, and the British government allows him four thousand dollars a year while in captivity. But his majesty does not like the gilded cage: he wants to get out. There did not seem to be any clear reason why the King of Bonny was in captivity. The nearest approach I could make to the cause of it was, that British merchants wanted to buy all the palm oil at lower rates than he would dispose of it or allow it to be sold by his subjects; therefore he was imprisoned for interfering with trade. At first he was kept upon the coast, but managing to send an order to his dominions, still prohibiting the sale on any but his own terms, it was thought expedient to send him more remote from his dominions. He himself said the English were great rascals, they shut the Emperor Napoleon up in St. Helena, and him in Ascension. The truth is, the principle is the same in both cases, only the magnitude of the Napoleonic crime makes the parallel of his sable majesty ridiculous. The officers at Ascension spoke of his confinement as an injustice.

We were told of a singular sea phenomenon which sometimes occurs at Ascension and St. Helena. Having no opportunity of witnessing it I quote the following description, by a Mr. Webster, from Purdy's Ethiopic Directory. He says:

"One of the most interesting phenomena that the island affords is that of the Rollers; in other words a heavy swell, producing a high surf on the leeward shores of the island, occurring without any apparent cause. All is tranquil in the distance, the sea breeze scarcely ripples the surface of the wave, when a high swelling wave is suddenly observed rolling towards the island. At first it appears to move slowly forward, till at length it breaks on the outer reefs. The swell then increases, wave urges on wave, until it reaches the beach, where it bursts with tremendous fury. The Rollers now set in and augment in violence until they attain a terrific and awful grandeur, affording a magnificent sight to the spectator, and one which I have witnessed with mingled terror and delight. A towering sea rolls forward on the island like a vast ridge of waters, threatening as it were to envelope it; pile on pile succeeds with resistless force, until meeting with the rushing offset from the shore beneath they rise like a wall and are dashed with impetuous fury on the long line of the coast, producing a stunning noise. The beach is now mantled over with foam, the mighty waters sweep over the plain, and the very houses in the town are shaken by the fury of the waves. But the principal beauty of the scene consists in the continuous ridge of water, crested on its summit with foam and spray; for, as the wind blows off the shore, the overarching top of the wave meets resistance, and is carried, as it were, back against the curl of the swell; and thus it plays elegantly above it as it rolls furiously onward, graceful as a bending plume; while, to add more to its beauty, the sunbeams are reflected from it, in all the varied tints of the rainbow.

"Amid the tranquillity which prevails around, it is a matter of speculation to account for this commotion of the waters, as great as if the most awful tempest or the wildest hurricane had swept the bosom of the deep. It occurs in situations where no such swell would be expected, in sheltered bays and where the wind never reaches the shore. The strong and well built jetty of the town has once been washed away by the Rollers, which sometimes make a complete breach over it, although it is twenty feet above high water mark. On these occasions the crane at its extremity is washed around in various directions, as the weather-cock is turned by the wind, and landing becomes impracticable for the space of two or three days. Such are the Rollers of Ascension, and like unto them are those of St. Helena and Fernando Noronha.

"The season in which the Rollers prevail is from December to April, not but that they do occur at other periods, and they have been felt severely in July. Ships at the anchorage are perfectly secure, and they have to apprehend no danger unless within the immediate influence of the breakers. Not only are the seasons of the Rollers the same at Ascension and St. Helena, but they sometimes are simultaneous in occurrence. The Chanticleer, while at anchor at St. Helena on the 17th and 18th of January, 1830, experienced some very high Rollers. On our subsequent arrival at Ascension I inspected the meteorological journal of my friend Mitchell, the surgeon of the island, and found it noted that the Rollers were so high on the 15th, 16th, and 17th of January that landing was impossible. Here then is a coincidence as to time."

The cause of the Rollers has been speculated upon, and various conjectures formed of them. Some have attributed them to the effects of the moon,

> "Whom Ocean feels through all his countless waves,
> And owns her power on every sphere he laves;"

and others have attributed them to the tides; but it is evident these have nothing to do with them. They occur in the most tranquil season of the year, when the southeast trade-wind is very light, when the vast volume of water is impelled in one direction. There is then a tendency to a back-set, or to a rush of water in a contrary direction, and a tumultuous swell is produced whenever it meets with the resistance from the islands, and banks upon which they are based, as well as the shores of a continent. The long, steep beaches of Ascension are admirably adapted for the full display of the effect which has just been described.

Having been hospitably welcomed by the gentlemen on shore, and on board the harbor ship the "Tortoise," on the 12th of December we closed our relations with them, and took our departure from Ascension.

As I looked back upon its red hills and green central mountain, I thought it somewhat emblematic of the people whose flag it bore. Planting themselves with volcanic energy and violence in the most remote wastes of the ocean, but with hearts and minds a central source of freshness and vigor, reanimating the ages of the dead past, and from the ashes and cinders of an extinct civilization calling up that which is new, energetic, and of world-wide usefulness.

Having steamed out of the port, our fires were put out, the clanking of the engine ceased, and sail was made on the ship. It was now pretty generally understood that instead of steaming to the Cape of Good Hope, which would require about eighteen days, we were to sail there, which would occupy from thirty to forty. Besides, to make the winds fair, we were necessarily compelled to steer away from our point of destination, or at best to make a right-angled instead of a diagonal course to it, conditions not gratifying to those impatient of long sea voyages. However, good fortune was with us, and the wind diverted us less from our course than we might have expected. On Christmas day, it is true, we had made only about five hundred miles, not quite so much, on our way, although we had sailed about one thousand four hundred, but the day was a beautiful specimen of the charming climate which had been around us, and which might well tempt us to dally on our way to the Indies. The sea was smooth as a lake, and with the blue transparency of a clear atmosphere, the south-east trade-wind was gentle and steady, and the temperature, although the sun was vertical, in harmony with every sensation of comfort, without imparting the least feeling of languor and lassitude. Thermometrically it was steadily 76° Fahrenheit.

Our whole ship's company greeted the first hour of this festal day, for just before midnight the drums beat to night quarters, and roused every one from his slumbers. And when Christmas came, on board the San Jacinto, it was amid the rolling of the big guns, the sounding of rattles to call away boarders, or the ringing of bells to extinguish imaginary fires. This lasted nearly two hours, when the retreat was sounded, and all except the watch again retired to rest. On the following day all labor in the ship was suspended, and the men generally occupied themselves in reading under the shade of the awnings, the band playing old familiar tunes, and most of us talked much and thought more of our distant homes. But then fine nights are an enjoyment, and the Southern Cross glitters like a jewel on the dark brow of the firmament for our admiration

—but admiration is not affection, and we world-wide wanderers have even astronomical affections.

"Look," said one of my lieutenant friends to me, a few nights before we crossed the line, "at that little dim star in the north. It is the last night perhaps you will see it for some time to come."

The belt of clouds and rain which intervenes between the trade-wind of the northern and those of the southern hemisphere shut out the north star sooner than we would lose it by our progress south, and as the unpretending emblem of fidelity, associated with our northern home, sank behind the dark curtain, we felt like parting from an old and tried friend, and by no means favorably inclined to the brilliant seductions of the Southern Cross. It is natural for travelers to see every thing in exaggeration, both because it is new and because we have an associated importance with that of the wonders we see, but nevertheless I am bound to agree with the sententious remark of a practical friend who, upon seeing the constellation for the first time, said it was "no great shakes" after all. It may be that I judge it under the indignation of its usurping the place of my northern friend, but it is neither proportioned, straight in its arms, nor brilliant in the four stars only which make it up. It bears no comparison with our Ursa Major, and at least half a dozen as good crosses may be imagined in any part of the heavens.

Our pleasant meteorological condition continued up to the 20th of the month, when the wind came out ahead and chilly. We were turned towards Cape Horn, the sea rolled up into fresh, brisk waves, pitching the ship into uneasy motions, and stirring up bilge-water. The air ports, those precious round holes which, about the size of a breakfast plate, let in the air and light to our dungeons, were closed—thick glass plates screwed into them, shutting out of course all air, and reducing the light to that dim, watery kind of a gleam which must reach the fishes in their sea depths. Albatrosses, too, were sailing magnificently through the air, and skimming the cresting waves. Some of our sensitive natures thought themselves sea-sick, and resorted to small glasses of porter, brandy and water, and horizontal positions.

That little puff did not last long, and now, January 1st, 1856, we have another beautiful day, but oh! so tiresome. We have made nothing on our way. Here we are, about where we have been for a week past, and with plenty of coal in our bunkers, a smooth sea, through which our engines could urge us without impediment; our port only about ten days off. Yet here we lay. The same daily routine: rise at six bells, seven o'clock—hear the drums roll for the men's grog, while shaving—breakfast at eight—quarters for inspection at two bells, nine o'clock—this lasts ten minutes—then the Doctor prescribes, and every one goes to what he has to do, some to duty, and others to reading, sleeping, smoking, walking the deck, and no more break in the day until the drum again rolls for grog at seven bells, half past eleven o'clock, and the Master gets an observation of the sun at meridian, when he tells us all it is twelve o'clock, and mechanically remarks what the latitude is, and the men are whistled or piped to dinner — then we read, and sleep, and walk again. Then, at four bells, two o'clock, the drum beats to our dinner, and this is a grand event, not as a dinner, but as a time mark. We grumble at our food and the caterer, criticise our captain and commodore in particular, and all other captains and commodores in general; are very wise and learned upon the books from which we have, in self-defense, been cramming all the morning, but as our learning is only for the occsaion, it wears out in one day, and is replaced by a new stock for the morrow. By the way, I must expatiate a little upon this peculiarity of man-of-war students, or rather readers. If a man were to have a sum of money loaned him for a temporary use, or even had suddenly acquired it, and was to go about arrogantly boasting of his wealth, and despising men permanently better off but not so inflated for the day, we should think him both silly and vulgar. We regard it as such for the really wealthy to obtrude their superiority upon us, and it is no better taste for a man to rush from his room and, with facts and principles gathered fresh for the occasion, obtrude them as substantial learning. With this episode of ward-room ethics, I go on with our routine. Dinner over, more reading, smoking, sleeping, until again the drums beat for evening inspection quarters, after the crew, at four or five o'clock, have had their supper—ten minutes at that—the medical officers do the evening prescribing—the men have their hammocks piped down, that is, the boatswain's mates blow their whistles for those men to come and get their hammocks who have the watch below, or whose turn it is to sleep in, and then we have our supper—chat a little. The officers who have the mid and morning watches soon retire to their rooms. He who has the sleep in gossips with those who have no watch. Eight o'clock puts out the lights on the berth deck, nine o'clock extinguishes those of the steerage, and ten puts out ours in the ward-room, and then the day is done. This, with daily exercise of divisions at the guns, occasional drilling in small arms, and twice a week general quarters for a grand battle exercise, make up the routine of our existence. There is occupation enough—leisure enough—but the occupation is an unvarying form, the leisure, a weary interval of wearying pursuits. No freshness, no change, no novelty.

> "Lovely seemed any object that should sweep
> Away the vast, salt, dread, eternal deep."

Here we lay upon its bosom in a calm—the winds lulled, the engines and the engineers rusting, the occupation of coal-heavers and firemen gone. We pity Mr. Marcy, if he wants that treaty with Siam made. We pity the King of Siam for the delay in receiving all these magnificent mirrors, these chandeliers, and other presents of our liberal minded Uncle. We pity Mr. Harris, who is delayed in making that treaty, and may be cut out by some swifter keeled nation. We mourn for Manifest Destiny, which is so long delayed in its diplomatic entrance to Siam. We mourn for those who are awaiting our relief in the China seas, but, most of all, we mourn for our pent up selves, and grieve that we are not rich enough to refund to the national treasury the cost of the coal which would take us to the Cape of Good Hope.

Hope—it is a cheering sentiment for this New Year's day, and a propitious word to close this chapter. It is a ray from a future sun gilding the clouds of present affliction.

"Weather braces! Weather braces!" cries out the officer of the watch.

"A fair wind at last," says an officer at the ward-room table, looking up in pleased emotion from the book over which he was dozing, and once again we all hope.

VII.

WATER.

"LUDLOW, you black rascal, what are you at, drawing water out of that filterer?"

"It 's for the Doctor, sir," said my sable servant, in reply to this peremptory demand of our most worthy caterer.

"The Doctor has his allowance, three pints a day, and keeps it in his room; you've no business with the filterer—"

"The Doctor wants to borrow some, sir; he'll 'turn it, sir."

"Well, take it along, but if the Doctor borrows water from that filterer, he must return it with interest. Some is always wasted in filtering—you hear?"

"Yes, sir."

Worse, Mr. Caterer, than Shylock. He took only the pound of flesh nearest the heart, but you take interest on the fluid of life. But after all, the caterer was right—as a just man he was right.

It was only a few days before this interesting conversation, that the Master, the young gentleman who has charge of our water expenditure, rushed into the ward-room, exclaiming with emotion—

"Well, in all my service, this is the first time I have been upon an allowance of water, even in sailing ships—but, here, in a steamer, I have been ordered to serve out only three quarts a day to each man."

This announcement created a sensation. Three quarts a day is certainly not a suffering limitation. Poor Bligh of the Bounty, with his boat's crew, got on with about a gill a day—got along very uncomfortably, it is true, and had no choice. But Bligh had no coffee, tea or soup to make. He had no hams, pork, beef, codfish to boil, nor beans either. He did not shave every day during that voyage, nor care much whether his face or any other part of his person were washed. Now let any of you who tap the Croton when you will, or let the bucket down the mossy well, or dip from the bubbling spring, make the calculation and see how far three quarts will go for all these purposes, and for what you may require to drink on a melting summer day, and you will see there was cause for a sensation.

Measures were to be taken in this emergency. We were, in the tropics, the sun was vertical, our cells were close and sudorific. Such was the condition of those of us most lucky. But the men had to move about, twice a week, with great activity, to pull and haul at the great guns, and run about with swords, pikes and pistols in their hands—sweating prodigiously.

Physiologists tell us that the skin is very leaky—runs off about five pounds of water a day; and certain workmen in gas factories lose from two to three pounds an hour. Six pounds a day, to supply such a run upon the fountain of life, would hardly keep it solvent. I will mention another physiological fact, and it is, that when men know themselves to be on allowance, the desire for drink wonderfully increases. Nature resists the force put upon her; and if it must be done, it were well to do it secretly.

However, manly hearts meet stern necessities without complaint, and this must have been a case of necessity. There must have been reasons for it—but as these were none of our business, of course we could not judge from them, and the thinking apparatus is such a busy machine, it will work upon what materials it has for want of better. At one gallon a day each man, there were forty days' water in our ship, and even trusting to winds we were not more than twenty days from any supposed port, and having coal and steam could have commanded our time. There was a mystery in it—a ship mystery which the reader will bye-and-bye have solved.

But, as I said, measures were to be taken in this emergency. There was our filterer which we had bought to purify our drinking water, and preserve our health—if the water was all put in that, and every one had the run of it, those who drank early would have an advantage over those who drank late, and those with camel-like capacities might leave the less favored dry. Those of us who had little faith, met this difficulty by bottling up our supplies in our rooms. But then there were tea, coffee and cooking generally. We made a close calculation, and agreed to allow from our share one half, or three pints, for general mess purposes; that left only three pints for shaving, cleansing teeth, washing and drinking. Such were my water relations leading to the collision between Ludlow and the caterer.

These solemn circumstances impressed us seriously; and as at the witching hour of night, and in suspected places, we have an irresistible propensity to tell ghost stories, so we drew around the mess-table and told terrible tales of thirst.

Captain Bligh, and his gaunt boat's crew, glided before us. One Navy captain, one of our Navy captains, was told of who so tenaciously held to an allowance of water that it held even in port. Finding a boat's crew bringing off a small keg for their own use, he commanded it to be thrown into the sea. Another was remembered who washed his cabin with fresh water, while his crew were parching with thirst, and some of these sucked the wet swabs or mops with which the washing had been done. These were all doomed to Tantalian torments or to the scurvy blotches and boils which they are supposed to have inflicted upon their luckless shipmates. I myself had a vision of my youth. A beautiful scene in Florida, a wooded hill-side sloping down to a pretty winding stream, and just where the margin of the creek washed the hill-side, shaded by a branching tree, welled up a gurgling spring. There, by that spring-side, during the hot summer days, day after day, sat a weather-beaten man, with an honest and benevolent countenance. A broad-brimmed white hat generally lay on the ground beside him, while the cool breeze played with locks which were beginning to whiten with age, although he was but a Lieutenant in the Navy. He was a native of Virginia. One day I remarked to him as I walked by,

"This seems a favorite spot of yours, Mr. Goodwin."

He sprang to his feet and exclaimed, "Sir, it 's a paradise. In my section, sir, are many such springs as that, and I 've been free to drink my fill, sir, all my life. But, sir, during the whole of this * * * * cruise, I 've been on an allowance of water, and I sit here, sir, and I drink, drink," he exclaimed with energy, "till I can drink no more, just to spite Captain C.; then I call to him, sir, to come here and put me on an allowance if he dare."

He sat down again remarking, "Yes, sir, this place resembles my section very much." Poor Goodwin!

> "The mossy marbles rest
> Upon his breast
> Long ago;"

and I suspect it must be near some one of the cool, bubbling springs of his section.

The allowance of water, by strict economy and some privation, got along pretty well for a day or two. The first visible effect of it was ethical. Many moralists contend that there is a close sympathy between a clean skin and rectitude of deportment. Be that as it may, one of the messes found that its whole allowance had been stolen early in the day, and had to ask a fresh supply.

The next was chemical. Salines preponderated in the blood. Ham and mackerel for breasfast, ham, tongue, salt beef and pork for dinner, were found to be aqueducts which ran off the whole supply before the day was done, and we were limited to those delectable uniformities put up in tin cans, whose chief distinction is the labels on the outside. I will except the lobster, the salmon and the soups.

Next came a meeting at the mast between a delegate from the ship's company, the officer of the deck and the First Lieutenant. The men had found out that rice and beans were great soakers, and sponged too heavily upon their limited means, and therefore wanted permission to leave them in Uncle Sam's possession, restricting their diet to salt meat alone. The men had no tin cans of fresh meats. So far, at least, we were better off than the men.

Sometimes I got very tired of my cell life, and by way of change would develop—ascend to the region of sovereignty, and make a call upon my friends, the Commodore and the Captain. The first was an old friend, and the latter I had known when he was midshipman; but as I held the important-sounding title of "Surgeon of the Fleet," perhaps I might have ventured in there independent of my amicable relations, but I do n't know. I had no right to walk on any part of the quarter deck except the port side—the remainder was reserved for the Commodore, Captain, First Lieutenant and officer of the deck. The space of plank which I had the right to walk, in common with twenty-four other officers, was about twenty-five feet long by six wide. Under the "ancient discipline," over whose mouldering bones so many lament, no such restrictions were imposed upon me in my inferior position.

Well, I made the call, and I should not mention it but for its great scientific results. Talk no more of the fall of the apple. Let Archimedes go on crying "Eureka," and Prichard prose about the unity of races. Let Geoffrey St. Hilaire defend, against Cuvier, his theory of "Unity of Composition" with such animation as, "On the eve of the revolution of 1830, withdrew for a moment the attention of politicians from politics, and which completely overshadowed, in Gœthe's mind, the importance of the revolution itself; for he knew that a whole revolution in thought, far deeper and far more important to humanity than twenty July days, was germinating there." All their discoveries were as nothing to mine, and I am prepared to prove all their unities of races and compositions a complete humbug.

I entered the cabin, and took my seat, at the polite request of the ever courteous Commodore. After a few words of more general conversation, I asked—

"How does the allowance of water hold out with you?"

"Oh, very well—we have plenty."

"Plenty to cook with, plenty to wash with, plenty to drink?"

"Yes."

"More than enough, may be?"

"Oh no; we have to manage and economize."

"Why, is it possible you use your allowance every day?" When there is an allowance, it is alike to all in the ship, the reader will understand.

"Certainly."

I here began to fall into that painful mental puzzle which precedes the birth of a great thought.

I looked around the cool and airy cabin, with the breeze playing in and out its ports. I thought of my own sweating cell. I thought of more: of cases of claret, and casks of ale, with which we officers might eke out our allowance; of the difference between cases of fresh meat and chunks of salt junk. I thought of the difference between those sitting in a cool cabin, and those pulling at the gun-tackles, or working in the fire-room, and in these facts and contrasts I had enough to erect a theory upon—more indeed, than the basis of many theories. How is it, I asked, that the same allowance of water which is just enough for men under the most favorable circumstances, is fully sufficient for others in such different conditions? Here the apple hit me on the head. I remembered that the works upon the laws of life are entitled, "Principles of Human Physiology." It is then evident that these pretenders to science have overlooked one fact just under their noses. *Human* physiology should embrace all men; but these observers have failed to study either sailors or officers, inasmuch as naval law so distinctly recognizes a difference in their natures that one or the other must be excepted from "humanity."

I might be satisfied with resting my fame upon this discovery, but I made others.

I promised the reader to solve the mystery of what may be called, "privations without necessity," and it shall now be done.

In the "good old days," under "the ancient discipline" of the service, when men were flogged, and officers were committing themselves by getting drunk, breaking their liberty, and other violations of propriety, captains had a glorious time; they could daily give tangible evidence of their authority, and roll it as a "sweet morsel under their tongues." They could get into great passions, swear, and cry out at the top of their voices, "Go below, sir, and consider yourself suspended from duty," and feel relieved and comfortable. But what can they do in these days of staid propriety? When officers do their duty from a conscientious sense of obligation, and respect themselves more than they fear authority, the captain's occupation seems nearly gone. What there may be stormy in his nature, is "cabined, cribbed, confined" by an invisible circle of conscientious deportment which will not let him blow out. His existence might be overlooked, and so—he stops your allowance of water, and you feel his power in every moving fibre and flowing vein. Is that not reason enough, unreasonable doubters?

No matter where you may be sitting at this moment reading my sea-cell developments, just for a short time imagine yourself sitting quietly alone in an elegantly-furnished upper room of a large house. There are two or three hundred people engaged in various avocations in the rooms beneath you, and although acknowledging your superiority, thinking more of their work than of you. This wounds your vanity. You throw yourself back in your chair; you stretch out your legs, and cross one over the other, and think. Suddenly it occurs to you to chain down the handle of the pump in the yard for one half the day, and stick up a notice that it was done by your authority. You may then feel assured that your existence is felt, and may enjoy the consciousness of power. And this mystery of water is the secret of more than half of what is called military discipline. I think, however, that naval government in this respect is essentially defective, so long as there is no sufficient means of serving out allotments of light and air at the instigation of whim and caprice, and am very certain that a Navy board could be found capable of organizing the system; but at the very beginning I protest against its appropriating the originality of the suggestion.

My friend, Lieutenant Bryan Boroihme, as he came in, trumpet in hand, after being relieved from the forenoon watch, sat himself down and looked serious, even sad; after a few moments he remarked slowly, half speaking to himself, "I shall be glad when this allowance of water is at an end."

I must, however, make my reader acquainted with Bryan, although I am not sure that the course of this history will give them the pleasure which I had, of an extended association. He was one of those who, being a law unto themselves, fortunately had that law resting upon a right heart and a sound head. His sympathies were with his fellow-man in the widest sense, and he recognized the rights and claims of humanity, independent of external circumstances, and as superior to those of any individual. His mental stores had been gathered from a wide field of literary ranging, and he was equally ready to hurl a sturdy oak of principle at wrong, or to cast the flowers of poesy upon the angry waters of discussion as they rolled by him. Such was the man to whose involuntary remark I replied, by asking what suggested it.

"I 'll tell you. During my last mid-watch, I was standing near the binnacle, when I heard a sort of sigh or grunt of discomfort from Turner the quartermaster, who was at the 'conn.' It attracted my attention, and I asked him what was the matter.

"'I was thinking, sir, of a hard time I had once on account of a shipwreck.'

"I have no objection myself to talking to the men and learning their experience, so I encouraged him to go on and tell me about it, which he did very graphically; but the gist of the whole matter was, that he and others, eleven in all, were sixteen days in a boat, on only four gallons of water, and he did not suffer so much from thirst as he was then doing.

"'But, Turner, how could that be—you have much more now?'

"'Know it, sir. Can't tell, except I was kind of anxious, and I knowed it could n't be helped.'

"'Are you very thirsty now?'

"'My tongue is like a dried shark's skin. Allowance gave out about four o'clock.'

"I fortunately had some of my own allowance in a bottle in my room, which I sent for, and moistened Turner's shark-skin tongue.

"But that is not all," continued Boroihme; "just now, before I left the deck—"

However, as I can not tell the incident in the manner of my friend, I will tell it in my own.

I must premise that this conversation occurred after we had left Ascension, where we had laid in a large supply both of water and green turtle.

Green turtle soup! After writing these words, reader, both you and I ought not to hurry on, but pause and think upon them, that is, if the flavor of the compound has ever rested upon your palate as it has upon mine—which I doubt. Rich in substantial gelatine, perfumed, gently perfumed, with varied spices, tinted with rosy wine, gemmed with emeralds of callipash, and garnished with golden lemons. We had a French cook, and such was the kind of soup our caterer gave us. But the men had turtle soup too—quasi turtle soup; all except one mess.

Just before my friend left the deck his attention was invited to a man standing at the mast with a big tin pan. All such conferences are held at the mast. It is the neutral ground between the quarter deck and the forecastle —the bar of impromptu justice, and the exchange where conflicting opinion meets. The Lieutenant walked forward and looked into the pan. On its bottom lay a turtle's bony and skinny fin, boiled to rags, and exhausted of juices. The man asked the officer respectfully whether that was a suitable dinner for their mess. The officer did not think it was, and the ship's cook being sent for, explained that this mess had not contributed of their allowance of water to make the soup, and therefore the dry turtle flipper which they gave to him, he returned to them more dry and less substantial.

"Why sir," quoted my friend with animation, as he concluded the story, "it was the play of Hamlet with Hamlet left out."

The turtle flipper and the shark's tongue of Turner caused Boroihme to wish the allowance at an end. There was no real suffering, but the men were uncomfortable.

All that kind of floating and unsubstantial gossip which on shore has its source in "on dit," and "they say," is on shipboard called "galley news." Reports from this quarter have reached us that we, instead of running our course, are running for rains. This I take to be a mere scandal, inasmuch as, in three days' loss of time, we might not catch one day's water. However, whether running for rains or not we fell in them, and the waters of the skies intoxicated our ship's company. There was a tremendous excitement; every man set up in the water line upon his own hook. The awnings were spread, and in their deep cavities the floods gathered. Every tub, pitcher, basin, bucket, bottle, or other vessel which would contain water was brought into use and stowed in our rooms. Our cells became water cells.

That the allowance of water on shipboard is often diminished without necessity, to the great detriment of health, the history of the service proves. It is too important an element of existence to be at the caprices of a tyrannical disposition, or a monomaniacal folly. It should be made a solemn and important thing. The commanding officer should convene a board of officers, of which the medical officer should be a member, and then, if this board does not concur in the propriety of diminishing the allowance, still let the commanding officer have the power of doing so, entering on the log, and reporting to the Department, his reasons for differing with the views of the board.

VIII.

SIMON'S BAY.

Before we were led off by this water excursion, our last word was Hope. And hope was fulfilled. That fair breeze came gliding over the water, rippling its bright blue surface, and gemming it with sparkling spray. Before it we swept on over the Southern ocean, and as we approached the southern continent we found the ocean rolling in long and magnificent swells. Without much wind, our ship running from three to five miles an hour only, they came sweeping down, rolling and tossing us about terribly, and when the wind freshened, it seemed to raise supplemental hillocks of water upon the top of these swells. Looking over a large expanse of ocean, it had the appearance of smooth rolling hills, with lesser hills cresting their tops. Ports closed in darkness, rolling and staggering over this heaving ocean, we sped on our way. January 12th, 1856, was a white day in my geographical calendar, as it was then I, for the first time, rested my eyes upon the black continent whose people have given the world more political and religious trouble than their physical strength has ever given it aid. It was a white day, not only on account of this geographical wonder, but because, after thirty-one days of sea rolling and ship dietetics, we were to have the quiet of port, the fresh fruits of the earth, and to tread once more its solid, motherly bosom. When I went upon deck at an earlier hour in the morning than usual, there were the great rocky buttresses, the ragged mountains of South Africa, jutting out into the sea, which rolled in upon them from the pole, or, at nearest, the Antarctic continent. Table Mountain, and all the individualized and named peaks of this renowned Cape were in sight as we ran along the shores of "Good Hope," rounded its promontory, and entered the smooth green waters of Simon's Bay. There a few neat-looking English houses clustered on the beach, at the foot of the gray, naked mountain towering behind them. We cast our anchor in front of Simon's Town—of about one thousand inhabitants—another of the tapping-places of England's world-encircling drum.

The anchor being down, then came all the bustle and preparation of an arrival in port. We tried to brighten up, mentally and vestimentally; our better and brighter uniforms were put on, straw hats hung up, and laced and embroidered caps substituted. The marines were brightly costumed, ready to be paraded as a guard of honor for any distinguished visitor; and such of them as stood sentry were placed on post, musket in hand, at the gangways. The boats were lowered from their davits, and one of the lieutenants, in cocked hat and sword, dispatched to wait on the authorities and arrange the salutes.

Various boats were hurrying off to us. One was that of the health officer and harbor master, before whose visit we must not communicate with the shore. Another, with the United States flag flying, brought the American Consul. A third, with a pennon in the bow, and the British ensign in the stern, brought a lieutenant from the English commodore's flag-ship, the Castor, to tender us the courtesies of the port. Then came the salutes, twenty-one guns for the British flag, and next thirteen guns for the British commodore, both of which were returned from the Castor, and we were fairly introduced.

The salutes over, the string of small boats which had been lying astern to be out of the way of the guns, now pull up to the gangway, and their occupants, each one hurrying before his neighbor, climb the ship's side and step on board. There are provision dealers, grocers, tailors, bumboat men, washermen and women, zealous to show their cards and recommendations from preceding ships, and to secure the custom of the various messes. The bumboat man is the most useful of all these water merchants. He may be all in one. His boat is the peddling shop, the corner grocery to the people shut up on board the ship. At designated hours he comes alongside with his store of fresh fruits, fresh bread, cooked fish and meats, with tempting varieties of articles peculiar to the locality in which we may be. He is a convenience also for communicating with the shore, making purchases, and bringing off small packages, of which we all avail ourselves, preferring the independence of this private arrangement to the *ifs* and *ands*, the cumbrous contingencies, the weighty concession which attends, so often, the getting the use of a ship's boat. Of course a man in such close association with the people of the ship must have the guarantee of a certain amount of reputable character, or he may do much mischief by smuggling liquor and other improper articles on board.

Upon this occasion a tall, slender, neatly dressed Malay, with a red Madras kerchief on his head, won the most general favor. He had a package of recommendations from the officers of British and American men-of-war, and one of recent date from an English commodore, recommending him to the special favor of all British men-of-war, because he had supplied H. M. S. Nankin with provisions despite the anti-convict restrictions. A ship came here to land convicts—the settlement resisted the landing, and prohibited its citizens from furnishing supplies. Treacherous to his town and true to his pocket, the Malay, Tiffley Manuel, supplied the ship at midnight with every thing needful, even to bullocks. The convicts, however, were not landed.

As one of our welcome-giving visitors sat in the

cabin, pointing to a neighboring mountain, he said, "The Muizenberg has its cap on; it's going to blow fresh from the south-east before to-morrow morning, and you are lying so far out you will feel it." And such we found to be the case. Whenever the cloud cap gathered around the brow of the Muizenberg, the south-easters whistled through our rigging. We dropped another anchor, and our communication with the shore was interrupted, difficult and dangerous.

The winds on the south-east coast of Africa are violently fitful, changing instantly from south-east to north-west, without a moment's warning; and our new acquaintances of the Cape were now mourning the melancholy destructiveness of these gales in the loss of the brig Nerbudda, which, having left Algoa Bay, had been hoped for from day to day, but never heard of.

Such a disappearance of a ship into the mysterious depths of the ocean with her whole living crew—of those with whom you have been in recent association, and for whose return you confidently look—is one of the most painful manifestations of the terrors of the ocean. The very uncertainty of the moment gives a dark and gloomy freedom to the imagination, and it will pertinaciously call up the horrors of that moment when an entire community of familiar friends, in full life and vigor, and in the consciousness of an inevitable doom, sank beneath the ingulfing waves. Our own recent national and personal losses in the Porpoise and Albany, enabled us to sympathize with our new friends in the loss of the Nerbudda. But this south-east wind has its compensations: its tempestuous flight bears healing on its wings. Blowing from the cold regions of the south, it is found to purify the atmosphere, and drive away disease. Although Simon's Bay has the annoyance of this wind, Simon's Town owes its existence to its being sheltered from the fierce winds which roll the

Atlantic in before Table Bay and Cape Town. It is also the site of the government dockyard, and the anchorage of the government shipping.

We are now receiving some of the physical compensations of our sea existence. Those things which are an ever present and little appreciated circumstance of shore life, came to us as a lucky accident; we were therefore much gratified at seeing our table, on the first day of our arrival, loaded with plums, pears and melons; pyramids of purple and white grapes, and most delicious peaches. We were now comfortable enough to afford some pity for our distant friends who were housed from the winds and snows of a northern winter.

Without going out of the ship we can supply our tables with most delicious fish. A line over the ship's side will reward the most exacting fisherman. Solid, substantial, silver-scaled Cape salmon, weighing from fifteen to eighteen pounds, were nightly taken in numbers from the waters alongside the ship, and enlivened the night watches by flapping the deck, as they were one after another thrown upon it. This lordly fellow was only one among many smaller fry. But there was death in the pot.

Upon our first arrival the harbor master placed in my hands the following printed paper:

CAUTION.

There is a fish in Simon's Bay, commonly called Toad Fish; it is about six inches long, back dark, with deep black stripes; belly white, with faint yellow patches; it swims near the surface, and is a constant attendant on lines employed fishing. When taken from the water, it puffs out considerably. Should any portion of this fish be eaten, DEATH ENSUES in a few minutes.

W. P. JAMISON, Harbor Master.

Port Office, Simon's Town, November 22, 1848.

Although we have not yet put our feet on shore, we are reminded that we are in Africa by the advertisements of some local papers which have found their way on board. "Rhinoceros horns—ostrich eggs and feathers—basket and drinking-cups made of ostrich eggs—Kaffir karasses, and native weapons of various tribes—lion, tiger, and other skins—a fine live tiger, and a variety of articles too numerous to particularize."

We must go ashore and see all these things, and more. I hope the reader will go with us, help us make our carriage bargain, and see things as we saw them, little and big. The south-easter had puffed itself out and left a smooth time, when, in the early morning, Commodore Armstrong, Lieutenant Rutledge and I, with carpet-bags and valises, started for the shore and a journey to Cape Town.

The proprietor of horses and carriages expected us, and was awaiting our arrival with a cart and horses ready harnessed—a cart on two wheels, with yellow painted canvas cover, but fortunately a cart on springs.

"What are we to pay?"

"Two pun ten sir"—two pounds ten shillings—"for Cape Town and back." The distance is twenty-four miles.

"How much to leave us there, and we find our own way back?"

"Same, sir. Two pun ten."

"How much time do you give us there?"

"Forty-eight hours from starting—we keep the horses. Ten shillings a-day for all detention over that."

"Very well."

We stow our luggage, take our seats, a native Sierra Leone negro, with teeth filed sharp, mounts the fourth seat as driver, and while the bright sun is gleaming on the water, and lifting the misty night-caps from the bald mountain-heads, we rattle out of Simon's Town, shaking the lingering slumber from the eyes of the few enterprising individuals who came to their doors and windows to see what was going on. The first thing we ran against was an institution of civilization—a toll-gate—sixpence. There were two others on our road. But what do we pay for? Here we are rolling over a better road than man could ever build, made by that Power, and at the same time, who lifted these rugged, rocky, bare, gray mountains, close on our left hand, from the ocean depths; a broad, level, white, firm sand beach, which for myriads of ages has been daily relaid by that same flowing tide which is now gently rippling over and washing out our wheel-tracks and hoof-marks. But we come to the end of our sea-washed road, and then we find that our road-tax is not for nothing. Over the point of high land which juts out into the sea, a fine macadamized road has been built. We have, however, two other fine bay beaches, with intervening points of high land. Along all this part of the road there is nothing to attract our attention from the wild grandeur of nature. Here and there a thatched fisherman's hut, or on the edge of a bank overlooking the bay, a small stone house, as a look-out for whales. As we proceed, and the settlement thickens, we notice a peculiar fence surrounding the inclosures—symmetrical white posts tapering toward the ground, and, in some places, more slender arches, with one end on the ground and the other curving up to and supporting a light wicker fence. All these are whalebones—the post the heavier, and the outside curving supports the lighter, ribs. Some fanciful individuals, standing two of the largest ribs erect, and bringing their tapering points together, had made pointed arches for gateway entrances.

We are now approaching a village, Kalk Bay, and the air is loaded with odors—an ancient and fish-like smell—

that of codfish. As we enter the village, we see on all hands the source of the smell and the settlement, in heaps and piles of dried fish—Cape salmon. There were kilns for drying them artificially, and wagons in which they were loaded, piled up like shingles. They are largely exported to the interior, and supplied to the shipping. Kalk Bay is also a hygeian resort for the invalids of the city, who come here to inhale fresh from the water the salutary breezes of the south-east wind.

Leaving Kalk Bay, our road takes us from the waterside, our gray rocky mountains recede further to the left, and do not threaten us with an avalanche of the great masses which, pivot-hung, appear ready to crash down into the road. On either hand we have a dry, sandy plain, greened over with an undergrowth of strange and varied vegetation. It would be terrible on such a hot day as this, the 16th of January, to have dragged our cart through such a heavy, sandy soil as this around us, but thanks to our road maker, we are rolling still over a hard, smooth, red macadamized highway, and therefore at the Muizenberg gate, we pay our sixpence with grateful, and, I hope, graceful freedom. Over the sandy plain to our left, where it approaches the slopes of the mountains, we notice several large white houses or country seats, surrounded by a richer vegetation, from which rolls up, in long round swells, the oak groves and avenues which bower in the houses of the vineyards of Constancia. I hope we shall see them more closely before getting back to Simon's Bay.

Having reached Rathfelder's, a neat wayside inn, we stopped an hour for breakfast, and to rest our horses. Our table was here supplied with finer grapes and peaches than we had yet seen, and we found some interest in walking through his large, rich, and well-cultivated garden of varied fruits and substantial vegetables. We here too saw, for the first time, in his slaughter-house, the carcasses of several of the peculiar Cape sheep, with the enormous broad masses of fat, of several pounds' weight, forming the tail. Subsequently meeting several flocks of these sheep, I was surprised to notice how little unwieldy and cumbrous these fatty masses appeared, terminating in a taper extremity slightly curved up.

Associating, as we do, the short woolly hair with the dark African skin, my attention was arrested by the very black skins of the female servants, combined with a beautiful delicacy of feature, and long black glossy hair. They were Malays, or rather a mixture of Malay and negro. Most of the colored women we saw were of this character. They are great favorites as domestics, having more docility, intelligence, and finer sensibilities than the negro.

From this pleasant half-way house on to Cape Town the country wonderfully improves. The road is beautiful—a shaded avenue, passing between rows of pine trees, and under an arched arbor of oaks. Farms, plantations and vineyards cover the country; and around the village of Rondebosh, near which is the residence of the Governor, Sir George Grey, are gathered pleasant country seats.

The road, too, is an animated picture for us. Specimens of various negro tribes and Malays, with English and Dutch laborers, are pursuing their way on foot.

What is this approaching us—a forest of horns? One—two—three—four—five—six—seven—eight pair of oxen in a single team—long horns and broadly-extended horns, three to four feet between the tips, yoked to one little, and what would be with us a one-horse wagon! We are meeting many of these little wagons, with pyramid-hatted Malay drivers—some of them, instead of oxen, have eight mules, donkeys, or horses. Amid this throng of laboring vehicles come rolling along English carriages, with servants in livery, and some stiff and stately John Bull inside—Cockneydom grafted upon Africa. I am not responsible for this ill-natured insinuation. It came from one among themselves. Aristocracy, he said, ran tremendously high among the placemen and successful adventurers of the colony One of the latter, wishing to be particularly distinguished, upon achieving fortune sent home to London an order for the most expensive books and most expensive wines. "Of course," remarked my informant, "he was no gentleman, but only a Cockney. For wines they sent him the Constancia which had gone home from his very door."

Occasionally, in these stately little liveried vehicles, we were cheered by the sight of neatly dressed English ladies, and could not refrain from the courtesy of a bow to that sex which has the most undoubted right to take airs upon itself.

Among so many vehicles, and tramping and driving, the red, iron-rust-colored dust of the road began to be annoying, and we were glad to find ourselves, after a four hours' journey, driving past the barracks, with its rolling drums and red-coated soldiers, and through the substantial English streets of Cape Town, and dismounted at the Masonic Hotel. A nearer look at the "Table Mountain" and the "Lion's Rump" and "Head"—a stroll through the city—a look out upon Table Bay and its shipping—a walk through the Botanical Garden, and beneath the mile long oak avenue, a thousand old oaks, of the government grounds—a visit to the museum of native animals—genial evenings at the hospitable tables of those gentlemen who kindly looked us up—visits to the curiosity shops;—these made up the sum of our occupation in Cape Town, which has between twenty and thirty thousand inhabitants. But it is the metropolis of a colony destined to a great future, toward which it is making rapid strides. It has a similitude to our own country in the phenomenon of a European civilization pressing for two hundred years upon, and pressing back, and out of existence, ferocious, barbarous tribes—carrying its frontier against those tribes, and against the most ferocious and powerful wild beasts and reptiles—the lion, the leopard, and the cobra—until it is arrested by the arid desert.

There is much to interest every man who thinks at all, every thing to interest the American in the social and political features of this colony.

By Dutch and English the colony has now been settled for over two hundred years; for over forty years it has been an English possession; and the act for the abolition of slavery in all British territories was carried into effect over twenty years ago.

Besides the old original Cape district, by conquest and by occupation twenty other districts have been added. The wilderness, once the possession of the Hottentot and quadrupedal savages, is now covered with grain fields, orchards, and vineyards producing the most luscious of wines; farms yielding that which is literally the "golden fleece" of the colony—wool, whose increase of export has gone on from a few thousand pounds to many and increasing millions, and whose progressive increase is beyond estimate. Yet, amid all these farmers, plantation proprietors, and wool-growers, where is the aboriginal inhabitant? Is he of them? He is the servant of servants, the laborer to Dutch laboring Boers, or he is a child-killing, parent-slaying savage. These facts should be suggestive to the theoretical philanthropists, who are regulating the social problems of the age by the benevolence of their own hearts. The free and protected black British citizens of Cape Colony are yielding their lands to the farms and vineyards of the white man, and the world and civilization are the gainers.

Twenty of the districts, we found, have grown out of the original Cape settlement, and sought their varied fortunes up the eastern and western coasts, and in the interior of the African continent. A glance at these various districts will give us a more definite idea of the present character and future destiny of this part of the continent, and we shall be drawing near to two strange republics:

The CAPE DIVISION has the metropolis, fine farms, various manufactures, extensive fisheries, and the Constancia vineyards.

MALMESBURY is called the granary of the colony, from its cereal abundance, and is distinguished by a warm mineral spring.

STELLENBOSCH.—Simon Vander Stell, the Governor, founded the town of this district in 1681. It is, therefore, one of the oldest in the colony. It is a populous and productive district, of picturesque and varied scenery, and fertile vineyards.

PAARL is another rich vineyard district. The wine of Paarl village is considered the best made in the colony. The sweet wine nearly equals the celebrated Constancia. I am tempted to quote the flattering account of Paarl, from its resemblance to some local paper's account of some village in Kansas or Nebraska: "This village makes excellent progress. Two banks have already been established, and landed property is rising."

WORCESTER gives us cool summers, frosty winters, and the finest flavored apples, pears, and cherries.

CLAN WILLIAM.—Herds, tobacco, rice, copper, mineral springs, hat factories, and cedar boards.

GEORGE.—Wool, butter, aloes, grain, cattle. It has a safe bay and wonderful caverns.

BEAUFORT.—Principally grazing, skins and ostrich feathers.

ALBANY.—A pastoral district, more populous than any other at the Cape, and has in it the flourishing city, Graham's Town.

FORT BEAUFORT.—We are now drawing near to Kaffirland, but still this division has some of the finest sheep and grain farms in the colony, several of which are worth from twenty to twenty-five thousand dollars.

The district of Stockenstrom, in this division, is of the most interesting and remarkable character. "It may, in general terms, be described as a basin encircled by a chain of mountains, from which issue the numerous streams that give fertility to the soil, and render it so eligible for a numerous population.

"This district was formerly occupied wholly by Hottentots, but, in consequence of the large number of its inhabitants (one half at least) who joined in the late rebellion, the Governor, Sir George Cathcart, at the end of the war," had steps taken to break up an exclusively national settlement—a measure (*i. e.* the settlement) which his excellency considered to have proved not only a failure, but was attended with dangerous and inconvenient consequences, prejudicial alike to the inhabitants themselves and to the community at large.

"From the town of Fort Beaufort can be seen a long range of dark and rugged hills, fringed with wood, and intersected by dark and precipitous ravines, and overlooking the country to this place, from which it is not generally more than five miles distant, as the crow flies. Here it was that Macomo and the rebel Hottentots took up their abode during the war, and here likewise has been the scene of the various conflicts and disasters which had for so long a time followed the attempts to expel the enemy."*

GRAAF REINET.—Wool and cattle are the chief pro-

* Cape Almanac.

ducts—principally wool. Large tracts of country in this division are entirely destitute of wood, the farmers using cattle dung for fuel. This is dug out of the kraals when softened by rain; it is then cut into square pieces and stacked, as is done with turf or peat in many parts of Great Britain. When sufficiently dry it is preferred, as fuel, to wood, giving a stronger heat, and causing less trouble. It is frequently used by blacksmiths at the forge, instead of coal.

Game of all kinds is plentiful—sometimes far too superabundant. Long droughts in the interior compel the spring-bok to forsake the extensive plains which are then its favorite haunts, and to migrate into the colony. This it occasionally does in such incredible numbers that their visit is felt as a serious calamity—the herbage being entirely consumed by them. The capital of the division is a beautiful village, planted on each side with lemon trees, interspersed with the acacia and Ceylon rose.

COLESBURGH lies north, on the Orange River. In cattle, sheep and horses it is the richest in the colony, although subject to violent snow storms.

These notes, condensed from the Cape Almanac, enable us to form some idea of the general character and resources of the country. We now pass on to the

SOVEREIGNTY

on Orange River, to the north of which it lies. It is three hundred and seventy-five miles from south to north. "In 1836 it was described by Sir C. W. Harris as a trackless desert, a howling wilderness, a land in which, though thinly populated by skulking hordes of Bushmen, and by the starving remnants of nomadic pastoral tribes which had been broken up by war and violence, no man permanently dwelt, neither was the soil any man's property—a land in which for hundreds of miles the eye was not greeted by the smallest trace of human industry, or by any vestige of human habitation—the wild and interminable expanse ever presenting the same appearance —*that of one vast, uninhabited solitude.*" This tract is generally a heavy grazing country. It is now occupied by fine farms and a flourishing population, making large exports of wool, and sending its droves even to Cape Colony. It is well watered, abounds in mill seats, produces various grains and fruits, and coal is found among its as yet little known mineral productions. Its towns and villages have their school houses, churches of various denominations, club houses and theatres. And this is an independent, self-governing, republican sovereignty. Independent by the voluntary act of the British authorities, and adjoining it, beyond the river Vaal is the

TRANS VAAL, OR DUTCH REPUBLIC.

Although expediency, and even necessity, beget much alliance and social union between the original Dutch population and the more recent English graft, still there is a marked line of uncongeniality, composed of contempt on the part of the English, and a mitigated dislike upon the part of the Dutch. Many years ago, Andries Wilhelmus, Jacobus Pretorius emigrated from the colony to seek a home, as many of his countrymen had done, in the wilderness, away from all interference by British authority. He went to Natal, when the country was independent of the British government. But British authority pursued the emigrant farmers in that retreat. A conflict ensued between the British troops and Dutch farmers, led by Pretorius. He was eventually defeated. The British government took possession of the country, chiefly, if not solely, *with a view of protecting the natives*, and a price was set upon his head.

He was subsequently pardoned, and resided at Natal several years under the administration of Lieutenant Governor West. He complained bitterly of the encroachments of the natives in the neighborhood, and upon his property, and traveled by land to Graham's Town to represent his grievances to Sir H. Pottinger, but that governor did not admit him even to a private audience. He afterwards saw Sir Harry Smith whilst this governor was on his way to Natal, and was afterwards very indignant when he heard Sir Harry had proclaimed the Sovereignty British territory—his version of the interview, as reported at the time, being, that that governor had promised not to do so unless the majority of the residents in that country were in favor of the measure—which majority, Pretorius declared, were not in favor of it. It will probably never be known with accuracy what passed between Sir Harry Smith and Pretorius, but the result of making the Sovereignty a British possession led Pretorius to invite his countrymen to take up arms, and the result was the battle of Boomplaats, since which time the country has not been disturbed by the Dutch emigrants. After this battle, Pretorius appears to have lived very quietly at Magoliesburgh, notwithstanding that a price was again set upon his head, and to have busied himself with endeavoring to consolidate a Dutch republic beyond the Vaal. He continued to be thus occupied until Major Hogge and Mr. Owen were associated with Sir Harry Smith, and subsequently he was again pardoned, and then was made the convention with him which acknowledged the independence of the Trans Vaal republic. In this convention the darling wish of his heart, which he had nourished for years, appears to have been gratified. He had wished all his lifetime to establish an independent Dutch State in southern Africa, and had at length succeeded. This republic, with its own President and laws, still exists, and is the second independent State adjoining the British possessions in southern Africa.

Honest-hearted American patriots, who are devoting themselves to the abolition of slavery in the United States, must have their confidence in the sincerity and principle of their English coadjutors very much shaken by the testimony of Lord Palmerston before a committee of Parliament—that English West India sugar growing interests are opposed to the existence of slavery in other nations; and the inconsistency of English statesmen upon this unhappy subject is prominent in the fact that both these republics are slave States. They are to all intents English States. No one can for a moment believe that England would permit their independence, if it were not convenient to do so. By permitting it, the boast of no slave foot upon English soil is maintained, in name. The independence of any small and weak State adjoining English military territory and power would be a phenomenon; the independence of such a State, with the ports of export and import in the possession of the English, is a farce.

An English local writer, speaking of the government of the free State, says, "We now expect that the laws (except with regard to slavery) will be as well, if not more efficiently carried out as under the English government." Speaking of the aggressive wars of the citizens of these republics over the Vaal River, this writer says, "Wars are there made for the express purpose of capturing children, and kidnapping is carried on in many parts. The consequence of this will in all probability be that the thin vail which has been cast over slavery by calling it the sale of services, or indentures, will soon be thrown away, and that they will keep them in bondage for their lifetime, and sell their children and children's children, and as the interest of the people in this system or trade increases, laws will be made from time to time protective of it.

"But one thing is plain, that if England does not use the influence in South Africa which God has given her, to put a stop to slavery, it will become a thorn in her side which will cause her much trouble yet.

"It is the policy of the government, in order to avoid future Kaffir wars, in order to prove to them that we wish to deal justly by them, and that we are actuated by high and Christian principles. Our permitting and countenancing slavery on our borders will give this the lie, and embitter them against us. They will say, 'We interfere when the blacks steal cattle from the whites, and then countenance the whites when they steal children from the blacks.'

"I stated before that no clergyman, to my knowledge, had hitherto risked his reputation or influence in that part of South Africa, by preaching or speaking to their flocks about slavery, or about the duties of the white Christians to instruct the black heathen in their households, or to look upon them as human, soul-possessing beings."

There are three distinct types of negro to be found in Cape Colony. The thick-lipped, sturdy, woolly-headed prominent-chinned, flat-nosed Congo, or West Coast Negro—the equally black, tall, graceful, delicately-featured Kaffir and Zulo, and the diminutive, light yellow, thin, tufty-headed Hottentot and Bushman, and who presents other peculiar physical formations, it would be as difficult to educe from external causes, as it would be to produce by these causes the analogical fat-tailed sheep of the Cape of Good Hope.

IX.

WINE AND WELCOME.

HAVING seen such sights and learned such facts as our short stay in Cape Town permitted, our cart was ordered up and we took our departure for Simon's Bay. Our return to this place was to be varied by a ride through the village of Wynberg, and a visit to the vineyard of Constancia.

After we had passed through, Wynberg, and had some ecstacies, such as are incident to sailors on shore, over its rural charms and prettily embowered houses, we found ourselves on the road to the residence of Mr. Cloete, the proprietor of the Constancia estate, and began to think it would be better had we the claim of some note or letter of introduction. As, however, our intention was to get permission merely to walk through the vineyard, and not to intrude ourselves upon the family, we came to the conclusion that, as we could not help ourselves, it was just as well as it was, by the time our cart trundled into an avenue of noble old oaks and brought up in front of Mr. Cloete's large and comfortable-looking mansion.

A Malay servant came to the door; received our cards; promptly threw open the drawing-room doors with a manner which showed that a prompt welcome was the rule of the house. Crouched upon the floor, upon one side of this room, was the stuffed skin of the largest and finest-looking leopard I ever saw. Its hide was of the brightest yellow with the blackest spots, and it was well and naturally set up. We had scarcely more than glanced at these things when two young ladies entered the room, welcoming us with graceful courtesy, and saying that their father, who would be in presently, would be delighted at our calling, without waiting for the visit he intended to pay us. Soon after, Mr. Cloete, a fine specimen of the colonial Dutch gentleman, entered the room and gave us a welcome as cordial and courteous as that of his daughters had been graceful. One after the other entering the room, we found ourselves at home with this very agreeable family, and almost forgot the vineyard.

Showing the way to the vineyard, Mr. Cloete explained to us the character of the grapes from which the four kinds of Constancia wines are made. The dry Pontac or Cape port; the sweet Pontac, a black, rich, sweet wine; and two beautifully ruby-looking wines, sweet and cordial-like to the taste, called Frontignac, and I think white Constancia. It is difficult for any one familiar with the spirituous taste of most wines, to believe that any such rich syrupy fluids can be produced from the grape alone, without the addition of sugar. But such is the fact. The grapes are permitted to almost wilt upon the vines before they are plucked, and to facilitate this saccharizing process the leaves are thinned from the vines. One accustomed to the mode of raising the grape in use with us, would scarcely recognize a Cape of Good Hope vineyard. At a little distance he would not distinguish it from a potato field—the vines being not over three feet high, bunches of fresh shoots supported on old knotty, venerable, gray looking stocks, many of which were probably as old as the vineyard, and this was near two hundred years of age, having been planted by one of the first governors, and gallantly called after his wife, "Constancia." These old Dutch governors must have been gallant knights, from the honors paid their wives; the division of Stellenbosch being called after the then governor himself, and the Maiden Bosch who became Madam Van der Stell, and Graef Reinet from Governor Graef, and his good wife Reinet. The days of chivalry were then, when these old gray wine stocks were new, and Constancia first flowed in ruby sweetness. It was better, however, Mr. Cloete told me, not to have the vines over one hundred years old—a vineyard of one hundred thousand vines should have a thousand renewed every year.

Waving his hand over a tract of a few acres, our host remarked, that in this tract alone, and in no other place, is raised the genuine original Constancia. Pointing to an adjoining field he remarked, "I can extend that vineyard as much as I please, but it will not, no matter what grape is used, produce 'Constancia' wine." I supposed, at the time, that this opinion might have been the result of partiality for his own homestead, but others testified to the same fact. An English gentleman—a competing planter—observed to me, "That is true: the Constancia is grown only there; but wines of the same character, and so near in quality, that scarcely any one can distinguish them, are grown upon other estates." It will also be noticed what is said, in the preceding description of the districts, on the wines of Paarl.

From the vineyard we took our way to the wine store, a neat, orderly, cool, white-washed stone building, decorated by a classic relief over the main entrance. Inside it was but an avenue between two ranges of immense ornamentally fronted butts, with polished brass cocks, each containing twelve hundred gallons. A capacious entrance, for cleaning these butts, was made by an oblong opening cut through the central plank of the head, with the edge so beveled that the smaller opening was external, and the pressure from within tightened the gate, which was also drawn firm by a screw passing through a bar. A servant brought us glasses, and we tasted on the spot each of the four kinds of costly Constancia. The nature of these wines would have pleased Athenæus, who, in his "Banquet of the Learned," says, "But that which is sweet, (as is the case with even white and yellow wine also,) is the most nutritious of all, for it softens all the ducts and passages, and thickens the fluid parts of the body, and does not at all confuse the head. For in reality the nature of sweet wine lingers about the ribs, and engenders spittle as Diocles and Pythagoras assert."

We have, in these modern days, a sufficiently wide range of wine taste, from the pale acid wines of the Rhine through claret to Port and Madeira, and from these to the rich syrups of the Cape of Good Hope, by the side of which grows also a delicately flavored Hock. But these old sensual heathens had such medicated wine tastes as to indicate a medicinal purpose in their wine drinking.

Athenæus again tells us, "Now the wines which have been carefully prepared with sea-water never cause headaches," and produce certain wholesome effects. "But Theophrastus says, that the wine of Thaos is wonderfully delicious, for it is well seasoned; for they knead up dough and honey, and put that into the earthern jars, so that the wine receives fragrance from itself and sweetness from the honey."

But with all this mixing of sea water and dough, the poets of those days had to sing "Temperance," if not "Total Abstinence," songs. It seems to have been the idea of Eubulus that three glasses of wine were enough for any man, as he introduces Bacchus, as saying,

"Let them three parts of wine all duly season,
With nine of water, who 'd preserve their reason;
The first gives health, the second sweet desire;
The third tranquillity and sleep inspire:
These are the wholesome draughts which wise men please,
Who from the banquet home return in peace.
From a fourth measure insolence proceeds:

Uproar a fifth; a sixth wild license breeds;
A seventh brings black eyes and livid bruises;
The eighth the constable next introduces;
Black gall and hatred lurk the ninth beneath;
The tenth is madness, arms, and fearful death.
For too much wine poured in one little vessel,
Trips up all those who seek with it to wrestle."

Very good advice of Mr. Bacchus; and as the three glasses of wine imply three tumblers of water, they may very safely be taken, we think.

Having seen the wonders of the wine store, we proposed taking leave of the family and continuing our way, but Mr. Cloete had had the horses taken out of our cart, and prohibited all such movements by saying we were all now going in to "tiffin"—for already do they begin to talk East Indian—and so in to tiffin we went. Our arrival had hit a happy occasion. A large number of his very large relationship, including nephews and nieces, had met at Mr. Cloete's house to celebrate his birthday, and upon our return we found the whole party assembled in the drawing-room, not stiff and stately, but easy, joyous, and chatty; so unconscious of the presence of strangers that we forgot we were such.

"Tiffin" seems a light and ethereal sort of a name enough, but call it, more substantially, lunch, and yet the word does not give a correct idea to our minds of the full meal which it really is—in fact one of our most solid family dinners.

We had hot meats and vegetables, ale and wine, followed by preserves and the most delicious peaches, melons, and grapes of "Constancia."

The magnificent leopard we had noticed on the floor, Mr. Cloete told us he had shot himself, about twelve miles from his house, and shot him with buck-shot, when the distance between the parties was little more than two gun lengths, and the leopard crouched on a limb ready for a spring. But in pleasant social intercourse and anecdotes of colonial life,

> "As bees flee hame wi' lades of treasure,
> The minutes winged their way with pleasure;
> Nae man can tether time nor tide;
> The hour approaches, we maun ride."

And therefore, taking leave of this agreeable family, we once more trundled on in our cart to Simon's Bay, much of our talk being of the enjoyment which a courteous hospitality had thrown into a few hours of our wanderings, and making those unknown to us yesterday, associated for the future with pleasant memories.

There is, necessarily, an intercourse of formal courtesy in our association abroad with the official representatives of foreign powers and the members of services corresponding to our own, with whom we may come into contact. With every nation but the English, this formality scarcely ever becomes any thing else; but with the English, our relations are scarcely ever stationary. They run into intimate friendship or strong repulsion, and the whole difference may depend upon the most trivial and accidental circumstances of a first meeting. The tempers and peculiarities of the individual who makes the first official call, either freezes our association into the stiffened formality by no means agreeable or congenial to any party, tinges it with bitterness, or throws down the barriers of national difference, and mingles us in such friendly union that we are almost inclined to ask, occasionally, whether a different flag flies over us. The latter was the character of our associations with the naval authorities of the Cape. The time, and the purposes of politicians, were then threatening a hostile conflict between ourselves and those from whom we were then receiving so many cordial kindnesses and courtesies. Having ridden over from Cape Town to Simon's Bay upon a day when there had been an arrival from Europe bringing, in all the papers, the letters of Caleb Cushing and the articles of the London Times, we found some of our English friends, including three lieutenants of the Royal Navy, awaiting our arrival, with a comfortable dinner—a desirable terminus to a ride of twenty-four miles. In mid-meal, and its social friendships, I mentioned the recent war news: it fell with startling effect upon this little group. One of the party was proud of a medal given him by the Congress of the United States for deeds of courageous humanity; and the others had survived the battle of Inkermann, and other Crimean horrors. One of these remarked,

"It will be hard, if after associating so pleasantly and so friendly together, they set us to cutting each other's throats."

I think that English officers do not interest themselves so much as we do in the politics which may place them in hostile positions with other nations.

"What 's it all about?" said one. "I do not understand what we are to fight for. I know we do not want your country, and I suppose you do not want ours."

I explained to him the mysteries of foreign enlistment, San Juan, Cuba, etc., as well as I could. He was a true man, a bold, yet modest, bluff, and single-hearted sailor, by no means given to sentimentality; and hence almost picturesque was the deep sadness which fell over his strongly marked face, as he laid down his knife, leaned on the table, and bowed his head, and in a meditative manner, as if thinking aloud, said,

"Alas! alas! they do n't know the horrors of such a war. If they did, they would be careful how they bring it about."

As the following concluding correspondence between

Commodore, now Admiral, Trotter, and Commodore Armstrong, has a semi-official character, I can see no impropriety in its insertion here.

"UNITED STATES FLAG SHIP SAN JACINTO,
"SIMON'S BAY, *January* 28, 1856.

"MY DEAR COMMODORE,

"I should have done myself the honor to have made you a call this morning, but pressing duties have prevented me from doing so.

"I embrace this occasion to thank you officially and personally for the assistance rendered this ship, and for the many civilities extended to myself and officers since our arrival at Simon's Bay.

"Have the kindness to present my respectful compliments to your lady and niece.

"Believe me your
"Obliged friend and
"Obedient servant,
"JAMES ARMSTRONG,
"Commanding United States Naval Forces,
"East India and China Seas."

"COMMODORE TROTTER,
"Commanding Her Majesty's Naval Forces and Station,
"Simon's Bay,
"Cape of Good Hope."

"HER MAJESTY'S SHIP CASTOR,
"SIMON'S BAY, 28*th January*, 1856.

"MY DEAR COMMODORE,

"I have the honor to acknowledge the receipt of your letter of this date, and I beg most sincerely to thank you for the kind manner in which you are good enough to express yourself in reference to the little assistance it has been in our power to afford the 'San Jacinto,' and to the endeavors to make your stay here agreeable.

"Permit me to say, and I express the feeling not only of myself and family and the officers of the squadron, but of the community in general, that your visit has been an especial pleasure to us all, and Mrs. Trotter and my niece beg me to say how much they regret not having had the pleasure of seeing you once more.

"Wishing you a pleasant voyage, and every success and happiness in your interesting and important command,

"I beg you will believe me very truly,
"And with much respect,
"Your obliged friend and humble servant,
"H. D. Trotter,
"Commodore, Commanding Her Majesty's Naval Forces
"on the Cape of Good Hope Station.

"Commodore Armstrong,
"Commanding the United States
"Naval Forces in the East India and China Seas, etc., etc."

X.

MAURITIUS.

On the 28th of January we sailed from Simon's Bay, and passed into the Indian Ocean, bound for Mauritius. On the evening of the following day the wind freshened, the sea dashed in shorter waves and with more angry fury; every thing set was close-reefed, and things looked like the beginning of a gale. As the night closed darkly over us the sea foamed and roared wildly around us; but every thing was snug and comfortable inboard. The jib had been hauled down, and the captain of the forecastle sent some forecastle hands out to stow it. Among them was an Irish boy by the name of McFarren. With the exception of the roll, and the pitch, which made one grasp at something for support, as I said, every thing was snug and comfortable inboard. One of the lieutenants and I were chatting at the ward-room table, when suddenly there came from the deck, that sound which, without hearing a single word, you know means a life in danger. "What's that!" I exclaimed involuntarily, but I spoke to the air. With the first alarm that reached us, my companion had sprung to the deck. I followed him. A man overboard —overboard on such a night, in such a sea! Every one feels that something ought to be done, but what? It was not a night to order any one out upon the water. There was no necessity for such an order—a crew of volunteers, headed by the gentleman who had so suddenly left me in the ward-room, stood ready for the hazardous duty.

The most suitable boat, the whale-boat, happened to be on the weather side. They commenced lowering a lee boat, but the attempt was abandoned as useless. Where were they now to pull for? We had already plunged on some distance in the darkness. At the stern hung two life buoys, with port-fires attached, intended to explode and burn some time after reaching the water, to show a drowning man where to find them, and a boat where to find him. The strings had been pulled, both had broken, and neither port-fire lighted. The boy was heard shrieking and gurgling in two successive moments, first near the gangway, and then under the stern, and this was the last of our first tribute to the Indian Ocean.

On the 14th of February we had Mauritius in sight early in the morning. The weather was hot and gusty, with heavy thunder squalls. It was a race with daylight and our getting into port, and as the day wore on in haze and gloom, our hopes sank. At dark, when off the port, and the shipping in sight, we fired a gun and hoisted a jack for a pilot, but no pilot came. We, therefore, lay off the harbor of Port Louis until the following morning, when the pilot came to us, and we ran into the narrow channel which forms the harbor. Now we had, clear and distinct, all the peculiar features of the scenery. Back against the sky cut the clear outline of the mountains, and nowhere are they more remarkable, Peter Botte being, however, the most conspicuous. In front of the mountain range rose a bright green hill, and around this hill clustered the houses of Port Louis. On our left, as we ran in, was a rock-built fortress, and the point on our right, also fortified, was covered with groves of palms.

The activity of the harbor was a surprise. I expected to see some shipping, but here before us was a dense forest of masts, moored in rows on each side of a central channel. We moored outside this commercial marine, and in due season banged away our salute. A Babel confusion of tongues shook the air of this crowded harbor. Crews of more than half-naked darkies were singing and yelling at the various labors of the port—loading and unloading vessels, arranging moorings, etc., etc. A loud cry of human voices arose with swelling and not unpleasant cadence upon the air. It came from a pyramid of copper-colored human beings, some clad in gay colored rags and some not clad at all, who thronged the decks, lined the sides, and rose one above another on the various elevated points of the ship—all shouting and singing. These were Coolies, and East Indians who had served out their five years' labor, and were returning to their homes.

Our entrance to the harbor of Port Louis, and the discovery of our peaceable designs and character, relieved the inhabitants from quite a panic. The war talk between the United States and England reached these remote regions with exaggerated effect, and when, on the preceding evening, we were discovered off the island, an impression was originated which, growing like the three black crows, by the morning had exaggerated us into three American frigates, and an allied Russian force, coming to take the island.

Mauritius celebrities are "Peter Botte," hurricanes, and its being the scene of the truth-founded romance of Paul and Virginia. Its support is sugar. Sugar is the practical thing; it swallows up all romance; it roots up jungle, cuts down ornamental groves, destroys aromatic forests —nutmegs, cinnamon and cloves. The efforts of the earlier settlers, their lives and labors, were given to making Mauritius a spice island—and the spice trees succeeded. Where are they now?—given way to sugar. Why do n't you grow this, and why do n't you grow that?—necessaries and luxuries. They would do well, but every thing must give way to sugar. Sugar is dollars. It was not the rise and fall of empires, the results of battles, which were signalized from the telegraph posts perched on Signal hill, but "Sugar has risen," "Sugar has fallen, fallen, fallen," was the depressing news at the time of our presence; and throughout this volcanic speck of mountain and plain, thirty-five miles long by thirty broad, and its mottled population of over one hundred thousand souls, it caused quite a panic. Of the population, about fifty thousand are in the city of Port Louis.

Discovered by Mascaregnas, the Portuguese, in 1505, it was merely looked at and abandoned, being, however, named Cerne. Nearly a century afterwards, in 1598, a Dutch admiral accidentally found it, and using it to recover his sick, the Dutch also abandoned it, but called it after their Prince Maurice—Mauritius. Nearly half a century afterwards, in 1644, the Dutch settled it, but in about another fifty years they abandoned it, being driven away by slaves whom they had stolen from the neighboring island of Madagascar, and who, escaped to the woods, became wild maroons. The prodigious number of rats, it is said, also assisted in this expulsion. Then, in 1715, came along the French, and called it the "Isle of France," and set themselves to work to make it a spice island. Still it was a hard case, and was about being again abandoned to its loneliness, when fortunately it came under the genius of M. La Bourdonnais as governor, who strengthened, defended, and watered the capital, gave security to the population, developed its resources, and directed it to such results as now crowd its ports with shipping to carry away one hundred thousand tons of sugar a year. But M. La Bourdonnais, to do all this, had to be very superior to everybody around him, and consequently had to earn their hate and calumny, to endure persecution, imprisonment, and to die an obscure and impoverished death. But what need M. La Bourdonnais care for all this? He has been dead now one hundred years, and the English are about to erect a monument to so great a man.

By the treaty of Paris, in 1814, the island passed into the hands of the British government, by which it is now held, and garrisoned by her troops. The French residents submit to this with a very bad grace, and there is but little intercourse between the English and French. Louis Napoleon has rechristened the neighboring isle of Bourbon, in view of the present alliance, "Reunion," but the French of Mauritius express the hope that the final settlement of this war will find Mauritius restored to themselves.

One of the most striking features of Port Louis is the motley population and motley costumes which are met in the streets. In mid-ocean, on the high-road between Asia, Africa, Europe and America, it seems to have gathered in the peoples and peculiarities of all quarters of the globe.

As in architecture there are certain fundamental principles derived from the simple forms and teachings of nature, and from which, by taste and utility, are educed the elaborate finish of the most complicated structures, so, in the streets of Port Louis, it is seen there are similar natural fundamental principles of costume, from which ascend by gradation every addition, until dress reaches the high finish of the French and English ladies and gentlemen, who are driving among their more simply clad bronze-colored brethren. The first and most simple necessity of dress seems to be a cloth about the size of a napkin, substituted for the primitive fig-leaf, and many are met in the thronged streets of the city with only this much of a garment. The next grows to a sheet folded around the loins in fuller covering. The head seems then to claim the attention of the more dressy. In addition to the articles already named, some have a tight-fitting skull cap of figured calico upon the head, but turbans, full and flowing, white, colored and scarlet, are the more fashionable head-dress. And in the streets and on the roads many a slender Lascar and Hindoo is met, whose only costume is the loin cloth and a scarlet turban, with long tails hanging down his bronzed back. The next addition is a bright figured muslin, though scant, jacket, buttoned lightly over the shoulders and breast. What the females want in muslin they endeavor to make up in the weight of metal thrust through their noses and ears. So it is bright and heavy, shape and symmetry seem to be of little consequence. Not only the lobe of the ears is heavy with the irregular pendants, but all along the outer rim and the top are perforations distended with golden-colored bars, plugs and rings. An especially favorite ornament is a ring of about the circumference of a tea-plate, dependent from the nose. But with all this barbaric decoration, the gay colors, the caps, the turbans, the dark hues of the slender, wiry, graceful figures are picturesque, and the snowy flowing robes, full trowsers and spotless turbans of the full-clad Parsees and Arab merchants, moving among all this variety, give and receive a pleasing effect from the contrast of spotless white and full clothing with varied colors and naked skins. These lightly-costumed Indians are the laborers, small farmers, hucksters, mechanics, market tenders, etc. Their villages of small filthy straw huts are clustered around the outskirts of the city, and rude signs, with unspellable and unpronounceable Hindoo names, announce that they are jewelers, tailors, shoemakers, carpenters and cabinet-makers. As a specimen of some of the names found among these people, I will give the following from the top of a quarter box of cigars which I bought:

MA SOO SA NA VA ROW YOU LOO.
(Ra Va.)
AT JAGGERNAIKPOORAM.

These people were originally brought into the island by the British government as a substitute for the negro population, rendered worthless by the emancipation of 1835. They are compelled to serve five years of what is called "industrial residence," and the best of these men get three dollars a month wages. At the end of the five years, if they desire it, they are returned to their own country, but most prefer to remain where they are, and enter into various pursuits upon their own account. During their term of servitude they are liable to coercion, but can complain against undue severity. A regular slave-trade transaction has just taken place. A ship came in from the coast of Africa with a cargo of negroes, and they were sold at eighty dollars each, nominally for the passage money. They had been kidnapped and stolen from Africa. This in an English possession!

One of the necessary and agreeable pilgrimages of Mauritius is a visit to the Canton Pampelmousses, about six miles from Port Louis, where tradition deposits the remains of Paul and Virginia. Whether this be true or not, it is but a just tribute to the beauty of the story to visit the scenes associated with it; besides, the drive is a beautiful one, and near the reputed tombs is the botanical garden.

I am not, however, disposed to accord in the incredulous view which some have been disposed to take of this beautiful tale. It is certain the St. Geran was wrecked in 1745, and St. Pierre, in his preface, says:—"I can give the assurance that those of whom I speak truly existed, and that the history is true in its principal events. They have been certified to me by many inhabitants whom I knew in the Isle of France, and I have only added some indifferent circumstances." The reputed tombs are shabby, crumbling little monuments of brick and plaster, standing in a bamboo grove on a private estate, and having neither inscription nor name.

Remarkable and conspicuous is the mountain of Peter Botte. From the sharp, steeple-like pinnacle of a mountain rises a mass of rock, shaped like an inverted pyramid resting on its apex, and the base overhanging the sides of the mountain. To ascend to the top of this capping rock is at once seen to be an achievement of great difficulty and danger. The name is derived from an unfortunate Frenchman, who, having made the ascent, lost his life in returning. It was, however, successfully made by a party of English officers, in 1832, and one of them, Lieutenant Taylor, wrote an account of the feat, which was published in the third volume of the Royal Geographical Society. The following extracts from this narrative will give some idea of the difficulty of the enterprise: With much labor they had ascended to the shoulder of the mountain, from which rises, for over three hundred feet, the neck or pinnacle upon which rests Peter Botte. To ascend this neck was in itself a great difficulty. A negro, who held on with hands and feet like a monkey, climbed up the sides with a rope, which he made fast above, and up this rope the party shinned. Mr. Taylor informs us "it was awful work. In several places the ridge ran to an edge not a foot broad; and I could, as I held on half sitting, half kneeling across the ridge, have kicked my right shoe down to the plain on one side, and my left into the bottom of the ravine upon the other. I held on uncommonly hard, and was very well satisfied when I was safe under the neck. And a more extraordinary situation I never was in. The head, which is an enormous mass of rock, about thirty-five feet in height, overhangs its base many feet on every side. A ledge of tolerably level rock runs round three sides of the base, about six feet in width, bounded everywhere by the abrupt edge of the precipice, except in the spot where it is joined by the ridge, up which we climbed. In one spot the head, though overhanging *its* base several feet, reaches only perpendicular over the edge of the precipice, and most fortunately it was at the very spot where we mounted. Here it was we reckoned on getting up. Lloyd had prepared some iron arrows with thongs to fire over, and, having got up a gun, he made a line fast around his body, which we all held on, and going over the edge of the precipice on the opposite side, he leaned back against the line, and fired over the least projecting part. Had the line broken he would have fallen eighteen hundred feet. Twice this failed, and then he had recourse to a large stone with a lead line, which swung diagonally, and seemed to be a feasible plan. Several times he made beautiful heaves, but the provoking line would not catch, and away went the stones far down below, till at length Æolus, pleased, I suppose, with his performance, gave us a shift of wind for about a minute, and over went the stone, and was eagerly seized on the opposite side. 'Hurrah, my lads, steady 's the word!' Three lengths of ladder were put together on the ledge; a large line was attached to the one which was over the head, and carefully drawn up, and finally a two inch rope, to the extremity of which we lashed the top of our ladder, then lowered it gently over the precipice until it hung perpendicularly, and was steadied by two negroes on the ridge below. 'All right now, hoist away!' and up went the ladder until the foot came to the edge of our ledge, where it was lashed in firmly to the neck. We then hauled away on the guy to steady it, and made it fast. A line was passed over by the lead line to hold on, and up went Lloyd, screeching and hallooing, and we all three scrambled after him. The Union Jack and a boat-hook were passed up, and old England's flag waved freely and gallantly on the redoubted Peter Botte."

On the 21st of February we cast off from our moorings, and got under way for Ceylon.

XI.

CEYLON.

"Ebony and topaz." Not the sentimental contrasted blackness and brightness of the thrice venerable John Quincy Adams, but real material ebony chairs, sofas, bureaus, boxes, canes richly carved, and glittering masses of topaz, in the shops and on the streets, with sapphires, rubies and amethysts, are the prominent first impressions of Ceylon, as we are introduced to it at the pretty walled and embowered town of Galle.

Bishop Heber's beautiful missionary hymn has so associated the fragrance of spices and poesy with this island that one feels reluctant to break the bonds of genius which have thus bound them together; but true it is, the "spicy breezes" are wafted only by the poet's imagination.

In the first watch of the night of March 5th, 1856, we made the light of Point de Galle, gleaming over the sea like a "star on life's tremulous ocean," and on the following morning the tall and graceful white shaft, standing on the extreme point of Ceylon, indicated to us the "fort" and city. A pilot boarded us and took us in.

It was a quiet and lonely looking spot, with but few vessels at the anchorage. As we ran in, however, the harbor became suddenly alive. A crowd of boats, thronged with bronzed Cingalese, announced their rapid approach to us by the confused clattering of many voices.

Queer looking boats they were, and won much of our attention. They seemed to be two planks, about six inches apart, coming end on to us, floating on the edge and carrying a heavy press of canvas. The planks rested upon a canoe beneath them, and out-riggers to a log, sharpened at both ends, kept them up in the water when under sail. Models of these boats are among the curiosities sold visitors.

From these unique boats our glance is to the chattering, jabbering, shrieking, scolding, quarreling human beings on board of them. Their costume is attractive. At Galle a little book has been published called the "Guide to Galle," in which, alluding to a part of Ceylon, it is said: "The rainy season extends from December to May, and from May to December the season is wet." So, in describing the costume of our new acquaintance, I would say—from the head to the hips there are no clothes, and from the hips to the heels about the same.

On shore we found ourselves among a varied population of Asiatics. The Cingalese, with glossy jet-black hair smoothly put back from the forehead by a semicircular tortoise-shell comb, and done up in a knot at the back of the head. Beneath this feminine arrangement are features covered with a fine skin, only less dark than the hair, of delicate and feminine form and expression, so that all the young look like girls to our unskilled eyes, a confusion which is increased by the white or bright-colored "comeboy"—a shawl folded as a petticoat around the waist, and worn alike by the more respectable of either sex. The women, however, wear a short jacket, dropping over the breasts, and leaving the body exposed between that and the comeboy. Like the boatmen we first saw, the lords of the lower class indulge in no such waste of muslin, but are content with that amount of costume which is a bare insufficiency. All have black teeth and bloody looking mouths, from the use of betel, mixed with lime, and pepper leaves.

Moormen, in Arab parti-colored caps, with shaven heads, and voluminous shawls wrapped around their waists, are everywhere at our heels, on the shores, in the streets, in the hotels and the halls of private houses; even on the road-side, to the distance of some miles in the country, they appear importuningly. These Moormen are the traders in jewelry and precious stones. Jewel boxes are taken from the folds of their shawls, and sapphires, rubies, amethysts, carbuncles, emeralds, cat's eyes, and moon stones, displayed in gorgeous abundance, or else good English and French imitations of these valuables.

Prices are coolly asked for these little glittering ornaments which would indicate that money was in great abundance at Point de Galle. Fifty, seventy-five, one, two hundred dollars for what, in your uneducated judgment, you hoped to win a wife or sweetheart's smile, at the cost of only five or ten. One of these street peddlers proffered to sell me a sapphire for fifteen hundred dollars;

and in a shop having over its door a sign, "Guaranteed Jewelry," I was shown a cat's eye, which the proprietor professed to value at two thousand dollars.

Ethnographers, in their classification of races, should make one of the mendicant or begging races; and this characteristic would give us at once all the subordinate and inferior qualities which fill the vacuum of absent self-respect. While to the Malabar or Moorman is left this trade in jewels and gold-mounted tortoise-shell bracelets, the Cingalese himself follows you with porcupine-quill baskets, carved ebony boxes, canes, etc.; and if he has nothing in the shape of trade by which to rob the passing stranger, he still thinks he has the right of contribution, and if you glance at him on the wayside, out comes his soliciting hand with a salaam; and smirking fathers will hold forth the hand of the infant in arms, to beg of the passer-by.

It would be curious to know what idea a Cingalese resident of Point de Galle has of Europeans. This place is the first Indian touching-point of those young adventurers to whom, being fresh from home, every thing is new. With life, and hope, and Indian fortunes in the future, they are reckless of their present limited means, and in the excitement of novelty, scatter what is to be so readily and richly replaced.

On the other hand, it is the last stopping-place in India of those golden-skinned, liver-grown few, who in the race against death for wealth, have jumped so often over the open graves into which their fellows have fallen; and when they reach this point on their homeward voyage, they begin to feel as though they had distanced their grim competitor forever. They boast already of their renewed strength, their freshness and vigor; and in the exultation of their spirits are willing to buy, at any cost, trinkets as tribute to the homes of their childish memories, and those whom they hope yet to find in them. The jewel merchant of Galle is a keen observer of human nature, or rather "passenger" nature, and has a home and a "passenger" price for his wares. After some little detention at Galle had made me familiar with these things, I said to one of these peddlers, "You scamp, what do you mean by asking me so much for this thing, when you know the regular price is so and so?" "I thought master was a passenger, and that is what the passengers give us."

Soon after our arrival, one of these peddlers was showing his wares to a group of officers at the ward-room table, when I, looking on, remarked of a neat and tastefully-set ring, "That is the prettiest thing he has shown." The man, with a graceful salaam, at once handed it to me, and said, "I'm sure you'll buy that." I had no intention of buying any thing, and wishing to be rid of his continued persuasive importunity, I asked the price. "Twelve pounds." "I'll give you one." In a dramatic manner, he laid his hand on his breast, and said, "I thank you. I know, though, you are but jesting; it is not in my heart to ask more than the real value;" and with a mortified air, he put up his ring and went on with his sales to those who were satisfied with his prices. I felt somewhat sorry for having hurt the poor man's feelings. Having concluded his sales, he returned to me, saying, "I am very much in want of money, and must take the one pound for the ring." I knew now that even at my own offer I was paying too much. Having made it, would have given it, but not having so much money by me, I told the man he must wait until the Purser came on board, or return to the ship in an hour or two. This did not suit him, and he urged me to say what I would give on the spot. "All that I have in my purse," as I laid it on the table. He eyed it keenly for a moment, pushed the ring toward me, and emptied the purse. It contained one dollar and seventy-five cents, with which he went off satisfied, having made a dollar and a half by the sale of his sixty dollar ring. What precious stones passengers must buy at Galle! There are, however, beautiful gems to be had there by the exercise of care and skill.

We are talking about some of the people and usages of Galle without getting into the place. Where is it? Most that we see are tall cocoa-nut groves, here and there and everywhere waving their graceful branches in the breeze, and promising to sea-parched throats the sweet refreshment of the sparkling water of the young fruit—a promise which is fully kept. There stands the tall light-house, from amid the trees rise the roof and gable of a church, and surrounding all are the walls of a fortress. Galle is a fort. Behind those walls and green ramparts, hidden beneath those trees, are the houses, churches, shops, hotels, and clean, quiet streets of a population of three thousand Portuguese, Dutch, English, Cingalese, and a mixture of all—Catholic, Protestant, Mohammedan, and Boodhists; and the only entrance to them is beneath a stone arch in the wall at the sea-side, through which are constantly passing, foot-passengers and merchandise, carriages, wagons, and queer little bull-carts—small carts drawn by small bulls or oxen, and trotting rapidly with one inside passenger. The highest elevation of this fort-town is occupied by the old Dutch church, with the exception of a small Wesleyan chapel, the only church in the place; and it presents an illustration of that Christian fellowship which should everywhere characterize Christian denominations. From early morn until night, it is, on the Sabbath, occupied for religious worship, and by three different denominations—two forms of Dutch Presbyterian, and an Episcopal congregation.

The congregations were of various degrees of color, from black, through shades of red and yellow, to white, and all dressed with great neatness, mostly in European style, but some in the native costume of the "comeboy," surmounted by light loose jackets. The spectacle to us spectators was strange—and a pleasant one—to see Hin doos, in Hindoo costume, coming devoutly, book in hand, to a Christian church, and kneeling reverently a few moments before taking their seats.

Most of the congregation was made up of half-caste descendants of the Dutch and Portuguese. Many of the Portuguese residents are either Presbyterian or Methodist; some of the church members are Cingalese. The Bible is freely distributed in the Cingalese language, which is that of the south of Ceylon; and also in the Tamil, which is that of the north of Ceylon, and the neighboring part of Hindostan.

Among the necessary excursions of visitors to Galle, is a ride to the cinnamon gardens, and to the Boodhist temples; and to those points of interest we of course went in a palanquin—a carriage cross between a "Black Maria" and a hearse, with four seats, roofed over and shut in, drawn by a miserable poor little horse, and conducted by a turbaned native, who, with well-timed consideration, gets the concern under full headway, and runs along for some distance by the horse's side, before mounting the box. During our drive, we met one of the carriages of the aristocratic residents, and the coachmen were picturesquely clad in white dresses, with turbans of intertwined crimson and white.

The cinnamon gardens on the banks of the Gindurah, are about four or five miles from the fort—a pleasant drive, passing out into the country beneath the shade of thick groves of cocoa-nut trees. The cinnamon plantation is a mere thicket of bushy shrubs, although if permitted to grow it would be a tree twenty feet high. Their branches are cut off close to the ground, and the growth is so rapid that they are replaced in a season. On our way to the cinnamon garden, we had stopped at a Boodhist temple, perched on an elevation a little distance from the road-side. The temple consisted of an interior chamber, with an outer hall, or passage, going all around it. In this interior chamber were great carved images of Boodha, one sitting and the other lying in front of the former. These images are about ten feet long. On each side of the same chamber are painted images of Sevà and Vishnu, the saving and the destroying deities. The outside passages, from roof to ceiling, were painted with allegorical or historical designs. Some of them seemed to have an elevated and spiritual significance, and there was enough besides the Trinity to show the corrupted relationship of Boodhism to a lost but pure revelation. The predominant color in every thing—paintings and idols—was a bright golden yellow. The crowd of Indians who followed us into the temple, and who, from their residence about it, I presume were Boodhists, seemed to have no veneration for it as a sacred edifice, but rather gave their own admiration to, and expected ours for it, as a work of art.

Immediately to the right, outside of the temple, was a dirty-looking shed, under which were two priests, wearing soiled mantles, of the sacred yellow color, hanging over their otherwise naked, and by no means cleanly-looking shoulders. One of them was, in a rapid, monotonous tone, reading from a bundle of narrow strips of bark, or rather the tough leaves of the tallpot (a palm) tree, closely written. The other followed the reader, silently looking on a similar bundle of bark strips. It appeared to be proof-reading, as the silent man occasionally corrected the reader. They did not interrupt their work to look at us, and the only break in the rapid utterance, was the spitting of the blood-colored saliva, caused by the betel-nut, into a brass spittoon, as filthy as the whole party and its surroundings.

As we drove along the road in the neighborhood of this temple, and of the cinnamon garden, our palanquin was surrounded by a crowd of children and men, who kept pace with us by a steady trot, begging—offering canes of cinnamon-wood, the ever-present boxes of jewelry, and, in the immediate neighborhood of the Temple, carved heads of the Boodhist Trinity. One lad, of about sixteen, with no clothing but the fold of muslin tied around his waist, was very persevering in showing a box of glittering jewelry at the palanquin window. I said to him, "Go away—I do n't want any thing—I am too poor—have no money to spare." He, with a laugh, promptly replied, in good English, "Oh no, sir, you are rich—you are as rich as Crœsus." The classical allusion, and the speaker, and the place, all taken together, were rather interesting.

There were other temples in the neighborhood. One of them, called "Minnangodde Parama Muda Vihare," instead of being under the direction of the chief Boodhist priest of Ceylon, is of the Siamese sect, the priest being ordained by the high priest of Siam. This functionary, and also the King of Siam and his brother, have sent some valuable presents to this temple, among them books in the Burmese characters, splendidly gilded and ornamented, and supposed to be worth over one thousand dollars; a betel-box, wrapped in cloth of gold; silk robes, richly embroidered with the same metal; paintings on cloth of the temple of Rangoon; and the foot of Boodha, as carved in a rock in the Nerbudda river. One of the small statues of this temple is said to be two thousand years old.

Among the points of beauty and interest in the vicinity of Galle generally visited by strangers, is an eminence known as "Garstin's Hill," being the property of the Rev. Dr. Garstin, military chaplain, and the site of his bungalow, or country cottage. It ascends, covered with a thick tropical growth, amid which chatter hundreds of monkeys, rather abruptly from the plain, and when the summit is reached, from the piazzas surrounding the bungalow, the eye sweeps over an extent of rich scenery—plain, river, ocean, village, hills—and away to the interior mountains of Ceylon, and can distinguish the peculiar and interesting point called Adam's Peak, or Mallua Sri Pade, the Hill of the Sacred Foot. From this peak, according to the Boodhist tradition, Boodha made a step into Siam, leaving the foot-mark of his last step from Ceylon impressed upon the rocky summit of this elevation, seven thousand four hundred and twenty feet above the sea. The Mussulmans change the foot-mark from Boodha to Adam, and both Mussulmans and Boodhists make it holy ground, and a point of meritorious pilgrimage. The Boodhists have the nine points of the law advantage of possession, and from their pilgrims quite a revenue is collected for the treasury of the high priest at Kandy. The approach to this sacred pinnacle is very difficult and laborious, as is also its ascent. Dr. Garstin had accomplished the feat, and told me the foot-mark was a mere weather-worn depression in the rock, assisted, by chiseling and additions of mortar, into the form of a foot.

The indolent effeminacy of East Indian life makes itself apparent at Galle. Every house seems to be crowded with a multiplicity of servants, all of whom do not do more than one good stout house-servant in the United States. There is a servant for almost every individual at table, besides one to stand pulling the punka, or great fan, suspended in the middle of the apartment. Two or three seem to be necessary to take care of one chamber, each having his separate function. This all looks very comfortable, and promises an easy kind of a life. It is such for a guest, but when the burden and charge upon the lady of the house are considered—the neglect of duty, the caprice of changing places, the jealousy and bickering among each other—it becomes a servile tyranny, to which the free expectoration of betel, in all directions, is no ornament.

The demoralizing influence upon the young is more than that attributed to slavery in our southern States. No matter what pains European parents may take to prevent their children becoming indolent and dependent, the result seems inevitable ; and an energetic lady, who had exercised a most vigilant precaution, told me that her children thought it the greatest hardship to have to take off their own shoes and stockings. There is much more real comfort in our New England and western homes, where one servant or more is kept, and where each individual develops a self-dependent and vigorous character by the necessity of personal exertion, than in all this abundance of oriental servility.

From the tyranny of this crowd of Cingalese domestics there is no refuge, as the number is a law of fashion and a measure of respectability. It requires, however, some habituation to the customs of the country passively to submit to it.

Upon taking my seat in a friend's office, to write a letter, I noticed that a fellow was at once set to fanning me with the punka. A whole man, physical, moral and intellectual, working with all his energy for such a result, made me nervous, and I could not write until I sent the fellow away. There was a want of proportion between the power and the end.

During one of my visits to Ceylon, being detained there several weeks, an agreeable poetical friend, Dr. James Cruice, of the British army, the author of Psyche and other poems, and I, determined to fly from the glittering tempters, the jewel merchants of Galle—from the gastronomic delights of its hotels, and to take refuge in a rural bungalow, five miles from the fort, amid the natural beauties of the picturesque vale of Walkwelle. Such an eremetical flight from hot, glowing streets—from the resources of the billiard room, and the loafing lounges of the hotel verandahs—from society—was easily enough accounted for by our friends, as regarded Dr. Cruice, from the fact of his being a poet, but as for myself, no satisfactory reason for the move, short of insanity, could be imagined. Nor was I personally dependant upon the mercies of the hotels, Commodore Armstrong and myself being made at home by the attentive hospitality of Mr. John Black, United States Consul, to whom the petty income of his office can be no compensation for the hospitalities of himself and family, extended to such of our countrymen as the passing steamers bring to Galle. One enterprising gentleman formed the bold theory that I might be a poet in disguise. I gave no reasons then and there. I will now give them in an appeal to a public jury "de lunatico inquirendo."

The bungalow of Walkwelle stood upon the point of a lofty promontory, which in one direction looked over palm-covered hills and valleys, out upon the blue sea and the sails upon its surface, from which the breezes came freshly, rustling among our cocoa-nut and palm groves. We looked down from each side upon grove-covered valleys, which meeting at the foot of our promontory, wound away as one expanse, dotted with cattle and island groves, between ranges of hills far as the eye could see; and over these boundary hills, dim and misty, were seen the distant mountains of Ceylon, suggestive of a wonderful interior. Down from those far hills, and away through our valley, on the right hand, in serpentine turns, flowed the Gindurah, now resting in the dark shadows of the overhanging forest, then gleaming in the open sunlight, as it sought its westward way to the sea. At sunset as the seaward sky was crimson, the river was a stream of bright gold. It was a place and a time to realize the opening of my friend's Psyche.

"It was the hour when, in his flight,
 The sun along the western sky
Leaveth a track of golden light
 To trace his radiant chariot by;
The hour when from the lofty pine
The shadows fall in lengthened line,
And song birds chant their vesper hymn—
The dying day's sweet requiem;
When feebly falls the slanting ray
On rivulets winding their weary way,
By shallow ford and tangled brake,
To rest that night in tranquil lake;
And flowers are closing their drooping eyes,
  And softly the gales
Are breathing around their amorous sighs."

The birds loved this scenery and lonely spot (we were the only inhabitants) as well as we, and sang among our trees their morning welcome; while certain grave and bearded old monkeys seemed to hold an evening mass meeting upon our presence, which, from the earnestness and confusion of the debate, may have originated some new political party in the state—from the chattering they certainly were not all of the same opinion. And the night cries of the jackal announced a wide-awake party in the forest.

Such was our Cingalese retreat, in which, after a few days, I was, with the exception of the servants, left the solitary inhabitant, and thenceforth occupied myself in making the acquaintance of the various inhabitants around my dwelling. The triangular point of the hill before my door, looking up the receding valley, had been at one time cleared and leveled a little, forming a small plain. Several large trees were, however, left standing, a row of cocoa-nuts fringed the edges near the house, and wild vines those at the point. Below these hill margins, the sides were a mass of wild jungle, and, for purposes of business or pleasure, the inhabitants of the jungle made frequent visits to my clearing, and gave me a good opportunity, as I sat in the verandah, of observing them with my opera glass; and I found this moral in my study, that throughout all animal existence, high and low, that manifestation of selfishness which displays itself in self-importance, is the one uniform character. This, however, may be truly a virtue—the consciousness of individual humility, in aspiration after a higher state of existence. As I half dreamed over the spectacle before me, I sometimes fancied I saw the various phases of human society, including those of our twenty-by-ten feet world, the quarter deck of a man-of-war.

I was a spectator and a listener at a natural and varied opera, more harmonious to my untutored ear than the clanging of instruments in crowded halls, beneath the glare of gas-light. The performance opened merrily at daylight, and continued with varying notes through the day.

The most numerous, restless, and dissipated members of this mixed society, were the brown-coated, striped chipmunks, who arrogated to themselves the right to discard all duties, and to sport now on the ground and then amid the leaves and branches of the trees. With no steadiness of pursuit, they sought only the excitement of the moment among high and low.

There were five or six families of lizards, some in grave and some in gay costume, with puffed-out throats, hurrying to and fro as if bearing messages of importance to the state—consequential as Mediterranean men-of-war, in inverse proportion to their usefulness. Occasionally two of these busy cruisers would stop a moment, exchange quiet signals, and then each hurry on his way.

Heavy-bodied, long-tailed iguanas, some of them three feet long, would waddle up into view, and after looking around the scene for a comfortable place, recline half on one side while they lazily raked the ground with one fore paw and nibbled at the exposed roots. Fat vulgarians lying on the velvet benches and nibbling ground nuts. Industrious gatherers of the surrounding sweets, but making their industry heard in the world, buzzing a contribution to the general harmony, were tiny, sober-clad, long-billed humming-birds.

Among my most frequent visitors, on the ground and in the trees, were pert, dandy, dapper little fellows, with black, velvety heads, black satin coat and vest, white satin breeches, coat tail lined with the same, and a narrow slashing of white along the sleeves, or wings. They hopped about, and sometimes, most impudently, up into the verandah, with their white-lined tails stuck perpendicularly up into the air, with a defiant "none like me" kind of air; but notwithstanding all their conceit and pretensions, they were very nervous and timid, so that I was compelled to be motionless or put them in a panic. While thus still and quiet myself, looking and listening, an enthusiastic chap, up in the tree-top galleries, startles me by calling out in good English, fast and loud, just what I thought, "Pretty, pretty, pretty."

But thorns among roses—bitters with sweets—and dangers amid the delights of Walkwelle. Whilst bathing in the Gindurah one is vividly conscious of the vicinity of crocodiles, and when coming from this refreshment early on the morning of the memorable 22d of February, I was in time to assist, at my own door, in the death of a fatal cobra; that is, I looked on, while the native servants mashed his head, extracted with great care four sharp-pointed fangs, and then held his contorting body in the flames.

To vary my residence at Walkwelle, I extemporized a vagabonding cruise of a day up the Gindurah. My boat was got up for the occasion. Two old and leaky canoes, one double the size of the other and doubly as rotten, with a bridge uniting them, upon which was laid, as a floor, a broad and golden yellow plank of the jack-fruit tree, and some twigs bowed over the machine, supporting a roof of dried palm leaves, completed our establishment. A cushion, carried with us from the bungalow, and extended on the jack-fruit plank, gave me a reasonably comfortable resting-place. Three naked Cingalese were my crew. The point of the river from which we took our departure was a ferry, and the country people were crossing it, on the way to the fort with their products. These were done up in baskets made of fresh taro or banana leaves, and suspended in green ribbons of some strong and fibrous leaf or grass, all having an inviting, fresh and tasteful appearance. Some carried suspended in these vegetable ribbons earthen bowls covered with green leaves, fixed by neat and regular rolls turned around the edges. Curiosity led me to look into these bowls, when I was pleased to see them filled with smooth and snow-white curdled milk, nothing less than the old-fashioned bonney-clabber, so bountifully associated with youthful years, country life and puzzling orthography in my childhood's early Maryland home. Thenceforth I had a bowl of this discovery and a bottle of fresh milk brought daily to my hermitage, and if its intrinsic merits, as a cool and refreshing food, had not been sufficient reason, I should have been tempted to do so by the renewed youth of early associations. A bit of brown fresh johnny cake beside the earthen bowl, would have absorbed all the intervening years and made the illusion complete. It is, though, a curious fact, that amid the spice groves of Ceylon, and with a nutmeg plantation within a short walk, I could not get a fragment of the aromatic nut to add its flavor to the cream's flakes, although it was always present in the North American farm-house. The wooden nutmeg, illustrative of the ingenious knavery of our eastern brethren, loses the originality of the invention, either as a fact or a caricature, by the natural products of Ceylon. The wild nutmeg of Ceylon resembles, in all external characteristics, the true spice, but the nut upon being cut is so completely insipid and wooden, that it is difficult to believe it any thing else than an ingenious artificial imitation. The probability is, that a fraudulent or accidental exportation of the wild nutmeg to Boston or to Salem, gave rise to this persistent sectional scandal.

Cingalese all chew betel; their mouths are blood-red with it; streets and houses are spotted with the saliva; the shops keep it for sale in tempting combination with the green pepper leaves, and lime. Galle exports cocoanut oil, ebony, spices, and the betel nut, the fourth in value being this nut.

From Point de Galle our destination was to the paradise of the East, to Pulo Pinang, in the Straits of Malacca. On the evening of March the 18th we made the south end of Nicobar, and on the evening of the 20th we were passing Pulo Rondo, and the several peculiar looking rocky eminences or islets which lie near it, and form a good land-mark for the Straits of Malacca. Pulo Wey, a very large island off the north of Sumatra. The waters are now of a dark green color, and we are running through their surface, unbroken by a wave, and, save the rippling of a gentle breeze, as smooth as a floor.

On the morning of the 21st we had the rocky islet of Pera close aboard. The surface of the waters is covered with drift-wood, upon which are floating, in quiet dignity, many large birds. Myriads of a dull yellow snake—from three or four inches to a foot in length—are rapidly gliding over the surface of the water. I endeavored to have one taken, but, fortunately, without success; as I subsequently learned from Dr. Bradley, United States Consul at Singapore, that these snakes had been ascertained to be deadly in their bite. That same day, as night closed in, we made the dark mountain island of Pulo Pinang, with heavy clouds resting on its summit, and the lights of habitations twinkling along its base. We had looked forward with the most pleasant anticipations to our arrival at this place, on account of the glowing descriptions which travelers have given of it; and in addition, we had the special and great interest in its being the point at which we were to receive our first letters from home. But as we could not run in to-night, we came to anchor, and postponed our anticipations until to-morrow.

We had been lying quietly at our anchorage for about an hour, when suddenly there glided up from the surrounding darkness a beautiful sharp and graceful boat, in which were, besides the dark-skinned native rowers, four or five Mohammedans, in full white turbans, and loose white robes. This was the boat of an old bearded Mussulman pilot, accompanied by his friends, seeking the business of the ship.

There is one very annoying peculiarity of the East, and it is, that a man loses all right to proprietorship in himself and his own services. An exaggeration of luxury, by which an individual has no *right* to exert himself in his own personal matters—his free agency has gone. He is the slave of his servants—the property of the dark-skinned men who put their hands on their foreheads, bow to the ground, and kiss the dust of your feet. One of these joint-proprietors of your individuality is the "dubosch," and one of the turbaned companions of the pilot aspired to be the "dubosch" of our ship; that is, to attend to all your shopping, marketing, and purchases in general. Our caterer explained that we had no occasion for his agency—that we had a good steward, who would do our marketing, etc. The dubosch explained that such was not the custom; the steward would not be able to get many articles, would get none so good as he would, and would pay more for them. All of which was true; and we necessarily fell into the hands of our dubosch, the willing and unresisting victims of his knavery, but still cheated to our profit.

"Where are you going?" said my host upon one occasion. "To the shops to get so and so." "Not at all," said my host in surprise; "you are not going to get it. Let the butler or your dubosch attend to that for you." I really neither needed nor wanted the article; but I have a woman's fondness for shopping in store or bazaar, for now all market places are called bazaars. I shop to see the people and things, the manners and customs; and I buy as a pleasant fee for the pleasure afforded me. These enjoyments taken from me, I had no object in shopping, and therefore sank back into the deep cane-seat chair in which I had been semi-reclining; replaced my legs upon its broad flat arms, lengthened out two feet for the purpose of supporting the whole limb from knee to heel, and resigned myself in despair to the servitude of luxury, and the torments of inaction.

On the following morning we again got under way, and ran into an anchorage off the town.

XII.

PINANG,

THE GEM OF THE INDIES.

PINANG, or Pulo Pinang, as it is variously written, has been called the "Gem of the Indies." A recent French traveler thus rhapsodises respecting this spot: "'To see

Naples, and then to die,' say the Italians, in their enthusiasm for that city, bathed by a capricious sea, whose waves are tossed by the cold winds of the north. What, then, would this poetical people say, if they knew Pulo Pinang, which, placed in the middle of Malaysia, is the Paradise of this Eden of the universe. It is upon this corner of the earth that the Deity has realized the vision of a perpetual spring." Such extravagant eulogy is unjust to persons or to places, and prepares one for disappointment. The whole effect of an intimate acquaintanceship, is vainly looked for in a first impression, and although Pinang did not burst upon us as a dream of paradise, we shall find increasing charms in our continued acquaintance.

Pulo being the general term for island, Pinang is the Malayan name of the betel or areca-nut, and is so called either from the immense number of the beautiful areca palm found on the island, or, as some say, from its resemblance, when seen from the sea, to the betel-nut in shape. It lies within two miles of the Malayan peninsula, and separated from the continental island of Sumatra by the Straits of Malacca. It is a forest-covered mountain, green and luxuriant, where its summit, two thousand three hundred feet high, catches the flying vapor, and sends it tumbling down ravine and rivulet, to water a plain of about four miles' width, which laps out irregularly from the base of the mountain into the sea. Upon this plain are the palm-groves and nutmeg-orchards, and the residences of the inhabitants. A few bungalows, or one-storied cottages, are perched along the hill-sides, and crown their very summits.

As we look around us from the deck of our ship, new features are before our eyes; here and there, among the shipping, are lying Chinese junks, with their confused pile of red-painted wood-work, and great goggle-eyes painted on their bows. Among the small boats pulling round and passing our ship, are two kinds—one long, sharp, canoe-built, with four or five half-naked, dark-skinned Klings sitting down and rowing; but everywhere is seen a curious triangular affair, with eyes painted on each side of the sharp bow. These are the Chinese "sampans," and are propelled by grave-looking Chinamen, who, with blue cotton trowsers, no upper garment, shaved head, and broad-brimmed, conical hat, are standing up, each alone, in his own boat, swaying himself to and fro, as he slowly, but steadily, sculls his sampan. It is India, but it is still England. There, on shore, floats the omnipresent cross of St. George. If there were no such mark of nationality, we might guess it by the evidences of comfort and order which meet us when we first put foot on shore at the substantial and convenient jetty. We are in the midst of a picturesque crowd, and pillared over our heads, protecting us from sun or rain, is an appropriate roof, so that we can bare our heads to the sea-breeze, and take a look at the people around — Malays, Hindoos, Mohammedans, Chinamen, Europeans; a mingling of bright colors, white and crimson predominating; Chinamen, with all the head shaved but the crown, and the hair from this depending in a long plait, or queue, to the ground, or else wrapped in circles around the head; Mussulmans, with the entire head shaved, and covered with close-fitting, many-colored straw or rush-plaited caps, or else with full crimson or white turbans. White or red striped petticoats or sarongs fell from the waists of some, and a few wore bright-colored iackets, but many encumbered with no more clothing than would meet the demands of decency. Here and there a dark native, fully clad and stiffly buttoned up, represented the existing authority. These were native policemen.

Ranged along on one side of the mole, were several cunning, sagacious-looking little ponies, harnessed to the palki-garis, or palanquin-carriages — low, oblong, close vehicles, with a back and front seat, each attended by a native oriental-looking Syce, light, graceful and delicately-limbed. Go as far as you will, as fast as you can, through the most burning sun, whilst you are fanning yourself in the carriage, the Syce runs a-foot at his pony's head, and from morning until night, at a dollar a day. These graceful grooms salaamed to us, and solicited us to employ their vehicles, but as our consul's house was in sight only a few steps off, we declined a conveyance. In this we showed our ignorance of customs. No one walks any distance. After having visited the consul's house, I stepped over to his office, but a little distance off, and when about to return, a gentleman whom I met there, said, "You had better not walk; I will take you over in my gari." I began to think that, in a fit of mental abstraction, I had lost the idea of the distance; but no; we got in, closed the door, whisked around the corner in a minute, opened the door and got out at the house. We soon fell into the custom of a gari and Syce for any distance, however small.

I have heard of a gentleman who professed very little apprehension of the punishments of a future world, unless they should make him a United States Consul, and although no such satiric remark could ever acidulate the bland speech of Mr. Currier, our most estimable consul at Pinang, none could have had greater reason to utter the reproach. His quiet and orderly establishment, fitted with all the comforts of a fastidious single blessedness, was, in all its large extent, freely and hospitably given to our accommodation during the ten days of our stay, and each day he seemed happy in crowding his dinner table with his countrymen as guests. The grave old black Mohammedan butler, and the long-tailed Chinaman who had charge of the *menage*, seemed in no way startled from their propriety by this sudden invasion, but, catching the spirit of their master, made each one at home, and as one of the family. I believe that the Pinang consulate has no salary, so that the chief merit of the office is this privilege of keeping open house and extending a courteous hospitality to his countrymen, with the honor of doing all this at the expense of the incumbent. The foundation of our consular system may be traced to that custom of the ancients by which each nation sent one of its own citizens to reside in foreign countries, to extend the rites of hospitality to those of its subjects who might wander thus far, and have no claim for entertainment. Mr. Currier seems to have revived the classic usage, without the national cause to sustain it. But there seems to be a law of compensation in all things, and the man who has not only the honors of an unsalaried consulate, but the most pleasantly situated home, the most delicious curries, and, better than all, the smile of sincere welcome which springs from a kind heart, must consent, for all these good things and qualities, to the penalty of giving a temporary home to his less fortunate countrymen. Of course, the East Indies is the only place to eat curry—and, as yet, I have seen the dish nowhere in such perfection as at the table of our consul. Who that has ever had the turbaned servant hand him the piled-up dish of snowy rice, with the giant silver spoon silently indicating the volume you were expected to consume, and then moistening his full plate with the cream-colored cocoa-nut Malay curry, following this with the richer and more pungent curry, almost solidified by the most delicate shrimp—who that has ever eaten this combination would again call the yellow-peppered turmeric-dyed dishes—curry? It was really surprising to see how this dish adapted itself to our taste, and some of my friends seemed to involve in doubt the necessity for the thing containing being larger than the thing contained.

An evening seat on the paved flat roof of the portico brings before us the advantages of this delightful residence. We are, behind our wall, and air-perfuming trees, sufficiently removed from the smooth road to the jetty, passing in front of the house, which forms the morning and evening promenade and drive. In front, on the other side of the road, spreads the green lawn of the parade ground; this is bounded by the waters of the strait, with its shipping, its junks and moving boats; two miles across are the low lands of the province of Wellesley, sweeping away until they are bounded by the blue mountains of the dominions of Siam. And now we may give some attention to the passers by on the road. The palki-garis are rolling by with the turbaned "Syces" running rapidly at the ponies' heads, and in these garis are various occupants—European sailors and residents, Chinamen sufficiently well to do to ride, Armenian and Arabian gentlemen, occasionally a European lady. The variously costumed natives whom we met at the landing are passing to and fro, and, in addition, a Malay "ayah," or nurse, with one or two white children; the ayah wears the sarong or petticoat twisted around her waist, and, in addition, a short loose badja or jacket dropping over her breasts. Their beautiful black hair is handsomely done up with silver or even gold ornaments. Sauntering down the road in a stately manner, come two of the dominant race, two Englishmen, with folds of white muslin rolled around their hats, and dropping in a short curtain over the neck—a compromise between a hat and a turban, to protect the head from the sun's rays. Across the parade ground is marching a specimen of the physical force by which a small collection of English brains rules this Indian empire. It is a detachment of Sepoys, the Madras Native Infantry, Hindoos taken out of petticoats and put into stiff English uniform and more constraining military drill, to help

Englishmen rule their country. Here comes one of the benefits of that rule—our ears catch a tinkling, clinking sound, and turning our eyes in its direction we see coming from their labor upon an adjoining public building, a gang of convicts, mingled Indians and Chinamen; slender wire chains pass from one of their ankles to their loins. They are in charge of a single native Peon. These are thieves, rascals, and murderers, punished by exile from their homes, as well as by forced useful occupation. The corresponding gentry of this place are sent to return the visits of these guests. They are the laborers on all the public works, and to them we owe the good repair of the excellent roads. Gradually the night draws on; the passers by are fewer and fewer, until the road is quite deserted, and all would be very quiet but for the sound of tom-toms, drums, gongs, and all the discordant noises which make a Chinaman's harmony, and which reach us obscurely from the more dense part of the town. Around us, too, we have a noisy animated nature of night birds and insects. The limpid cocoa-nut oil lamps are lighted in the house; the Chinese servant, in Chinese costume, hands us tea in Chinese cups, which is taking the beverage with all appropriate concomitants.

A quiet chat in lounging chairs, with cigars for the smokers, closed our first day in Pinang; and we were shown to our comfortable, large and airy rooms in the second story, with open movable Venetian blinds next the sea, and the back looking, by capacious windows, upon the surrounding enclosure, or "campong," as such yards are called in the East, so that our sleeping might be fanned by every breath of air—a very pleasant arrangement, but accompanied by some contingencies, which afterward appeared, and took a little from the full enjoyment of such airy apartments. The sleeping garments of this climate are peculiarly convenient. They consist of very loose, light-flowing trowsers, made of white or striped muslin or silk—one style being fashionable in one locality, and one in another. These trowsers are fastened with a drawing string around the waist, and called panjammas. Over this is worn a badjo, or loose, shirt-like jacket, without a collar. By those who do not go out of the house, these are worn as a loose morning costume, or *déshabille*, until the breakfast toilet is made.

From dawn to sunrise, and from sunset till dark, are the only hours for out-door exercise; and accordingly, accompanied by a friend, I started, at the freshest hour of day, for a stroll through the streets of the foreign residents. It was like a walk through a garden. Smooth white-graveled roads, bordered by green sward, passed through avenues of cocoa and palm trees, flowering shrubs, and bamboo hedges—walls, almost concealed by foliage, enclosed campongs of nutmeg trees and other shrubbery, and in the midst of these stood the dwelling, generally large, square, and airy, built of brick, stuccoed, washed cream color, and roofed with tiles; the second story, and sometimes the first, surrounded by Venetian verandahs. In front of every house is built a portico, projecting twenty or thirty feet, and resting upon stone columns. Under this the carriages drive, and are well protected from the weather. The roof, being flat and paved, forms a pleasant lounging place in the cool, shady hours of the day. Returning from our stroll, we bathe, throw on the badjo and panjammas, take coffee, and read or write until it is necessary to dress for breakfast, which is ready from ten to twelve o'clock, and is a meal worthy of the appetites which approach it. Tiffin is on the table from one to three, and dinner from five to eight.

The bathing arrangements of the East, are very simple. The bather stands besides a tub or bucket of water, and with a dipper pours it over himself. This douche bath, without the shock of the shower bath, is considered more tonic than getting into the water, and not so dangerous, as having no tendency to produce congestion of the brain. Any one who can get a bucket of water, and a convenient place to stand, can take such a bath.

A walk through the business part of the town has no such attractions as that through the villa streets of the foreign residents. It is a complete Chinese town—all the mechanics, carpenters, cabinet-makers, blacksmiths, shoemakers, tailors, jewelers, are Chinese, and also the shopkeepers. The streets are generally narrow, with foul-smelling ditches on each side. The houses are closely built, the second story, or dwelling part, overhanging the lower, or stores and shops. Long, narrow signs, with Chinese characters, hang perpendicularly at the sides of the doors, and strips of red paper, with Chinese characters, are suspended from the top of the door. Queer-looking Chinese children, with shaved heads and young queues, are playing in the dirt before the doors. Joss-houses, or places of worship, with Chinese lanterns suspended before them, are frequent; and almost, if not every habitation, has its private joss, with a lamp burning before it, and slips of paper in a vessel ready to be lighted and burned before the deity. "Licensed Spirit Shop," "Licensed Toddy and Bang Shop," "Licensed Opium Shop," are signs seen in every wretched street. Toddy is the intoxicating fermented sap of the cocoa-nut tree, and bang is a liquid preparation of the maddening hachish, or Indian hemp. These evidences of gross indulgence seem scarcely reconcileable with the untiring and persevering industry of the Chinese. All day long, in the hottest weather, in shop and at forge, they are at their labor; and bowed beneath the weight suspended from each end of a long stick across their shoulder, they are met in the street and on the road, from youth to old men, hurrying along with their burdens. Some are bringing in loads of marketing, others are bearing miniature peddling shops. One man is a peripatetic meat market; on the top of a large covered basket is lying a quarter of mutton or pork, and each of his suspended baskets contain his butcher wares. Another travels around with a cook-shop and eating-house—his furnace in a box at one end of the pole, and his cooking materials in another box, at the opposite end.

As we get on the outskirts and along the water-courses, the houses are built on posts five or six feet above the ground, and reached by a ladder. The domestic animals harbor under the shelter of their proprietors, and when the tide flows, it washes in and out under these tenements.

Among the street and road sights, few things are more singular than the large, docile, unwieldy, patient-looking draft-buffalo. They are naked, quite destitute of hair, generally of a bluish black, and sometimes of a pinkish flesh color. They have a hump on the shoulder, and flat, corrugated horns. It was a comfort to see them all look fat and in good keeping.

Among the most repulsive resorts of this population are the opium-smoking shops. Situated generally in filthy localities, the door is closed by a curtain of dirty coarse canvas, and no care seems taken to gild the horrible vice. At night, accompanied by a friend, I visited one of the principal of these establishments, over which hung the sign "Opium Farm." In attempting to open the lower half-door of this establishment, a Chinaman on the inside refused us admittance, and pointed to a window closed by upright wooden bars wide enough apart to admit the hand. A crowd was gathered around this window, inside of which were two men, one busy in taking money, and the other in passing the opium to the squalid-looking purchasers outside. It was some minutes before our turn came, when, handing a rupee (about forty-five cents) through the window, I received about a teaspoonful of a dark, semi-fluid preparation of opium folded in a piece of corn-husk. All who purchased while we were there went off, I presume to their homes, to smoke it.

With ours as a ticket of admission, we again approached the door, which was now immediately opened to us. The apartment was gloomy, dirty and comfortless. A small lamp burning before a "joss" threw an obscure light over the place. On one side were piled chests of opium. In the shadows of the apartment one or two figures could be seen lying upon benches. These we supposed to be individuals laid away in the deep intoxication of the drug. Near the idol altar, lying in a recess, were reclining two Chinamen, with a small lamp between them, smoking the opium pipe. One of these men seemed to be half servant, half friend of the other, as he steadily filled the pipe and handed it to his companion, only occasionally and at long intervals taking a whiff himself. The pasty opium was introduced into the small cup by means of a slender wire, and one, or at most two whiffs, the smoke being gradually breathed through the nose, seemed to exhaust it. The effect was instantaneous. The countenance took on a rapt, but unpleasantly contracted expression, during which he lay with his fingers resting on his forehead. The effect was of very short duration, and while the pipe was being refilled he sat up and conversed with a natural expression, occasionally smoking a pipe of tobacco in the intervals between those of opium. With an habitual smoker some hours are necessary to bring on the full intoxication. These individuals seemed rather gratified than otherwise at our attention. The superior ordered seats to be brought us near them, and the opium-pipe being filled, courteously offered it to us.

I have alluded to the discordant tom-toms and screeching gongs which invaded our quiet residence on our first night ashore. Following up these sounds until they grew louder and more intolerable, they brought us to a motley crowd, over whose faces glared the lights from a covered platform in an open space before the principal Chinese temple. It was a Chinese theatre supported by a subscription of the Celestials for public performances. All I could make of it was this confounding noise of all imaginable discordant instruments—a crowd of people moving about the stage in various Chinese costumes, including silken royal robes, with masked faces, and in the pause of the instruments screeching to each other in voices no less discordant. I made a very short stay. Inferring that my readers are as tired as I am of these degraded and senseless exhibitions of a degraded humanity, we will refresh ourselves in more natural and invigorating scenes.

Although, under the influence of fresh sea-breezes and the calm pulses of a quiet life, there is no great inconvenience from the heat of Pinang, yet the inhabitants have the choice, in an hour's ride, of a cooler and more bracing climate. Mr. Greene, a partner of Mr. Currier's house, was residing at his bungalow on the hill-top, at an elevation of two thousand five hundred feet above the sea. This gentleman was kind enough to invite us to make him a visit at his elevated home, an invitation which we gladly accepted. Leaving the city at four o'clock in the afternoon, we rode, in palki-garis, four miles, over graveled roads winding through palm and nutmeg groves, to the foot of the hill, and here we found saddled ponies, and their attendant Syces, who had been sent out in advance of us. Mounting these little ponies, which seemed scarcely able to bear our weight, especially as two of our party were in the neighborhood of two hundred pounds, we commenced the ascent, the animals moving off with astonishing briskness. The whole distance of the winding road was three miles to reach the two thousand five hundred feet elevation. The road passed through the most luxuriant forest of shrubs, vines, and towering trees, while the ground was carpeted with mosses and varied ferns. Birds and insects were sounding their notes through the forest; but, above all, rang out the notes of the trumpet-beetle, a rapid succession of whirring notes, terminating in a series of shrieks like that of the Guinea-fowl. It is difficult to conceive of so much noise coming from an insect so small. It is of a bright green color, and in form a mixture of locust and katydid. Monkeys dwelt in myriads along our route, but concealed themselves on our approach. Much of the road overhung deep ravines and precipices, and occasionally an opening in the foliage gave us a view of the distant sea. We were about half way up when the evening clouds came sweeping in smoky mist upon us, and we had every promise of a drenching rain, for which we were by no means prepared. It would be cruel and useless to urge our ponies, who dug their hoofs with spiteful energy into the earth, and pulled us up with all their might. The clouds grew thicker and darker, and soon down came the rain in torrents, in sheets of water—such a rain as only can rain in a tropical forest of a mountain island with a steamy sea around it. It was such a rain as relieves one of all responsibility of guarding against it, and induces one to submit in pleasureable despair, anticipating the comfort of dry garments, no matter where; nor how they fit. It was nearly dark before we reached the bungalow, and quite so before we were in dry garments, therefore all picturesque views were postponed until the morning; and for the sentimental, we gladly accepted the actuality of a substantial and most welcome mountain-summit Pinang dinner—thanks to the kindness of Mr. Greene and to the enduring fortitude of the bazaar man. Daily he comes out from town a-foot, with the loaded baskets of provisions suspended from the stick across his shoulders; walking all these eight miles, ascending these two thousand five hundred feet, and bearing this burden, for twenty cents. Besides the convenience of such cheap transportation of their marketing, the mountain bungalow residents have a convenience rarely if ever enjoyed by the rural residents of any country. In their immediate neighborhood is the government bungalow, and at the government bungalow is a semaphoric telegraph; so that if any change in the marketing is required, an extra duck or chicken, any inquiry to be made, or the physician needed, in a few minutes the order or message is conveyed and an answer returned. We had, during our stay at Pinang, several occasions to appreciate the advantages of the telegraph.

As we sat after dinner in the piazza in front of the drawing-room door, we found that we were still enveloped in passing clouds, for the astral lamp behind us reflected our shadows upon the flying vapor. The thermometer stood at 74° Fahrenheit, about 12° below the temperature of the plain, a difference which produced chilliness, made thoughts of cloth clothes agreeable, and a blanket at night desirable. Then, there were no mosquitoes. But stories and traditions of gigantic scorpions and long centipedes, were a little calculated to derange our sleeping comfort.

By the earliest dawn one of our company came to my room in quite a fit of enthusiasm, calling me to look at the wonderful scenery lying spread out before us. It was just one of those views which one feels his incompetency to convey, by description, all their grandeur and all their delicacy. The air was intensely, keenly clear, and far down below us lay the plain, extending in a triangular form into the sea. Like white lines, the roads curved through the nutmeg groves to the extreme point of the triangle upon which rested the city, and the shipping lay like toys upon the water. But the whole plain of the opposite province of Wellesley lay far below us covered in a fleecy white cloud, tossed into gentle hillocks, with here and there a larger bank, looking like a broad snow-covered prairie, sweeping away to the distant Siam mountains, which stood out clear, blue and distinct—so clear, that a gentleman familiar with the view, said there was one peak visible he had never seen before. Here and there a nearer peak rose through the cloud-frill like a detached island. Our point of view faced directly toward the east, and as the sun came over the highest mountain summit, his faint rays falling on the velvety, snowy hillocks, beautifully tinged them with pink, violet and golden hues. As the sun gained power, the cloud covering was removed from the rice and corn fields of the plain, and gathering around the mountain tops for the day, shut them from our sight. Our morning stroll about the grounds was in an atmosphere perfumed with the greatest profusion and variety of roses. The gardener, each morning, replaced the mammoth bouquet, of the day before, in the rooms by fresh ones, without fear of exhausting his stock. We extended our morning's walk beyond Mr. Greene's premises to the government bungalow, about two hundred feet higher up. We there heard that the Lord Bishop of Calcutta was momentarily expected to spend some days in this cool retirement. His servants were already there, and before we left his lordship arrived, borne in a palanquin on the shoulders of six Coolies. For his age, seventy-eight years, he was a fine-looking, hale, cheery old gentleman. As the Rev. Daniel Wilson he had earned some reputation, and was the author of a work on the Evidences of Christianity. All accounts represented him as a good, earnest and benevolent man, but even our high churchmen thought his bearing too authoritative and lordly to meet our republican notions of a clergyman's demeanor. If it was so, it was more the fault of the institutions under which he lived than of the man. We can not judge justly those placed under influences to which we have never been exposed.

> "Who made the heart—'tis He alone
>   Decidedly can try us;
> He knows each chord, its various tone,
>   Each spring, its various bias.
> Then at the balance let's be mute,
>   We never can adjust it;
> What's done, we partly may compute,
>   But know not what resisted."

And the man who has lived for many years of a long life in the command of a large revenue, in the enjoyment of high power and prerogative, among a people deferential to that power—a churchman, whose progress is marked by salvos of artillery—may have had struggles of humble self-teaching, and have accomplished a personal discipline unknown and unnecessary to those who have not been thus exposed. In the afternoon, the Lord Bishop, supported on the arms of his friends, walked over to our bungalow, and made us a cheerful and pleasant visit. On the following morning we left our cool mountain nest, and before the heat of the day had come, we were back in the town.

During our absence, the first death had occurred in our ship, in the person of a German marine, who had been long sinking under consumption. With three volleys of musketry over his grave, we left him in the Roman Catholic cemetery of this beautiful island.

The Roman Catholics have a French mission at this

place. In the town is a female seminary under their charge, and a few miles out quite an extensive college for the education of youth from Siam, Cochin China, and other points of the East. These youths are taken from their homes and fitted for such priestly and missionary duties as may seem to suit their natural talent. It is a principle not to interfere with their national peculiarities in costume, etc., so that they may be returned to their people with no external peculiarities marking their difference of faith. In company with Mr. Harris, who was well acquainted with the priests, I rode out to this college. We reached there just as dinner was over, and as we entered the corridor, the youths, from fourteen to twenty years of age, were walking about, some with books in their hands, but all, including the youngest, smoking long pipes of tobacco. The fathers were amusing themselves over a billiard-table. Father Martin, a gentleman of great urbanity and courtesy, showed us over the whole institution. He was an enthusiastic naturalist, and we had great pleasure in looking at his collections, which, among other curious preparations, had several specimens of the flying fox, a very singular animal. There was one fine large tiger which had been killed close by the institution. Laid out in serpentine length along the top of the apartment, was a large boa constrictor. Thirteen feet was its actual length. To say such a reptile is thirteen feet long, gives no true ideal of the measurement of impression. Exaggeration seems necessary to tell the truth, so far as effect goes; and without knowing the length in feet, had I been asked the length of this snake after I had left it, I should have said from twenty to thirty feet. To such mental impressions I attribute the incredible size which it is said, as sober truth, these reptiles sometimes reach. Individuals have told me they have seen them over one hundred feet long, and record their capacity to swallow full-grown cattle or buffalos, and naturalists record it as a fact that they do so. The largest, however, of which I had positive evidence, was twenty-three feet long, and from it was taken a pig weighing one hundred and six pounds—so that a man might not be too large a mouthful to swallow. If the snake I saw dead grew upon me in impression from thirteen to thirty feet, I imagine he would have looked much larger had I met him writhing in the forest, and can easily suppose that one of thirty feet would with truthful purpose be reported one hundred.

Upon our return to Mr. Currier's, the roof of a back building in the campong, a few feet from the back windows of our airy apartments, was indicated as the spot where the boa constrictor I had just seen, had been killed only a few weeks before.

During our stay at Pinang, I had two opportunities of attending the Free Scotch Church in charge of the Rev. Mr. Moir, an intelligent, earnest, and able divine. Upon first entering the church, I was surprised, and at first unpleasantly so, at seeing two long punkas swaying to and fro over each range of pews, and a smaller one over the pulpit. These punkas were pulled by native Mohammedans in the side aisle. The moving fans, the turbaned Mussulmans, the labor of fanning Christians at their devotions, seemed incongruous. But the silent moving punkas were no disturbance to the worship, and the clattering of an infinitude of fans would be. Less manual labor was done in the aggregate by the three Mussulmans than would be done in detail by the individual fanners. Again, the Mohammedans did not regard the Sunday as a Sabbath, and if not there, would be engaged in active labor elsewhere. If they could understand the teachings of the sanctuary, there was nothing in their punka-pulling to prevent their profiting by them. I was told that the men doing this work had all been condemned for murder.

The punka affords an illustration of the servile condition of the native races. Dining with an English gentleman, I remarked upon the comfort of such an arrangement in such a climate. "Yes," he said; "but we can not here hire a man to pull one all night over our beds, for less than $4 a month. In Madras, I paid only $1.50." "But, did one man pull all night?" "Certainly. You put him on a high stool, off of which he is sure to fall if he goes to sleep. If you hear him come down, go and give him a kicking, and he will be sure not to do it again."

This is Indian British liberty. I would not adduce the single remark as the foundation of a general rule, but it was made in such a matter-of-course manner as to show that it was the rule; and further, it is consistent with all my observations of India. Since rounding the Cape of Good Hope I have not yet seen the first white man at any manual labor, excepting only the seamen of our own and other foreign vessels, and from all I hear, all I read, as well as all I see, I suppose such an instance would be a marvel. In all the intercourse between white and native, the demeanor of the latter is more servile, the language used toward him more harsh, habitually, than is the usage between master and slave in our southern States. Yet these are, in name, free British subjects. What is the difference between the abstract liberty of the Hindoo and the actual slavery of the African? I state facts, which those who are honest in solving the problems of humanity ought to know and consider. "I thrash them; I am obliged to thrash them," said a sugar planter to me. "To be sure they have the right to complain, but we take care to prevent that."

During our stay at Pinang, I saw much of an intelligent commander of a pepper ship, from Sumatra. Most of the pepper trade is carried on by American ships, and yet he told me that there were no surveys of the coasts excepting those made by necessity by merchant captains. He thought, however, that any of our national vessels cruising on the coast, would chance to do as much harm as good, as the latter had been the result of past proceedings. An outrage is committed upon some Americans by a small body of individuals, and this outrage, perhaps, provoked by the abduction of some female—the severest offense which can be committed against them—or by smuggling off pepper at night. Without inquiry, or the means of adjudicating the facts, a man-of-war comes along and batters down the town and the houses of some rajah and his people entirely innocent of the matter, and then goes away. This naturally excites a feeling of bitter hostility and a desire for vengeance, which may be wreaked upon the crew of the first unsuspecting pepper ship which comes along.

The eclat of vindicating American rights, by battering down some semi-barbarian town, may be brilliant in the home papers, but ten or twelve thousand miles' distance, and the absence of a press among the punished people, may prevent many contingencies appearing to tarnish that brilliancy.

One would little suppose that the quiet town of Pinang has the business which is really done, reaching the amount of ten millions of dollars. Nearly one million of this is with the United States. The exports are tin, brought from the tin mines of Siam, India rubber, gutta percha, cocoa-nut oil, nutmegs, pepper from Sumatra, and rattan.

Pinang was once a possession of the rajah of the opposite province of Queda, but was a beautiful jewel dowering the rajah's daughter, and, undoubtedly, rendering more brilliant her charms, when she married an English gentleman by the name of Knight, who subsequently transferred his possession to the India Company.

Our repairs being all completed, on Wednesday morning, April 2d, with an English pilot on board, we got underway for Singapore, where our friends in the frigate Macedonian were anxiously awaiting our arrival, and had been doing so for two months, that they might return to the United States from their protracted cruise of three years.

XIII.

SINGAPORE.

Any one who will look at the geographical position of Singapore, and its relations to the commerce between the East and West passing through the Straits of Sunda and the Straits of Malacca, will readily understand how, in a few years, a thriving city of forty thousand people has been planted in the jungle. Although the papers record that in the surrounding thickets of Singapore island the tigers destroy an average of a Chinaman a day—three hundred and sixty-five a year—the voyager finds its harbor floating the models and the flags of all nations, from great lumbering, red-painted, goggle-eyed Chinese junks, to the fine, large and elegant clipper-ship of the States; and among the flags of Europe and America we saw the white elephant banner of Siam, and the gaudy-hued flags of other eastern nations.

Another characteristic of the wide-spread interests of Singapore and varied nationalities here gathered together, is found in the names of the business houses:

Syed Abdoal Al Junied, merchant; Seyd Abbobaker, Arab merchant; Eng Wat, Moh Guan & Brothers; Raab Quay; Cursetgee & Co.; Whampoa & Co.; Shungiebhay Humusjee, Parsee merchant, etc. Such specimens are scattered numerously among those of European houses, and no men stand higher in the commercial world than the Arab merchants.

Our anchorage was necessarily a long distance, from two to three miles, from the shore, and falling readily into the usage which makes the native the servile laborer, we employed two native boats to run between the ship and shore, instead of using our own boats and seamen. These boats were narrow, sharp, flat-bottomed, ticklish, wabbling things, roofed over the middle with matting, and rowed by three or four natives. They were very neat and clean.

Singapore is Pinang enlarged. There are the same neat, garden-surrounded, stylish houses of the foreign residents, with pleasant promenades and drives through them, and the same long, narrow, close-crowded, opium-smoking, toddy and bang drinking streets of the pounding, blowing, filing, sewing, stitching, laboring Chinamen; but the two sections are, in this instance, separated from each other by a stream crossed at several points by bridges. The street which runs along the business side of this river is lumbered with piles of the products of the East and the West, and crowded with the buffalo carts carrying away, or laborers passing it into the adjoining stores. Rising above all, for five hundred feet, is the foliage-covered government hill, with the British flag flying before the house which tops the summit. From this hill is a good view of the town, the harbor and the nutmeg groves of the surrounding country. The Chinese are in such numbers and wealth that their joss-house or temple is said to be one of the finest to be seen. I directed my Syce to drive there. Admission was given us by a Mohammedan native, who had his quarters in one corner of the temple paved court. Before unlocking the door he cast over his shoulder and breast a band with a silver plate engraved "Chinese church." This individual conducted us around, pronouncing in English the names of the various things he thought objects of interest. The idols were three behind each of two altars, representing a higher and two lower deities, and on each side of the collection was a figure the size of life, and whose character was easily read in his demoniac face and long tail curled over his shoulder, even if our guide had not said, shortly, pointing his finger at them—"Devil." The whole affair was a collection of confused carving in wood and stone, of gilding and tinsel, with distorted figures of human beings and animals. There was nothing to admire, and but little to wonder at, where absurdity and stupidity are the rule, and therefore, after a glance around, I put some buckskeesh in the guide's hand when he immediately, under the roof of the sanctuary, said, "You take some beer, good English beer." My companion and I assented for the novelty of the thing. He conducted us to his room in the court corner, took down a bottle of Scotch ale from a high shelf, and drew it for us. An old woman and another man came in and squatted on the brick floor —his mother and brother. We offered our host and his relatives some of our ale, but they all declined, being Mohammedans. Double the usual price being charged for the prohibited liquor, made the Mussulman's fee for showing the Chinese temple to Christian visitors.

Among the individuals of whom the stranger first hears in Singapore, is Whampoa, the Chinese merchant. Not to allude to Whampoa would be to cast a doubt over one's having really been in Singapore. In the first place he has the reputation of being a strictly honest man, which, being a noble reputation everywhere, has the merit of being a particularly rare one in the East. Of my own knowledge I can not speak to this fact. You will go to Whampoa's, and you will find him at his desk behind an inclosure in his ship-chandlery store, and will be introduced to a good looking, stout-bodied, round-faced, Chinese gentleman. In this apartment, settling bills, buying stores, or merely looking on, you will find English, French, and American officers, with citizens of all countries. The great attraction, however, is the second story. There, handsomely arranged in cases and shelves around the sides and through the centre of the apartment, are the shawls and embroideries of cashmere from India, sandal wood, card cases, boxes, work baskets handsomely inlaid in colored metals, carved ebony work. From China the hundred useful things and toys in ivory, sandal wood, silver, besides shawls, paintings, and silks; and mingled with these are the products of western elegance and art. Whampoa has a handsome country residence, amid spice groves and gardens, about five miles from town. Here he entertains strangers with courteous hospitality, and very kindly, during his business avocations in the city, gives visitors a ticket of admission to his house and grounds. With one of these tickets, three or four lines of Chinese characters run off rapidly with a brush up and down a piece of yellow blotting paper, I drove out there. The house was profusely furnished in a mingled Chinese and European style. Handsome cabinets of minerals and bijouterie; paintings; a good English library, and one of Chinese books. Nothing could look more comfortable and appropriate than his sleeping apartment. The bedstead was in size a chamber itself, shut in by a fine gauze frame, and closed by a gauze door. The bed was covered with a fine mat, and around its side lay different styles of cushions and pillows. A punka was suspended across the bed, the cord of which led into an adjoining dressing-room. In his drawing-room the portrait of Commodore Perry was paired with that of Lord Nelson.

Whampoa is a gentleman of many enterprises, and among them he has a flouring-mill which I had the curiosity to visit. It was alive with Chinamen, all the operations being carried on by hand. Chinamen ran round with the mill-stones by means of hand-spikes in the upper stone. The bolting was a very curious process. A section of a round piece of timber rested with its convex surface like a rocker upon the floor. On its upper flat surface was fixed a short board projecting a little over the edge of the rocker. A Chinaman, standing with a foot on each end of this board, by rapid motion of his legs up and down, agitated to and fro a lever connected with the bolting-cloth, and conveying to it the sifting motion. Every Chinaman, with the perspiration rolling down his body, naked to the waist, was fanning himself in time with the rapid motion kept up by his legs. When but the lower part of the legs were concealed, as they were in most instances, by articles lying around the room, these men had the ridiculous appearance of dancing jigs and fanning themselves in competition with each other. The inference is, that Chinaman power is cheaper than that of steam in Singapore.

The exports of Singapore are the same as those from Pinang, with the addition, to a large extent, of sago. A sago factory was next to the flour-mill of Whampoa. This was also thronged with laboring Chinese. The fecula of the sago palm is brought to Singapore in a crude state in mat baskets. It is here washed to snowy whiteness, and formed into the small pearls in which it is found in commerce by passing through sieves, and dried in ranges of pans set in a furnace. With the exception of a part of Sunday, one day was all the time I had for my observation of Singapore. At its close, after dining with our consul, Dr. Bradley, I returned to our ship, and the following day we started for Siam.

FANKWEI.

II.

SIAM AND THE SIAMESE.

SIAM AND THE SIAMESE.

XIV.

KINGDOM OF THE WHITE ELEPHANT.

At Singapore we were at another end of the earth, at a city within less than two degrees of the equator, and at the extreme point of Asia. Rounding this termination of the eastern continent, our way was now to that kingdom which lies immediately north of this Malayan peninsula—the southern kingdom of the Asiatic continent, lying between the 6th and 20th degrees of north latitude, a territory bounded by mountains unexplored by civilization, but presenting the testimony of being rich in mineral wealth. It is watered by the Menam, whose course is eight hundred miles, and much of it through luxuriant forests of the valuable teak wood, and plains of great fertility; producing rice and sugar at the lowest cost of production, spices, and an abundance of the most choice fruits.

All this old eastern world is very young. Its age is like that of the rock or tree-inclosed frog who is again born to the light after the centuries of structure which have grown around him falls beneath the ax or is shattered by the explosion of a new civilization. The teachers of that old eastern world are themselves but just born. The great Anglo-Saxon republic of Australia, and the other-day-planted republic of the same race on the western coast of America—when their power, commerce, civilization and Christianity are brought to bear upon the nations of Asia, who can anticipate the result? However, we people, older in all that which the world values, are already looking for that result and bringing it about. Hence the special mission of the Hon. Townsend Harris, Consul General to Japan, to this White Elephant kingdom.

On Sunday, the 16th of April, we anchored in an expanse of muddy water, over whose surface, distant twelve or fourteen miles, could be seen the tops of the trees on the banks of the Menam. A few small native craft were lying off what we supposed to be the mouth of the river, and near our anchorage was a group of American, English, Dutch and French ships.

A boat and an officer were immediately detailed to visit the shore, announce our arrival, and make arrangements for the landing of the mission suite and presents. However, some Americans who were visiting a ship at the anchorage came on board of us. They were about returning to the large city of Bangkok, distant forty-five miles, and the official communications were committed to them, and I sent a communication with which I had been intrusted to one of the brothers of the king, who was a physician, and member of the New York Academy of Medicine. The detail for accompanying the Commissioner was made out, including the marine guard and the band.

All day Monday we expected some reply to the message sent up to Bangkok, but none came. Early on Tuesday morning, the quartermaster of the look-out reported the appearance of steam over the distant land, and this, as we inferred, was from a small steamer belonging to the King of Siam, coming down the Menam. In the course of a few hours, this tiny commencement of the Menam's future steam marine, painted bright blue, came puffing towards us, as if worn out by her exertions. The bustle of preparation for the departure of our large party now commenced—the packing of trunks and bedding, cooking provisions and rations for the men. The steamer anchored near us, and our boats being sent her, brought to our ship the Pra Kallahone or Prime Minister of the kingdom, and suite of his younger brothers, sons, servants, sword-bearer, gold teapot, and betel-nut-box bearers. They are of a light mulatto color, short stature, light bodies, small features, but heavy stout limbs. Their teeth were jet black from the use of betel-nut and lime, while the saliva, colored by its use, crimsoned their mouths. They wore loose sarongs, or loin cloths, of rich silk, passing around the hips and between the legs, one corner fastened by tucking in at the waist in front, and the other at the back, so that the loose side of the garment fell like full trowsers as low as the calf; the remainder of the legs and the feet were entirely bare. No upper garment is generally worn, except upon state occasions, and this being one of them, they wore silk jackets of bright colors. The head was bare, and with the hair cropped short, or shaved, all excepting three or four inches of top-knot on the front of the head, giving them the appearance of what are known as Polish chickens. The contrast between the rich silken jackets and sarongs, the cropped heads, black teeth, bloody-looking mouths, and bare feet, was very great.

The scabbards of the swords and the betel-nut-boxes were of solid, handsomely-wrought gold, thickly studded with jewels, and were of native workmanship. The box borne by the prime minister's servant was nearly a foot long by about four inches broad, and two deep. Inside of it were several small boxes of wrought gold.

One of the striking characteristics of the people, and

prominently shown in this our first introduction to them, is the claim of rank and primogeniture. No man of inferior position must be, in place or position, on the same level with his superior, and there are scarcely such relations among any as equals. If a superior appears, all inferiors seat themselves on the ground, or squat below him, with their feet concealed from view. If they are compelled to be in the same apartment, as in audience chambers, there are floors of elevation for each grade. Every man takes his meals at a small table by himself. The younger brothers kneel in addressing their elders, or handing any thing to them.

The prime minister was walking along the deck of our ship, and his cigar became extinguished. He turned to one of his brothers, a stout young man, handsomely clad in silken sarong and blue silk jacket, and asked for a light; the brother sank immediately to his knee, and remained in that position until his distinguished relative had lighted his cigar and passed in.

It is said that when Sir John Bowring was negotiating the British treaty, Sir John and his suite were seated in the room of a second story, and the Siamese, to reach it, must pass through the lower story, and consequently beneath their visitors. To obviate the degradation of such a position, a ladder was placed at a window of the upper story, and by this the Siamese princes and nobles ascended to the audience chamber. There were two lads of twelve or fourteen with the party. These lads were too young to have any specific title, but all young persons who are likely by birth to acquire title are called young "coons." They passed all over the ship, examining it with great care, and the prime minister and his son seemed to take special interest in every thing they saw. The young man was a naval architect, and had modeled and built the little blue steamer which brought them to us.

The engine they got out from the United States, and put together themselves, although they had no practical instruction in engineering, or any other than casual informants, or from books. The government is administered by two kings, who are brothers. The first king has a general control over all affairs, and the second king commands the military. According to the usage of the monarchy, so far as there is any usage, the second king succeeds the first upon his death; but this right is not admitted by the first king if he has heirs, and the matter would be decided by the nobles. Under other names these sovereigns hold the relations to each other of our President, Vice-President, and Commander-in-chief of the army. Under the name of Fa-Chou, the second king has been extensively known to foreigners and Americans, from his knowledge of the English language, its literature and science.

The second king has, with his own hands, constructed a steam engine in all its parts. Both brothers have considerable attainments in astronomy, calculate eclipses, etc., and are members of the "Asiatic Astronomical Society."

The proper names and titles of these princes will be seen when we come to the treaty, and Chou-Fa is a general term for those princes who are noble by both parents.

Our visitors remained with us several hours, partook of refreshments, and finally took their leave, giving us no satisfaction as to our future movements, and making all our hurried preparation useless. Mr. Parkes, who brought out the English ratified treaty, is still here, and has been for some weeks endeavoring to launch it into successful operation, in which he has found some difficulty and many obstacles. Mr. Parkes is uncertain when he will get through. The presence of this gentleman is no doubt some obstacle to our negotiations being commenced. He occupies the best quarters; and, although they have built large bamboo houses for the accommodation of our own and the French mission, the prime minister said we would not be so comfortable in them as in that now occupied by the British envoy. I suspect they do not want too much on their hands at once; and soon the French mission will be pressing them.

They must be impressed with their increasing importance to the western powers. This treaty-making is a difficult and responsible business among such a people. It is contrary to the traditions, notions and habits of the masses to be in appearance surrendering rights to foreign powers, and especially western powers. It is contrary to the interest of the nobles to be opening for general competition a trade of which they now have the monopoly. The enlightenment and education of the two kings, being so far in advance of their nation, may prove their ruin. It may be regarded as the evidence of treachery to the interests of the nation, or incompetency to comprehend them. The first king, in his character of Buddhist priest, has expunged from their books the cosmogony, retaining only the moral precepts, because the teachings of that cosmogony were adverse to the introduction of western science.

We well know that no important treaty is made, or other political step taken, among civilized nations, without exciting the hostility and opposition of certain parties and factions. The same influences necessarily agitate these semi-civilized nations; and many who, before the making of one treaty, might be favorable to it, might, by the rivalries and jealousies of its progress, disappointment in presents, etc., be thrown into opposition to another; so that I am prepared to expect more difficulties in our negotiations than now appear, unless great address is used in meeting them. After the departure of our visitors, to whom we gave a salute with the Siamese flag at the fore, there was great impatience got up on board at our detention. Shipboard weariness, lying in this monotonous gulf, was excessive. We are now within a few days of our letters, and anxious to reach them; and various indignant and belligerent opinions burst forth.

"Well, if I had this treaty to make," said one, "I would just say to them, 'I have only so many days to stay, and if the treaty is not made by that time, I shall clear out.'"

"But," it was replied, "they may answer, 'You came here seeking us, and forcing this negotiation upon us, and have the same freedom to go as you had to come.'"

"Then I should go," said another. "A treaty with such a country as this can be no advantage to us."

"Not worth a damn," says a third.

"The statesmen of three such commercial powers as the United States, England and France, appear to think differently, by the costly squadrons, the presents, and the large salaried envoys they send here treaty seeking," was the answer to this ship-board diplomacy.

The betel-nut chewing—the semi-nude nobility—the excessive reverence for age and rank, and all its formal external manifestations, were things to wonder at in contrast with our own usages; and called from many expressions of contempt as evidences of barbarism; but I could imagine a Siamese going home and relating his experience of a visit to our ship. I can see him take a seat on his cool mat, surrounded by his large family, and say, "It is wonderful that a people who have acquired so much skill in building ships, and make so many useful instruments, should yet be so stupid and benighted in many of the usages which make life comfortable; and I am not surprised that they desire association with us, to learn some of our wise customs."

The old gentleman now stops for breath, and makes a

sign to one of the females sitting around him. She handed him an elegantly-wrought golden box, tinted with reddish hues. Looking at it for a moment before he opened it, he said, "Among their rich presents, I have seen nothing equal to our skill in gold, or to the elegance of this box."

Opening it he took from it a pawn, of which it contained several. The pawn is a globe of green fresh leaf, containing the betel-nut preparation. They are prepared by the females, and deposited all ready in the betel-nut-box.

"Instead," continued the old gentleman, "of this bracing nut, mingled with fragrant spices, and tinging the mouth vermillion, they fill their mouths with the poison tobacco plant, made more black and disgusting by some mode of preparation. It makes the saliva flow from their mouths in dark yellow streams; and all about their rooms they have small vessels to catch the offensive fluid and to receive the black remains of the tobacco, whose juices have been pressed out by their teeth. These, in their very harsh language, are called quids."

"Horrible beasts!" exclaimed Ronta, the ebony-teethed and pinky-lipped favorite wife.

"Do such wretches have any other wives than those they buy?" asked Mou, the last and youngest addition to the harem.

"I have not told you the worst," replied their lord. "The physician informed me that the effect of this poison was to make them weak and trembling, to take away the desire for food, and to keep them wakeful and restless; but such is their devotion to this poison, that they even leave the company of their wives to enjoy it, it being against their laws to have the vessel for holding the yellow spittle in the same rooms with their wives."

"That," said Ronta, "must be to keep their wives from enjoying whatever pleasures their husbands find in the poison."

"Were I the king, I would make no treaty with such filthy barbarians," said Mou.

"They have no idea," said the old gentleman, "of the use of garments. Instead of dressing themselves for comfort, decency and cleanliness, they envelop all parts of the person, those which show its symmetry and health, in close, heavy garments, hiding all blemishes, and retaining the moisture of the skin about it instead of allowing them to be swept away by the free atmosphere, or washed away by the free and daily bathing which we use."

"How," asked Ronta, "do they manage such filthy arrangements?"

"It was a great mystery to me, but I was very particular to inquire, and wrote it all down on a piece of paper." He took the golden box, turning up the pawns; in the bottom were several folds of paper, from which he read as follows:

"'First, they draw on the feet two long cotton bags, pressing the toes together; over this they draw a long cotton garment, which ties with strings around the lower parts of the legs, and shuts them up in two tight bags, keeping the blood up in the legs until the veins almost burst.'"

"Terrible!" breathed out the listeners, with rapt attention.

"'Then,' went on the narrator, 'they draw over this a long woolen garment, which, with thick folds, comes up around the middle of the body, and fastens with heavy straps and buckles across the shoulders. Before putting over these straps, they take a light loose cotton jacket, which would be almost as pleasant as our own if they permitted it to hang loosely, but they tuck it in tightly around their hot and constrained bodies, and over this they fasten a gloomy, dark-colored, woolen garment, covering them from the hips to the hands in its close folds.'"

"But that," asked Ronta, "is only in their own horrid

country, where the sun does not shine and the running water turns to stone?"

"You fool, you, no! I've not been there, and I tell you what I saw under the burning sun of Siam. They do make these outer garments sometimes of white cotton, but it is only by stealth. I believe it is against the precepts of their religion to do so, and I shall record in the annals of Siam that those who dress in white are outcasts and heretics. Poor wretches, how I pity them!

"I have not read you yet about what they put on their heads."

"Their heads! why, do n't they leave them exposed to the free air?"

"Not at all. They put on their heads black, iron-looking things with rims, which look as though they would make good rice pots, or they cover them up with thick folds of cotton and cloth, with a stiff piece of leather in front."

"How stupid!"

"By close observation and some inquiry, I ascertained that there was a mysterious meaning in these garments, which led the poor people to endure them, notwithstanding their filthy and uncomfortable character. There really seemed to be more in the dress than in the unhappy beings to whom it belonged.

"There is a kind of officer among them who walks all day on the deck of the ship and sees every thing properly done. I was talking to one of these officers just before he was called to his post. It was in a lower chamber, and he had on the unlawful white clothes. When they called him to go up on the deck he pulled off his white jacket. I was glad to see that, as I thought he would be cooler; but then he put on one of the dark woolen jackets with heavy metal buttons, and looked terribly hot and uncomfortable as he walked up and down in the hot sun."

Such, possibly, may be the Siamese criticism upon our habits, corresponding to that we pass upon them.

After the departure of our noble friends, time hung in heavy monotony and hourly expectancy until Thursday morning, when we were boarded by a large boat with mat sails and two rudders, one on each side of the sharp stern. Its appearance was announced by the clamor of Siamese, the squealing of pigs and the mingled cries of ducks and fowls. It proved a boat of presents from the king. Twelve hundred pounds of sugar, four chests of fine tea, piles of fruit, and hundreds of cocoa-nuts and fowls, with four pigs, all to keep us in good humor while we waited the slow progress of diplomacy.

XV.

THE WHITE ELEPHANT AT HOME.

EARLY on the morning of April 21st, two enormous teak-wood boats or canoes, and the little sky-blue steamer were seen approaching our ship. The canoes were manned by from thirty to forty rowers in crimson jackets and caps, and from various points of the canoes bright-colored small silk banners were fluttering in the breeze—some blue, some white, and others crimson. The bow and stern of the boats were built up high, and in the centre, dividing the rowers into two bodies fore and aft, was a small house, or roofed shed, for the passengers. There are no seats in Siamese boats; a mat, a Persian rug, and a hard triangular leather pillow to support the back, or throw the arm over in a semi-recumbent posture, is the mode.

A small schooner which had previously come down, was hauled alongside the San Jacinto to receive the presents, and all was again in a stir and bustle of preparation for our departure. With our baggage, some extemporized bedding, and stores of provisions, we were all on board the steamer, with a name as long as herself, "The Royal Seat of Siamese Naval Force," and under way for the Menam by half-past ten o'clock. The marine guard, with Lieutenant Tyler in command, had gone ahead in the boats with the crimson rowers and bright flags.

Mr. Harris, the Consul General, Commodore Armstrong, Lieutenants Lewis, Rutledge, Carter, Assistant Surgeon Daniels, Chief Engineer Isherwood, the secretaries to Mr. Harris and to the Commodore, Mr. Heuskin and Mr. Vanden Heuvel, with the band and our servants, composed the party in the steamer. This vessel looked scarcely more than a toy, and not competent to carry such a party in addition to the natives already on board. We however stowed in her small cabin snugly, the band in her bows. As we steamed away from the San Jacinto, her battery poured forth a salute to the President's letter, to the Consul General, to the Commodore, or all together. The band struck up "Hail Columbia," which was changed into "God Save the Queen" as we passed under the stern of Her Majesty's brig Saracen, which dipped her ensign in acknowledgment of the compliment. On our way in, we passed several merchant ships at anchor, all of which were being loaded by Mr. King, an enterprising American merchant of Bangkok, and also lines of fishing-stakes, around which were Siamese boats receiving the gatherings of the nets. In about two hours and a half of puffing and paddling, we were passing between the low, green, mangrove-covered shores which form the mouth of the Menam, the muddy waters of which were clouding those of the gulf some miles out. On our left lay a large Siamese ship which had missed the channel and run aground. To shun such accident our pilots sounded their way with bamboo poles. At a short distance above the mouth of the river, the Siamese flag was floating from a look-out station. This flag, nationally, is a white elephant upon a red ground. The king's individual banner, in yellow upon a green ground, represents the throne in the centre, between two of what are called the royal umbrellas. There are from five to nine circles supported on a staff, and diminishing in size upward. These wheels are covered with embroidered silk or gold cloth, which hangs in a curtain about a foot deep from the circumference of each circle. About four miles from the entrance of the Menam is the town of Packnam, and as we drew near it long lines of white fortifications were seen glittering in the sun, and through their embrasures were jutting the muzzles of large-sized cannon. These fortifications are built of brick and white-washed. Their brilliant whiteness was strongly contrasted with the surrounding and equally brilliant green of the rich and heavy vegetation.

As we drew near the landing, our band crashing forth its loud harmony, it was difficult to look at any thing else than the mass of yellow-skinned humanity lying crouched upon the banks, watching in silent interest the strangers who had come from a far western world to form more extended relations with them. This mutual and earnest gaze of Anglo-American and Siamese, has a future for both people beyond the curiosity of the moment. Our steamer anchored in the stream; and a boat, with a small wooden house built in the middle, came off to us. In the house was an officer who, from his glittering costume, might be one of importance. He was a sallow, old, attenuated creature, dressed in a caricature of European military costume, bedizened with gold and silver tinsel, with epaulets on his shoulders, and diamond-shaped figures of ruby-colored glass set, like rows of buttons on each side of the breast of his bright silk coat. I am amused now at the stately stiffness with which we all sat to receive poor old Gabrielle, not certain which was the great man, whether we were or he was. This military-looking gentleman was one of the descendants of the early and proud Portuguese settlers. They still call themselves Christians, and attend a Catholic chapel which sometimes flies a flag with the words "Vivat Jesus;" but they have assimilated with and degenerated below the Siamese, are all in the service of the king, although they have a head and officers of their own to administer their affairs. Our visitor was next to the chief of these Christians, but notwithstanding this high position, and all his finery, he held a very humble Siamese appointment. He came aboard as a messenger on the part of the governor of Packnam, to tender us welcome, and to say a feast was prepared for us. Afterwards, in our association with the old gentleman, we found him useful and willing in any humble service. The Siamese are said to have some wit, and I could almost believe there was an intention of satire in their dressing up this caricature of a man in such a caricature of our costume, epaulets and all. How much more elegant and simple to their eyes must seem the ample folds of rich silks around the loins, with their naked busts and limbs; a contrast the more marked, when he was, as I have since often seen him, crawling in all his silk and tinsel, on hands and knees, at the feet of some half-naked noble!

Guided by this gilded Gabrielle, we landed on the soil of Siam. A guard in crimson coats, white trowsers and English soldier caps was drawn up in two lines at the landing, and as we passed through them they rolled drums and presented arms to an order given in English. We passed on a short distance to a palm-leaf and bamboo building open at all sides, the roof supported on posts and ceiled with white muslin. The floor was a series of platforms rising one above another, so that the inferior ranks should not be upon a level with the higher. In the middle of the highest floor a dinner-table was set out in European style—white table-cloth, napkins, wine-glasses, porcelain and decanters of wines. We were here received by two of our first acquaintances, the visitors to the ship, the stout, good-looking brother of the Pra Kallahone, or prime minister, and Pra-nai-wai, the Pra Kallahone's son. These individuals were dressed in their silken jackets, were attended by their retinues, and the bearers of the golden vessels belonging to their rank. There being none superior to them here, they had the privilege of sitting upon chairs, although afterwards I have seen these same men crouching and crawling in presence of their superiors. The dinner was immediately served, and was very abundant, being a roast pig, boar's head, chickens, ducks, various curries, shrimps and crabs. There was a dessert of puddings, preserves, confectionery and ornamental cakes, and jellies of rice, flour, eggs and sugar. Fruits followed this, of which there were a great variety, the best, however, being the mango. Tea and coffee were served, and cocoa-nut milk in young cocoa-nuts from which the husk had been stripped and the top cut into a circular lid. Dinner was prepared for the marine guard and band in separate sheds. The dishes for our table were kept, until placed upon it, under conical covers made of some light frame-work covered with red cotton cloth. These covers were, I afterwards found, in very general use, being on sale in many of the shops, and placed on the brass trays on which dishes and delicacies were sent as presents.*

It was expected that from this boat we would go up the river in a number of the long boats, such as brought in

* During our meal, all the descending platform of our apartment was a throng of Siamese men, women and children sitting on the floor and looking silently upon us.

the guard from the ship, and several of them appeared to be gathered at Packnam for the purpose; but we had found ourselves so comfortable in the steamer, that we concluded to continue in her to Bangkok. Taking the marines from the long boat into the steamer, we were all again under way about three o'clock, leaving Packnam under a salute from the battery. Pra-nai-wai saw us aboard, and left our steamer just as we got under way. We had now about twenty-five miles to go, the river being very tortuous and about five hundred yards in width. The banks were fringed with the desert jungle vegetation. One species of the bamboo grew to a lofty and feathery tree. Groves of various palms everywhere drooped their gracefully-curving branches. In the background they crowned the top of the tall and slender areca-tree, and close along the water's edge a dwarf variety shot up clusters of leaves, curving like plumes, directly from the root. As we ran close along first one and then the other bank of the river, we saw beneath these dark, green groves, and lying among their branches, countless men, women and children, looking like river animals who had crawled upon the shore. Through openings in the trees we could see their sharp-roofed bamboo and palm-leaf huts, built up five or six feet from the ground on poles, with a ladder to reach the door; and all along were tied their boats, their principal and almost sole means of passing to and fro. At frequent intervals we passed narrow wharves or platforms of planks pushing through the trees to the river's side, and these were crowded with boys and men with shaved heads, and yellow cotton mantles over their shoulders. These were Buddhist priests and novitiates belonging to some wat or temple planted amid groves in the background. Occasionally we would see several of the neat-looking salas, an open hall with tiled roof supported on white-washed brick and stucco pillars—

a kind of garden summer-house for shade and rest—which is freely planted through the grounds of the wats, and give them a pleasant and ornamental appearance. Our band was the first one of western music ever heard upon the Menam, and as we passed along its waters our approach was made known to the natives by the notes of its bugles and drums, sounding, besides our national airs, German waltzes, the "Old Dog Tray," "Old Folks at Home," etc., etc.

We passed in the river, some under way and some at anchor, several large vessels, barks, and ships, which had been lightened sufficiently to go over the bar. Most of them bore the Siamese flag, but one fine ship carried our own. At Packlat we passed another extensive range of fortifications, similar in appearance to those at Packnam. Here a boat came alongside, with a present of fruit from the governor. It was all sent on board in trays or tables of sheet-brass, about eighteen inches high, and two feet diameter, with pedestals of the same metal cut into open-work figures; a narrow border of similar work ran around the top. A great quantity of the smaller fruits —lichis, mangoes, etc., were sent aboard in these trays, besides a boat-load of water-melons and cocoanuts.

At a point on the river, some distance above Packlat, two of the large boats we had seen at Packnam came shooting through the bushes of the right bank. They had by a canal, accessible only to such boats, cut off a large curve which we were compelled to make, and they came upon the river with loud shouts of triumph at their success in overtaking us.

Day was just closing as we ran alongside the bank at the lower end of the city. Here were the quarters which the king had caused to be erected for us, and to which we were welcomed by Mr. King, several of the missionaries, and Pra-nai-wai himself, who had succeeded in reaching here as soon as we.

Our quarters were a collection of new-dried palm-leaf and bamboo houses, inclosed by a bamboo fence, with a flag-staff planted in front of the gate. The whole place was lighted up, and in the large central room an inviting-looking table was set, with a handsome silver and porcelain service, and just the number of plates and chairs for our party. Before the dinner or supper is ready we shall have time to look round the premises. The main building was set on posts ten feet high, so that there was a clear open space underneath, giving the soldiers and men a shady retreat during the heat of the day. This building contained one large central dining and sitting-room, with two smaller rooms for pantry, servants, and stores at each end. Outside of this, at the back and one end, were open galleries or passages, along which were ranged the sleeping apartments, those at the back having a covered hall between the rooms and the open passage. At one end of each passage was a bath-room, with several large jars of water for bathing, according to the method of this country, the water being poured over the person, and running through the planks to the ground beneath. One suite of sleeping apartments was divided by a portable Chinese partition of carved and painted wood work. The other rooms, and all the remainder of the building, were inclosed and divided by dried palm-leaves, neatly and smoothly laid into bamboo frames. The roof was of the same material, and the whistling of the wind through the dried leaves had the sound of a heavy pouring rain.* There was not a nail or piece of iron in the whole structure, all being laid up by notching, mortising, and lashing. The rain poured in

* The windows were railed with light bamboo rods, and the shutters of close palm-leaf thatch, swung from the top, and opened by propping out the lower end, so as to screen against sun or rain.

torrents during our first week, and yet our temporary home was quite dry. The slender stock of bedding which we had brought along, in case of necessity, was not needed, for every room was supplied with a high-posted bedstead, mattrass, and pillows, and hung with green silk gauze mosquito curtains, and ornamented with two slips of silk a foot wide, one blue, one crimson, tacked along the edge of the tester.

There was a separate and lower building, though still elevated from the ground, for the marines and musicians, and another for the kitchen. A new, light mattrass, made of white muslin, with red edges, filled with a light silk cotton; a mat, mosquito curtain, and pillow, were all ready for every man and servant.

All the cooks, servants, and the provisions of this establishment, together with three boats, with from twenty to thirty rowers, or rather paddlers, in each, were furnished by the king. And the expense of our reception and entertainment must have more than equaled the value of our presents to the king.

On the morning following our arrival we ran the American flag up at the flag-staff, played "Hail Columbia," "Yankee Doodle," the "Star-Spangled Banner," and made ourselves at home in Siam. A few nails knocked into the posts of my room, two empty packing-boxes tacked over with brown paper—one for a table and one for a closet—made my room quite snug and comfortable.

Now we may look about us and catch the general appearance of this Bangkok—this city of four hundred thousand Siamese and Chinese. We find that our quarters are on a point with one of the city canals running close up to our fence on the right, and a broad ditch bounding us as closely upon the left, while back of us is a closely-built, confused jumble of native thatched houses, without apparent street, lane, or alley between them. So that by land we are prisoners. But before us rolls the broad Menam, and the king, as stated, has placed boats and men at our disposal. Even in these we are not free. In the "land of the free" we felt at once the hand of oriental despotism. With each boat is an obliging individual as director, captain, or interpreter. When we want a boat manned, we hint it to him, and it is done. These men are all Portuguese, speak Portuguese, some Spanish, and a little English. Courteously, they are our interpreters and guides; loyally, they are close spies upon all our words and movements. At the close of the day their report is given in—the places and the persons we have visited, our gestures, expressions, mood, tempers, words, so far as understood, if only a single one; and I am told by one familiar with the secrets of this espionage, that the accuracy with which character and the tenor of conversation will be inferred from such fragmentary reports, is astonishing.

But we are all now in a good humor; we have sights to see, are not in the spirit of treason, and may furnish the materials of a report favorable to ourselves and country. Old gilded Gabrielle, in more simple attire, is our guide for the day, and he and I have entered into such pleasant relations, that he has begged me to leave him my old shoes to attend mass in, and I have bought of him a red flannel chicken cock, made by a female of his household, at three times its value, and upon which the custom-house appraisers at New York, not appreciating my intentions to favor our relations with the Siamese, made me pay duties at twice its cost. Under such favorable auspices, we get into the wooden house in the middle of the boat, draw up the curtains which shut in its open sides and back, sit upon the Persian rug and mat, leaning against the triangular morocco cushions, the rows of half-naked men ranged along each side of the boat strike their paddles into the water, and with animating shouts shoot us out upon the Menam. These loud cries are the peculiar privilege of persons and boats of consequence; and when the king is making a progress on the water, they are rung out in the loudest tones from his boat.

We are now upon the literally Broadway of Bangkok. Instead of omnibuses, horses and carriages, it is thronged with boats of various forms and use. Its shops are lines of small houses of wood, with palm-leaf roofs resting on bamboo rafts or floats, all along each bank, rising and falling with the tide. They have each a small platform before them, and the whole front is open, exposing the neatly arranged shelves and counters of goods—mostly from China: silks, muslins, chests of tea, lacquered ware; and also the products of the country: ivory, deer horns, skeletons and skins of tigers and leopards, snake and shark skins. The skeletons and the snake skins are exported to China for medical uses. Some of these houses are tin and leather shops, these being generally combined; some are eating-houses, with strings of peppers, dressed poultry, and slices of fresh pork suspended invitingly in front. Most of them are the dwellings as well as business places of their proprietors; some are solely dwelling houses; and many wealthy persons who have their dwellings back on the solid ground, have a floating store in front. Canoes and boats are fastened to the projecting platform; little children are running about them, or playing on their very edge, and almost at every hour some member of the family may be seen taking a bath by dipping buckets of water from the river and pouring over their persons without any change in their usual attire.

Beyond these river houses, and a confused mingling of tiled roofs just on the shore back of them, we see very little of the habitations of Bangkok, as they are hidden beneath the thick groves of trees and shrubbery covering the rich alluvial plain. These houses are generally built on posts, and are either of atap, the palm-leaf, or of wood framed in panels. The roofs, either palm-leaf or red tiles, have a very steep pitch, and their edges at the gables are faced with plank, meeting in a sharp peak above. These sharp points are seen, here and there, sticking above the leaves. Some of the better houses are built of brick, stuccoed and painted, and have their grounds inclosed with brick and plaster walls. Those of the nobles are generally of this character, as are also the dwellings of the wealthier Chinamen. In every direction flag-staffs are seen. These are in the grounds of the nobles, each one of whom flies his own banner and devices.

A most conspicuous, indeed, the commanding feature of Bangkok, is the roofs of the wats, and their graceful pagoda spires or pra-da-chis. These wats are surrounded by grounds of from twenty to thirty acres, through which are built the salas, or resting places, and numerous temples. The roofs of these temples are in sight on both sides of the river. They are built very high, the ridge being, in some, one hundred feet, and are, in most instances, a succession of roofs, three or four in number, with the pitch of the legs of the letter A, diminishing in size both from the gables and the eaves, as one roof rises a few feet above the other. Each corner of each roof and ridge is surmounted by a curving, horn-shaped projection. The whole are covered with gold and green-colored, glazed tiles. One roof will be a field of gold, with borders of white and green; and another, a green field with golden borders; and the whole of the gable ends or fronts of these temples, are massively gilded over figured stucco work. As we passed the grounds of one of these temples, the many white-columned salas, or summer-houses, the white, needle-like spires of the pra-da-chis, the surrounding flowers and shrubbery, the figured and gilded gable fronts of both the salas and the lofty temples, and bright cornices rising one above another, all the roofs of green and gold glittering in a bright sun, presented a scene of splendor which one could well wish was the proof and the product of a national elegance and prosperity, rather than, as it is, the result of an absorbing superstition. Far up the river, at least two miles from our quarters, we see the lofty pagoda of one of their principal wats rising, not with a needle spire, but with a rounded steeple summit, to the height of two hundred and fifty feet. Such is the general appearance of Bangkok, as we see it from the river.

But our most animated scene is on the river itself. Ships and junks are anchored in the stream. Some of these junks are enormous masses of timber of a thousand tons burden, and almost defy description. The bottom is a large square scow, upon which are built sides of heavy plank; the bow end of each side is rounded off like the runners of a boy's sled, but all the square bow is open to the winds, the waves and the water gods, for whose admission it is left so; and in this open space lies the anchor, made all of wood nearly as heavy as iron. The middle of the sides of this craft are open chasms, down almost to the water edge. Through these the cargo is taken in, and then they are closed for sea by gates let down into grooves. The stern is built up into platforms of cabins; and three heavy, naked sticks, without yards, make the masts. Every junk has its joss-house, or temple, and each with a lamp steadily burning to make offerings to the god. The whole vessel glares in bright paint outside, and is black and rank with filth inside. The sides are generally bright red, with two large eyes in the rounded terminations of the front. The stern is a confused mingling of dragons, gods, etc., in green, yellow, red and white paint. The rudder is a heavy mass of timber, about ten feet square, and swings in a wide opening in the stern.

The junks now before us have about completed their cargoes, and are ready for the south-west monsoon, which is just commencing. As they can sail only with the wind, of course they make but one voyage a year, going with one monsoon and returning with the other. Sapan wood seems the chief cargo of the junks now before us, and it is piled up in every part of the vessel, and suspended in large bundles over the sides.

The small boats crowding the river, gliding rapidly with the favoring tide, or struggling against it, are frail tiny toy and graceful canoes, in the centre of which sits a man or woman bringing the boat to within an inch of the water, and requiring a lifetime of practice to keep the thing from upsetting or filling. But this lifetime of practice they all have, for we see in some of these canoes a naked child or children, not more than six or eight years of age. Another form of boat, somewhat larger, may be regarded as the family carriage; the front and bows are open for from one to two paddles in each, but the middle is rounded over, and completely inclosed by a basket work of wattled bamboo, painted and water-tight. This basket apartment generally accommodates two persons. The after part is permanently closed with a wooden screen having a round window or port in it, and the front has a curtain to be drawn at pleasure.

Large boats of this kind are the dwelling places and shops of whole families. The substitution, for the matted cover, of a small wooden house, with open-curtained or Venetian-closed sides, makes a better class of boat; and these vary in size from two to four paddles of plain individuals, up to the large and noisy crew of between twenty and thirty of the state and aristocratic boats, such as are now paddling us through these scenes of the Menam. In the larger boats, they are propelled by the men sitting along each side, and dipping the paddles close to the boat. Where there are a small number of rowers, a compromise is made between a paddle and an oar. A short, strong staff, about eighteen inches high, is set into the side of the boat, and the oar works in a strong cord which fastens it to the top of this staff. The oar has a short handle on its upper end, at right angles to its length; the rowers, generally one in the stern and one in the bow on opposite sides, standing up and grasping the oars with their left hands, the handle with their right, propel and steer the boat at the same time. As many, if not more females than males, exposing the whole upper part of the person, are seen rowing these boats; and often two females will be seen laboring in the sun at the oar, while a lazy whelp of a Siamese husband is lying in the shade of the covered part of the boat. We have passed many boats of the shape of half an egg, divided lengthwise; two Chinamen, one in the bow and one in the stern, with broad-rimmed, sharp, conical-crowned bamboo hats, are paddling it, sitting with their legs turned under them; and between the two the open deck is piled neatly with dry-goods, kept in place by boxes of ribbons, needles and other small wares. Similar boats are laden with crockery, brass and tin ware; these are the equivalents for the peddlers' wagons of the United States—Chinese peddling boats. Here comes a single peddler, seated among plates and pans, with a small furnace, stews odorous of garlic and onions, and the raw material to prepare them—a peddling cook shop. Now a much neater boat is approaching us, of which the sole occupant and proprietor is a woman. In front, laid up in neat circles, are piles of fresh green leaves, and behind them are large jars filled up with beautiful pink pasty masses looking like strawberry ice-cream. She is a vendor of the cirrhi, or pepper leaves, and the colored lime for smearing them with, as they are rolled around the betel-nut for chewing. Now we are passing by a line of large basket-covered boats fastened close to the shore, in the front of which are exposed for sale, vessels of eggs, onions, strings of pod pepper, beeswax, etc.; small grocery stores, with the family living under the basket roof; and many canoes are passing about with covered jars in them, the paddler, woman or boy, crying out, in monotonous tones, the articles for sale.

In such a crowded and busy thoroughfare, there seems to be but one law of the road, and that is, that the smaller boats must keep out of the way of the larger ones, or take the consequences. If a woman with all her stock in trade is upset, no one takes any notice of her, but all leave her to right her boat and look out for herself; and the very boat in which we are making this excursion, ran into and upset a canoe in which were two small boys; passing on without the least attention to the accident. I looked back, and was glad to see that one had reached the platform of a floating house near by, and the other was quietly swimming, laughing and pushing his canoe before him. Siamese are at home in the water, and scarcely ever drown.

One of the preliminary steps of the negotiations to be carried on, was calling upon some of the principal and most influential nobles. Accordingly, on the afternoon of the second day of our arrival, Mr. Harris, accompanied by Mr. Mattoon, and two or three other officers and myself, proceeded to the house of the Grand Prah Klan, or minister of foreign affairs.

The entrance to his house was through a heavy gateway to an open marble-paved court, ornamented with stucco figures of men and animals carved in stone, with a few vases of flowers and shrubs. From this we passed into the house, the front of which, supported on pillars, was open to the court. The floors rose in the usual ascending platforms, and on the highest, which was carpeted, were two rows of chairs for twelve persons facing each other; at the upper end of the chairs a table and seat, or divan behind it. The more domestic or private parts of the house were behind this reception room, the openings to it screened by curtains, common engravings and mirrors.

The Prah Klan, about forty years of age, was a heavy, solid, sober-faced man, dressed in a blue figured silk mantle, fastened around the waist by a yellow silk sash, and received us in an easy and dignified manner, but seemed disappointed that a larger number of officers had not come, and immediately inquired the reason. He signed us to the chairs, and took his seat on the divan. His subordinates and retainers were lying around, crouched upon the floor, and just off from one side, on his knees, was a man with a large feather fan at the end of a long handle; this he would bring down slowly towards his master, and then make a sudden dash, as if casting a current of air upon him, which is the true principle of fanning, instead of continuous uniform motions.

After a few common-places of opening conversation, he at once entered upon the subject of the treaty, and said, "There would be no difficulty in regard to it."

The commissioner said he thought there could be none, as the British treaty of Sir John Bowring would be the basis.

"No more than that yielded could be granted," replied the Prah Klan, adding, with a faint smile,

"The boat was already full, pressed to the water's edge, and would bear no more."

The commissioner commented upon the good feeling of the United States' government towards them, and its general desire for justice and relations mutually beneficial.

The Prah Klan was well convinced of all this himself, but was not sure that the Siamese people understood it, and the responsibility of treaties, was from the fact that their own people might break them.

The commissioner thought that judicious negotiations upon the part of each nation could readily arrange any threatening difficulty.

"Such," said the Prah Klan, "is our confidence in the justice and good disposition of the American government, that we would like to have an article in the treaty providing, that in case of any trouble with any western power (England or France,) the United States would act as umpire."

The commissioner thanked him for the compliment, and assured him no such provision would be necessary, as the United States felt it an obligation of friendship to comply with any such request. The Prah Klan looked a little disappointed, but did not again allude to the subject. Upon our arrival here annoying reports had reached us, that the Siamese government, in consequence of our not representing a crowned head, had determined not to receive our embassy with the same honors as had been extended to Sir John Bowring, and as would be awarded the daily expected mission from the Emperor of France; and that the king, instead of receiving the President's letter personally from the hands of the commissioner, would only receive it through a subordinate officer.

I suspect that these views had more ground than mere rumor, and were put forth as feelers as to our temper in the matter. Mr. Harris had determined firmly to resist any such indignities, and any humiliating forms in a public audience. It was therefore very satisfactory to hear the Prah Klan voluntarily allude to this subject, and say that our formal reception was to be the same as that given the English, and the President's letter to be received directly by the king from the hands of the commissioner. He suggested that Mr. Harris draw up his views in advance of a public audience, so that they might be under consideration.

Tea was served us out of a golden tea-pot in delicate porcelain cups, and cigars from a golden salver. From these nobles we went to the house of the king's brother, the Prince Kroma Luang Wongsa, the medical prince to whom I had addressed a note, on the part of the New York Academy of Medicine, respecting his diploma. He was now residing in the old palace which had been built after the removal of the seat of government from Yuthia to Bangkok. Prince Wongsa was a short and very fat man, with a broad, benevolent and somewhat jocular face, though at the time of our call the expression was rather sad. He wore a simple grass-cloth jacket, fastened with golden filagree buttons. He received us very cordially, held me by the hand, while he inquired if I was the person who had written him, and then gave me an embrace of professional fraternity, which edified me very much, as he was the only royal doctor I have ever seen. He exhibited the most friendly disposition towards our mission, and made many kind suggestions, such as, being strangers, we might not know what nobles to call on, and therefore might unintentionally give some offense. He suggested that Mr. Harris had better address a note to the prime minister, asking him to designate who were to be waited on, and then, if any were neglected, the responsibility would be the king's and not ours.

Coffee was served in delicate French china. He asked if we would have any thing stronger, and when we declined, he said, "Do as you like; I can not drink wine myself, but of late have felt forced to make the effort." During our conversation, a very fine boy of six years old, his youngest and favorite child, was playing around his knees with more freedom than is usual. The retainers were lying crouched on the floor. The boy was decorated with golden chains, bracelets and anklets; his hair done up in a knot fastened with a golden arrow. Prince Wongsa hoped we would visit him often and freely. If apprised of our coming, he would receive us in state; but, for himself, he much preferred to see us freely and privately; he had become wearied of ceremony and state. I remarked that "I should claim the freedom of a professional brother." "It was a great gratification," he said, "to see me. The diploma sent him had been injured in framing, and he hoped I could have it replaced; though since he had been in a political position, business had so crowded upon him that he did not practice, except in the royal family." He requested me to come down and have a talk with him respecting a brother then lying under paralysis; and asked me to let him have, if possible, a few cups, and another surgical instrument.

The prince asked Mr. Harris if he could let him have a copy of his credentials, and also of the address to be delivered at the public audience. We took leave of the old gentleman, I trust, with feelings of mutual regard and admiration.

These two visits had carried us well into the evening, but the Pra Kallahone, or prime minister, was expecting us. To reach his house we turned from the Menam into what in the dark appeared a labyrinthine canal, and pushed our way among what seemed a maze of boats. A blaze of torches of a fragrant gum resin lighted us into the large and richly ornamented marble-paved court. This palace of the prime minister is a large, new and truly elegant building. The audience room, of ascending floors, must have been near one hundred feet deep. It was handsomely finished with carving and gilding, the upper part of the walls being of open ornamental work, giving free ventilation to the adjoining apartments. A decorated partition separated this large hall from one of equal length back of it; but the whole length of both apartments was exposed to view by an oval opening in the partition, looking, with its border of carved wood work, at the first glance, like an immense oval mirror. In front of this opening was placed the divan, and immediately back of it a silken lounge, so as to catch any air which might be passing through these capacious apartments. Through all their length a row of glass shade lamps was suspended from the ceiling, and lighted up.

The Pra Kallahone, it will be remembered, is our first acquaintance, having visited us on ship-board. His small and light figure was enveloped in a yellow silk robe. He came forward gracefully, and taking Mr. Harris by the hand, led him to a chair, inviting us, at the same time, to be seated, placing himself in a large arm-chair. The prime minister has the reputation, on all hands, of being the ablest man in the kingdom; and the impression of ability is given by his high and broad forehead, and melancholy, thoughtful countenance. The horrible black teeth, and filthy betel-nut chewing in universal use, diminished very much, at first, the agreeable impression made upon us by such men. The prime minister was the intimate friend of the present king before he reached the throne. They were supposed to represent "Young Siam," or a party of progress, and great expectations were held as to their joint influence in the advance of their country. Since reaching the monarchy, the king has not shown himself such a progressive, and is supposed to entertain some jealousy of the prime minister's influence and abilities.

Pra-nai-wai, his son, was present, but, like the other dependents, lying crouched on the floor, and would not rise off his knees as we spoke to him.

The Pra Kallahone invited free conversation upon the treaty, although he was by no means well.

Some allusion of a general character was made to the increased wealth and prosperity which would accrue to Siam from these treaties with western nations.

The Pra Kallahone replied that his earnest desire was for the prosperity and happiness of the people, but with them there was nothing to secure permanency. They had no Congress, no Parliament. The accidental disposition and intelligence of the monarch controlled every thing, and kings, in a few generations, forgot that they sprung from the people, and lost all sympathy with them. It was essential to the prosperity of a nation that it should have fixed laws, and that the nobles should be restrained from oppressing the people, otherwise the latter were like chickens who, instead of being kept for their eggs, were killed off.

The commissioner again remarked upon the many advantages of our treaty alliance.

The Pra Kallahone spoke in a low, but clear and musical voice, and raising his hands gracefully to the shade lamp hanging overhead, he said, "Treaties are like that glass, beautiful and useful while whole, but requiring great and constant care to keep them from being broken."

He then, as the Prah Klan had done, spoke of their confidence in our country, and repeated the request to insert an article in the treaty, making us the umpire in case of difficulty with the other western powers. Mr. Harris replied as he had done to the Prah Klan, respecting our general obligation to prevent difficulty.

The Pra Kallahone said something more specific was needed: that if a misunderstanding were to arise between the governments of Siam, and England or France, the United States Consul might, while it was a small matter, interfere so as to prevent its becoming a greater; but if there was no obligation upon him to do so, he would naturally say, "It's none of my business," and the trouble would increase.

Mr. Harris said that no United States Consul could, consistently with his duty, refuse his friendly offices to prevent national difficulties.

The prime minister said no more upon the subject, but asked Mr. Harris to draw up the treaty.

A conversation then took place respecting the various natural products of the country, and Mr. Harris very judiciously directed the conversation so as to show how the product, the commerce in, and the revenue from, these articles might be greatly increased, and the advantage of throwing the mines open to any who would work them and pay ten per cent. of the product into the treasury. The Pra Kallahone seemed to understand and assent to all this, as though it were already familiar to his mind, and suggested that an article be added to the treaty, opening the mines upon the payment of ten per cent.

Mr. Harris suggested the advantage they would have from their young men traveling in Europe and America.

The Pra Kallahone thought it would be of little use unless they were men of ability, and these were very scarce. He requested my advice respecting an inflammation of his mouth, and as we had expressed our admiration of his palace, he invited us to walk through it. On each side of the large room back of the audience hall were passages leading to the sleeping apartments; all was new, clean, and neatly matted. At the lower end of the range of rooms was his own chamber, in which was a high-post gilded bedstead, with crimson silk curtains. Around this palace, within its inclosures, were settled a village of retainers, a thousand or more in all.

A hundred servants, at least, are in the household of

each of these nobles, and seldom less than thirty attend them when going out.

Immediately after breakfast, on the following morning, our quarters were visited by the fat, good-tempered, but shrewd and intelligent Prince Wongsa, and a crowd of his retainers in his train. Soon after taking his chair, he seemed to be so annoyed by the heat that he threw off his grass-cloth jacket, leaving his broad person entirely naked down to the loins. He had scarcely more than taken his seat, when the Grand Pra Kallahone came in without any other dress than the sarong.

They had come to return our visit, and to say that the public reception, or audience, was fixed for the tenth of waning moon, being, according to our reckoning, Wednesday, the 30th of April. The names of the nobles, upon whom we were to call, were also announced, and the style of our calling suggested—the marine guard and band being to accompany us. Prince Wongsa expressed a wish to hear the band, and preferred to have it up in the room where we were. The crash of "Hail Columbia," "The Star Spangled Banner," and "Yankee Doodle," on base drum, drum and fife, with horns in proportion, was tremendous. The Pra-nai-wai came crawling in, but we rose, and, shaking him by the hand, insisted upon his taking a chair. He seemed very reluctant to do so in the presence of his father and of royalty, and looked, all the time he was sitting, as if conscious of an offense or impropriety.

Just before the entrance of his son, the Pra Kallahone had inquired which was the Engineer. Mr. Isherwood being pointed out to him, was at once asked if he understood machinery.

"I do."

"I would be glad to have you visit me, and look at mine."

"At any time when his excellency will send for me, I am at his service."

Mr. Isherwood remarked how much Prince Wongsa resembled the Bourbons.

The prince laughed, and said, "I believe they were driven from the throne."

Mr. Isherwood.—"But the one you most resemble died on the throne."

The prince arranged with me for visiting him to-night, for a consultation respecting his palsied brother, if Mr. Mattoon were sufficiently disengaged to accompany me.

In the evening, Commodore Armstrong, Dr. Daniel, and myself went up to the prince's. We found there Mr. Parkes and several officers of the Auckland. The prince was in a more cheerful and jocular mood than I had yet seen him in. The lady of Mr. Parkes had been making a visit to the wives of the king, and the prince wanted to know what she thought of them, saying, that she had seen more than he ever had, as he never saw but two of the king's wives.

Mr. Parkes, laughingly, remarked: "I don't know what right you had to see even that many."

"I will account for it satisfactorily," replied Prince Wongsa; "one I saw professionally, and the other is a relative."

Immediately after the departure of the English gentlemen, the prince invited us to walk up stairs to his private room. It was quite an armory. At each end, rifles and other fire-arms were suspended, one above another, against the wall. We had a long talk about the condition of his brother, and the only conclusion to which we came was that he must die in a day or two, which he did. He said he had exhausted his own medical resources, but such were the prejudices of the Siamese, he dare not call in another foreign physician. The Surgeon of the Auckland had seen him, but found great difficulty in procuring the observance of his prescriptions.

We remained chatting with the prince until a late hour, and as we returned down the river, against a strong flood tide, the lights had disappeared from the fronts of the floating houses, and our way was in darkness; but a beautiful appearance was seen on the river bank, the fire-flies, instead of being diffused through air, were gathered around certain trees, and the whole assemblage, from lower branches to summit, would flash out simultaneously like glittering diamonds, taking the form of the tree. Opposite to our quarters was a tree which gave the fantastic form of a dancing harlequin, alternately flashing into brilliancy and sinking into darkness.

On the next day after this, being April 25, the commissioner, accompanied by the Commodore and the entire suite, with the band, proceeded to make the calls upon the nobles, as suggested the day before.

We started up the river in four boats, and had got but little way when we met a procession of large state boats coming down. These boats had crimson and gilded canopies and hangings; in one was a Siamese band, and all were propelled by men in crimson caps and jackets. The procession moved slowly to the sound of funeral music, and was on its way to cast into the river the fetid fluids of a deceased noble of whose burning we had the day before breathed the smoke.

Upon the death of any one of rank, the body is closely wrapped and pressed with bandages so as to expel the fluids from it. It is then placed in a vessel in an apartment of the dwelling. From this vessel a tube passes through the roof, so as to carry off all exhalations; another tube passes from the bottom to a jar for receiving the fluids. In this condition the body remains for many months, when it is burned with much ceremony upon a platform of damp clay, and the collected ashes are molded into a small idol, and gilded for future preservation and reverence. The collected fluids are carried in great state down the river and cast into it.

The burning of a noble had taken place a day or two ago, and we would have been very glad to have witnessed it, but it was intimated that the king was to be present, and our presence, before our reception, would not be proper. On the following day, being in the neighborhood of the wat where the burning had taken place, I was enveloped in a cloud of smoke still coming from the funeral pyre.

XVI.

SIAMESE AND CHRISTIAN NOBLES.

OUR first visit was to the somdecht, an aged noble, the uncle of the minister of foreign affairs and of the prime minister. He is said to head the party of "Old Siam," especially opposed to reform and progress, and keeps himself very much aloof from strangers. He is the individual who defeated Mr. Balestiere's attempt to form a treaty. The somdecht is one of the highest titles of nobility, being a royal designation. It was given to this old gentleman and a brother now dead, as a retiring honor, to bring on their sons to their active places and offices. We found him seated upon a carved and gilded divan, wearing only a sarong of changeable silk. It is somewhat remarkable that notwithstanding the scant attire used by the Siamese, they exhibit the best taste in the materials and colors of what they do wear. I was told by a lady that some one, attributing to them a barbarian taste for tawdry materials of glittering colors, had brought in a lot of such goods for sale, but the Siamese rejected them as vulgar.

The table along which we were seated was furnished with sixteen golden and jeweled vessels, betel-nut-boxes, tea-pot, water vessels, etc. The old gentleman had an affable and pleasant expression, but at the same time one of great penetration and sagacity. I observed a habit of watching intently any one speaking, with his black, bright eyes half closed, as if wishing to conceal the earnestness of his gaze.

He at once expressed a wish to hear the music of our band, and when it had finished, directed his own to play. It contained about ten instruments, the principal of which were gongs, or cymbals, of different sizes, with an elevated centre, arranged on cords in a circle, in the middle of which was the player, who struck the cymbals with a cushioned hammer. Another frequent instrument is a series of metal or bamboo bars, laid on cords suspended over a hollow log, generally of the shape of a boat. These are sounded similarly to the former, and the ringing, musical, metallic sound of the bamboo bars is surprising. During the whole of our visit, a number of the females and children of the harem, the former wearing yellow silk scarfs crossing their breasts, and the latter golden chains and bracelets, were seated or crawling over the floor of a raised apartment back of us, and just seen over a balustrade which separated them from us. Some of these females were handsomer than any I have yet seen in Bangkok. But when they opened their mouths, exposing the rough, black teeth, no semblance of beauty remained. The band, crouching on the floor before us, having finished its performance, the somdecht waved his hand toward the apartment behind us, and immediately a large band of female musicians, concealed by a light screen, struck up their tinkling notes. The music and the airs were very harmonious to my ear, the music resembling that of a piano combined with the tinkling of bells. A refined and elegant entertainment was served us. An ornamental golden stand, of the size of a small table, was placed on the table before each two officers, and upon each of these stands were four smaller ones of enameled gold, containing confectionery, preserves and fresh fruits, the fruits, where they required peeling, being prepared and arranged in a showy and tasteful manner. Before each of us was a fresh cocoa-nut made into a temporary goblet, and filled with the sweetest cocoa-nut milk I ever tasted. The variety is peculiar to Siam. Tea was served in delicate gilded porcelain, and in similar cups the sweetened water and white pulp of the napa palm.

Here, for the first time, I saw the celebrated "durian," a fruit of which I have heard ever since our arrival in the East, and in such superlative terms, both of its disgusting repulsiveness and subsequent fascinations, that I regarded all descriptions of it as exaggeration and affectation. The fruit is about the size of a cocoa-nut with the outer husk. It is green, and covered with sharp short points. This outer prickly pod is divided into four or five lobes, in each of which are three or four smooth brown stones, enveloped in a stringy custardy pulp—which is the edible portion, there being very little fruit for the great show. The odor of this fruit is very strong, and may be perceived in all parts of the house in which a durian may be. This odor has been described, and truly, as a mixture of sulphureted hydrogen gas and garlic. All are driven from the fruit when they first see it, and when they venture to put it in their mouths the taste is worse than the smell, and yet all who continue eating it become extravagantly fond of it, preferring it to every other fruit. One gentleman told me that the first ever brought into his presence was under a dish-cover, and, without knowing what it was, he fled the table in disgust. He lived six years in yearly contact with the durian before he was able to put it in his mouth. A lady, in another region of the East, told me that she was longer than this before she could taste it, and now both these persons preferred the durian to all other fruits. This on the somdecht's table was not opened, as none of us ventured to taste it, and it was sent, very much to the disgust of some of our party, with other delicacies to our boat. That evening, the young German secretary to the Consul General came out of the room in which he had been writing, with an expression of disgust upon his countenance. I asked what was the matter. He said, "That thing is hanging outside the window, and I can not possibly sit in the room." A day or two after this, I made my first attempt to swallow some, and succeeded with great difficulty. The following morning I put another morsel in my mouth, and was compelled immediately to eject it. At dinner of the same day I ate a little with some relish; on the following day I wished for it, and, since then, have found no fruits a compensation for the durian.

From the somdecht's we went to the palace of the Chief of the Judiciary, the Lord Mayor of the city, and, what is better than all, the father of the king's favorite wife. Here refreshments were also offered us. On the table were some peculiarly-shaped black clay water bottles. Having noticed them, he said he had been on a war expedition to the province of Laos, and brought them from there. Upon taking leave, one of these bottles was presented to each officer.

On our return, having called at the house of the Rev. Mr. Mattoon, Prince Wongsa, living opposite, sent for us, to have a social chat; and the old gentleman, as we took leave of him, sent a bag of rock candy into our boat, as he had noticed, he said, upon the occasion of his visit to our quarters, that the sugar we had on the table was very bad.

On the following morning—Saturday, the 26th of

April—the son-in-law of the somdecht, in a handsome sarong, came to announce that the old somdecht was on his way to see us, and soon after the old gentleman made his appearance in a most stately manner, wearing a long yellow silk mantle, and sandals of crimson cloth—the first of the nobles I have seen with shoes of any kind. He was accompanied by his band of wind instruments, which in the aggregate produced a music resembling that of the bagpipes. I asked which of his bands he preferred, and was answered: "They are of different characters, as is European music, and I like each in their way." This visit of the old somdecht was remarkable as the first he had ever been known to pay foreigners. We were sorry that we could not approach his style of entertainment, being able to give him nothing but tea and ship's bread.

After the departure of the somdecht, two or three of us, accompanied by the Rev. Mr. Ashmore, of the Baptist mission, undertook a walk through what may be called the business street of Bangkok. Winding our way a few steps through the maze of thatched houses back of our quarters, we came upon a narrow pavement of very heavy bricks. This pavement was a kind of alley-way for miles through rows of closely-joined shops of Chinese goods, gambling-houses, etc. It led through the bazaar or market, in which vegetables, fruits, fish, crabs, shrimps, half-naked women, wholly-naked children, and myriads of yelping yellow curs were seen. The entire dwelling places of the families seemed to be the sheds in which their wares were exposed. A covering of bamboo slats in many places crossed this lane, from the roof of the houses on one side to those of another; and if no other testimony existed of Siamese stature, this covering would give it, as most of our party had to stoop in passing under it—the average height of the Siamese being but five feet three inches. Besides this business alley, similar paved ways wind off for miles through the jungle, crossing the canals on bridges of one or two planks, which may be removed when the king makes a passage, so that no inferior foot may, by any chance, tread over his sacred head. In following one of these rough pavements, which are generally not more than two or three bricks wide, it is so overgrown with grass, passes through such a wild thicket, and is so hedged with jungle, that one would think he was treading the scant remains of some ruined and overgrown city of a past age; but, scattered through the thickets on each side, may be seen, on their posts, the thatched huts of the Siamese.

While following one of these walks, upon another occasion, we came upon a group of men shooting at a black squirrel on a neighboring tree. They used bows with two strings, separated in the middle by a small cup, or basket, of bamboo fibres, from which they shot clay balls, and with much accuracy; for, although they did not hit the squirrel, the balls passed immediately beside him, and sometimes shook the small limb directly beneath him. My companion, Lieutenant Lewis, was so taken with this archery that he attempted it himself, amusing the Siamese very much by his failures; but, after a few attempts and a little teaching, he surprised them by his success.

Our first Sunday in Siam, although no Sabbath to the Siamese, was to us a gratifying day, as we had the opportunity of assembling at the house of Dr. Bradley, of the Presbyterian, or rather Congregational mission, for the accustomed worship of our country. There are three missions, the Presbyterian and the Congregational, which are up the river, and the Baptist, which is two miles below. Each member of these missions has his prescribed duties—some as Chinese preachers and teachers, some as Siamese. One gentleman has charge of the press, and those skilled in medicine give their services and their remedies to all needing them and willing to take them. They constitute a community active for good, according to their own conscientious convictions. At first it would seem that the fact of three differing Protestant sects being represented by the missionaries at Bangkok would be adverse to their making any progress in their teaching, as the heathen might well say, "Why teach us, when you disagree among yourselves?" but, in the providence of God, these diversities become the evidence of truth and sincerity, because, although known to be of different sects, they are seen mingling in harmonious worship, and united in teaching the same great religious truths. But the great question is, What success have their teachings met? No matter what the reply, it can in no way affect the convictions of religious communities and individuals, because they acknowledge the command, and have faith in the promises of God, leaving their fulfillment to His own time and ultimate designs. It is sufficient for such that God has said,

"Go ye therefore and teach all nations, baptizing them in the name of the Father, and of the Son, and of the Holy Ghost; teaching them to observe all things whatsoever I have commanded you; and lo, I am with you always, even unto the end of the world."

"Ask of me, and I shall give thee the heathen for thine inheritance, and the uttermost parts of the earth for thy possession."

"The seventh angel sounded; and there were great voices in heaven, saying, The kingdoms of this world are become the kingdoms of our Lord, and of his Christ; and he shall reign for ever and ever."

But there are many persons who profess to believe the Bible, and who would be very much surprised if told they had no faith in it, who yet persist in limiting and judging the Deity's vast arrangements by their own ever-erring and fallible judgment. Such persons judge of the value of a sect, indeed, of the success of Christ's kingdom, by the worldly eloquence and wisdom of those preaching in the sect and proclaiming the kingdom, forgetting that inspiration has declared, not by, but against, worldly wisdom and philosophy shall the power of the gospel be made known, that it may be seen to be of God, and not of man.

"And my speech and my preaching was not with enticing words of man's wisdom, but in demonstration of the Spirit, and of power: that your faith should not stand in the wisdom of men, but in the power of God."

"For it is written, I will destroy the wisdom of the wise, and will bring to nothing the understanding of the prudent.

"Where is the wise? where is the scribe? where is the disputer of this world? hath not God made foolish the wisdom of this world?

"For after that in the wisdom of God the world by wisdom knew not God, it pleased God by the foolishness of preaching to save them that believe."

But reasoning after the wisdom of this world, men professing faith in the Bible exclaim, "Missions to the heathen are useless; it is labor and money thrown away;" when they look upon so barren a field as Siam. "For a quarter of a century, missionaries have labored in Bangkok," and have yet to be assured of one Siamese convert. This certainly seems discouraging enough, but those who have labored longest and most assiduously still keep at their work in full faith in the promises of a truthful God. Why should they not? A quarter of a century is much in man's life; centuries added to it, in the eternal designs of God, may not be the brief moment of the lightning-flash. Centuries after the first proclamation of Christianity, and in the countries nearest to its origin, pagan rites and ceremonies were in use among the most enlightened and powerful existing nations. And as I have before remarked, the national teachers of these peoples are but just born.

But is it not presumptuous to say that nothing has been done—that God has neglected His own work? In these twenty-five years may not the foundation of great and permanent future changes have been laid? Indeed, the apparent results of missionary teaching and residence are far more encouraging than might be inferred from the absence of personal conversion.

At the house of Mr. Telford, of the Baptist mission, there are, every Sunday, several services by Mr. Telford and those of Mr. Ashmore, in Chinese, are attended by about thirty Chinese Christians, some of whom take part in the service. At the house of Mr. Smith there are similar Siamese services, and also at the house of the Rev. Mr. Mattoon, of the Presbyterian mission. It is true, these are attended chiefly by their pupils and various persons employed by the mission families; still they are attended respectfully, and hear the gospel intelligibly. Again, the Bible has been freely translated into the Siamese language; it is read eagerly, and I have seen Buddhist priests, in their yellow garments, several times applying for some parts of these translations. It is a very significant fact, too, that the more intelligent and better informed among the Siamese, in defending Buddhism, do so apologetically, saying its moral precepts are similar to those of the Christian religion, apparently valuing their faith according to its approach to Christianity. The king, who, previous to his reaching the throne, was a talapoin, or priest, and who now records himself as professor of the Bali language (the sacred language) and of Buddhistical literature, has expunged the whole Buddhistical cosmogony, and retained only its moral injunctions.

Then, again, the kindness and devotion of the missionaries to the interests of the natives without the expectation of reward—their patience, sincerity, and truthfulness, have won their confidence and esteem, and, in some degree, transferred those sentiments to the nation represented by the missions, and prepared the way for the free national intercourse now commencing. Nothing could more strongly illustrate the influence personally exerted by the missionaries, and the confidence reposed in them, than the fact of their being freely consulted and advised with by the kings and nobles, even in affairs between the Siamese government and that of the missionaries themselves. It was reported to me that Sir John Bowring had said that his own success in negotiating the British treaty had been so far beyond his expectations, that he could but acknowledge the finger of God in it. True, whether Sir John piously said so or not; and part of the chain of these successful events was the planting of American missionaries in Siam, for the confidence reposed in them extends to kindred western people. It was very evident that much of the apprehension they felt in taking upon themselves the responsibilities of a treaty with us would be diminished if they could have the Rev. Mr. Mattoon as the first United States Consul to set the treaty in motion. Finally, among the quiet means by which the missionaries, unperceived by themselves, have been extending the influence of their religion, has been the moral force of that virtue which is said to be next to godliness—cleanliness. The neatness, quiet system and order of their houses, excite the wonder and admiration of the Siamese, and stimulate some of them to a wholesome imitation, and many express their admiration of the cleanliness their confirmed habits of filth unfit them to imitate.

Truthfulness, unfortunately, is not a Siamese virtue, but they can understand the value and the obligation of truth among those who do appreciate it. This was shown in a contest between two Siamese in the employ of one of the missionaries, and I record the anecdote as evidence of the unperceived influence of missionary residence among such a people. The dispute was referred to their employer for settlement, and one of the party made a statement directly contrary to what he had previously asserted to his competitor. His competitor reminded him of the difference between his present statement and that he had previously made.

"Certainly," he replied, "but between ourselves, you know, we all lie as much as we can, but in talking to the Doctor, I must tell the truth."

Admitting, however, that missionary influence in Siam has been slow in its results, there are peculiar reasons for such a delayed progress, without implying the uselessness of missions upon mere human reasoning. In the first place, the whole nation is of the priesthood. Every man is obliged to serve some portion of his life as a priest, and, directly or indirectly, every family is allied with, and interested, in the priesthood.

Again, the servility and humiliation of the masses is yielding and submissive beyond conception. I have never seen any approach to it, except among the serfs of Russia in relation to their Emperor and Patriarch. In Siam every man belongs to some superior, and that superior is to the man, what man is to the dog—his God. He prostrates himself upon the ground, and presses his face into the earth before him, and is happy in doing so. To think in opposition to his master, is a treason and a heresy. Of course there can be no independence of thought, no spirit of investigation among such a people. Some of them have said to the missionaries, "We are interested in what you say, and would like to study the matter further, but we dare not — we are forbid." The power of this despotic control is shown by the fact, that of the large and more independent Chinese population, many have become sincere and practical professing Christians.

A third, and a great obstacle, arises out of the nature of the Buddhist faith. It is a doctrine of works of merit, a belief that future happiness is purchased by human effort, by charities, by building temples, pagodas, etc., and, as in all such doctrines, the result is corrupting. It is a debtor and creditor account, which is left altogether in the hands of one of the parties, and to the bias of his own interests. A freedom to sin is felt to be in proportion to the ability of compensation — according to the sinning individual's judgment of what is a fair price. It recognizes none of that purity of heart, of which good deeds are but the blossoms and the fruits. Hence, while admitting all the virtues of the missionaries, and commending their self-denial, patience, benevolence, etc., they say, of course, it is all on the debtor and credit principle, to lay up for themselves a store of purchase money for the happiness of futurity.

I have written what I believe to be my honest convictions respecting the necessity and utility, upon human reasoning, of missionary influence among heathen nations. Religious men will wonder that I have wasted any argument upon so settled a question, but my life throws me among the honest, sincere, and well meaning, who will insist upon seeing every thing by the dim twinkling of human experience and observation, instead of by the sunlight of revelation. Looking at the matter through the same imperfect organs, I have felt it an obligation of duty to point out its hopeful appearance.

To many of us the missionaries of Siam are a grateful remembrance. Our duty had placed us geographically in a broad level physical swamp, but there lay around us a more mephitic moral marsh of humanity, and from this dreary level the homes of the missionaries rose like healthful and refreshing eminences. The association of intelligent and honest countrymen and women, the kindly-tendered hospitalities, the invoked blessing at the neat meal, the morning and evening family worship, carried us back to our country and to its best observances. We left them surrounded by dark clouds of heathenism, but gleaming like stars through their thick vapor, and offering the promise of a coming day of unveiled brilliancy —Christian nobles.

XVII.

DIPLOMACY INAUGURATED.

The principal part of the city of Bangkok stands upon a projection of land, around which the river curves, and the two extremities of the curve or horse-shoe, three miles apart, are united by a broad canal, thus leaving the site of the city an island, or rather a collection of islets, for a number of minor canals, private and public highways, pass from the river to the canal, and intersect each other. The whole city is inclosed by a heavy turreted wall.

Although it was quite a gloomy, rainy day, and the rainy season appeared to have fairly set in, the Rev. Messrs. Telford and Ashmore, of the Baptist mission, called with their boat to make a tour of observation. The small boat of these gentlemen was a much more convenient affair for penetrating the by-ways than one of the stately government boats furnished the commission; and then we were free from the constant espionage of Pedro, Gabrielle, Macko, and the whole tribe of Siamese-Portuguese spies who hung at our heels wherever we went in the official boats.

Vultures—dirty, disgusting vultures—were continually seen from our quarters, wending their way ever in one direction. It was toward the grounds of one of the larger wats in the centre of the city, where the daily dead were generally consumed. The gloomy rainy day was a congenial one for a visit to such a scene of burning, corrupting mortality. We took our way through the new canal—the one above mentioned, there being an older and a shorter one close to the city wall. In passing through these canals we see the practical good sense of paddling instead of using long sweeping oars; for the latter there would be no room, but the paddles, kept close to the sides of the boats, enabled them to pass each other with facility.

Soon after leaving the mouth of the river, we turned into an intersecting canal to visit the "king's wat." It was not so extensive as many others, but was very neat, the grounds decorated with the lotus and other flowers as usual. The main temple was curious from having, above the Buddhistical paintings which decorated the walls, a correct representation of the solar system. Immediately back of the main temple was a smaller one, looking like a vault, but closed by a doorway about five feet by three, which was a perfect gem. It was of solid ebony inlaid with the most delicate mother-of-pearl, and so inlaid and covered that just enough of lines of the dark ebony were seen to relieve the pearly gleaming of its decorations. These were finely, beautifully and smoothly wrought, and represented, in the upper and lower part of each half of the door, the triple-headed elephant, and other royal insignia, surrounded by leaves, scrolls and flowing plumes. The slightest change of the point of view threw the whole into opaline scintillations or irridescence. On our way to this place we passed acres covered with sheds, under which were the large war boats or canoes of the kingdom.

We next pulled along another intersecting canal to the wat of the "burnings." The grounds and buildings of this place are said to occupy about thirty acres. The buildings make a village of themselves; and as we passed along the avenues, they had a forlorn, dilapidated appearance.

We slopped our way through mud and puddles of water to the grass and weed-grown ground where the bodies were consumed. Here, in several points, were masses of coals, ashes, and half-burned human bones. Near by were some elevated, smoke-blackened frames, looking like gibbets. These were for the arrangement of fire-works by those who were well enough off to burn their friends amid such celebrations and displays. On these gallows-looking frames and the ridges of some adjoining tumble-down buildings, sat confidently at home lines of dark-gray, dirty-draggled vultures, with drooping wings, their breasts and necks stripped of feathers, and their filthy crops hanging like balls of black flesh. What did they among these dry bones and ashes? The weeds grew in rank patches, and looking into one of these clumps of vegetation, I saw a human body with the flesh partly stripped from its bones. Near by was a broken wall with an opening in it. Curiosity led me to look through it, and though it has been my lot to witness many disgusting scenes, I hurried with revolting from what there met my eyes. In shallow puddles of water lay several naked bodies, as if just thrown there. Off of some, vultures were making a ravenous meal, and a gaunt dog was tearing the flesh from the cheek of another. This wat, I understood, has an allowance for burning the bodies of those whose friends can not afford this office for them, and to economize the fuel, they leave the dogs and vultures to consume the flesh, and charge themselves with burning only the dry bones. I had heard that such was the economical mode of disposing of the bodies of the poorer people, but could not believe it until this offensive sight lay before my eyes.

Continuing our way through this canal, we came, at its upper terminus, upon the river again, and visited a factory of some acres' extent, on which, under sheds, were piled up in fragments rising from circular brick inclosures, tons of pink-colored mortar, all of which was to be passed into the mouths of the Siamese, this being the place for preparing the lime used with their betel-nut. The beautiful pink hue is given by the mixture of turmeric. This process was going on in several brick-lined pits.

Upon our return to our quarters, we found that a message had been received from the king postponing the public audience from Wednesday, April 30th, to Thursday, May 1st, upon the alleged ground that it would be in a more lucky month, according to the month of our calendar. This, however, was supposed to be a mere pretext to meet some convenience of the king. That evening the order and manner of our reception, which had been a subject of some uneasiness, were all satisfactorily arranged. The Siamese have the most exalted notions of monarchy, and as before stated, they had either conceived the notion, or it had been suggested to them, that as we represented no monarch, but *only* a republic, the reception ought not to be so distinguished as that of the British embassy, and the letter of the President, instead of being received by the king directly from the hands of the commissioner, must be handed to some subordinate functionary. If they did entertain such notions, they readily and liberally changed them upon proper explanations, and it was determined that our reception was to be of the most honorable character which pomp and circumstance could give. The letter of the President was to be borne alone in a royal throne boat, with a proper escort, and received by the king directly from the hands of the commissioner. No degrading humiliations were to be exacted from us. Upon our entrance to the audience hall, we were all to bow; then, walking up the hall to our places, we were to bow again before taking our seats on the carpet; then velvet cushions were provided for the commissioner and Commodore. Upon the conclusion of the commissioner's address, we were to rise, bow, and resume our seats.

The rain, which had been almost constant since our arrival in Bangkok, would have interfered very much both with the comfort and brilliancy of our procession, but the morning of May 1st was beautifully bright and clear, and about twelve o'clock we started from our quarters in the large state barges which the king had sent for us. First went boats containing the band; then followed the boat with the President's letter, which was deposited upon an elevated and canopied throne. In this boat were five standard-bearers with triangular silk banners. The letter itself was laid in a portfolio of embossed purple velvet; heavy white silk cords attached the seal, which was shut in a silver box ornamented in relief with the arms of the United States. The cords passing through the seal and box were terminated by two heavy white silk cord-tassels; the whole was inclosed in a box in the form of a book bound in purple and gold; over this was thrown a cover of yellow satin. The marine guard, in two boats under command of Lieutenant Tyler, escorted that containing the letter. Next came a richly-canopied and curtained boat containing specimens of the presents from the United States to the king. This was followed by the barge containing the commissioner, his interpreter, Rev. Mr. Mattoon, and his secretary, Mr. Heuskin, with one of the ship's coxswains carrying the United States flag. The Commodore, his secretary and I, occupied the next

9*

boat; and then followed the remaining officers of the suite, Purser Bradford, Lieutenants Rutledge and Carter, Chief Engineer Isherwood, and Assistant Surgeon Daniels. The whole procession must have extended along the river for at least half a mile. The river fronts, the floating houses, were covered with a dense mass of Siamese, through which we were pulled for two miles, our rowers shouting and whooping like wild Indians, as their paddles rapidly struck the water; this being one of the modes of indicating that they bore what they consider honorable burthens.

Arrived at the palace landing we were received by one of the king's brothers, over whom was borne a large golden umbrella, and a salute of artillery was fired in honor of the President's letter, or, may be, of all of us. It was some distance through the paved streets of the town, it may be called, which lies within the palace walls, to the audience hall. Two chairs, carried on men's shoulders, were provided for the Commodore and commissioner, and for the remainder of us simply red cushions upon a seat without back or sides, and supported on arms resting on the men's shoulders. The bearers stooped that we might take our seats, and as they rose suddenly with us, during the irregular steps of their progress our seats were very uncertain. We must have sat there very awkwardly, for the crowds of Siamese through which we passed rent the air with shouts of laughter. Besides our own marine guard and the band, a large company of Siamese, carrying silken banners, accompanied the palanquin, upon which the letter was borne, and also a company of men in transparent muslin robes. These latter were the sheriffs and constables of the kingdom. Our way was through files of the varied military companies—some in European costume, with muskets, some in red calico gowns and caps, archers, single-headed spear companies, trident-shaped spear companies, some with pikes, some with single swords, and other companies in which each man carried two swords; some carried oval shields and others long narrow shields, protecting only the arms. Passing this military line we came upon one, of about a dozen elephants, in holiday attire and decoration. Each elephant was mounted by three men in fancy costume, and on the backs of several of them were small pieces of artillery.

We were dismounted and detained some little time at a building still some little distance from the audience hall. Presently a messenger came to usher us into the royal presence—the guard and band to remain outside of the inmost gate, through which no arms were allowed to pass. As we turned a corner we came suddenly upon an appalling sight—files of a hundred men on each side of our road, and each man had under his left arm an oblong drum; in his right hand was a bone, looking like a deer's antler. The moment we made our appearance, these two hundred drums received simultaneously a single blow—and the crash was awful; and then, after a short pause, another. Having passed through the drums, a band of wind instruments received us, and then we were at the door of the audience hall. All of the Siamese officials in attendance upon us fell prostrate to the ground. The lofty doors were thrown open, and a spectacle at once magnificent and humiliating was before us. Along each side of the long hall, in two rows, lay the nobles of the kingdom, resting upon their elbows and knees upon red velvet cushions. They were clothed in the richest golden tissues, some having golden muslins over under garments of rich silk, and some fine muslins over tunics of uniform gold. My old friend, Prince Wongsa, and the prime minister were among those most richly and tastefully costumed. The former wore a robe of purple silk and gold, the latter a fine white muslin, or lace, over a golden tunic. Before each noble was arranged his paraphernalia of golden vessels, some of them as large as a soup-tureen. There must have been from ten to twenty thousand dollars before each noble. Behind the nobles, along each side of the hall, were ranges of the pyramid-shaped standards of lessening silken circles, called the royal umbrellas. Glancing our eyes along these rows of glittering prostrate nobles to the upper part of the hall we see depending from its lofty roof two curtains of gold cloth. These are drawn back, and we see an elevated throne of gold cloth, covered with a graceful pointed canopy. The curtains of the front of this throne are drawn back, and in the open space is seated the king, also clad in golden fabrics, and upon his head a crown of purple velvet, glittering with jewels, and having a single bird-of-paradise plume falling over to one side. He is a small, thin, pleasant and intelligent-faced man, of a hue scarcely differing from that of his dress and surroundings.

We made the arranged bows and took our seats. Mr. Harris placed the President's letter in the king's hands and delivered the following address:

"May it please your Majesty—

"I have the honor to present to your Majesty a letter from the President of the United States, containing a most friendly salutation to your Majesty and also accrediting me as his representative at your court.

"I am directed to express on the President's behalf the great respect and esteem that he feels for you, and his warm wishes for the health and welfare of your Majesty, and for the prosperity of your dominions.

"The fame of your Majesty's great acquirements in many difficult languages and in the higher branches of science has crossed the great oceans that separate Siam from the United States, and has caused high admiration in the breast of the President.

"The United States possesses a fertile soil and is rich in all the products of the temperate zone. Its people are devoted to agriculture, manufactures and commerce. The sails of its ships whiten every sea. Its flag is seen in every port. The gold mines of the country are among the richest in the world.

"Siam produces many things that can not be grown in the United States, and the Americans will gladly exchange their products, their gold and their silver, for the surplus produce of Siam. A commerce so conducted will be beneficial to both nations, and will increase the friendship happily existing between them. I esteem it a high honor that I have been selected by the President to represent my country at the court of the wisest and most enlightened monarch of the East, and if I shall succeed in my sincere wish to strengthen the ties of amity that unite Siam to the United States, I shall consider it the happiest event of my life."

At the conclusion of this address we all rose, made the stipulated bows, and resumed our seats. The king then commenced a conversation with the commissioner. Although he spoke and read English, it was carried on through Mr. Mattoon, who sat near Mr. Harris, and a Siamese official interpreter, who lay next Mr. Mattoon with his head bowed to the floor, and his hands pressed together before his face. At each communication he raised his head slightly, and prefaced his message by some of the magniloquent titles of the king. During the first part of the conversation, the king was loosening the clasps of the President's letter, which he seemed impatient to get at. He asked how long Mr. Pierce had been President, and how many Presidents there had been. Having by this time got out the letter, he noticed the seal, and asked if we had a new seal with each President. He then opened the letter, and read it aloud in English, with a French accent, and then said to the commissioner,

"Did you understand me?"

"Perfectly."

"I will now read it in Siamese," and he did so to his nobles.

He then inquired how many treaties we had with the East, and with what nations. He remarked, that in any treaty we might make with Siam we could expect no exclusive privileges. The commissioner replied that we desired none.

The king then went on with quite a long history of the various embassies which had visited Siam, and held up a gold-scabbarded sword which had been presented through Mr. Roberts to the then king, and had fallen to him. He seemed to prize it highly.

He then inquired what were our usages in receiving presents, and was told by Mr. Harris that the Constitution of our country prohibited our receiving any. He inquired what was done with such presents as had been made to officers of our government, and was told they were deposited in the State Department. I suppose he made the inquiries, because he had heard that such were our arrangements.

He then called up the commissioner and the Commodore, and handed them cards for each one present. They were neatly engraved on silver-edged cards, and inclosed in glazed silver-bordered envelopes.

Somdet Phra
Paramendr Maha Mongkut.

The Commodore and commissioner then backed to their seats; the golden curtains were drawn across the throne; the nobles all rose on their knees, and with their face toward the throne, and hands pressed together before their faces, made three simultaneous salaams, and the audience was closed. During the audience I felt some one lightly pushing my elbow; and, looking around, found it was a young man, the nephew and private secretary of the king, on his hands and knees, pushing before him a silver cup of cigars and box of lucifer matches, and also a small stand of wine in cut rose-tinted decanters, and with glasses to correspond.

Notwithstanding the sacredness of "the presence," smoking was not against etiquette, and was therefore freely indulged by the commissioner and others of us smokers during the hour and a half that the audience continued.

Returning to the first reception-room, we found an elegant and profuse dinner prepared for us. The French have a reputation for artificial cookery; but the Siamese can teach them savory and elegant complications, somewhat obnoxious, it is true, to some unsophisticated tastes, by the free sprinkling of garlic. We had but just taken our seats at the dinner-table, when our old and substantial friend, Prince Wongsa, joined us, stripped, undoubtedly to his great delight, of all his court trappings, and wearing nothing but his silken sarong, entirely exposing his broad chest. He took a seat in an open window, and saw that all the arrangements for our table were properly conducted. The King of Siam was drunk with three cheers, all *pro forma*, as we were not a cheering or drinking set. Prince Wongsa remarked that we did not give our hurrahs with the same energy as those who drank more brandy.

On the following day we had a public audience with the second king, very similar to that with the first. He also made many inquiries respecting our Presidents, and seemed to have a particular affection for General Jackson, respecting whom he made minute inquiries.

Some of the officers present he requested to stand up as their names and stations were individually mentioned.

After the audience was closed, the somdecht said he wished to see me, at my convenience, at his house. Dinner was served as yesterday, and Prince Wongsa again made his appearance in the same Eden-like costume, but said that he must apologize for leaving us, as the king was about making a progress on the water, and it was his duty to attend him. During dinner a message was received from the second king, that he wished to see the Commodore privately; and just as the remainder of us had embarked on our return, a hurried message came for Lieutenant Carter. The king takes great interest in arms, and desired some information from Mr. Carter upon the subject.

Having separated from the rest of our party to make a professional visit, on my way down the river I met the king's procession; he was attended by a large number of barges, in a line, paddling with great rapidity, and with the usual loud shouts. In the king's own boat were several men with long staffs, from which were streamers of white horse-tails; these they threw into the air and brought down, striking violently in the bottom of the boat, in time with each shout of the crew. All other boats on the river stopped and their crews crouched down to the seats.

The following morning the second king sent for several officers and myself, who had not previously done so, to visit him privately. We were first conducted to a large guard-room or armory. Bright muskets were neatly arranged around the walls; over them were suspended cartouch boxes and knapsacks. Several men were busy burnishing up arms. Every thing was in neatness and order.

After some detention at the guard-room, a messenger

came to conduct us to the king. We passed through a gateway, at which were stationed guards, into a large and handsome garden of fruit and ornamental trees. At specified distances through this garden were small boards, on which were painted distances for target-shooting. Guards, two and two, were walking on a semicircular pavement in front of the portico of the palace. We ascended a flight of marble steps to this portico, which was on a level with the second story, and all paved with marble. From this we entered a large room, and passed from one end of it into a royal snuggery. Here the king received us in an unostentatious and gentlemanly manner. He wore a rich black satin jacket over an embroidered skirt, and a changeable peach-blossom sarong, with embroidered slippers. The room had a long table in the centre covered with a maroon silk cloth, and over it hung a punka. On each side of the room were hair-seat sofas, and over that on one side, was a colored lithograph of Queen Victoria, Prince Albert, and five of their children —a present to the king. Over the opposite sofa was hung a map of the United States; and at each side of it an oil portrait of Presidents Washington and Pierce—recently presented. A very large alabaster vase, and several small paintings, were among the decorations of the apartment; and in the corners were correct statuettes of Napoleon, Wellington, Prince Albert and Victoria, modeled by a Siamese artist, after engravings. One end of this apartment opened upon a smaller one, in which, neatly arranged, were his electrical and philosophical apparatus; and one side of it opened into a secluded study, in which were many elegant and convenient arrangements: chemical apparatus and tests; a silver mounted desk; handsome brass field bed, and brass, morocco-covered rocking-chair. In this study, and in the main apartment, were book-cases, filled with standard authors, American and English; in general literature, history, science, theology and military affairs.

He inquired particularly after my friend Dr. Ruschenberger, of the United States Navy, of whom he had a distinct recollection, and called my attention to a volume of the Doctor's works in his library. Upon saying I would like to look at it, he took it from the library, and pulling around the rocking-chair, said, "Take and read it, and make yourself at home, and look at it as long as you please," which of course was a very condescending act of royalty, but I trust had more value as the act of a gentleman. He drew a seal ring from my finger and inquired about the device, and then showed me a fine collection of his own, as also a gold pencil-case and sword scabbards made by his artists in the palace. Tea, coffee, fruit and cigars were placed upon the satin-covered table, and the king poured out for us. His son, George Washington, a young man of eighteen years, was moving about the apartments, but whenever he came in the presence of his father stooped to the floor. It was, however, a pleasant fact that neither father nor son used the disgusting betel, and therefore had white instead of ebony teeth.

Whilst dining at Dr. Bradley's after my return from the second king's, I received a message from the somdetch to visit him. The Rev. Mr. Smith of the Baptist mission accompanied me as interpreter. When the somdetch saw Mr. Smith with me he seemed startled, and stepping up to Mr. S., asked him, as this gentleman afterward told me, whether he might regard him as friendly in any conversation he might have.

It was in this very room, and with the somdetch himself, that an angry conversation occurred with Mr. Balestiere, defeating his attempt to make a treaty. Mr. Smith was present at the time, and had not, until now, been in the house since.

After a short professional conversation, the somdetch made many inquiries respecting our mode of rationing our ships, how the supplies were kept up, the value of each man's ration, and who had the privilege of supplying themselves. He also inquired where the coffee used in the United States was grown, and whether we used most tea or coffee. He inquired the amount of salary paid to the President of the United States, and expressed the greatest surprise that it should be so little, repeating several times that it was impossible it could be so little, as no man, he said, could maintain such a position upon so trivial an amount. I was not at all annoyed at the evident contempt he felt for our chief magistrate's salary. I rather enjoyed it, as I thought it gave me an opportunity of reading him a lesson upon republican dignities, and I helped the contempt to settle well upon his mind.

"He can not make any thing by his office," said the somdetch.

"Upon the contrary," I replied, "he may leave it poorer than he entered it."

The old gentleman looked puzzled. "Now, Mr. Smith," I said, "tell him the ablest men in our country seek the presidential chair, not for its salary, but because we think it the highest honor on earth to be the chosen ruler of a nation of thirty millions of people."

He immediately asked, "How old is the United States?"

"Eighty years. And eighty years ago it had only the present population of Siam."

"How did it grow to be so large, and where did such vast numbers of people come from?"

"By liberality and toleration, by inviting all nations and all religions into the country, and allowing any one who would to improve their condition and develop its resources —by avoiding taxation and monopolies."

He handed me a book, and asked me to write in it the

names of the nations from which our population is derived. I wrote in it all the nations of Europe and the East, including the Siamese, and as I handed it I called his attention to his own nation, saying I had written it because I knew there were two of them, the Siamese twins, farming in one of our southern States. He seemed much amused by this, and said he wanted to know something about those boys.

In the course of a little further conversation he asked which had the better disposition and temper, the Commodore or the commissioner. I replied that I had known the Commodore many years and the commissioner but a few months, and therefore did not think it just to draw a comparison between them. The old gentleman smiled, and, turning to Mr. Smith, remarked, "A very appropriate answer."

He asked me if I liked curries, and what time I breakfasted. "Yes, and eight o'clock." He said it was an early hour, but he would send me two such as they esteemed their best.

I passed a very pleasant evening with this fine-looking, intelligent, shrewd old gentleman; and although he was unadorned by any garments but the sarong around his loins, I had the evidence that evening, from some things which occurred in our conversation, that he was a person of much natural delicacy and refinement. He has, from honest convictions, been opposed to innovation and intercourse with foreigners. Until now he has kept aloof from them, but finding that circumstances are against his old fogyism, he yields gracefully. During the twenty-seven years that the missionaries have been here he had never been in one of their houses, but during our visit he called at Mr. Mattoon's, and took tea at Dr. Bradley's.

When I took leave of him he ordered a small bag of coffee to be put in my boat, and the next morning, by breakfast-time, a train of servants came bearing the two tureens of promised curries.

Understanding that there were services in Chinese to a small congregation at the Baptist mission, I walked around there.

The congregation consisted of about thirty men. The services commenced with singing a hymn, after which a Chinaman of the congregation made a prayer, and another read a chapter in the Bible from the desk. Mr. Ashmore then preached a short sermon, which was listened to with much apparent attention. Mr. Ashmore has the reputation of being a good Chinese scholar, and seemed to use the language as if he were thoroughly imbued with its nature.

The room in which the service was held was upon the thoroughfare, and a man was stationed at the door to invite in all passers-by. Some came in laughing, some with an expression of earnest curiosity. One of these chance auditors was on his way to market with a basket of salad and other vegetables, which he deposited at the door. He remained, as did several, an attentive listener until the close of the service. Most of them, upon entering, squatted immediately upon their haunches until shown to seats.

At the close of the service, in the interval between the first and second service, tea was handed the congregation.

On account of the health of Mrs. Ashmore, she and her husband are about leaving for China, and the present was the last service they would attend previous to their departure. Much feeling was exhibited by the regular congregation, the members of which came up, salaamed, and shook them by the hands, expressing their kindly feelings and regrets for their departure.

At the same time a Siamese service was being held at the neighboring house of Mr. Smith, and as I saw the neatly-attired servants of the missionaries going into the worship, I thought that much had been gained in the poetry of decent dress by the missionary influence, if nothing more. We nations who are familiarized to the artistic arrangements of silk, wool, flax and cotton, are all like the old lady, who, when Christie Johnstone entered, "a beautiful young lady in a black silk gown, a plain but duck-like plaid shawl," exclaimed, "Oh, my child, if I had seen you in that dress I should never have said a word against you."

An invitation was received from the second king for the officers to visit him privately. Commodore Armstrong, in assertion of our national character, replied to the messenger that "we must be excused. It was a sacred day with Christians, on which we neither visited nor did work, but attended the worship of God." This course, irrespective of the acknowledgment of any religious obligation, was a wise and judicious one. It asserted our national character, and the independence of principle. Besides, our country had hitherto been represented only by two classes of persons—the missionaries, who taught the sanctity of the Sabbath, and too many adventuring, reckless Americans, who belied the teachings of the missionaries and of all moral precepts. The king's messenger spoke English, and replied that "he knew enough of Sunday to know that we would not go when he was sent for us; but he dare not say 'No' to the king, and he hoped we would not be angry—the king had great reverence for Americans."

Into the scale of the long-laboring missionaries, was thrown the weight of our position as official representatives of our government, and the encouragement it might convey.

The mingling of Christian prayers and hymns with the tinkling of air-rung bells on heathen pagodas, is a strange and startling combination; but it was presented to most of us on this Sabbath afternoon, who attended church service at the house of Rev. Mr. Mattoon. His house is situated directly adjoining, almost on the ground of, a large and elegant wat, the pagodas or pra-di-chis of which tower above the roof and cast their shadows upon it. It is the great pagoda or pra-di-chi, already alluded to as the loftiest in the city, and as being, it is said, two hundred and fifty feet high. From base to summit it is of most elaborate finish. The shape is an octagon, with sides of about eighty feet in length, and built in retiring and projecting angles, like steps laid on their sides. Through four of these sides, precipitous steps ascend to galleries, one about twenty feet above the other. The outer inclosure, and the inner wall of these galleries, are of the same niched or receding and projecting angles as the foundation. The outer inclosure is of heavy, open-work porcelain plates, and it is surmounted at each outer end, and inner point, by a red freestone vase. The receding niches of the inner wall of these galleries are occupied by grotesque human figures. The steeple, as it springs above each of these galleries, appears to be supported on rows of figures of Buddha resting on one knee and the foot of the other leg, the leg being at right angles at the knee. The arms are thrown above the head, supporting the superincumbent weight. Above every gallery is a range of these supporting figures, and then the steeple, diminishing in size, rises for some distance, when it takes the form of four niches like ornamented windows, and in these niches stand nearly life-size figures of triple-headed white elephants with fantastic riders. Over each of these niches rises a graceful pagoda tower, and from the midst of these four towers rises the diminishing terminus of the steeple ending in an oval summit, surmounted by a light ornamental decoration of gilded metal. At a proper distance off from the corners of the base of this grand pagoda stand four smaller ones like it—except that the niches, instead of elephants, have horses. On the sides between these smaller towers are handsome ornamental temples. The whole of these structures are brilliant with green and white, and red and gold, representing symmetrical figures, flowers, leaves, etc.

If I say that all this dazzling bright work was made of porcelain tiles, molded for the purpose, the dignity of the material would seem to be consistent with the elegance of its effect. And it is made of porcelain flower-work, but it is the fragments of broken china plates, cups, and saucers; and now, I dare say, word-enslaved reader, you lose all admiration of the ingenuity and the effect of the application, in your contempt for the humble nature of the material. Yet these structures are beautiful in form and coloring. In architecture they are studies. From every niche and point hangs a gilded bell, and from the clapper of each a heart-shaped plate of thin gilded metal. As I have sate, of an evening, looking at the lofty steeples glowing in the setting sun, and the breeze came first rustling through the trees, and then gently tinkling these gilded bells, it was the realization of fairy scenes, with fairy music in the air.

The most important and elegant wat in the city is the wat Chi, the P'on-a-ram, or, as it is generally called, wat Po, on the left bank of the river, near the palace. The lofty and bright-colored roofs of its temples look like the buildings of a separate city. Its grounds inclose beautiful salas, with broad stone seats, surrounded by shrubbery. There are miniature mountains and artificial lakes, with pet alligators in their waters. Forests of graceful pra-di-chis shoot up their tapering spires; conspicuous among these are three in a line, said to be one for each king of the present dynasty.

Colossal human figures, hewn out of granite, and

dragons, of the same material, guard the entrances. The broad green leaves of the sacred lotus, growing in vases, are seen in every direction.

Within these grounds are ten corridors for medical prescriptions. In niches of the wall are figures representing various affections, and against the columns in front, written on stone, are directions for cure.

One of the temples of this wat has a more elegant and substantial finish than any I have seen elsewhere. A range of substantial buildings, with four entrances, inclose a large square. These buildings, with bright-tiled roofs and fronts of open-work green porcelain plates, have around their whole extent ranges of gilded idols, of life size, all precisely alike, and sitting with their limbs folded under them. From each corner of this quadrangle there are projected recesses, also filled with the same idols. I estimated about four hundred in all. These buildings inclose a large square, in each corner of which is a pra-di-chi, and in the centre a large temple. The pra-di-chis are not needle-like, as are those of the wats, and, instead of being covered with fragmentary porcelain, they are all faced with blue and white marble. A wall four feet high, of the same material, laid up in panels, surrounds the temple. Within this wall, pillars, four feet square and fifty high, support the roof.

The windows, surmounted with ornamental cornices, are closed by heavy carved and gilded shutters. The doors are ebony, inlaid with mother-of-pearl. The floor of this building is paved with marble, and the inside pillars, the walls, and ceiling, are entirely covered with crimson paint, and gilding. At the upper end, as in all these temples, is one gigantic and several smaller gilded idols.

But the greatest curiosity of this wat Po—a wonder of the world—is "the reclining god."

When I entered the building in which this is contained, I saw a wall of gold rising before me. I looked up—and still it rose to near the roof of the building for more than forty feet, and then took shape. I was at the back of the idol as it lay. The head profusely covered with stiff golden ringlets, and the shoulders of the idol, the head resting on the hand and bended elbows, were before my eyes. I was behind the figure. As I looked along down its glittering length, it stretched away a human figure one hundred and fifty feet long, resting upon a bed of masonry three or four feet high. This figure is built of bricks, smoothly covered with plaster and thickly gilt. The soles of the feet, which are perfectly smooth and flat, are inlaid with mother-of-pearl.

Of the various wats there are over one hundred in Bangkok, and connected with them are armies of priests. Some wats alone have as many as five hundred, and there are said to be thirty thousand altogether. Many of them are mere lads or novitiates. They all wear turmeric-dyed garments, and are supported by contributions—not charity—as the favor is supposed to be done by the recipients. In the early morning they are to be seen in their boats upon the river, and passing through the town collecting their dues. The remainder of their time, with the exception of a few routine services, is passed in idleness. The sacred language of the Buddhistical literature and services—the Bali or Pali—is entirely different from the secular language; and if the priests did not make themselves acquainted with it, they would be called upon to exercise some study and labor.

There is not the least reverence in their manner while in the temple or in the performance of their services. Childish levity and inattention mark their deportment. Frequently upon entering their temples we found a group of them sitting upon the floor in front of their god, one reading from their sacred books, the others chatting and smoking, and even lighting their cigars from the lamp burning on the altar. Upon our entrance sometimes the reading would stop, and all comment upon us and laugh at us; at others the reader would go on while the remainder amused themselves with us.

These talapoins, or priests, are supposed to be regulated by a code of one hundred and forty odd precepts. The following specimen will show the nature of them, and lead to much doubt as whether any of them are regarded:

"After twelve o'clock, M., eat nothing. Attend no shows. Listen to no music. Use no perfumes. Wear no jewels. Contract no debts. Look at nothing as you pass along. Touch no money. Do not dig the earth. Have nothing to do with state affairs. Do not laugh loud nor make a noise with the feet. Never revile, backbite or threaten. Do not cough so as to attract attention, nor extend the feet as you sit."

The high or ruling priest is appointed by the king, and every man is obliged to serve as a talapoin at least three months. He quits at any time after this that he pleases; but if he enters a second time, it must be for life.

Crowds of people assembled to take part in the show and spectacle and ceremonies of launching a ship, and then they scatter, few thinking of the storms and rocks, and labor which are before her future; or they gather around a balloon, and rend the air with cheering shouts as she springs into the upper air, and as the first cloud shuts her in, each goes his way, leaving her to expand to bursting in the regions of space, or to come safely and successfully to earth again as the skill or luck of the lone æronaut may determine.

Thus had we, amid music, and glitter, and pomp, and spectacle, performed the dramatic part of our treaty-seeking enterprise, and on Monday, the 5th of May, there was a scattering of our party. The Commodore and most of the officers returned to the ship that the Captain and other officers might visit Bangkok, and now, the show being over, the practical work of negotiation was to commence.

On the following day, "The Royal Seat of Siamese Naval Force" returned, bringing Captain Bell, Lieutenants Williamson and Bryant, Sailing Master Bowen, Assistant Surgeon Semple, and Captain's Clerk, Ashe. I now gladly accepted an invitation to move up to the Rev. Mr. Mattoon's, where Lieutenant Lewis, an invalid, was already staying. Instead now of being on a mud-bank, with a ditch on one side and a canal on the other, I was surrounded by shrubbery, flowers and verdure, and from the porch at the back of my room, I looked upon the grounds, temples and pagodas of the wat before mentioned; and from that in front, I had before me one of the historic buildings of Siam, the old palace built by the monarch who abandoned Ayuthia, the old capital, for Bangkok. The story, briefly is this: the present dynasty obtained the throne in 1782. Previous to that, Siam had been conquered by the Burmans. It was liberated by a half Chinese nobleman, with so many names that, upon the authority of the present king, I give him only that of Phya Tarksing. This noble became king by the best of all titles, common consent, and, during the early part of his reign, displayed great wisdom, liberality, and prudence — removed to Bangkok and built this old palace. But in later years he is accused of being mad, imagining himself a god, and committing great excesses; thereupon they knocked out his brains with perfumed sandal-wood clubs, and the grandfather of the present king ascended the throne. He was succeeded by his son, and upon his death the present first and second kings were the proper successors, because they were chaufas, that is, royal by both father and mother; but being young, they were displaced by an older half-brother (the late king), royal by the father only. The present king, thinking his claims somewhat detrimental to the security of his life, took refuge in a monastery and became a priest. His brother, the present second king, then Prince Noomfanor, occupied this old palace, and being then in the freshness of his mechanical and scientific pursuits, had the following English sign over his work-shop: "Clocks and watches repaired here." From these circumstances it is seen that the throne of Siam is rather in an unsettled succession. The office of second king, seems to be for the purpose of filling the superior vacancy, and as such many hold it, but the first kings are naturally anxious to convey it in their line. Such is the steady purpose of the present king, and the rivalry and unsettled claims, it is, perhaps scandalously said, beget bad feeling between the brothers, besides offering a temptation to any strong politician to seize the throne.

When the late semi-usurper died, the nobles assembled to determine who should be his successor. One claimant and another were brought forward without a decision, but our sagacious old friend, the somdecht, and his late equally sagacious brother, the older and greater somdecht, had quietly got control of the military, and remarked to the assemblage that it seemed to have forgotten the rightful heirs, and at once named them to the throne, and offered, themselves, to settle any objections to such an arrangement.

The nobles were surprised at their oversight, and at once sent to the monastery for the talapoin, and to the work-bench for the watchmaker, and thus they became their golden-feeted majesties of Siam.

XVIII.

BUDDHISM.

In touching upon a religion which influences the character and habits of four hundred millions of the population of the globe, we approach a subject which in its magnitude alone should win some attention from the most superficial observer; and now, amid these gorgeous temples and sacred groves, those who have this volume in hand may be willing to learn what little my own limited glance at the subject may impart.

In our general idea of idolatry and heathenism, we picture to ourselves a stupid and degraded people, bowing in unmeaning reverence to inanimate images; and, although this may be the practical result, we too much lose sight of the encouraging and elevated elements or influence of human nature, however derived, of which that idolatry is but the perverted expression. He who claims his religion to be essentially one of charity, owes some respect to that which professes to embody itself in these two maxims,

"Whatever happiness there is in the world, it has arisen from a wish for the welfare of others."

"Whatever misery is in the world, it has all arisen from a wish for our own welfare."

It is certainly encouraging proof that man is made in the image of his Maker, to see him, without the light of divine revelation, constructing theories of moral government, and subjecting whole races and nations to those theories, although they inculcate the rigid suppression of all his appetites, desires and passions—the subjection of his animal to his spiritual nature.

In this struggle and in its results are seen the want and

the necessity of revelation. Man struggles with all his trembling power to lift himself from the ruin into which he has fallen, but only sinks lower, unless God takes him by the hand.

Professor Salisbury, of Yale, proposes as a theory of the origin of Buddhism, "A quickening of moral feeling against the pantheism of the Brahmins. The tendency of the Brahmin philosophy was to confound the Deity with the works of his creation.

"There was a sort of necessity, in opposing pantheism, to deny all attributes to God—to conceive of simple abstract existence as the highest Being."

Upon the inference of such an abstract non-existent Deity is formed the idea of the highest human virtue, called by the Buddhists the state of Nirvanha. There being some doubts as to whether Buddha was an historical personage or a mythological creation, various proofs of his personal existence have been offered. The period of his birth is determined to have been about five hundred years before Christ. He is said to have belonged to the warrior caste, being the son of a prince who ruled over a territory in the north-western corner of the province of Oude, on the edge of the Himalaya, the distinctive color of the principality being probably yellow; it has become that of the badge of the Buddhists.

Several Buddhist nations trace the origin of their religion to Ceylon; and the Buddhists of India have referred to that island the origin of their faith, but recent investigation shows that its primitive seat was India itself.

In Nepaul, written in Sanscrit, have been discovered the original Buddhist works, from which those of Thibet Mongolia and China have been translated, and thus fixes upon India the origin of Buddhism.

The scriptural canon of the Buddhists has three divisions—the Sutra, Vinaya and Abhidharma. The Tripitaka. The Sutra is made up of familiar discourses attributed to Buddha himself, is composed of fundamental maxims and axioms, and is divided into sections, each of which, according to an apparently prescribed form, begins,

"This was what was heard by me one day when Bhagavat was in such a place, when such were his auditors," and ends thus, "When he had finished his discourse, all present were greatly delighted, and approved his doctrine."

The Vinaya is devoid of these formal commencements and terminations, and consists of legends "illustrating ceremonial duties by examples of conduct."

The Abhidharma is held not to have emanated directly from Buddha, but to be a sort of digest of the metaphysical views involved in what he taught.

As examples of each of these books, Professor Salisbury, from M. Brunouf, gives the following, as the simple Sutra: "This is what I have heard. One day Bhagavat was at Vaisali by the side of the pond called Markalahrada, in the hall called Kutagara. So then, Bhagavat having dressed before noon, taking his mantle and pitcher, entered Vaisali to receive alms; and having gone through the city for this purpose, he took his repast. When he had eaten, he ceased gathering alms; and, having put up his pitcher, and arranged his mantle, repaired to the place where stood the Tchapala-tchaitya, and there sought the trunk of a tree, and sat down by it to pass the day."

After some conversation between Buddha and a disciple called Ananda, and various terrific natural phenomena, earthquakes, meteors, a burning horizon, Ananda finds out that his master is about to be translated to the state of complete extinction.

"Even now, O Ananda, Bhagavat having made himself master of the elements of life, has renounced existence.

Any being who has investigated, comprehended, propagated the four principles of supernatural power may, if it is asked of him, "live either to the end of a kalpa, or a whole kalpa."

M. Brunouf defines the four grounds of supernatural power to be—1st. The faculty of conceiving the abandonment of every idea of desire; 2d. The abandonment of every idea of thought; 3d. The abandonment of every idea of energy; 4th. The abandonment of every idea of knowledge.

"From all which it results that the Buddhists attribute supernatural faculties to him who has reached the point of imagining that he has renounced all idea of desire, of thought, of effort, and of investigation, or meditation—that is, to him who has, as it were, disengaged himself from all mental activity."

The following quotation, made by Professor Salisbury, from M. Brunouf, seems to present more fully the doctrine of Buddha. The devotees to whom the words are addressed, are assembled in a hall, for the purpose of hearing them:

"All compounds, O, devotees, are perishable; they are not enduring, they can not be relied upon with confidence; their condition of being is change, so absolutely that it is not proper either to think of or to please oneself with any thing, as a compound. Therefore, O, devotees, here or elsewhere, when I shall be no more, must the laws which exist for the benefit of the passing world, and the happiness of the passing world, as well for its benefit and happiness hereafter, be compiled and comprehended by the devotees, and through their instrumentality be preserved, preached and comprehended by others, in order that the religious law may continue long, be received by many people, and be everywhere propagated, until it shall have been completely made manifest to devas and to men.

"Now, O, devotees, there are laws which exist for the benefit of the passing world, and the happiness of the passing world, as well as for its benefit and happiness hereafter, which must be compiled and comprehended by the devotees, and through their instrumentality be preserved, preached and comprehended by others, in order that the religious law may continue long, be received by many people, and everywhere propagated, until it shall have been completely made manifest to devas and to men. These laws are the four applications of thought: '1. The body; 2. Sensation; 3. Thought; 4. The law.' 'The four complete renunciations,' already given; 'the four principles of supernatural power, the five senses, the five powers, the seven constituent elements of the state of Buddha; the sublime way consisting of eight parts, *i. e.*, the sublime course of life, consisting of right, or just and regular right, will, effort, action, life, language, thought, meditation.'

"Such are the laws, O, devotees, which exist for the benefit of the passing world, and the happiness of the passing world, as well as for its benefit and happiness hereafter, and which the devotees, having compiled and comprehended, must cause to be preserved, preached and comprehended by others, in order that the religious law may continue long, be received by many people, and be everywhere propagated, until it shall have been completely made manifest to devas and to men. 'Let us go, Ananda, towards Kusigramaha.' 'Be it so, O venerable,' replied the respectable Ananda, 'to Bhagavat.'"

As a specimen of the Vinaya, given by the treatise from which we are quoting, we have the legend of a certain commercial adventurer, named Purna, who, on one of his voyages, hears, accidentally, of Buddha and his doctrine, and determines to become a devotee and recluse. He, therefore, holds personal communion with Buddha, and addresses him in the following words: "Let Bhagavat consent to teach me the law briefly, and having thus heard it from the lips of Bhagarot, I may live alone, retired from the world, in some desert place, exposed to no distraction, with mind attentive, intent, and collected. After I have lived retired from the world in solitude, exposed to no distraction, with mind intent, attentive and collected, might I, having known by my own immediate cognizance, having seen, face to face, the supreme end of the life of a devotee, that is, the life led by the sons of a family, when, after shaving the hair of the head and beard, and putting on yellow garments, they leave home with a perfect faith, and become mendicants—might I, I say, having myself received the investiture, cause others to adopt the life of a devotee? I am no more subject to the condition of birth; I have fulfilled the duties of the life of a devotee; I have accomplished what I had to do; I know no other state than that in which I am."

Buddha then explains to Purna the doctrine of Nirvanha. "When there is no pleasure, there is neither satisfaction nor complacence. When there is neither satisfaction nor complacence, there is no passion. When there is no passion, there is no enjoyment. When there is no enjoyment, the devotee, O, Purna, the devotee who is affected neither with pleasure, passion, nor enjoyment, is said to be very near to Nirvanha. There are, O Purna, sounds adapted to the ear, odors to the smell, tastes to the sense of taste, feelings to the touch, laws to the mind, all which are qualities desired, sought after, loved, transporting, giving rise to passion, and exciting the desires. If a devotee, perceiving these qualities, has no satisfaction in them, seeks not after them, feels no inclination towards them, has no complacence in them, it results that he has no pleasure — he is said to be very near to Nirvanha."

The following are specimens of the Abhidharma: "Again, O Bhagavat, the Bodhisattva, to whom it belongs to live in perfection of wisdom, to meditate on that must not stop at form, nor at sensation, nor at idea, nor at conception, nor at consciousness. Why so? Because, if he stops at form, he lives in the notion that form exists — he lives not in perfection of wisdom. And so if he stops at sensation, at idea, at conception, at consciousness, he lives in the notion that all these have an existence — he lives not in perfection of wisdom. Why so? Because he who lives in that notion, grasps not at perfection of wisdom, brings not his faculties up to it, does not attain it. Not attaining to perfection of wisdom, he will not reach omniscience, because he grasps at that which is intangible. Why so? Because to one in the state of perfection of wisdom, form is intangible; and the same is true of sensation, idea, conceptions, consciousness — all which are things intangible to one in the state of perfection of wisdom."

From such a transcendental and unintelligible an ideality—such an abstraction into annihilation—such an effort to leap, not alone from earth and corporeal existence, but even from spiritual existence—has naturally grown their wide gardens and deep solitudes, their banyan-tree groves and marbles seats and temples, with the lotus-leaved lakes upon which they are placed. And from such an attempt to make or substitute the works and deeds of man as an atonement for the corruptions of his heart, have arisen the waste of gilded temples and idols, the wide-spread beggary and dead stagnation of armies of Buddhist monks.

It was an attempt of human reason to avoid, by an earthly existence, the penalty of Brahminical transmigration, and to reach at once the tranquillity of Nirvanha.

In the words of Professor Salisbury, "The means which Buddha directed to be used for obtaining the supreme good were chiefly moral. It was the sum of his teachings that desire must be loosed from all objects of sense, 'as a drop of water falls off from the lotus leaf.' He, however, enforced this detachment from sensible objects on principles which involved the denial of reality in any thing objective, and he required his disciples to possess themselves of these principles by deep meditation, as a condition of their reaching Nirvanha. Voluntary poverty, chastity, knowledge, energy, patience, charity, or self-sacrifice for the good of others, which, in the course of time, received the name of the 'six transcendent perfections,' were the special duties inculcated by the new teacher; and it is worthy of notice that a pure spirit pervades the ancient Buddhist legends, which, as contrasted with the moral laxity of those of the Brahmins, evinces, at least, a temporary reformation of morals in India, effected by Buddha. It can not be doubted, indeed, that the more elevated idea of the social position of woman, belonging, as we have reason to suppose, to primitive Buddhism, must itself have exerted no little influence in favor of a superior tone of morality."

XIX.

DIPLOMACY; THE HAREM IN THE HALL.

It was seen that we arrived in Siam on the 10th of April, and it was not until a month later that the first meeting relative to the treaty took place between the commissioner on the part of the United States, and those on the part of the King of Siam. So long as the British negotiator was present, there seemed to be a reluctance to undertake any thing else, and various were the causes of delay.

On Monday, the 12th of May, we thought the work would begin, but then it was found there had been a mistake in the translation of the precept. On Wednesday, 14th, Mr. Parkes was to have an audience; on Thursday, one was given the Portuguese Consul, who had been waiting for the chance more than a year, and on that same day Mr. Parkes took his departure. The next day, Friday, they were ready for us.

The commissioners on the part of the King of Siam were:

His Royal Highness the Prince Krom Hluang Wongsa D'Hiraj Snidh;

His Excellency Somdecht Chau Phaya Param Maha Bijai Neate;

His Excellency Chau Phaya Sri Suriwongse Samaha Pra Kallahone;

His Excellency Chau Phaya Rawe Wangu Maha Kosa Dhipade, the Prah Klan; and

His Excellency Chau Phaya Romraj, the Lord Mayor.

The first interview was at the house of our friend, Prince Wongsa, and the Pra Kallahone came to it in some annoyance. He had been ordered by the king, as the other nobles had, to provide a wreath of flowers for some festival on Monday. He said he could not do it in time. He might be deprived of his office or his head, but it was impossible, and he must abide the consequences.

The recently-made British treaty was read over, and, in its main features, adopted as the model of ours. That treaty provides that, after ten years' residence, British subjects shall have the right of purchasing and holding property in the city of Bangkok. The reason assigned for requiring this time is, that they may learn something of the language and habits of the people. This was unhesitatingly incorporated in the British treaty, because the time was altogether prospective, there being at the time no known British residents. But the commissioners were startled when such an article was about to become part of an American treaty, because the American missionaries, had already been the prescribed time, and more, and at once acquired the right of purchase. The proposition was the more annoying to them, because of a serious difficulty which had recently arisen. A Siamese female, in the family of one of the missionaries, had bought a piece of property in her own name, but for the use of the family in which she resided. For this she had been imprisoned, and tried by the Siamese authorities, but subsequently acquitted, the property remaining with her. The commissioners wished to make this ten years' residence, as applicable to Americans, prospective also; but it was argued, upon their own ground, that there was no reason for it, as the required knowledge had been obtain- by their past residence.

An article of the British treaty provides for the mutual protection of British subjects in Siam, and Siamese in British territory. This, the Pra Kallahone very justly remarked, meant something between the English and themselves, because the English had neighboring territory; but, as Siamese were not likely to fall into the United States, there could be but little reciprocity. He therefore suggested, as an equivalent for this protection granted our people, that United States government ships shall be required to protect Siamese vessels against piracy and accidents of the seas, and that United States consuls in foreign ports extend their protection to distressed Siamese.

On Saturday, May 24th, the last meeting was held, and

the negotiations complete, to the great delight of all of us, who were getting very tired of Siam, especially those who were confined to the monotony of the ship in the shoal waters of the Gulf of Siam.

When all the papers were written up and signed, on the 29th of May, the important fact was announced to the world by the Siamese batteries. The king being relieved from the burden of the business matter, was desirous of having an opportunity of continuing his hospitality to us, and of amusing us. But, the business over, we took our departure. The king sent the United States commissioner the following letter:

SUPERSCRIPTION.

The Siamese royal credentials, given in hands of Honorable Townsend Harris, Esquire, the American envoy for receipts of the letter and valued presents brought from United States of America, and complying the necessity concerned therein and promised for royal letter in answer and proper presents on other opportunity:

"Somdecht Pra Paramendre Maha Mongkut. By the blessing of highest and greatest superagency of universe.

"The King of Siam and Sovereign of all tributary countries adjacent, in every direction, namely, Laos, Cambodia, Kariangs, and most of Malay Peninsula, and professor of Pali language and Buddhistical literature, etc., etc. To all and a singular to whom these presents shall come greeting:

"We have acknowledged the receipt of the letter of the President of United States of America, whose name is Franklin Pierce, dated City Washington, 12th of September, 1855, handed us by Hon. Townsend Harris, Esq., who is the envoy appointed to make a new treaty with us, as amending the old treaty of the said country with ours, for being improved and more advantageous to both sides, in similar manner of that with English government just done. We have the said letter perused at present of our supreme court, on the 1st day of May, 1856.

"Agreeably to request of government of United States of America we have counsel of whole royalty and our counsel, and appointed one of our royal brothers, three high ministers, officers of state, who were totally four individuals, ever have been appointed plenipotentiaries in our part and held the consultation and made the new treaty with Sir John Bowring, English plenipotentiary, on last year, and add the other one in place of our first regent, who had been one of the five plenipotentiaries in last year and lost his life in the time of the treaty with English was just sealed and signed on 18th April, 1855, so our plenipotentiaries were full five individuals, invested with full power to make the new treaty of friendship and commerce between Siam and United States of America, in our part and hold consultation with Townsend Harris, Esquire, the envoy plenipotentiary of United States of America. Their names and offices were fully mentioned in the form of the treaty. Although they were appointed by us on very early part of current month, but in consequence of their business in being our royal commissioners to make the agreement—which is a commentary of the treaty with English, both old and new—with Mr. Harry Smith Parkes, who was the bearer of ratification of the new treaty from England for exchange here and prepare all its provisions after that agreement was done on late of the present month. They have held the consultation with Townsend Harris, Esquire, on a few occasions. The American envoy has formed the new treaty in very similar manner of that of English and wrote in duplicates which were concluded by signatures of both Siamese and American plenipotentiaries, on the 29th of May, 1856.

"After which date Townsend Harris, Esquire, was in greatest hurrying for his departure on 31st of May; we could not postpone his departure for a few days more in next week; we regret very much we could not furnish proper royal letter, in answer to the letter addressed us from President of United States of America, and already in picking and preparing the suitable royal presents for the President, who have goodness enough to offer us his good friendship, remarked by his valued presents designed to us on this occasion. As the time is very narrow between the day of the conclusion of the treaty and departure of the envoy, therefore, for declaration our being sincerely gratitude to the President of United States of America indeed, and for our further promise that we send our royal letter and suitable royal presents to America on other occasion by any rate when good opportunity allow. We wrote these present with our royal hand and seal, with great seal of our kingdom and our official and particular seal for our royal standard, to be a credentials from us in hand of Hon. Townsend Harris, Esq., the envoy.

"Given at our court of Bangkok, on the Saturday 12th, the waning moon in the lunar month of Wesakh, in the year of Quadruped Serpent, bearing the number of Siamese astronomical era, 1218, corresponding to the 31st May, 1856, of Christian era, which is the sixth of our reign.

"S. P. MONGKUT,
"*First King of Siam.*"

List of Presents sent the Kings of Siam by the United States Government.

Two splendid mirrors, very thick plates, measuring eighty inches by fifty-six inches, with frames finely carved out of solid wood, and richly gilt.

Two superior solar chandeliers, each eight lights, ormolu gildings, after the premium models of the World's Exhibition in 1851. Thirty-six cut glass globes for the same. Thirty-six plain glass chimneys. Seventy-two dozen of lamp-wicks.

One compound achromatic microscope, of the most approved form, for the magnifying of minute objects, with three eye-pieces of different powers.

Four sets of achromatic object-glasses of different focusses, double mirror, movable stage, diagonal eye-piece, condenser, dissecting instruments, box of objects, and camera lucida, by which an accurate drawing of any object viewed in the microscope may be taken.

One solar microscope, by which a magnified image of any object is represented on a white wall or screen; has three rack adjustments, three-inch condensing lens, three object-glasses of different magnifying powers, and three objects finely prepared.

A small box containing twelve finely-prepared objects for the solar microscope.

One small box, containing twelve finely-prepared objects for the compound achromatic microscope.

A book descriptive of the objects most interesting for the microscope, with many plates.

One Sharpe's patent primer rifle, octagon barrel, globe sight, No. 32 guage, and German silver mounted. Two lbs. of Sharpe's primers. One hundred cartridges.

One rich-engraved, extra fine finished, richly-gilt ivory-handled Colt's five-inch pistol, in rich, brass-bound rosewood case, velvet-lined, with fine extra plated flasks, molds, wrench-key, etc., best percussion caps, powder, balls, etc., complete.

One portrait, life size, of General Washington.

One portrait, life size, of General Pierce.

One Republican Court, or Society in the Days of General Washington, illustrated and splendidly bound, scarlet Turkey morocco, full gilt.

One Webster's American Dictionary, unabridged, bound in scarlet Turkey morocco, full gilt, and lettered, "Presented to His Majesty the King of Siam, by Franklin Pierce, President of the United States of America."

One colored view of the City of Washington.

One colored view of the City of New Orleans.

One colored view of the city of New York from St. Paul's Church.

One colored view of the City of New York from the Bay.

One colored view of the City of Boston.

One colored view of the Senate Chamber at Washington.

One colored view of the City of Philadelphia.

One colored view of West Point.

One colored view of the Crystal Palace, New York.

One tinted view of the City of New Orleans.

One view of an express railway train.

One map of the United States from Atlantic to Pacific Oceans, on rollers.

After the ratification of the treaty, the King of Siam sent, with the ratified copy, the following letter to the United States:

Letter of the King of Siam, written by him in English and accompanying the ratified treaty with the United States:

"This copy of the treaty, regulations and tariff have been written in both characters and languages of English and Siamese, and signed and sealed by each one of the respective plenipotentiaries of both sides, was received from

Townsend Harris, Esquire, by our officers of foreign affairs, and conveyed here and delivered to us for perusal and our approbation and ratification and signature with our royal manual signs and seals, and has been kept in this palace waiting to exchange with the ratified treaty returned from Washington. We have perused and seen and understood the whole contents of this treaty, and found both English and Siamese very nearly similar a copy of the treaty made with the English plenipotentiary, only such changes in names of persons and country and of form, as would be proper in a treaty between Siam and America. We consider that the treaty in this form will be favorable for foreign merchants who will trade and reside here, but we were waiting upon the President and Senate of the United States of America, who we have not yet ascertained will like all the articles of the new treaty, or will correct some portion, for what consequence we hesitate our ratification before the present time. Having waited twelve months, until at this occasion the envoy of the United States, Charles William Bradley, LL.D., has arrived, having credentials that he was sent by President James Buchanan, who entered upon the office of President on Wednesday, 4th of waxing moon, in the lunar month of Phagim, being fourth month in the year of Drugin (Dragon ?) in 1218 of Siamese era, corresponding to 4th of March, 1857, in the place of Franklin Pierce who sent Townsend Harris, Esq., to negotiate the treaty in the previous year. This American envoy has come at this time for the purpose of exchanging the treaty ratified and sealed with the seal of the United States for the one kept here, and will be sealed with our royal seals, and signed with our royal hand. Mr. Charles Wm. Bradley has informed to our officers of state that the new or recent President and Senate of the United States desire to amend the treaty by striking out the fifth article as one not inserted in any American treaty with other nations, all others to remain in force. The Siamese principal officers of state thought the fifth article could not be omitted, as it was found in the treaties with England, the ratification of which had been exchanged in the previous year, and in the treaty also with France concluded in ultimate year; and if it should be struck out of the American treaty it must also be struck out of the English and French treaties, and the foreign merchants would wander through the country without passports, and some difficulties would arise, and the Siamese officers could with difficulty protect them, and the seamen would desert, and they could not easily be retaken, or apprehended according to consider requisite. They therefore desired that it might remain.

"Mr. Bradley, the bearer of the ratification, has replied to our officers of state, that the ratification of the President, with the fifth article struck out, had already been placed after the end of the treaty which he had brought for exchange, as the President and Senate had trusted that the Siamese government would consent; but if they were unwilling it should be repealed altogether, he desired they would consent to strike out the fifth article of the treaty, and to enact it as a seventh regulation. To this the Siamese royal commissioners consented and agreed to be guided by; and as there was no room to place the seventh regulation at the close of the previous regulations, the Siamese royal commissioners, with Mr. Bradley, the American envoy, and Mr. Stephen Mattoon, the American consul, agreed to such regulation to be a new agreement, to be written in both Siamese and English style, and signatured with the seals of the Siamese royal commissioners and American envoy and American consul, and to attach it to the two copies of the treaty about to be exchanged at this time; and to this proposal we both do unanimously agree with great pleasure, and respectfully accept, and confirm and ratify, for ourselves, our heirs and successors, by placing our royal promise that we will sincerely, faithfully and carefully perform and observe all things here to be fulfilled and connected with all articles of the treaty, regulations and tariff; and will recommend our officers of state to be always circumspective in prohibiting every individual and party in our subjects, that none should violate or transgress the same in any manner, as far as in our ages and reign, according to our power and ability to govern the people of this half civilized and half barbarous nation, being of various races, languages, religions, etc.; for which nations we are still afraid that any one individual or party among such nations, being very ignorant of civilized and enlightened customs and usages, may misunderstand any thing or things contained or expressed in the treaty, and do according to his or their knowledge, which may be contradictory to some clauses of any articles of treaty; and yet we will observe accurately, and command our officers of state to correct the wrong as soon as possible, whenever the American consul might complain to our officers of state directly, with whom our officers of state will be joined in correction and adjustment of such matter of complaint. If there be different understanding between the American consul and our officers of state, we will cause our ministers to hold conference, asking true decision by consultation of United States government and the Siamese council, or every member of our government here unanimously concluded that this minor country shall have refuge under the grace, mercy and indulgence of superior powerful major country, such as the United States.

"We now have embraced the best opportunity to have made and exchanged the treaty of friendship and commerce with United States of America, and we shall be very glad to esteem the President of the United States, at present and in future, as our respected friend, and esteem the United States as united in close friendship, as we know that the government of the United States must ever act with justice, and is not often embroiled in difficulties with other nations; and if the treaty of friendship between the United States and Siam has been long preserved in harmony and peaceful manner, it will ever be the occasion of the highest praise among the Siamese people. And now for greater testimony of unanimous fulfilling of willfulness of whole Siamese government in this treaty, we have caused the great seals of Siamese kingdom, with its whole dependencies, to be pressed on first page of this document, one in the shape of the divine elephant, bearing three heads called ayerrubats, and the other to be affixed in figure of the Nazayn angel of four arms, standing on Grudh named Grudhabah; and we have also signed with our royal hands, and sealed with our respective official and standard royal seals, both impressing and affixing in the suitable parts therein.

"Given at our royal pyramidical residence, named Pra Tinang Dusit Moha Prasad, in the grand royal palace Ratnekosindr, Bangkok for exchanging to-day, on Monday the 8th of waning moon of the seventh month (Temar month of Jesh), being of the year of the Quadruplicate Serpent, answering to the 15th of June, 1857, which is the seventh of our reign.

"SUPREMUS REX,
"SÎAMENSIUM,
"S. P. R. MONGKUT,
"The First King of Siam and Dependencies, reigning 2223 days ago."

While we were waiting the tediousness of diplomacy, we were invited, on Friday, May 9th, by the first king, to attend, at the palace, a laokon, or ballet operatic performance, in which all the performers are females.

The king's boats were sent for us, and we were borne from the landing, in palanquins, upon men's shoulders, to the place of performance. This soon became apparent from the sounds of native music which greeted our ears, and the throng of natives and files of soldiers surrounding it. The theatre was a large and lofty shed, closed only at one end, the roof supported upon posts wrapped in red cotton cloth, and roofed, or rather ceiled with the same material of a blue color. The floor, of smooth plaster or cement, was matted. Our host, his golden-footed majesty—where is he? Along the whole length of the left side of the building, at an elevation of several feet, was an apartment or stage, shut in to the height of three feet by a fronting of gold and crimson cloth. From the lofty ceiling to this floor hung curtains of cloth of gold, but now drawn back upon their cords. In the centre of this apartment, close to its front, and slightly elevated above it, sat the king. He wore a tunic of white muslin, a purple sash crossed his body, from the shoulder, and a yellow one around his waist, a silken sarong of course, and on his head a purple velvet cap with a single large jewel in its front. Some of his higher and favorite nobles were lying on the same platform with himself—we could just see their heads—and others lay crouched on the floor below the platform, the same that was occupied by ourselves and the performers.

Near the ascent to the king's apartment was a rich gold palanquin throne, over the seat of which was thrown a crimson silk cloth with broad golden borders. Just outside of the theatre stood another gilded palanquin, but, unlike the first, roofed and curtained; near this were two Arabian horses, richly caparisoned, and with cloths of silk and gold thrown over their saddles, and reaching almost to the ground on either side. The closed end of the building contained the apartments of the performers;

at the opposite end, directly fronting the stage, and on a level with it, chairs were placed for our accommodation. Seated on the ground along the whole line of the theatre to our right, were the musicians, one band of male and one of female performers, the latter much the larger, and sung the story which was carried on by the actors in dumb show, only occasionally a few words passing between the actors on the stage. The performance was going on at the time of our arrival, and soon after taking our seats a party of twenty girls, from eight to eighteen years of age, came upon the stage. These represented the prince of the play and his attendants. The gorgeousness of costume was brilliantly magnificent and defies description, either in general effect or in detail. It was the realization of the imagery of eastern fairy tales, bewildering the imagination of our youth. If, in an attempted description, I speak of silken cloth of gold, although I mean one surface of the glittering metal laid on a silken fabric, it implies many hues and figures, from the bright metallic lustre of a smooth surface, to figured textures which by changing folds and the varied gleaming of the light, gave tints from almost silvery whiteness, through various depths of yellow, to orange-red, and yet all gold.

I will attempt to describe in detail the costume of the girl representing the prince, and it was in no respects more elegant than any of her attendant train. Her head was covered with a conical golden crown, glittering with jewels, many of which were diamonds. A jacket of diamond-shaped figured purple silk and gold, fitted tightly to her body; the arms were closely covered with sleeves woven in narrow rings of alternate light and darker shades of gold, and about six inches of the lower part of the arm were covered with heavy golden bracelets; the fingers were loaded with jewels, and terminated by artificial nails of gold diminishing to wires six inches long, curved back toward the wrist. The sarong or petticoat was of a delicate rose-colored, changeable silk, with narrow lines or bars of gold thread. It passed in full folds around the lower part of the body, and where it fell around each limb like the loose leg of short trowsers, had a figured border six inches wide. Her ankles and feet were bare. A sash of figured gold cloth, twelve inches broad, passed tightly around her waist, one end fell like an apron in front of her person, and the glitter of this was relieved by a centre of dark green silk, supporting a figure of gold embroidery, and the ends had a border of three oval spaces of maroon-colored silk, with central figures of gold. The other extremity of this sash was divided into two narrower slips of figured gold cloth, one hanging down the outside of each limb. A collar of gold and diamonds passed around the neck and hung low on the shoulders and breast, being fastened in front by a rosette of diamonds. With the exception that they wore much prettier golden and jeweled coronets instead of the conical crown, and the variety of colors of their silks, all the costumes of this bevy, representing males, were similar to those I have described. Some of the sarongs were maroon, some purple, some dark green, but all richly embroidered in gold, and all the silks were of that heavy, solid, cloth-like thickness which is characteristic of the richest and most costly material. In the train of the princess of the play there was a corresponding number of attendants, dressed in like manner, but all having, in addition, a rich mantle which, falling below the breast in front, passed over the shoulders and extending almost to the ground behind. Most of these mantles were of narrow stripes of cherry, green or purple silk and gold. Two of them were entirely covered with gold embroidery, glittering in changeable hues. The face, neck, arms, and feet of these girls—all exposed parts of the person—were rubbed with a mixture of some white powder and turmeric, and the effect of this coloring was, strange to say, not unpleasant, giving them a softer, whiter, and more delicate yellow than the natural complexion. The performance consisted mainly in a slow dancing, or rather posturing, sometimes of a single person, and sometimes of the entire company, in time with the music, and the singing by the musicians, of the romance the actors were illustrating. The measured motions of the limbs and body, though monotonous and little varied, were not ungraceful, and the grouping of these splendid costumes, and glittering crowns in regular figures, or in lines, sometimes sitting on the floor, sometimes standing the whole length of the stage, was dazzling in its effect.

I observed closely, during this performance, the king and the Pra Kallahone. The former has been charged with giving too much of his time to these dissipations to the detriment of the interests of the kingdom, but he seemed now to give no attention to the scenes of the stage; but to be busily engaged in writing, or in business consultations with the nobles about him. The prime minister was lying on the floor beneath the throne, on the same level with us. Much of the time he lay with his face to the wall and his back to the actors, and when facing them his intelligent, calm, and mysterious countenance was turned toward our party with a thoughtful and abstracted expression, and I fancied he was looking at the hand-writing upon the wall, and reading the future of his country.

XX.

ROYAL SIAMESE LITERATURE.

THE following account of the illness and death of the queen, wife of the present first king, has some interest, being written by the king himself, and showing his attainments; the condition of medicine in Siam, and also the nature of certain Siamese customs:

An account of the most lamentable illness and death of Her young and amiable Majesty the Queen Somanass Waddhanawathy, the lawful royal consort of His most excellent and gracious Majesty Somdetch Pra Paramender Maha Mongkut, the reigning King of Siam.

This princess was born on the 21st of December, 1834, and was the only daughter of his royal highness Prince Zaks Nanugun, who died in the beginning of June, 1855, six months after the birth of this princess, whereupon his late gracious Majesty Somdetch Phra, Nang Klau C. Y. H., took great compassion on the orphan princess, and took her to the grand royal palace, adopting her as his own daughter. She was placed under the care of her aunt, her royal highness the Princess Welasee, who also died during her niece's infancy. After this event, the late king had exceeding great compassion on his adopted child, and made a royal mandate endowing her with all the estate and retainers of her natural father, as also with those of her royal aunt. He also conferred upon her all the honors and privileges belonging to the highest rank of royal children, and gave her the title of Phra Ong Chau Somanass Waddhanawathy. At the ceremony of cutting off her hair, she being then twelve years of age, her adopted father made a royal procession suitable to princesses of the highest royal birth, who are entitled

Chau-fa, or children of royalty by a princess of royal birth. The ceremony of the hair's cutting of their present majesties, the first and the second kings, were also celebrated in the same manner, they both being of the highest royal birth. This princess was, therefore, respected by a great many people, both native and foreign, and by all the adjacent tributary countries during the late reign. On the demise of his majesty Somdetch Phra Nang Klau, C. Y. H., the late King of Siam, and accession to the throne of his successor, Somdetch Phra Paramender Maha Mongkut, the reigning king, the whole council of royalty and nobility, seeing that this princess was without a protector, had great compassion on her, and unanimously proposed that she should be united by marriage and coronation to his majesty, the reigning king, as his royal consort.

Not a single dissenting voice was heard at this proposition, as they knew that his majesty had just returned from the priesthood, (which he had avowed for twenty-seven years) and had no lawful consort by whom he might expect an heir to future royal authority. The ceremony of the royal nuptial and coronation took place on the 2d of January, 1852, his majesty being then forty-eight, and the queen sixteen years of age. Since she was married and crowned in full dignity as queen-consort, she was respected both in private and in public, and was treated with the highest honor by the whole Siamese nation, and often received respectful compliments and presents from the adjacent tributary communities, and even friendship presents from certain noble persons and gentlemen of foreign countries, who were formerly correspondents of his majesty, the present king, so that she was well and happy for six months. But alas! it was the pleasure of Superagency (God, merits and demerits, and demons, or, according to different faiths) that it should be otherwise; an unfortunate event befel her, and she became ill of a fatal disease, which at first appeared curable by all the physicians, both foreign and native, they professing it to be only a natural consequence of her condition. On the 25th of June, 1852, the disease first showed itself by great pains in the umbilical region, accompanied by vomiting; at this time the physicians then observed that the disease was in the abdomen. After the eclipse of the moon of the 1st of July, she seemed to recover her health; but alas! after forty days her former painful suffering returned, until the 18th of August, when her disease became serious. On the 21st of August (at 1 P.M.) her majesty was safely delivered of a male royal infant. Her royal son was alive, but very feeble, crying and giving the usual signs of infantile life. A great many persons of royalty and nobility were immediately assembled with the officers of the palace, and welcomed the royal heir's arrival by birth, with the highest order of music, and other demonstrations of joy. They made its bed in the golden seat, covered with white, and surrounded with valuable royal weapons, a book, pencil; and in accordance with the ancient royal custom. Alas, the weak royal infant only lived three hours after its birth! it died at 4 P.M., on the same day, its life being but a brief one.

The officers then secretly carried away the body, letting her majesty believe that it was well, and in another room, as her former sickness was still on her. That same night her majesty became worse, and vomited so frequently that she almost died from the attack. The Siamese official physicians tried to revive her, but they could not succeed to stop the painful vomiting even for half an hour.

His royal highness Prince Krom Hluang Wongsa Dhiraj Sniddh administered some homeopathic medicines, from the effect of which her majesty's frequent vomiting was relieved, and she had the happiness to have a good sleep, at four or five o'clock, A. M. Next day, the 23d of August, his majesty the king, and his royal highness the Prince Krom Hluang Wongsa Dhiraj Sniddh, and a great many princes and princesses, with the servants of her majesty, consulted with several Siamese physicians, and took the counsel of all who were in her service, as to placing her under the care of Dr. Bradley, one of the American physicians now in Siam, who had been called to consult with them. Dr. Bradley treated her majesty's disease according to the homeopathic mode, which has but lately been introduced into Siam by himself. His system of applying medicines is not so much believed in by the Siamese as it ought to be.

It was thought necessary to indulge her majesty a little in her desire to follow the Siamese mode of being confined. She, accordingly, lay alongside of a fire (the universal practice of Siamese females after child-birth),* although Dr. Bradley, and a few believers in his system of medicine, who were present, were of a contrary opinion; and her majesty was then placed under the homeopathic mode of treatment of Dr. Bradley. Under his care, her majesty was a little relieved from her frequent attacks of squeamishness, vomiting, and fever.

She had frequent attacks of this disease for seven or eight days, until the 28th of August, being the seventh day after the death of her royal son, Prince Chau-fa (an honored appellation applied to children and persons born of the king by the queen, or of any high prince by a pricenss of the rank of Chau-fa, or, in other words, born of parents that are both Chau-fa), when her majesty having known of the death of her royal son.

Their majesties (the king and queen) then prepared valuable presents, and offered them to an assembly of

* 14 days usually.

Buddhist priests, and scattered balls, containing coins, to the people, in every direction, from her majesty's residence. This money was prepared, as customary on such events, for offerings at the death of her majesty's son, Prince Chau-fa. Since the 29th and 30th of August, however, her majesty, unfortunately, became worse, and discharged from her stomach large quantities of bile, of a dark and yellowish color, and accompanied by fever. Dr. Bradley then begged of the princes and nobles that her majesty should withdraw from the fire, and entirely follow his mode of treatment. This was complied with, and, being entirely under the care of Dr. Bradley, at length her majesty seemed slowly to recover. The vomiting was less frequent, and the fever disappeared, but she continued gradually taking less food, and thereby became very feeble and thin. In this state her majesty continued until the 11th of September, when her feet appeared to be swollen, and other bad symptoms appeared, which much alarmed her friends and relatives. They consulted together, and resolved to try a Siamese physician. In fact, her majesty had not much belief in Dr. Bradley's system of medicine, as he was a foreigner, and she would not credit the statements of Dr. Bradley, and others that believed in homeopathy, that a few drops of spirits in a spoonful of water would cure her disease. Her majesty, therefore, tried again a Siamese physician, who administered to her medicines after the Siamese mode. But she got no better under his treatment, and even grew worse, so much so that no Siamese physician would take her case in hand. Dr. Bradley was, therefore, sent for again, who treated her after his own mode. While under the treatment of the Siamese physicians, the vomiting of black and yellow matter continued, accompanied by painful affections in her breathing, etc. These attacks occurred seven or eight times a day.

Since the return of Dr. Bradley to attend her majesty, up to the 16th of September, her majesty seemed to be a little better, as the vomiting of the black and yellow substance, supposed to be bile, became less frequent, and other bad symptoms being less than when she was under the treatment of the Siamese physicians; but alas! her majesty's weakness and refusal of sustenance yet prevailed on account of her continued vomiting. There was not a single day passed without severe vomiting, which obstinately refused to yield to any remedies. After the lapse of a few days, Dr. Bradley had not succeeded in making her vomiting less frequent, the intervals between her attacks of vomiting now became less distant, and unfavorable symptoms appeared, and her face and body presented a yellow appearance. In consequence of this, she was again put under the care of official Siamese physicians; but they refused to take her case in hand. Upon this a proclamation was issued, offering a reward of many peculs of money to any one who could restore her majesty to her former health. Since the time her majesty became worse under the hands of Dr. Bradley, her pulse became very quick and violent, and on the 27th of September she became delirious. On the same day a royal proclamation was issued to the people of the city, offering a reward of two peculs of money to any one who could make her better. An old Siamese official physician then came to examine her majesty, and wished to try his skill, and was therefore permitted to see her. On seeing her majesty he misunderstood her complaint, and attributed her disease to mismanagement during child-birth or time of confinement, because she did not lay near the fire. From his statements, it appeared that he would cure her majesty in a short time, and got the consent of her majesty's relatives and friends, and even that of his majesty, to try his skill. But alas, two or three hours after drinking three or four spoonfuls of his aromatic medicines, her majesty became so delirious that she could not speak so correctly as before, and occasionally cried out with a loud noise, and became much agitated, and continually moving to and fro. His majesty then immediately rejected the old ignorant and covetous physician, and again called Dr. Bradley, who attended her majesty till her death, of which she appeared to be soon a victim. The doctor restored her by homeopathic medicines, but his success was only partial, and, on the 1st day of October, her majesty's eyes became strangely fixed, and she remained silent, refusing medicines and nourishment. On this day it was observed that there was an abscess which must have occurred probably (early,) and had been broken by the violent agitations of her body during her illness; pus and matter, mixed with blood, found an outlet at her umbilicus; it continued to discharge freely and by degrees for days. Her majesty, by means of some remedies and applications in various ways, was restored to consciousness, although she was manifestly failing in strength, until the 6th of October. During this interval his majesty the king and her majesty's kindred brought many gifts of yellow cloths, etc., to her, and induced her to present them as her last offering to the priesthood, and to receive the sacred instructions for her last meditation from the high priests, according to Buddhistical tenets—in which her majesty placed her faith. Her majesty then offered these cloths, etc., to many hundreds of Buddhist priests, and received their instructions and benedictions, though laboring under painful attacks of vomiting, and which caused her daily to lose her strength. Alas, on the 6th of October, there was indubitable evidence that the abscess was also discharging its contents (internally). After this for three days her majesty sunk rapidly, and breathed her last on the 10th of October, 1852, at six o'clock, P. M., greatly lamented, and bewailed by all the royal household.

Her majesty's remains were bathed and adorned with golden ornaments used for the dead according to the royal custom, in the full style and dignity of a queen, and wrapped in many folds of white cloth. Her remains were then placed in the golden urn or vessel called Phra-Kate, with a queen's crown on her head, and then covered with the cover of the golden urn. On the same night her majesty's remains were removed from the queen's residence to the "Tusita Maha Prasad," a great and richly gilded hall of the grand palace, and placed in the same apartment in which the royal remains of his late majesty laid during thirteen months, from April, 1851, to May, 1852.

Her late majesty's remains now lie there in state, surrounded with all the insignia of rank, until the burning takes place in about four or five months more, and will be attended with considerable ceremonies suitable to her late majesty's exalted rank. This event will perhaps take place about March or April proximo. Her most amiable and youthful majesty the late Somanass Queen Waddhanawathy was the beloved and adopted royal daughter of his majesty Somdetch Phra, Nang Klau, C. Y. H., the late King of Siam, since her infancy. At the thirteenth year of her age she was dignified to the highest rank of royal daughter, called Chau-fa, and became the queen consort of his present majesty Somdetch Phra Paramender Maha Mongkut Phra Chau Klau Chau Yu Hud on the commencement of this present year, and lived happily with her much-esteemed and lawful royal husband, the King of Siam, for only seven months, from January to July, and from the 10th of August to the 10th of October, being sixty-two days and nights, her majesty was ill, making nine months and a few days that she lived as queen consort. Her majesty's death happening in her youth and amiableness, and after such great prosperity and happiness which she enjoyed but for a short time, was much lamented and bewailed by his majesty, by the people of the city, and by foreigners of tributary countries. After her majesty's death all the Siamese, Chinese and American physicians concluded that there was great reason to believe that the foundation of the disease which destroyed the valuable life of her majesty must have been laid some time previous to her espousal to his majesty, the present king, from her majesty's being uncommonly stout for a person of her age, and having suddenly become thin and emaciated, and being attacked at the same time with a severe fit of coughing; but the symptoms of her late majesty's disease did not show themselves till the 25th of June, as has already been stated. As her late majesty was an orphan, and became the adopted daughter of the late king, by whom she was made to inherit the whole estates and retinues of her late royal parents and aunt, and being the only daughter, she has no half or full brothers and sisters, and has consequently no heirs. The whole of her property and large amount of money, together with her annual income or private fortune, will be placed in the royal treasury till after the funeral ceremonies are concluded.

His majesty, the present king, has concluded that a portion of her late majesty's great property and money will be expended to refit the sacred places and monasteries belonging to her late royal father and aunt, and another portion will be expended in the construction of a sacred building within the new wall of this city, and will be called Somonapwihari. The remainder will be employed in the royal treasure for the use of the public. As there are many of her late majesty's acquaintances in almost every province of Siam and the adjacent countries, and among them are even some persons of foreign countries, of China, Batavia, Maulmain, etc., who were or are the intimate friends and agents of his majesty, and became her friends for his majesty's sake, his majesty therefore commanded that an account of the illness and death of her late majesty be prepared in Siamese, to be issued by proclamation throughout the kingdom of Siam and adjacent countries; and also to prepare an account of the same in the English language, to be printed and sent to all her English friends, so that they may know accurately about her.

Printed in lithographic press at the royal printing office, 21st December, 1852, which is the second year of the reign of his Siamese majesty Somdetch Phra Paramender Maha Mongkut.

XXI.

AN UNCOMMON COMMMONER.

Happening to be making some inquiries respecting the laws of Siam, Mr. Smith told me there was an imperfect copy of the laws printed in the Siamese. The written laws filled many volumes of the peculiar black slate paper books, and any one requiring a copy was necessarily compelled to employ a writer to make it, and, at the regular charge, the cost was over one hundred dollars.

A young Siamese conceived the idea of compiling the laws, and having them printed so that the whole code would cost but about five or six dollars, and thus, while benefiting his country, derive some pecuniary advantage for himself. He had completed the printing of one volume and a half of the two, which was to compose the work, when the king became jealous of such knowledge being accessible to foreigners and seized the whole work, severely censuring the enterprising young author and destroying his chance of reward. The present king, with better judgment and greater liberality, had restored the printed volumes, and by the sale of these the expense of the publication had been in some degree met.

I expressed the wish to make the acquaintance of a person of so much energy and foresight, and Mr. Smith called, on the evening of May the 9th, to take me to his house. We found him at an out-of-the-way place, a little removed from the back of the river. Having been apprised of our coming he received us very graciously, and conducted us to an upper room of his house, where tea and cakes were placed upon the table. To appreciate this man, the fact must be considered that the only language he understood was his Siamese, and in that language there are no works upon any of the sciences. In the commencement of our conversation, I paid him the little compliment of saying I had called on him in consequence of my respect for his enterprise in compiling laws, and for the acquirements I understood he had made. He said he had been working like a blind man with great difficulty, and that all he knew he owed to the missionaries; that he had been taunted by his countrymen with wishing to be a Christian, and charged with laboring for knowledge of no use to him; but when they found it was of some use, they were willing to avail themselves of it, and to learn of him to do the same things. Upon one occasion the king, in a public audience, handed him some percussion caps and asked him to make some. He did so, and this was a convincing proof of the utility of his studies. Several of his children were sitting around the table—boys from six to fifteen years of age. I remarked to him that having had so much difficulty himself, I supposed he would have his children taught English, in which were so many books upon all knowledge, to be had at little cost. He said he was anxious to do so if it were possible, and thought they ought to send some of their young men to the United States to be educated; he had repeatedly spoken to the king about it, and sometimes he seemed to regard the proposition favorably, but nothing had been done. His countrymen were not disposed to receive his suggestions favorably, because they thought he assumed upon the little knowledge he had. The Siamese were generally so ignorant themselves, they did not understand the advantage of knowledge for their children. I intimated that therefore it was the more incumbent upon him, who knew better, to give his children every possible advantage. Whilst he admitted this, he remarked there was little inducement to any to improve themselves, where there were no inducements to exercise their thoughts and their talents. He thought the true way to make the nation would be to draw forth the talent of the common people, and elevate those who showed any, and this they might learn from their own history. When the kingdom had been conquered by the Burmans and was liberated by the half Chinese who became king, he consulted with all persons who had ability, and found his best advisers among the common people, and these he promoted to the stations for which their talents fitted them, and thus accomplished the independence of his country.

He has arranged himself quite a laboratory and makes many chemicals—distils alcohol—nitric acid. I happened to complain of the annoyance of my lucifer matches, that in this damp weather scarce one would light.

"If they were prepared from the 'chloras potassa' you would not have so much trouble," was his reply.

He then gave me a Chinese tinder-box, which he remarked was rude and simple, but one of the best modes of procuring a light. A small roll of Chinese paper, charred at one end, and the end of it passed into a bamboo tube. The charred end protruded from the bamboo-tube is lighted by flint and steel and extinguished by being drawn back into the tube. The advantage it has, in common with all similar contrivances, over the match, is that it is readily lighted in the open air, and the advantage over similar methods is, that a puff of breath upon the ignited end lights it into a blaze. He also showed me a means, in common use, of getting a light by atmospheric compression—the piston working in a small tube of buffalo horn. He spoke of the various modes of procuring fire, in use among the savage nations, and said the double-convex lens, or sun-glass, was of comparative recent date in Siam. About the time of its introduction, a military officer was sent to conquer some jungle tribes, and took a sun-glass with him. He induced these people to believe that by the favor of celestial beings he could draw fire from heaven at will, and obtained such an ascendency over them, that he used their support to revolt against the kingdom and make himself independent, being afterwards conquered with much difficulty.

He alluded to the proneness of ignorant people to be imposed upon by such acts, and said there was a prevalent conviction among their own people that a man might become invincible, and be impregnable against the power of knives or bullets, neither of which could wound him. He first began to doubt the truth of this when he "was of the age of that boy," pointing to a son of twelve years, and yet he was puzzled by the doubt, for every one else believed it. He commenced by inquiring who had ever seen such a man, and could hear of none who had done so. He determined to study the subject fully, and either satisfy himself of its falsity or acquire the art. He applied himself to it, even after he entered the priesthood and until his twenty-fifth year, only becoming more and more convinced that the belief had no other foundation than ignorance and imposture. He had himself seen a man strike his arm repeatedly with a sharp razor without wounding the skin, but this he knew was a mere trick.

From his allusion to his having been in the priesthood, I hoped to obtain from him some information respecting the organization and internal management of this body; but he seemed to misunderstand me, and fear that I wished to lead him into some theological discussion which he was desirous of avoiding. He hastily replied that he was only in the priesthood the three months required by law; that he thought there were no more than nominal differences between their religion and ours, especially if their religion were purified, but that it was corrupted by the notions and usages of several ignorant natives; still, it and the Catholic religion were nearly identical—there was no difference worth talking about.

I merely asked how many priests there were.

"Ten thousand; an army we are compelled to support in idleness."

I was satisfied my friend had reached the true significance and value of Buddhism, and was timid lest his opinions should be discovered.

Wishing to make him some little useful present, I thought of a small and simply-constructed electro-galvanic apparatus in my possession. I inquired if he had paid any attention to the subject. "Oh, yes, much. I have made many batteries myself, and punish my servants by galvanizing them." Still hoping that mine might be a little better finished than those of his own hands, I asked to see one of his. He had none by him but the first he had ever made. This was brought in, and was so far superior to mine in power and finish, being inclosed in a handsome case, that I saw I could do nothing for him in this way.

His work-shop was in a lower room, about twenty feet

long. The whole of one side was occupied by a large and well-finished turning lathe which he had built himself. Along the wall, neatly arranged, was a variety of implements and mechanic's tools, and around lay several heavy solid brass wheels, some in the roughness of a fresh casting and some smoothly turned. He was then constructing in an outer shed a much larger lathe, and also a small steam engine to turn it. In the shed where he was putting up the frame of his large lathe there lay a pile of ship's blocks. These he was making for the use of the king.

I again alluded to the extent of his acquirements under such difficult circumstances. He replied that he owed it all to the missionaries, who were in all respects the best men he had ever met. When they were first expected there was a great apprehension among the Siamese lest they should be arrogant, annoying and troublesome, but he thought much upon the subject, and one remarkable fact impressed itself upon his mind. "I said," he continued, "all the people I know of have kings to rule over them except this people, and they are all equal and agree among themselves who shall be their head; and although they are all equal, we hear of no wars and dissensions among them. Therefore, I said, they must be a people of greater virtues and better hearts than those people who have to be kept in order by monarchs. He had known the missionaries intimately from their first coming, and their character and behavior had confirmed the judgment he had formed before he knew them, and the manners of Americans generally were more amiable than those of Europeans."

I replied that he had hit upon the true principle; that being all equal, no man had the right of talking arrogantly to another; that the President used the same courtesy to one of his fellow-citizens that he would to a member of his own family, and hence courteous deportment became a national characteristic, and was manifested in our association with other people; that we knew a republic could only exist with an intelligent and virtuous people, and therefore we endeavored to impart those qualities to our people by free schools all over the country, giving every one an education at no, or but little, cost.

This man had acquired by conversation with the missionaries all his scientific knowledge. His plan was to get them to read to him from English books what related to any matter he was studying, or what illustrated any engraving which attracted his attention. He would immediately make some practical application of his knowledge, and thus he learned from them what, practically, they did not know themselves.

I left him about ten o'clock. He thanked me for my visit, and promised soon to return it.

FANKWEI.

III.

IN CHINA

IN CHINA.

XXII.

HONG KONG.

On Saturday, May 31st, the "Siamese Seat of Naval Force" took the whole of our party away from Bangkok. We reached Packnam at night, where the governor had made arrangements for our accommodation until morning.

About eight o'clock the next morning, we reached the San Jacinto, after seven weeks' absence, and immediately got under way for Hong Kong, where awaited us our letters of eight months' accumulation, and all the incidents of joy or sorrow which, in a changing world, might in that time await our arrival. There was, also, the hope of liberty for our ship-sick, ship-imprisoned crew, nearly a year in this worse than penitentiary imprisonment, without their feet touching mother-earth.

When our legislators produced the act to "provide a more efficient discipline for the Navy," in their simplicity they assumed some natural human rights to exist on board a man-of-war, for they say: "Section 3. And be it further enacted, That it shall be the duty of commanders of any vessels in the Navy, in granting temporary leave of absence and liberty on shore, to exercise carefully a discrimination in favor of the faithful and obedient;" and among the legal penalties is, "deprivation of liberty on shore on foreign stations." They should first have ordered that the men should not, without great and urgent cause, or as a penalty, be deprived of the liberty of the shore; or some Secretary of the Navy should make such an acknowledgment of right a regulation of the Department. The usage is to keep the men on board ships for months, whereas officers, and officers' servants, go ashore daily in every port. This tantalizing and provoking contrast nurses and feeds the fever of the accumulated excitability of confinement to a water-bound prison; and then, when they are permitted to go ashore, it is in large gangs, for a twenty-four hours' debauch—the naval idea being that the nature of the sailor is to have this debauch, and, in ignorance of man-nature, overlooking the fact that the men have been brought into a morbid condition by the unnatural management of them.

The first touch of the foot to the shore, after such an estrangement, is an intoxication. I have experienced it myself after a long sea voyage; then to this excitement is added that of numbers, and the incitement to outrage which arises from the physical power of numbers turned loose for indulgence in a weak community. A great lever of punishment is lost, by the fact that no rights or indulgence are secured the good, and of which the bad may be deprived.

Instead of this unnatural management of the crew, suppose, when in port, the men were—such as behaved themselves—permitted to go ashore, daily, in small numbers, as they could be spared from their duties. The frequency of visiting the shore would diminish the wildness of excitement, the small numbers would lessen the incentives to turbulence, a lever of correction would be constantly on hand, and the bad would be separated from the good.

Some sensible commanders have had the good sense to

try this reasonable system, and the results are as favorable as might have been expected.

Owing to the defect in our engine, and some delay in repairing it, we did not arrive in Hong Kong until the 11th of June, 1856—within a few days of eight months since leaving New York.

From the lonely waters and level flats of the Gulf of Siam, to the green islands, rugged mountains, and thronging vessels of the harbor of Hong Kong, is a transition of marked contrast.

Our first contact with Chinese qualities introduced us to their indomitable energy, perseverance, and industry. An enterprising Chinese pilot had picked us up far out at sea, and another had been for a month steadily on the look-out for us; and, as we ran up to our anchorage, we encountered a Chinese invasion. A fleet of boats, propelled by mat sails, by sculls and oars, bore down upon us. The principal object of competition was to get the office of comprador—the privilege of supplying the various messes, and of being the ship's bum-boat; that is, trading with the men during certain fixed hours. This is a very profitable position, and those who engage in it get rich. Then, there were tailors, painters, shoemakers, peddlers, washermen and washerwomen, besides aspirants for the honorable appointment of "fast boat"—the boat which, being the home and dwelling-place of the proprietor and his family, wives and children, is employed, instead of the ship's boats, to take us to and from the shore.

On came the competing fleet, regardless, apparently, of being run down by our heavy steamer. We were not then familiar with the great skill with which these boats are managed—being suddenly turned and changing their course just as they appear to be rushing upon an object. Stimulated by the prize before them, and confident of their skill, they paid no attention to the orders to warn them off, if, indeed, these could be heard above the clamor and the screeching of their own tin-toned throats. Some of the greater tacticians had small American ensigns flying, and one bold diplomatist, determined to command success by assuming it, flew from his mast-head a white flag, painted in large characters—

BUM-BOAT.
U. S. STEAMER
SAN JACINTO.

Up alongside the ship they dashed, and, despite their skill, not without some damage to them, crashing bamboo spars. Men and women clambered up the ship's sides, and thrust forth bundles of certificates from their former patrons in our service, at the same time assuring us that he or she was No. 1 in their respective vocations.

A great and absorbing interest drew us for the time from these novel sights. Owing to the courtesy of the house of De Silver & Co., the accumulated letters of an interval of eight months' absence from home were sent on board to us by the time we had anchored, and the hopes, the fears, and the anxieties of all this time were to be confirmed or dispelled.

The hurry and bustle of a fresh arrival, the reception of visitors, and the firing of salutes having subsided, in a day or two we are in a state to make a more detailed examination of this fruit of English civilization which had sprung up in what, twelve years ago, was a den of Chinese pirates and a collection of miserable fishing huts.

The city of Victoria, in the island of Hong Kong, may be said to extend from Happy Valley on the extreme east to West Point on the extreme west, a winding road of about three miles in length, the Queen's road, skirting the bay and twisting along the foot of the mountains washed by the waters of the bay. The mass of the city lies within the central two miles of this space, straggling and adventurous settlements linking in the spaces beyond. Indeed, nearly a mile beyond the eastern point we have named, alone and separated from the rest of the city, are the extensive buildings of the large commercial firm of Jardine, Matheson & Co., which seems to be somewhat an independent though allied sovereignty of Hong Kong—firing its morning and evening gun, keeping its own police force, and running an individual line of steamers to the East Indies. After the city begins to leave the Queen's road with any lateral aspirations, there is nothing left for it but to climb up the mountain-side, and so it does, with sharp, angular features standing out with a general complexion of white and yellow ochre on two or three dark-green, granite-knobbed mountain spurs, along which wind terraced roads fringed with shrubbery and gardens. High up on these elevations stand the pretentious palaces of the successful merchants, or those which, built upon a hopeful future, have passed into the hands of those who have followed "one more unfortunate."

Also standing out to catch the breezes of the hill-top, with the union jack flying in its front, is the yellow-washed castle of the Governor, the residence of the Bishop of Victoria, and the cathedral, with fortifications and military quarters capping off nature's granite summits with the same material molded by the lines of architecture and masonry. Over all, from an elevation of eighteen hundred feet, looks down Victoria's Peak, over city and bay, ampan, lorcha and junk, the merchantmen of many nations soon to be lying in the stagnation of war and blockade.

Under English fortresses and men-of-war we are tolerably safe. But the opposite or Kowloon shore of the bay, inviting as it looks, only two miles away, is at all times pretty certain death to any wandering Fankwei. Hostility to the barbarian is increased by his proximity, as some unfortunate Englishmen have recently experienced.

A morning's stroll along the length of the Queen's road will present us with much of interest, and show us a variety of races and some of their habits. We will begin again at the Happy Valley, and to get there, we start before the sun is up, and find ourselves rapidly passed by early-rising, fast-walking foreign residents, who are doing up their daily amount of out-door exercise as energetically as possible, making this valley their general terminus. It is a little beauty of a basin of prairie, about a mile in circuit, shut in by the precipitous hills, through one of which our road is cut—a beautiful and inviting-looking spot to look at, but deadly to dwell in. Most of it is filled by the circuit of the race-course, and around it are placed the various cemeteries. By the time we are ready to return the sun is gilding the hill-tops, and the laboring life of Hong Kong is astir. As we reënter the suburbs of the city, the mechanics are busily at work in their open shops. The bamboo chair-maker and the rattan shaving mattrass-maker are topographical trades, but the blacksmiths, tinmen and braziers are numerous, and the barbers are everywhere, in shops and in the streets, shaving heads, plaiting queues, shampooing backs, cleaning out ears and eyes. Then we have a range of market-shops; the pork-butcher is dealing out his slender cutlets, the fruiterer his pines, banannas, oranges, and huge pomelons. Next to this golden-colored merchandise, are masses of green salad, cabbages, peas, beans, with radishes and tomatoes. There are dried fish and fresh, with bunches of dried ducks, split open, pressed flat, as if rolled between heavy rollers, and dried with transparent thinness.

The laboring coolies, with their burden-sticks across their shoulders, fill the streets, all dressed with much uniformity in broad-brimmed, sharp-peaked hats, made of palm-leaves, blue cotton shirts, or frocks, coming to their hips, trowsers of the same reaching half way down the leg, and either bare or straw sandal-shod feet. The women wear precisely the same costume, except that the outer frock hangs lower, and the trowsers reach the ankle. Even among the lower classes, a few small-footed women are seen tottering along like a child on short stilts, but most of them are either barefoot or wear a shoe with a sole two inches thick, shaped like a rocker skate; mothers are tottering along with children lashed to their backs by a square cloth, of which the prevailing fashion is crimson.

At a later hour, when we would meet the better classes of Chinese, another style of costume varies the streets. Black satin or embossed velvet shoes with thick white soles, white leggings reaching to the knees, and meeting blue silk breeches which are fastened by silk garters, or the silk breeches, may descend the leg, fitting it tightly and being fastened at the ankles with ribbons. The outside garment is either a figured silk or a woolen cape, or a long robe either light and flowing, or quilted and trimmed with rich furs, according to the season. In fact, although there is a general style of costume, it admits as much variety almost in fashion and material as is seen on Broadway. The cap of these gentry is a close-fitting skull cap made of eight sections, with a crimson knot on the top. Rain or shine, cold or warm, in the day time, cloudy or clear, every Chinaman has an umbrella, and at night a lantern.

By the time we have passed through the Chinese suburbs, and reached the large and capacious buildings of the European settlement we find we are bounded on all sides by the British government. First we come to a guard-house, and then a long range of granite buildings, called the war department; a little further, on the opposite side, the military hospital, a large central building with a fountain amid the shrubbery of the front yard, and two wings. Then on and on, other public buildings—a navy yard. Then again, on both sides of the street, long ranges of military quarters with shady walks under rows of trees in their front, and sentries posted at the gate. Here we fall in with specimens of the military guardians of the empire. European soldiers in the tight-fitting crimson jackets, or dark colored, curly-haired Sepoys, with loose white robes, flowing trowsers and crimson turbans; or the same fellows dressed in tight-fitting, European military dress, looking like flexible black snakes stiffened in tin jackets.

Having passed these military establishments, we come upon another small prairie expanse, the parade ground, opening to the bay on one side, and overlooked at the other by the Episcopal cathedral perched upon an eminence.

A row of trees on each side of the road shades our walk across this space, and at later hour of the day there would be much to keep us loitering along this thoroughfare. In the shade of these trees is the place of business of respectably dressed and sage looking old Chinamen—conjurors, physicians and magicians.

One of the "Faculty" has a large white cloth spread out, upon which is painted many human figures, and upon it the exact seat, or morbid effects of every disgusting disease which the doctor professes to remedy. This is an energetic looking individual who urges his talents upon the public notice. Another more dignified and grave looking person sits behind his table, spread with parcels of medicines, neatly spread plasters, and, absorbed in the study of a book, quietly awaits the calls of his patients. More numerous than these quack doctors, are the conjurors. Several of them have little cages containing beautiful and well-taught Java sparrows, and a box in which a variety of cards are packed on their edges. Any card may be selected from the pack, and being marked and returned to it, the sparrow, at the bid of his master, hops over the pack, plunges his beak into it, and draws forth the identical card which had been marked.

One shrewd, cunning-looking, sharp featured individual was very importunate. He had the countenance and expression of the keenest Yankee, crossed with the trickiest Chinaman. He stood in front of a suspended chart, on which were painted two busts, mapped off, and named or numbered as the organs of a phrenological bust. In his hand he held a small looking-glass, directed toward the passing crowd, to which he seemed to be addressing a constantly flowing lecture. Many passed him by without any notice, some halted for a moment, laughed, and passed on, but some stood fixed in gaping wonderment; to these he held up the small mirror, and, with rapid speech and moving fingers, pointed at various regions of the head and face, the subject, always with an anxious countenance, seeming to come more and more under the influence of the operator—whether medical or magical, I could not guess.

Having crossed this lively region, we are now amid the showy houses of business of the foreign merchants, the wholesale opium smugglers, and also the shops of the retailers. These, with the better class of Chinese lacquer, silk and ivory shops, extend along the Queen's road for half a mile, when the road, both topographically and morally, makes a descent into Tae-ping-shan, the dense Chinese settlement proper, where, amid native trades, pirates and robbers, painted courtesans, opium and tea shops, renegade foreigners keeping sailor boarding-houses and drinking shops, purvey to the depraved appetites of their countrymen. Such is Hong Kong from the beginning to the end of its great thoroughfare, the Queen's road. During the busy hours of the day it is thronged with pedestrians, native and foreign; sedan chairs, close and open; traveling cook-shops, and peddlers of cakes, confectioneries, oranges and olives. All these are regularly licensed and numbered, paying tribute undoubtedly to the colonial government. Cobblers of old shoes, workers in leather, repairers of broken china, with their implements of trade, are among the morning occupations of the street; while bands of labor coolies are carrying bales and heavy burdens from point to point. Among the throng are black, hyena-looking policemen, Indians in European clothes, with numbers embroidered on their collars, and these omit no opportunity of asserting their proud position as British subjects, by kicking over a peddling Chinaman's stock in trade, scattering his fruit, nuts and baskets in the street, lashing him with the short thick whip he carries under his arm, or beating him, as I have seen, with the flat of his sword.

Such is a glance at the capital of the island over which is ruler and governor Dr. Sir John Bowring, the philologist and philanthropist—the poet and philosopher—the statesman and chartist—an apparently worthy gentleman, whose literary reputation is far greater than that of his position of Governor of Hong Kong. According to the colonial press, he does not possess one good quality or a solitary virtue. Sir John, it has been said, has somewhat humorously said he was the great supporter of the colonial press, as but for abuse of him, the writers would have no material for their pens to work upon.

It seems so essential a condition of a Hong Kong governor's position to be abused, that, as a thing of course it resolves itself into a mere form of speech, and is diluted into a Pickwickian sense. After all, the governor, who has earned a world-wide reputation as a man of letters, may be as able as those of whom the world has never heard, and morally may be no worse than the commercial community of which the leading business is opium smuggling, and the daily excitement, gambling upon its price.

XXIII.

CANTON, THE CITY OF RAMS.

On this 10th day of July the first overland mail since our arrival left in the steamer for the Red Sea. We had all privately and officially been working up to this point The consul general for Japan had finished his dispatches, and they, with the Siamese treaty, were in the hands of Dr. Bradley, the bearer of the treaty for ratification, who went home by the mail.

The next morning, bright and early, we were off for Japan ; that is, we were to be. Steam was got up and the anchor weighed. Around went the propeller, when such a blow, such a shock, struck the San Jacinto in the stern, as made every timber in her quiver ; and everybody—those on duty and those awoke from their morning slumbers—began to wonder what was the matter. Slowly turned the propeller—thump—blow—shock—quiver. A five hundred horse power engine was applying the weight of fourteen thousand pounds of metal to some part of the ship not intended for such a state of things. Cyclopean poundings. Something was wrong, certainly. Away went the anchor again, a mile or so from where we had picked it up. The engineers examined the propeller, and came to the conclusion that the keys which kept the blades in place had been destroyed, and the blades consequently had fallen back so as to strike the stern rudder post. But before any thing could be definitely ascertained, and certainly, before any thing could be done, the ship must go into dock. The dock was at Whampoa, some eighty miles up the Canton river, and the San Jacinto, now entirely helpless, could not get to Whampoa herself, but must be humiliatingly towed there; and as she must be lightened to sixteen feet to enter the dock, all the coal, water and provisions with which she was filled up for her cruise must now come out, also her guns, and perhaps her masts.

On Saturday, the 13th of July, two steamers took us in tow, and by eight in the morning we were on our way to Whampoa. As we passed by the British frigate Nankin her band struck up "Hail Columbia," but as we were not moving proudly by our own forces, but humbly dragging in the wake of two steamboats, although intended as a compliment, it felt like a satire.

Our way up the river presented us with the interest of picturesque scenery. The waters, reddish yellow in color, were rolling, flowing around and between rocky islands, some of them clothed in green. The banks were a succession of lofty mountain hills, with intervening valleys and Chinese villages. It is most extraordinary that any one of observation should have spoken of these river borders as uninteresting or as thinly peopled. Every plain and cove has its populous town or village, and wherever the soil, washed from the hill-sides, has accumulated in masses large enough to support life, there life has planted itself. And in addition to this population supported on the shore, much of that which wins existence, honestly or dishonestly, from the water, makes its home along the banks of these waters. It is true that owing to the breadth of the stream, the little elevation of the dwellings, and the concealed coves and nooks in which they are nestled, but little of the population is seen by the traveler on the river.

Some of these green hill-sides were sprinkled over with large-sized, white semicircles. These were Chinese graves. They are constructed much like a large, old-fashioned, oval-backed sleigh, high behind and low in front. They are built with two semicircles, or horse-shoe shaped inclosures of masonry, one within another. The outer is built up two or three feet from the ground at the back part, and has a diameter of ten or twelve feet.

As we approached the Bogue, it could be recognized in the distance by the long lines of white walls running from the water-side to the hill-tops, and inclosing the forts built to defend the passage. These forts are extensive, but are now very much dilapidated. So narrow is the passage at the Bogue, and so favorably placed on the high lands overlooking it, that it might be made impregnable. After passing the Bogue, the hills recede, and low, flat rice or paddy fields, with an embankment or levee shutting out the waters, border the stream. Obliged to anchor at night, it was not until the following morning we found ourselves among the shipping of the miserable, marsh-surrounded, pestilential anchorage of Whampoa; and thus terminated our first effort to reach Japan.

Whampoa is a curious, but desolate-looking place—a Chinese town on shore, and a foreign one upon the water. I noticed a neat-looking boat in the river built over with a house, and having green Venetian blinds. That was the doctor's house and office. A similar boat, housed over, the windows Gothic, with other church-like adornments, was the church; and the boat from which I looked upon these things was itself a floating grocery and ship-chandler's store. The nature of the shore may be imagined where the water is a more agreeable abiding-place; but the insurance officers have arithmetically calculated the chances of having your throat cut and your property destroyed on shore or afloat, and have reached the money-measured conclusion that on shore they will not make insurance, on the river they will.

On Monday afternoon the steamer Willamette came along, on her way from Hong Kong to Canton, and Commodore Armstrong, his secretary and I took passage in her. As we approached the city we ran among lines of the most extraordinary-looking boats, armed junks, with all sorts of fantastic-looking cannon jutting out of their sterns, their sides and their bows. There were many very long, roofed-over boats, with rolls of black varnished matting laid along their roofs. These were canal boats bringing produce along the vast canals of the empire from the great interior. Their sails lay neatly protected beneath the rolls of black matting.

Almost hidden by this massing of boats — some belonging to the spot, and to the local river population, others strangers from the distant provinces—lies, on the Chukiang or Pearl river, the old "City of Rams," Kwangtung—Canton—associated, in the minds of antipodal merchants and ladies, with clean matting, aromatic tea, and bright silks; in those of juvenile patriots with firecrackers, fourths of July and Christmas. So globe-famed a city makes no show from the deck of the Willamette. Its low, tiled roof houses are just seen over the boat city in its front; but there it lies, within its seven miles of wall, with its million of population, and its age-accumulated horrors, vice and corruption, plethoric, and full—fattened and enfeebled by oriental luxury, facilitated, not controlled, by a material religion, and aided by art enough to concentrate without refining.

Travelers in the United States are constantly annoyed by the ferocious importunity and deafening cries with which hackmen are permitted to assail them at the railroad depots. All this is scarcely equal to the solicitations of the Tanka girls of China. These girls do all the boating on the river — such as carrying passengers and messages between the shipping and the shore. Their boats, roofed over with matting, are exceedingly neat, every thing being scrupulously clean, and the smallest thing having its proper place. Order and system are especially necessary to this neatness, as the boat is the permanent dwelling of its three or four inmates — their kitchen, dining-room and bed-chamber. The women wear loose Chinese trowsers and short frock of dark blue pongee silk, with heavy ear-rings, bracelets, and anklets of a pearl-colored stone,* or of silver. The young ones are, many of them, quite good looking, with cheerful faces, framed in a bright-colored kerchief thrown over the head, and fastened under the chin, and in the smiling, merry animation with which they urge you to employ their boats, many of them display beautifully regular and white teeth. Their feet are bare. These boats rushed and crowded upon our steamer, as we came to the anchorage, in the most reckless manner, and the captain told me they are frequently upset, and their inmates drowned.

We had anchored immediately in front of the Hongs, or Factories — that little spot, of all Canton, in which are shut up all the foreign residents. Its whole extent is about the size of two ordinary city blocks, two hundred and fifty yards in length. The front, immediately along the river, is laid out into walks, planted with shrubbery. In the middle of this park, or garden, stood the church, and on one corner, immediately on the river, the clubhouse, billiard-rooms, and boat-shed.

The houses and places of business of the foreign residents front on this park, or ranging back on narrow avenues running to the wall, which shuts them in from the Chinese streets. There are, however, gates at the end of these streets opening to the Chinese city. In the im-

* Jade-stone, very costly when the real stone.

mediate vicinity of these Hongs are two short streets — "Old China" and "New China" street — in which most of the business and shopping of foreigners are done, and these streets are the most they see of Canton. The whole extent of both is not over three city squares, but in that space, and in the small shops, scarcely more than boxes, which make its boundaries, what tempting wonders greet the eyes of the newly arrived foreigner—all the elaborate carvings and ingenious workings of ivory, pearl, tortoise shell, and sandal wood, carefully wrought ebony cabinets and tables, curious bronzes, bright painted porcelain, jetty lacquer-ware out-glittering in bright blackness its gilded decorations; work-boxes and tables, chess-tables, desks, book-cases, tea-poys. There are certain gloomy little shops, in which the passer-by sees scarcely any thing to attract his attention. The brick floor and every corner, as in all the shops, is particularly neat. A few high camphor-wood chests are ranged along the sides; behind a small polished counter are a few shelves, and these are generally concealed by long shutters of black varnished boards. One or two old respectable looking Chinamen, as neat as their shops, dressed in white silk or grass cloth, are sitting quiet, as though they had nothing, and wished for nothing, to do, and yet their shops are full of riches and temptations — embroidered shawls and silks. Upon inquiring for these articles, the chests are opened, or a board or two is taken down from before the shelves, and rolls of elegant silks are unrolled for your admiration; or handsome lacquered and gilded boxes are opened, in each of which is an embroidered crape shawl; any number of these will be taken out, held up for your inspection, or tossed into intricate and confused folds; and when your curiosity is satisfied, all will be as neatly folded and replaced as though they had never been disturbed. You may leave the shop, as most of us do, without buying a thing, there will not be the least display of annoyance or vexation, and you will be "chin chinned" out with as much courtesy of manner as though you had been a profitable purchaser; and yet these same men are accustomed to fill orders for silks and shawls of from fifty to one hundred thousand dollars.

Canton streets are the narrowest possible lanes. The crowd passes in single file in opposite currents, and the foot passenger hears ever behind him loud roaring cries from coolies bearing sedan chairs, or heavy burdens depending from poles, supported at either end upon a man's shoulders. The street is not wide enough to permit these chairs and loads to pass without the foot passengers giving way, and as the coolies so laden proceed at a very rapid walk—almost a dog-trot—unless their cry is heeded, and way made for them, the force of the burden will clear its own way at the cost of all resisting objects and persons.

These narrow and crowded streets have a gay and animated appearance. The shop-signs, about a foot wide by five or six in length, are suspended vertically beside the doors. They are of bright vermillion or jet black colors, finely varnished, and lettered in gold, and presenting, in the long vista of these narrow alleys, a very gay appearance. The shops themselves are perfect cabinets, especially those of the apothecaries and perfumers, the bottles and jars being gayly ornamented, so as to give a harmonious effect to the whole arrangement. The hat stores, with their elegant and plumed mandarin hats, are also very striking. The same neatness and order prevail in every shop. Every parcel, bundle, roll, etc., has its own shelf and niche in which it is deposited when not wanted for use.

The most fascinating street, however, to the stranger, is that whose character is well indicated by its name, "Curiosity street." This is slightly wider than the streets generally, and shows to good effect its bright lines of up and down signs. The stores on this street are museums, being filled with carved ebony furniture, tables of curious marbles, inlaid work, antique porcelain, fantastic bronzes, bijouterie cut from various stones, metallic mirrors reflecting from the polished front surface certain figures molded on the back, and many other rare and curious articles.

Convenient divisions of the streets, near the intersections of others, are assigned for marketing purposes. There are no market-houses, but the supplies are set out on each side of the street, and all in the neatest and most inviting manner; the meats and plucked poultry are clean and smooth, the latter very white; the vegetables look fresh, and the crabs are moving in a lively manner under fine streams of water, which also play over the fish laid on inclined planes. The narrowness of the streets of Canton at first appears to be in bad judgment, and would not seem to be favorable to cleanliness; but the protection which is secured from the burning sun, and the chimney-like drafts created in these narrow avenues, are great advantages. Sewers pass under the streets, which are washed out by the tides of the Canton river, carrying off the filth. Each street, too, where it passes into another, has heavy gates, so that the inhabitants and police of a limited district have it under their control. In case of a riot or violence in one street, by closing the gates by which it opens into others, the disturbance is limited to its origin, and more easily suppressed, and neighboring districts avoid all implication. At night all these gates are closed, and each district shut up within itself.

It rained, rained, day and night, in heavy torrents, during my visit to Canton, and when the flood-tides came in, the streets were under water. The water was particularly deep around the foreign factories, so that at first we were prisoners during several hours of the day; subsequently, the waters were so high that the lower floors or stories were entirely overflown, and the only mode of getting about was by boats. Thousands of the Cantonese lost their lives by this flood, and even this abundance of water did not save them from the affliction of fire; for, in the midst of the rains, a quarter of boats floating on the river —flower boats—gaily gilded and ornamented—the scenes of the grossest Chinese revelry and debauchery—took fire, and lives were lost, variously estimated from hundreds to a thousand. They were chiefly those of the women who had abandoned themselves to this life of licentiousness; but there were also several young Chinese students, who had just taken high collegiate honors, and were celebrating their triumph in these dens of dissipation—a terrible passage from an intellectual glory to a death of shame.

These terrible rains were an annoyance to us, but in the future, death and desolation to awful masses from the nearly four hundred millions of Chinese. There are now lying before me on my table a mass of dirty, green greasy-looking copper coin, each one about the size of a twelve and a half cent piece, and having a hole perforated through the centre. This coin is called Cash, and about twelve hundred of them make the dollar. They are strung on bamboo fibre in masses of one hundred each, or about eight cents, and immense masses of these are piled up on the counters of the bankers, brokers and money changers. Yet this small coin, a single "cash," this, in value, infinitesimal currency, is a medium of purchase with the Chinese, and becomes an index of the low cost of subsistence. One hundred cash may be considered a large daily expense, hence a rise in the price of rice, a doubling of its value, may put the means of subsistence out of the power of many families, and doom them to starvation. Three days' rain at the season of harvest will do this; what then must be the terrible consequences of these deluges at this time? Much of the grain is just ripening, much has been cut, and is in shock in the field. Rice has already doubled in value, and the first moans of the coming agony are heard in the report, the domestics bring in, of the pinching hunger, already experienced, among their families and in their association. Although families employ a host of servants in this country, by a curious system there are none of them fed in the family, but support themselves. They generally pay so much to a comprador to supply them; from a dollar and a half to two dollars a month.

During the last scarcity, a year or two ago, the suffering became so enormous as to paralyze even the hope of relief, and those taking their evening walk in the neighborhood of the cities, would pass not unfrequently on the road side the bodies of those who had laid them down and died for want of food. With such experiences as these, how greatly must every American rejoice in the freedom of his own happy country from such dire distress. Poverty is an inconvenience, and may entail the sweating brow, but, in drought and flood, there is enough for all; where one case of starvation rouses the indignant sympathies of whole communities, and none sit down in unfeeling apathy to see entire families of whole districts, the pining infant and indurated old age, passing out of life for want of food. There must be something radically wrong in the social arrangements of humanity to produce such results, or there must be some unseen ulterior designs of Providence to be effected by such sacrifices, like the good which grows out of the volcano, the storm, the earthquake and the pestilence. One age records the misery, another the tenfold blessing growing out of it.

These food necessities of China are driving its inhabitants over the face of the earth, and who shall foretell the result? The Coolie trade is carrying Chinese and Chinese institutions into various parts of the globe. The first and a heavy wave broke upon the United States at California, and they have even been imported for the use of Kentucky iron furnaces.

About the time we went up to Canton there seemed to be an unusual degree of fermentation in the Chinese mind of that city, and an increase of its hostility to foreigners. It was the first rumbling of the storm of war which broke forth the following fall. Inflammatory placards were put before the public, urging it to expel the foreign barbarians and drive them into the sea. This aggravated state of feeling is supposed to be caused by the outrages of the Coolie trade; in which public Chinese opinion implicates all foreigners.

This feeling of animosity is always sufficiently active among the Cantonese. It is correctly set forth by the following remarks from the *Chinese Repository*:*

"Foreigners, in their limited walks, are seldom or never accompanied by native gentlemen. Few, if any respectable Chinese, are willing to be seen abroad in company with Europeans; nor is this strange when we bear in mind the fact, that wherever the foreigner goes, he is sure to be assailed with offensive language, not to say sticks, stones, brickbats, and so forth.

"It is not so at the north; but here, no matter who the foreigner may be, or where he may go, if he but appears in European costume, and goes among the common people, he is sure to have volleys of vile epithets heaped on him. By some, by most, these are overlooked or unheeded. This is the cheapest and the wisest policy. By others, they are frowned at; and by now and then one they are recompensed *vi et armis*. The use of these

* Vol. xv.

terms does not give unequivocal evidence of malice prepense or of a malicious heart; but they always grate harshly on the ear, and ought not to be allowed. *Fán kwey, fán kwey po, fán kwey tsae*, and others too vile to be repeated, are the offspring of none other than base feelings, and as such they can not be too strongly reprobated."

In the month of June immediately preceding our visit in July to Canton, the following inflammatory handbill was placarded on the walls of Canton:—

TRANSLATION.

"The absence of interruption to the peace of the country is of the same vital importance, in our opinion, as the maintenance of regularity in the avocations of its inhabitants. We now call public attention to the fact that in the province of Canton, from the earliest to the present times, barbarians have never been allowed to go into the villages. Recently, however, a set of unprincipled vagabonds have been met with, who, without any fear of shame or exposure, carry on a secret intercourse with the barbarian dogs, and combine with them in a number of ways for working out their crafty schemes. Night and day, we see them entering the villages, and occasioning so much trouble by their irregularities, that gods and men must unite in detestation of their practices. To judge of the extent of the evil to which our provincial metropolis is thus exposed, we have only to look to Shanghae and Hong Kong, and take note of the iniquities that are there committed.

"Hereafter, therefore, whenever any barbarian dogs come within our limits, we ought, by calling together our families, to maintain the dignity of our city (or province), and, bravely rushing upon them, kill every one. Thus may we, in the first place, appease the anger of Heaven; in the second, give evidence of our loyalty and patriotism;

and, in the third, restore peace and quiet to our homes. How great would be the happiness we should thus secure."

Mr. Parkes, her Majesty's Consul, himself very familiar with Canton, very kindly proffered to accompany me in a walk around the walls of the city, a distance of seven miles.

But not wishing to impose upon him a labor of so little interest to himself, I declined his offer; and not realizing the danger of the hostile spirit of the Cantonese, although on the 2d of July two English gentlemen had been attacked while rowing, I arose early on the morning of the 22d of that month, and, with a sedan chair and three coolies, started on the exploration by myself. The chair I had taken as much to have the chair-coolies as guides, as for a conveyance, and, therefore, seldom used it except in the more filthy and muddy part of the route.

The high, heavy and parapeted city wall, through most of its circuit has small Chinese shops and dwellings built beyond it, with only a narrow filthy lane between them and the wall; and at the early hour of my journey the air was loaded with all villainous smells. Beyond these disgusts, and the occasional abuse of boys and cries of *Fan kwei*, I met no disturbance in the first part of my route; and things became more interesting as I came out back of the city into green fields and neat vegetable gardens. Here, however, on the path side, I saw the repulsive spectacle of a dead Chinaman lying just as he had sunk down to die, as his attenuated form indicated, of starvation. No more attention was paid to the body by the passers-by than if it had been that of a dog or a cat.

I had nearly passed this open space, and was again approaching the dense outside settlements which the wall penetrated, and was walking ahead of my chair, when I came under the observation of a group of rascals sitting in one of the parapet towers of the wall. From the energy with which they sprang to their feet and cried out, *Fan kwei*, I anticipated some mischief, but kept on my way, not taking any notice of them, until their loud curses were substantially accompanied by missiles. A stone struck me on the head, or rather on the thick-crowned rice paper or pith hat which I fortunately had on. It cut into the half-inch thickness of this with sufficient force to show how serious the blow would have been had I worn my cloth cap. Involuntarily I turned, and shaking my fist at the party, threatened them with the vengeance of the mandarins. As soon as I walked beyond their view I got into my chair. It was well I did so, for the crowded rabble among which I now passed in the narrow lanes manifested the greatest hostility. The obnoxious cries sounded ahead of me in the streets, before the chair could be, amid the crowd, visible to those uttering them; and men would rush up ferociously to the side of the chair, as if bent on violence. But my coolies were as anxious to get rid of their burden as I was to be released from the whole party. They kept on a very fast walk, approaching a dog-trot; and I suspect if any thing had arrested the progress of the chair, a violent assault would have been made upon me. I was very much gratified to find myself, after a three hours' journey around the walls of Canton, once more safely in the sanctuary of the foreign Hongs.

This ferocity of the Cantonese is not alone manifested in regard to foreigners; it is the essential character of the whole province, as described by native writers. So prone are they represented to be to fightings and disturbances, that conflicting and hostile parties will ally themselves to drive off the authorities who would seek to interfere with their amiable and affectionate sports — parents and children, brother and brethren engaged in conflict with each other; and the inhabitants of modern Kwangtung are, equally with those described by the ancient native historians, "fond of what belongs to demons." But since my visit, the foreign factories, Old China, New China, and Curiosity streets have all disappeared before the flames of war, and the sealed streets of the City of Rams have been opened to the free foot of the Fankwei.

XXIV.

MACAO,

THE CITY OF CAMOENS.

"My cradle was the couch of Care,
And Sorrow rocked me in it;
Fate seemed her saddest robe to wear
On the first day that saw me there,
And darkly shadowed with despair
My earliest minute.

"For I was made in Joy's despite,
And meant for Misery's slave;
And all my hours of brief delight
Fled, like the speedy winds of night,
Which soon shall wheel their sullen flight
Across my grave."
—*Camoens, translated by Lord Strangford.*

"Porta de Nomo de Deos," "Porta de Amacao," "Cidado de Santo Nomo de Deos de Macao," and, as a final contraction, "Macao" alone.

In these latter days Macao, to the traveler, is Camoens, as Stratford-upon-Avon is Shakspeare. Hence my melancholy quotations from the composition of the poet, as I draw near the place which is eminent as the refuge of the fortune-stricken bard, and the locality of the solitary cave in which he nursed his muse.

I have much respect and admiration for decayed gentry;

those who show forth the dignity and refinement of past state and pomp beneath the softening influences of present privation and adversity. They present the picturesque in the social scene, as the crumbling tower, touched by the setting sun, does in the natural.

Therefore such old towns as Macao are pleasant to me, made up of great massy old houses, surrounded by grounds darkened by trees and tangled in shrubbery, which, with the crabbed independence of age, has a will of its own, above all trimmings and trainings. The families occupying these homes—pleasant, quiet people, they are, every one says—how they live, no one knows—are polished, dignified, unobtrusive, and always seeming to say, by their amiable, mild deportment, "It is affection, not pride, which makes us cling to the old home, and the associations of all that is left us—our family history." What have such people to do with the fuss, and struggle, and turmoil of the present? Their lives are in the past; they are dreamy-looking people; even the children look so, and all the family have their hopes resting upon that thoughtful-looking boy and pensive girl, who are just coming into life. By them the sinking star of the house is to close in darkness or rise to its former brilliancy.

There is a charming contrasted repose in such a quiet old town as Macao to one who, three hours before, leaves the upstart, fussy pretension of Hong Kong, where everybody is trying to be somebody, and nobody believes that anybody else is any thing.

The natural site of Macao is picturesque. It climbs up the sides and through the ravines of a group of hills, the summits of which are topped by old castles and convents.

Conspicuous among the ruins of Macao, on one of these hill-tops, is the front wall of an old church, standing out sharp and clear upon its elevation. Only this front wall remains, its ragged edges and window-openings cushioned with moss and fringed with the wild foliage which time has planted.

The stone-faced mole, or praya, which curves in front of the city, was in former days the scene of a bustling commerce, but is now the pleasant, quiet promenade of those who have nothing better to do. Besides this Portuguese and foreign Macao, there is, in the low grounds of the city, a dense mass of a Chinese town; and the combined population, Portuguese, foreign, Chinese, Malay, and mixed, is about thirty thousand. At the mouth of the Tigris, and as a sea-port of Canton before Hong Kong sprung up, Macao had a day of commercial prosperity. For over three hundred years it has been a foreign settlement. The general impression is, that it was given the Portuguese as a reward for their having suppressed piracy on the coast. But there is no evidence that there has ever been any relinquishment of sovereignty on the part of the Chinese authorities. The Portuguese claim seems to be but that of possession, at first tolerated, then permitted, and now acknowledged, in fact if not in name.

Provisions are abundant and good; the climate pleasant and healthful, and it is the chosen retreat of the business-worn merchants of Canton and Hong Kong, the refuge of those whose fortunes have been broken, and the residence of the foreign legations, all of whom make up an agreeable society, whose chief occupation and amusement is social intercourse. The English and American difficulties with the Chinese, and the blockade of Canton have somewhat revived the activity of Macao. Even in the worst times there is always some animation on the praya, and the sea which washes it, in the group of Tanka boats, and the girls who, I was going to say, *man* them, and as these girls really do the hard labor of men, the nautical verb may remain. These picturesque, white-teethed, laughing-mouthed, bandana kerchief-headed nymphs, live on the water, and make their living by landing passengers from the steamers which run between Macao and Hong Kong—and did in time past run between this port and Canton—and in rowing to the bathing places the business and dissipation-worn wretches who retreat for a few weeks to Macao to tone up. And at these bathing places, too often the unblushing immodesty of the civilized Christian belies his country and his training, and outrages those whose necessities compel them to do him service.

The commercial foreign resident of China too often looks upon the native as in no wise superior to brute beasts, and an abiding contempt of the judgment and ability of missionaries on the part of the commercial community rests partly upon the fact that missionaries will regard Chinese as human beings; partly, perhaps, upon the fact that those who make wealth their aim, have a pity for the stupidity of those who live for other objects.

The Tanka boat people are said to be of an unknown race, distinct from Tartar or Chinese. They have their own customs; the females never contract their feet; they marry among themselves. Where the men live, and how, I do not know.

Among the various kinds of barometers, natural and artificial, few are more accurate than these Tanka boat-girls. The wind is a little fresh this evening—nothing remarkable; the bay is just tossed into short curling waves—not so rough, but that the freshness rather invites you to go before it, and take a pull in a Tanka boat. You can not do it. See now what an animated scene the praya presents. Life has rushed, or is rushing, up from the water to the land. The damsels are helping each other, pulling and tugging, dragging their boats up the inclined planes of the stone jetty, and moving them on rollers up and down the praya, until they form a village of mat-roofed houses. You had better not try your water excursion now, even if you could persuade the ladies to take you. Go home, if you happen to have a home, and care any thing for it; and put in your heavy typhoon bars over doors and windows, and most likely before morning comes these bars will be bending like twigs. I have heard the winds in these tempests come dashing against the windows in gusty blasts, until the stout bars bowed and bent, as though they must violently break and open the room to the tempest. During my residence on the coast of China, there came one of these typhoons so violently and suddenly at Macao, as to grind up the boats which were caught out, and destroy many lives.

Macao rests its association with genius not alone upon the fame of Camoens. It has also that of the painter Chinnery. "Who was Chinnery?" I dare say most of you will ask. He died at Macao where he had lived for some time, an octogenarian genius, too great a man intrinsically to be little great externally. He loved the productions of his talent better than he did fame or money. With a few single touches of his pen or unstudied dashes of his brush, he produced living effects which no care and elaboration of the less gifted could effect. Many, especially in Philadelphia, may have seen the engraving by Sartain of the old Chinese merchant, Howqua, after an original painting by Chinnery. In the twelfth chapter of "The Newcomes," Thackery pays a tribute to his skill in the words of Colonel Newcome: "Chinnery himself, sir, could not hit a likeness better."

After his death the fragments of his studio and portfolio were sold at very high rates.

Regarding Macao as associated with the only great poem the Portuguese have produced, there is a harmony in its decay which makes it the fitting monument of the man who wandered, the world over, the victim of thwarted first love; who, born noble, sustained his existence by the begging of his negro slave, and ended his life in a hospital. As a broken column emblems the useful life cut short, the lonely cavern and the crumbling city may emblem such a genius in ruin, and the gloom of its existence.

In admiration for a genius which has passed from earth, we lose sight of the great alloy which may have adulterated the pure metal of that genius, and are too prone to visit with our censure and indignation the age and the people which have failed to surround its possessor with wealth, luxury and splendor proportioned to the magnitude in which the immortal abstraction has come down to us.

We remember Camoens and the Lusiad, the beggar poet and the alms-house death-bed; we generously but unjustly forget how much the poet had to do with making his own bed. According to those compensations which conserve a healthful society, his life may have naturally tended to this one end. He had devoted himself to passion, to love, to licentious love, than which there can be no perversion of the human faculties more purely selfish, no exertion of them which makes so little claim upon society, none which so physically effeminates and morally indurates the individual, and renders him unfit for the love of useful labor which has its reward in accumulating comfort.

Camoens had evidently made his bargain with life and written it out:—

"Why should I pant for sordid gain?
Or why ambition's voice believe?
Since, dearest, thou dost not disdain
The only gift I have to give.

"Time would with speed of lightning flee,
And every hour a comfort bring,
And days and years, employed for thee,
Shake pleasures from their passing wing."

Such was his bargain, and verily he had his reward.

"Gallantry," says a biographer, "was the leading trait in the disposition of Camoens. His amours were various and successful. His own words, in his last days of poverty and wretchedness, are the most forcible commentary of the result of his bargain, and how rigidly he was held to it:—

"Alas, when I was a poet I was young, and happy, and blest with the love of ladies; but now, I am a folorn, devoted wretch! See, there stands my poor Antonio, vainly supplicating fourpence to purchase a little coals. I have them not to give him."

His own verse has hinted the justice of his experience:—

"I saw the virtuous man contend
With life's unnumbered woes,
And he was poor, without a friend,
Pressed by a thousand foes.

"I saw the Passions' pliant slave
In gallant trim and gay;
His course was Pleasure's placid wave,
His life a summer day.

"And I was caught in Folly s snare,
And joined her giddy train,
But found her soon the nurse of Care,
And Punishment, and Pain.

"There surely is some guiding power
Which rightly suffers wrong,
Gives vice to bloom its little hour,
But virtue late and long."

The cave of Camoens is in the grounds of a private residence. It has been so perverted by art as to lose all that is picturesque.

During the whole of my visit to Macao, of about two weeks' duration, it rained incessantly—the whole country was deluged—the prospects of rice diminished. Faggots of wood, sold as fuel by weight, increased in heaviness by the absorption of water, and also in the amount of cash to buy it; the cries of the poor increased, and many died of starvation.

It was during this residence in Macao I came first into contact with the strange language called "Pigeon Englese" (business English). It is in use not only between Chinese and English, but between the Chinese themselves, when they speak different dialects. "Why do n't you do so and so?" I said to my boy.

"My got too much pigeon" (I have too much business).

"How can do that pigeon?" or "My no makee that pigeon," "My no savee that pigeon," equivalent to "I can not do that."

"Missus havee got?" you say to the boy at the door, when you ask for the lady of the house, and he answers you, as she may be out, or up stairs, or down stairs,

"No got"—"Havee got topside"—"Havee got downside."

"Catchee me one piece glass of water—two piece of glass of water," or "Catchee me" any thing you want brought you.

"Take this to your mistress, and tell her I will direct her what to do with it when she comes down," I said to a Chinese boy in the presence of an old resident. He laughed at the wondering look of the boy, and then translated for me: "Talkee Missus, when come downside, Doctor talkee he how can do that thing."

Upon one occasion, when living on shore, I had made arrangements with the First Lieutenant for a sampan, or Chinese boat, our mess had employed, to call every morning at a certain place and wait a few minutes for me, in case I wished to go off at that hour. The man called several mornings in succession without my going down, and thinking it labor lost, he went to the First Lieutenant and said, in a tone of vexation—

"No good my go every day. No can catchee that piece of Doctor."

"A terrible incident associated itself with my visit to Macao. A Dutch ship, the Banca, loaded with coolies, had put in there—humanity swapping black skin for yellow. She anchored in full sight, some three or four miles off the town. As I walked to my lodgings, a light arose from that ship; soon her hull and spars were lighted up by a devouring conflagration, and amid the light, the human forms were leaping from place to place, and many into the sea. In the morning her burnt hull only remained. A mutiny had occurred on board; the captain and officers trained guns from the quarter-deck and fired among the dense mass; the conflagration ensued by accident or design, and of five hundred only about one hundred and fifty escaped.

XXV.

A LOOK AT JAPAN.

On Tuesday, August 12, we again left Hong Kong for that eremitical empire which prefers seclusion and domestic quiet to the activity of commerce and the cares of money-getting. This time every thing seemed to favor our voyage, and, with wind and steam, our ship did better than she had done yet this cruise—made twelve knots an hour. With this speed we ran through the channel between the mainland and Formosa; but in two days more, as we passed the north of the island, things changed. The barometer became unsettled, the weather rainy, wind unsteady and finally ahead, reducing our speed to six knots. The sea was heavy, and compelled the closing of our little vent-holes, the air-ports. It was comfortless above, and miserably wretched, sea-sick weather below.

Whilst thus glooming along, we were roused into some excitement by seeing the surface of the sea dotted with chests or cases of something. Every glass in the ship was brought to bear upon them. In every direction they were rising and falling with the waves—carefully wrapped and strapped boxes. Our avaricious imaginations looked upon them as valuable prizes. Chests of tea they might be, and then good for nothing; but cases of silk or opium might be worth picking up. A boat was lowered, and they proved, to our disappointment, nothing more than cases of dried lichis,* the deck-load, probably, of some wrecked junk. About an hour afterwards, another object was descried from the deck, not being seen by the look-out at the mast-head. At first it was made out to be a spar—then something like a man upon it—then some thought they saw him move his arms. Man or not, he was broad off abeam of us, and it was only a chance we did not pass the object by. A boat was lowered, in which Lieutenant Williamson went after him, and at the same time the ship headed in that direction.

It was a solitary Chinaman floating upon a slender bamboo raft. As the boat approached him, he threw up his hands, bowed his head and burst into tears. He had strength enough left to step into the boat, but immediately sank beneath exhaustion and the revulsion consequent upon his rapid change of circumstances. As he came over the side, he sank on his knees to the officer of the deck who received him at the gangway; and as I reached out my hand to feel his pulse, he grasped it with both his, and gave this expression of feeling toward every officer who approached him. His hands and feet were white, and shriveled by the action of the water.

The Chinese servants we had on board understood him but imperfectly, and we could not make much of his history. He had belonged to a junk, on its way from

* An abundant and very good fruit when fresh.

Canton to Shanghae; had been out now half a month; four days ago they were overtaken by the tempest, in which all of thirty, except himself, had been lost.

Not long after this a sail was cried from the mast-head, which was seen, as we came up with it, to be a dismasted and wrecked junk. At first we supposed it to be abandoned. There were, however, twenty to thirty persons on board. The masts were all gone, except the foremast, and the rudder lost. As we came up, the poor wretches seemed very much rejoiced, and by way of expressing their thankfulness and joy, a large gong was held up and pounded vigorously. A boat was sent on board the wreck, and after some time word was brought back that all on board were anxious to quit the wreck except two men, the captain and owner, who wished to be towed into safety. Upon hearing this report, orders were given to hoist up our boat, and leave them all as they were, except that a compass was sent them. Upon seeing our movements, the people on board the wreck sent forth the most heart-rending shrieks; some threw themselves on their knees, some jumped about frantically, and some were rapidly tossing their arms into the air. All of them, including the two who had declined abandoning the wreck, joined in these demonstrations of despair. They were supposed to be forty miles from an uninhabited island, over three hundred from the mainland, and about one hundred and twenty from Formosa, which they could make.

Whilst we were engaged with this wreck two others were discovered, both apparently dismasted—one stationary, and one, apparently a lorcha, with a small sail on a foremast, was under way, and firing guns of distress.

We stood first for the stationary wreck, and found her at anchor, with the rudder and all the masts gone. There were ninety-four persons on board, including eleven women. Understood them to say they did not wish to leave the wreck, and sent them a spar and sail. The officer who took these aboard says that, when he left, the captain commenced crying, and many of the others clung to his legs. It must be considered that our communication with these distressed wretches was very imperfect. Chinamen do not understand each other, unless from the same district, and the man we used as interpreter, spoke English imperfectly. It was melancholy to think of how many misunderstood, or unexpressed hopes and sighs there were on board that wreck.

We now turned our head, just before dark, to the lorcha, which had been firing signals of distress. She had approached more near to us whilst we were engaged with the other wreck. She was an armed government lorcha, and was altogether in much better condition than either of the others; but the captain and officers were willing to abandon her, although informed they must leave every thing behind, except their clothing. They did so, and all, to the number of fifty-three, came on board of us. The vessel had a cargo of sugar, and twelve barrels of powder in her magazine. She was, however, set fire to. During the night we came up with another junk, the people of which announced by loud cries their want of assistance. They were in want of water, and had been suffering for some days for food, the destitution of water preventing the cooking of their rice. We supplied them with four hundred gallons. A typhoon had preceded us.

On Sunday, the 17th, we were rolling every thing about in heavy, rough weather. There were constant rain-squalls, and the barometer fell to 29° 40′—a very, very uncomfortable day.

Monday 18th was better, though the sea was rough. The sky was clear, and we made the Lintochin group of lofty islands, the first of the Japanese empire; and after that, with a delighful temperature, a smooth sea, a gentle breeze and cool nights—such nights for sleeping!—we ran along the Japanese empire, but a solitary sail. Here we were, on the coast of an old nation of a population greater than that of the United States, and running along it for hundreds of miles, and not a sign of that prosperity which is indicated by the word so dear to western nations—commerce. Whether they have, in such isolation, happiness, is to be determined by a decision of the question whether this is most to be found in seclusion or in the activities of life.

On the 22d, we made the harbor of Simoda, off which we fell in with a large fishing-fleet of Japanese. They were comfortable-looking boats, filled with robust men, wearing generally broad straw flats and long blue calico gowns. They crowded their boats up on both sides of our ship, and supposing they wished to put a pilot on board, we stopped, but no one could be induced to enter the ship; they waved their hands in the direction of Simoda, and altogether seemed kindly disposed. As we drew in with the land the weather became thick and rainy, but about noon we ran into the harbor of Simoda. As we entered it a boat was seen pulling out bearing two flags, the Japanese, three horizontal stripes, two white and a black one between them, and the other one our own stars and stripes. This boat brought us a pilot, a short, full-faced, respectable individual, in straw sandals, blue stockings, with a separate place for the great toe, like the thumb of a mitten, and affording a holding-place for the string which retained the sandal to the foot; cotton trowsers, tight around the ankles and loose and baggy about the legs; a short gown of similar materials crossing the breast in intersected folds. Stuck through a girdle, on his left side, was a short, black-handled, black-scabbarded sword, but his head, as every male Japanese head I saw, was most peculiarly arranged and decorated.

The top, from the forehead to a little back of the vertex, and for a breadth of three inches, was clean-shaved. The hair, black and shining, was then brought up from the back and sides of the head, and formed into a smooth spike, with the end cut even. Being bound by a thread close to the scalp, this spike made first a short bend back, and then forward, resting like a piece of polished ebony upon the shaved surface. This functionary drew from the folds of his gown a box, in which, carefully protected by several wrappers, was his commission as pilot for American vessels, given him by Commodore Perry, and printed in English and Dutch, by the "Japan Expedition press." He spoke but a few words of English, and none of us spoke Japanese, but he gave us to understand, by the waving of his hand, when we were to go to starboard, or port, or ahead.

The San Jacinto was the first propeller he had ever seen, but our visitor made known his knowledge of the difference between a side-wheel steamer and a propeller, first paddling with both hands, and then pointing with one towards the stern, and moving it in rapid circles. The Captain and he carried on an animated conversation in gestures which employed both their bodies and all their limbs, and took up half the poop deck. It far exceeded that between the Spanish professor of signs and the one-eyed butcher at the University of Glasgow.

If, perchance, a traveler sets his eyes upon any foreign country, and pretends to give an account of it, it seems to be a modern expectation that he should give a whole history of it—its laws, institutions, manners, and customs. I have no such intuitively observing faculties. It is true, I might begin learnedly with Marco Polo and Engelfeldt Kampfer, but so many of late have disinterred these antiquities, that even their names are no longer a sign of special lore. As the knowledge of Japan seems to stop with old Kampfer, I am not sure that there would be any great want of charity in hoping that the Japanese would give our Consul General and his observant secretary a cage journey throughout their sealed empire. Of course we should promptly avenge their wrongs, shake down the walls of exclusion, and make peace by shaking hands with the Siogoun on his throne in Yedo, and then, for once, we should know all about modern Japan. Indeed, the interesting revelations and observations the prisoners would be able to make, the wonderful stories they would have to tell, might go far to shorten the duration of our national anger.*

In the meantime, I must paddle my little canoe near the shore. I was only thirteen days in Simoda, and did not even see that little fishing village; and to write an account of Japan from the most thorough observation of such a point would be as though one, entirely ignorant of our language, should write his views of the United States, east, west, north and south, from a two weeks' residence at Ocracoke Inlet.

What I could do to see something, I did. I studied the country in the only place where the people and the government could be seen together, and their characteristic relations developed—in the market-place, the bazaar—in Japanese, the *Goyosho.*

But we have not yet got in. I left the Captain and the dumpy pilot gesticulating on the poop deck.

As the ship ran into the harbor, its picturesque beauties called forth general admiration. The bay, bounded by a chain of pointed mountains, clothed with vegetation to their very summits, and the steep plains and valleys running up between these mountains are neatly cultivated in

* We are glad to learn that Mr. Harris has, by his diplomatic tact and skill, penetrated to the imperial residence in honorable freedom, and done away with the prospect of cage-traveling in the future.

terraces or shelves, rising one above another, and diminishing in breadth until they terminate in the deep angle of the nook. At the mouth of the bay we passed a rugged, rocky island, overgrown with trees, and having a cave, into which the sea rushed, arching through it; and in the middle of the bay a small, craggy rock looked as though it had been designedly thrown there as an ornamental support for the shrubbery which dressed without concealing it. At first we began to be suspicious as to the existence of any town, but presently a small village, with several junks lying in front of it, made its appearance in a nook to the right hand. This was the village of Kakizaki, at the south-eastern end of the bay; as we ran a little further in, we observed the low roofs of Simoda in a recess of the bay opposite to Kakizaki, concealed by a projecting point, and defended from the encroachments of the sea by a long, well-built, hewnstone breakwater, with a narrow channel between one end and the rocky shore, for the passage of small boats. About half way between the two towns, we dropped our anchor in nine fathoms water.

Soon after, a boat came off from the town, bringing a large number of Japanese—several persons of rank, with their attendants. Nothing of western costume can give an idea of the style of a Japanese gentleman's dress, unless it may be that of a plain, neat, but richly-dressed Quakeress, just attired for a street promenade. The pantaloons, of silk, rich in texture, but plain and soft in color and figure, have each leg broad and ample as a petticoat itself. Their colors are lead or dove-color, tea-green, rich browns, or fine blue and white stripes. These petticoat trowsers meet at the waist a mantle or vest of silk, which crosses the shoulders and breast in intersecting oblique folds, like what is called a surplice dress. Over this is worn a loose short gown of fine transparent silk gauze, generally black or dove-colored. The sleeves hang very large and loose. On each sleeve and on the shoulder of this gown, woven in white, is a delicate figure, a circle inclosing some device, a lozenge, three petals, or cross bars; the coat-of-arms of the individual; the same device is worked upon the mantle of his retainers. A long and a short sword, stuck through a girdle on the left side, the stiff, clumsy-looking spike lying along the centre of the head, and the stockings and sandals already described complete the costume. The manner and countenances of these men—indeed, of all the Japanese gentry I saw—were those of intelligent, polished gentlemen. They exhibited that kind of quiet, subdued courtesy which is the effect of excessive training, and the habitual suppression of emotions—that manner which is so characteristic of the polished clergy of the Romish church. The smiles which constantly lighted their countenances set forth a display of beautifully white and regular teeth. It is strange that those who can prize and appreciate such teeth, should tolerate the artificially blackened teeth of the married women.

As an illustration of their courteous deportment, and of their mode of salutation, I saw two gentlemen on shore about to pass each other—acquaintances I suppose. One rested his hands upon his circumflexed knees, and, with gracious smiles, lowly bowed his body forward; the other immediately did the same thing, each bow was repeated, and they passed on. Such is not only the salutation of inferiors to superiors, but the exchange of courtesy between equals.

Before leaving China for Japan we had entertained some anticipations of getting some of the pretty lacquer-work bijou for which the Japanese are celebrated, and have been from the earliest period of the acquaintance of European nations with them. Our hopes were not very sanguine, as some British officers with whom we made acquaintance had been very unsuccessful. One of their party had succeeded in procuring an old comb, or piece of a comb, the only thing obtained. Among the first inquiries made of our Japanese visitors was as to the chances of buying any of their productions, and the answer received was, "Goyosho." In the meantime, some of our officers, who had been visiting the shore, had accidentally discovered the Goyosho, and came off with such brilliant accounts of its lacquer-ware and mother-of-pearl inlaid articles, it seemed as though they had discovered some store-house of treasures in a fairy land. Curiosity was very much excited, and, with others, I took an early opportunity of visiting the shore. The "Goyosho" was built on the edge of a canal, walled with hewn stone, on one side of the town. It consisted of a range of one-storied wooden buildings, inclosing a hollow square, filled in with loose, small-sized pebble-stones. The front of the establishment was occupied as a town-hall, or rooms for the transaction of public business, and opened upon a yard similarly paved with loose pebble-stones, and shut in by gates from the street. The entrance to the commercial part of the establishment was on one side; and, immediately at the right hand, upon entering, was a small room for the porter or gatekeeper, messenger, guard, or whatever he might be. On the left hand was a much larger room, with broad lounges covered with matting, for the midday repose of those visiting the bazaar. At the entrance to this room sate a vessel of drinking-water, with a new smooth white pine cover, over which lay a wooden dipper, and alongside of it several small porcelain cups. The remainder of three sides of the "Goyosho" were shops entirely open in front to the court-yard, and filled with the finest lacquer-work of Japan. It was ranged along the open front side of the shops, and piled away at the back on shelves to the roof, with a convenient aisle or avenue between the front and back collection. The articles consisted of black and gold, black and inlaid scarlet maroon, gilded and inlaid boxes and cabinets, of various shapes and sizes, in value from fifty cents up to two hundred dollars. Lacquered cups, bowls, and waiters, of various sizes, shapes, and colors; maroon, scarlet, green and gold, predominating. There was also a small collection of silks and of porcelain.

The front or fourth side of the building, it has been said, was used as a public hall; but at the back where it opened upon the court-yard, was an elevated covered floor or platform, which was the office of the Goyosho. Here the clerks, secretaries, treasurer and interpreters sat on their heels, their legs folded under them, with their desks and writing apparatus. Next to this office, between it and the gatekeeper's room, was another small and elevated room, reached by several hewn stone steps. The floor was covered smoothly with white matting; around the sides were new white-pine benches, their legs not resting rudely upon the matting, but let into wooden bottoms. These benches were covered with matting framed tightly over them. On each bench was a shining black lacquered tray, on which was a porcelain jar containing coals of fire, a smaller jar to receive the ashes of cigars or pipes, and between them a small lacquer stand with a porcelain tea-cup. This was a room for rest and refreshment. Indeed, every ordinary want and necessity was neatly and commodiously provided for by these Japanese; and I have been thus minute in describing this building as it does much towards indicating certain characteristics. The whole was new and fresh, the timber was soft and satiny white pine, covered with black paint where exposed to the weather, and roofed with dark blue and white tiles with ornamental edges. All was neat, quiet, clean, fresh and toy like.

This place was our principal resort during our stay in

Simoda, not only for the purpose of purchasing, but on account of the beauty of the display and the comforts and conveniences of the establishment. Up to the last day of our stay in Simoda, a lively excitement of purchasing Japanese lacquer-ware was kept up; almost every boat-load of officers on leave made their way to the Goyosho, and every returning boat was piled with boxes, the result of their bargains, while in the evening our apartment was brilliant in the exhibition and comparison of the results of the day's work. The Goyosho had an additional charm from the fact of its being the only place in which could be seen at once the natural Japanese character, its modifications by their institutions, and the searching despotism of the government. The inconsistency of aristocratic distinctions being made to depend arbitrarily upon the business pursuits of individuals, was fully shown in this place. In the distinction of classes, merchants or traders are among the lowest; they may attain the honor of wearing one sword, but can not pretend to that of petticoat trowsers, and yet the high functionaries of the empire, the empire itself is a petty trader. In our dealings at the Goyosho, if any thing occurred out of the written line, involving it may be only a few cents, the matter was referred from the officers to the mysterious building in front, in which were the princely governors.

The mode of transacting business was as follows: every article in the shops was labeled with two labels, upon which the price was written in Japanese and in our own figures. No payments were made to the person from whom the article was purchased. The purchaser wrote his name upon the parcel, the shop-tender then tore off the labels, and pasted one firmly upon the parcel, the other was taken possession of by a secretary, who made a record of the transaction in a book. The purchaser and the free label were then sent to the office, where the purchaser, when he had completed his business in the shops, or at any time, was informed of the aggregate of his account, and upon making payment, received his articles, which, if of sufficient bulk, were sent by attendant porters to the landing.

It sometimes happened that in the small shops of the town, we saw articles which we wished to buy. It could only be done by having them sent to the "Goyosho," where they were priced, labeled and paid for. Notwithstanding this rigid system the people and the officers seemed to be free, genial and social. They were all fond of laughing and joking with us, and readily made themselves acquainted with our names. As I was a daily visitor to the place, when I entered of a morning and as I passed through the shops, every one seemed to pride himself upon calling me "Doctor," or "Doctor Bood." Several of them asked me to prescribe for them, and having done so in one case I gave the man a written prescription to take on board ship and get the medicine. In about an hour he brought it back and handed it to me. I signed that he was to keep it and take it on board ship. He still insisted upon returning it, and as a reason for doing so, bowed his head and made the sign of an axe passing through his neck. The argument was powerful and conclusive. I took back my prescription. Among themselves they appeared to be merry and cheerful; none of that gloomy depression which is the general result of such a despotism. Both from the functionaries of the office and from the shops in which there were several persons together, there would come shouts of laughter during the intervals of business. In fact, the Japanese present an anomaly in the contrast between the natural character of the people and the nature of their government; a contrast so great that the despotism of centuries has not been able to deaden their lively geniality. It is not difficult to see that almost every Japanese has two characters, that which is official and that which is personal. The official is a routine performance duly acted. This dual character would account for the contradictory accounts of them given by different writers, indeed by the same writer, as is the case with old Kampfer himself. Take the man in his official relations, he is distrustful, jealous, suspicious, cautious, unyielding, taciturn, cruel; while personally he is social, kind, trusting, communicative. I noticed this double existence in our diplomatic negotiations. Minute, earnest, exacting in carrying out the wishes or instructions of the government, a British or an American statesman would patriotically identify himself with his cause, but the Japanese, his business being over, has no personal interest in the matter. This enables them to be cool and equable during the most interesting and important discussions. It leads also to an inference that any supreme government set up in place of that of the Siogoun, would receive the sanction of the Japanese masses. This is, however, taking a very broad look through a very narrow opening.

The Japanese are an honest people — and this same Goyosho showed at once their personal honesty and personal confidence, with their official distrust. After a visit from any number of Japanese, no one would think of missing the smallest article; indeed, none could be induced to accept the most trifling present; and, upon one occasion, I discovered after leaving the Goyosho, that I had received thirty-seven cents too much change; an unusual thing, as they were generally exact. Upon returning the following day, I took it to the office, but as the interpreter was not there, I could not make them understand why I returned it, and they refused to receive it. I pushed it towards them, and they pushed it back to me, until I walked off, leaving it upon the floor; when, in an hour or so, the interpreter came in, and hunted me up in one of the shops to know why I returned the money. They seemed to have no distrust as to leaving us alone in the shops, with the innumerable articles lying around, a degree of confidence which strangers do not expect nor receive in their own country — in World Exhibitions, for instance, where a policeman's eye is on every individual person and thing.

While these private transactions and familiarities were going on between the officers and the Japanese, the functionaries were arranging for an interview with the Consul General. The Commodore was out of health, and could not be present, and yet the authorities seemed earnestly desirous that he should be. A day was appointed, but the Governor was taken suddenly with a sore foot, and the day was postponed until Monday, August 25th. I omitted to mention, that immediately upon our arrival the Consul General dispatched his communications to the government at Yedo, but was told it would take ten days to receive a reply, as the post went afoot. As the distance was only about eighty miles, we knew this to be a delay designed for a purpose, and were well assured that no action would be taken, of any kind, by the authorities of Simoda without instructions from Yedo. However, the day above mentioned was an important one in the annals of Japan, inasmuch as a courteous and amicable reception was given to a resident representative of a foreign power, and that power one of the youngest among nations. Mr. Harris was accompanied by Captain Bell and a party of officers of the San Jacinto, who were received in the front building of the Goyosho, and entertained by a repast of confectionery, soups, tea and sacké.

A week after this a reception was appointed for Commodore Armstrong, whose health had improved. The Consul General and a suite of officers, in all the glittering decorations of a full dress uniform, accompanied him.

We entered the council house by a hall, covered with

fine white matting, almost too neat and white for the tread of our boots. Indeed, in the Japanese private houses, they put off their shoes in a small area before treading upon the clean, neatly matted floor. One side of the upper end of this hall was screened off by a folded screen of gilded paper, and to the left of this we entered a light and airy room, almost toy-like in its delicate structure, and the superlative of Japanese nicety. The peculiar, soft, white wood used for the posts, ceiling joists, and window-frames, smoothly worked, was fresh and unpainted. Whenever bolt-heads came through, they were covered with neatly chased hexagonal brass nuts. The floor joists over head were exceedingly delicate — not thicker than the wrist. Light window-frames, covered with a silky, white, semi-transparent paper, formed the windows, but these were now freely opened to admit the air. The dead wall of the room was covered by a delicate light-colored, figured paper. Down the centre of the room were two lines of benches, with a red serge framed tightly over them. In front of one row of these benches were low tables, and upon each table a black lacquered tray, upon which lay two new, long-stemmed, brass pipes, a porcelain cup with fire, another for ashes, and a small lacquered box of tobacco.

A new Governor, we were informed, had just arrived from Yedo; in fact, an officer of high rank, especially commissioned for the circumstances of our case.

We were met at the entrance of this room by the Governors and their suite, and invited to the seats in front of the low table. The Japanese officers placed themselves, with their limbs bent under them, on the benches opposite; back of these was a row of inferior persons, note-takers, etc., and on the floor, at a distant end of the room, was a throng of domestics, all similarly resting upon their bended legs. These domestics appeared, from their costume and swords, to be young men of rank. At the upper end of the space between the Japanese officials and ourselves, was the raised seat of the interpreter, who, in this instance, appeared to be a gentleman of rank — the intelligent, polished, and courteous Moriamna. Thus placed, the council was ready. The servants immediately set before us porcelain cups of tea on small lacquer stands, and the talk began.

The Governors opened in Japanese. Moriamna bowed his head toward them, and at the conclusion of the speech, gave his head a lower inclination, and, turning to Mr. Heuskin, who sat next the Consul General, delivered the message in Dutch; this gentleman again delivered it in English. It was an inquiry after the health and well being of General Pierce. This being appropriately answered, another message came through the same channels — an inquiry after the health of the Consul General. Then the same ceremony in regard to the Commodore, and, finally, in regard to all of us. This important courtesy having been duly reciprocated, and the new Governor having informed us that he was very much broken and worn with his journey from Yedo, and I having offered my professional services to restore him to a state of health and vigor, some beautiful confectionery was placed before each of us, every parcel precisely alike. There were two oval cakes of sugar and rice-flour, one white and one pink, beautifully molded with flowers, resting against candies formed like the plume of a Highland bonnet, and these again supported by a scroll of candy. There was also a square mass of greenish jelly, sanded over with sugar-plums. With the parcel was a piece of thin, fine, silky paper, as strong as cloth itself, and a bundle of long filaments, some white and some red, bound together in the middle by a band of thin silvery metal. I, at first, thought these long threads were a kind of flexible candy.

It is a Japanese custom for each guest to have sent with him a part of the feast of which he has partaken, and the ornamental part was intended to be borne away, the strong paper to wrap it in, and the white and red filaments were paper twine to bind the parcel.

All this ceremonial conversation, though it had amounted to nothing, going through so many languages, had used up the morning. After this confectionary we were served with a lacquer tray placed before each gentleman, and containing several fine lacquer-covered cups of soup of various kinds—fish-soup, egg-soup, vermicelli, craw-fish. There were also small lacquer plates of delicious fried eels, and others of pickles. The plate of each guest had precisely the same articles, of the same size and shape, and the same arrangement. The implements for conveying this food to our mouths were two smooth new white chopsticks, and one thin small black lacquer fork. The Japanese were amused at our awkwardness, and very kindly offered to show us the mode of using these novel tools. During the feast, it was announced through the interpreters, that the new governor was an officer who had come from Yedo, with full powers to enter into any negotiations with the Consul General which might be necessary. They seemed disposed to enter upon business immediately, and said, "They knew very well that the treaty provided for the residence of a consul at Simoda, whenever either nation might think it necessary. What," they asked, "renders it necessary now?" Mr. Harris replied that he was not in the secrets of his government, and could not say why it had availed itself of the treaty to send a consul general to Japan. This reply having gone back, they then said, "We know you cannot be in the secrets of your government; but we think you must know the particular reason why you have been sent here."

Mr. Harris said he could only reply that he came under the treaty for such duties as are exercised by consuls in other countries—to provide for shipwrecked and distressed seamen, to decide differences between the commander and men of ships, and to prevent our lawless sailors from violating Japanese laws. This did not seem to satisfy them, and they answered that by the treaty they had agreed to treat kindly shipwrecked seamen, and unless there was a doubt of their sincerity, a resident consul was unnecessary.

They then turned to the Commodore, and asked if he had any power to treat respecting the residence of the Consul General. He replied, "None at all;" he commanded the military, and had received orders to bring Mr. Harris to Simoda, and, he added emphatically, "leave him there." They then inquired of the Commodore if he knew any reasons why Mr. Harris had been sent there? He answered, none other than the provision of the treaty. He was next asked if he did not think it would be better to receive a statement of their reasons for not receiving Mr. Harris, and take him away until some future time when more urgent reasons might exist. The Commodore replied that he had no discretion but to obey his orders. They asked if he would take a communication from them to the United States government. He would, he said, take any thing, but it must come through Mr. Harris. Some little difference had arisen during the conference as to the reading of a clause of the treaty. The Japanese had their copy before them. Mr. Harris remarked to them that this was a visit of ceremony, a call of the Commodore upon the Governors, and not one of business; that he had not come prepared for any negotiation, but would meet them at any time they might appoint for that purpose.

The Japanese functionaries, however, seemed to be

like men who had an appointed task, and were anxious to rid themselves of it. They would frequently, before putting a question or proposition, read from a paper, which one of them kept before him; and during what appeared to us must be to them the most earnest and interesting part of the discussion, they would converse in a pleasant, smiling manner with each other, and the most earnest arguments passed through Moriamna, without in the least disturbing the placidity of his countenance, or ruffling the courtesy of his demeanor. It was probable that these officials had instructions from the imperial government to get rid of the American Consul General if they could without an infraction of treaty obligations, and if they could not, to make the best of the circumstances.

After this skirmishing had been protracted for some hours, and they found no diversion in their favor could be expected from the Commodore, they apologized for having detained him so long, and suggested that he and the officers might at their pleasure take their leave, but would be glad if Mr. Harris and his secretary would remain and continue the negotiation. This was assented to. Mr. Harris requested me to remain over with him. The remainder of our party took their leave, accompanied by attendants, carrying their bundles of confectionery. After we had resumed our seats and refilled our pipes, the conversation was resumed by their stating general objections to receiving a Consul General. They said that Simoda had suffered very much by earthquakes; and if an American Consul came, a Russian and a French one might come, and this would involve a great deal of trouble and expense.

They were told that Simoda was the place of their own appointing, that any agreement they had with the Russian and French was of their own volition, and should not interfere with our admitted claims, and that no expense would be imposed upon them by our consulate, which bore its own expenses. It was then objected that there were additional articles appended to the treaty which had not been ratified, that when these articles were ratified, an ambassador would come out with them, and after that, it would be time enough to receive a consul. It was replied that those articles were merely explanatory of the treaty and needed no ratification; but that if they were, no ambassador would come with them, as they would be sent to the Consul General; and this was another of his functions, the transmission of communications of his own government to that of Japan. They now said they would receive Mr. Harris temporarily, and as there were no quarters suitable for him, they would accommodate him in the temple at the opposite village; but they would in the meantime forward their objections to our government, and asked if he would forward such a communication. Mr. Harris said, certainly, he was bound to forward such communications, even if they were complaints against himself. The inquiry was now made as to whether a verbal request of the Governors, addressed to the United States Secretary of State, would not be sufficient, and Mr. Harris told them no. They had a written communication fromMr. Marcy, the Secretary of State, and it was usual with western nations to acknowledge such communications in writing. This had not been done. They replied, it was not a Japanese custom, and as a high officer had been sent to receive the Consul General and to make a verbal communication to the United States through him, they thought this sufficient. (I understood them to intimate the most respectful mode.) They suggested that a written communication from the two Governors would be all that was necessary; but were told that the Secretary of State only corresponded with supreme governments, and no request preferred by any subordinates would receive any attention. They said Mr. Marcy's letter said Mr. Harris was to enter into new negotiations, and they wanted to know what these negotiations were. Here was the secret of their perseverance in asking what were the reasons of Mr. Harris's coming, and showed their dread of new business and demands being thrust upon them, and they were evidently little suprised at being informed that this was merely a general allusion to such business as might arise in the future, and had in view no definite point at the present time. In stating this, Mr. Harris instanced that he might open negotiations for a change of consular residence to some other places. This gave a little uneasiness, and they asked, at once, if any such changes would be made by him without the sanction of the Japanese government. He told them, certainly not, it must be a matter of mutual negotiation and consent.

During all this long, triply-translated discussion, there were as many changes of cloud and sunshine as mark an April day; but as the business drew toward a close, and difficulties gradually disappeared, the sunshine of cheerfulness and good humor rested abidingly upon us all. The Japanese felt the satisfaction of men who had done their duty, and the Consul General had done his, and accomplished his ends. I, having nothing to do but look on, had smoked comfortable pipes of mild tobacco, and drank small cups of sweet saki, and kept as calm and placid as Moriamna himself.

The Japanese finally remarked that Mr. Marcy's letter said the consul was treated with the same consideration and granted the same privileges as were usual among civilized nations. They said they were entirely ignorant as to what these were, and would be glad to be informed. This was done. They made frequent apologies, during the negotiation, for its length, the necessary tediousness of translating, and hoped that no offense would be taken at any of the questions, as they were ignorant upon the subjects under discussion, and asked many things only for information. We offered them the most positive assurances that we were delighted with their urbanity and glad to answer all their inquiries. They hoped that Mr. Harris would not object to their visiting him when he got settled, and talking over matters in his own residence. Upon the contrary, Mr. Harris would only be too happy to see them at any time, socially and on business, and they in turn assured Mr. Harris that every thing should be done to aid him in making himself comfortable; and amid smiles and bows we parted company for the day.

The Commodore, previous to his departure, had invited the Governors and their suites to visit our ship on the coming day. They came off, to the number, attendants, sword-bearers and all, of about thirty. They partook freely and with great zest of the entertainment set before them; ate ham, tongue, cold chicken, lobster-salad, hard bread, soft bread and cake; drank ale, white wine, champagne, brandy; laughed, talked merrily, jested and played practical jokes. Mustard and sweet oil seemed curiosities to them, but they used them freely. I mention these things to show that their natural appetites do not confine them to rice alone, and that they are glad to throw off official stiffness and reserve. The feast being ended, they drew from the folds of their fine silks, squares of paper, in which, after asking permission, they wrapped up fragmentary specimens of their entertainment. They partook of our viands with a complimentary vigor which chopsticks alone would not supply; and though they left us, gentlemanly and proper in deportment, their gleaming eyes and rubicund noses were inconsistent with the supposition of totally abstinent principles.

For their entertainment the crew had been exercised at quarters.

During these exchanges of hospitality business had not been neglected. The Japanese had been industriously preparing the allotted temple for the reception of the Consul General, and our carpenters had been actively preparing a suitable flag-staff for the first American flag which was to fly as a permanent emblem on the shores of Japan.

Soon after the departure of our Japanese guests, the Consul General and his secretary took their final leave of our ship; and early on Wednesday morning, September 3d, the Captain, Boatswain and Carpenter went ashore to raise this memorable and now completed staff. The temple before which it was to be planted stood in a nook of the mountain a little back of the village. Its roof could be seen rising against the dark-green background, somewhat above the houses of the village. An accident happened in the first attempt to raise the pole. It fell, breaking the cross-trees, so that new ones had to be made. Those who read omens, and read them gloomily, might interpret this into one of bad significance; but early in the afternoon the flag-staff, perfect in all its parts, rose triumphantly to its place, and we saw from our ship the stars and stripes fluttering in the breeze before the Japanese temple—the Consul General having the satisfaction of running it up with his own hand. May it there be the emblem of the final triumph of our country and its policy over all preceding obstacles, disappointments and difficulties.

This event accomplished, our working party returned to the ship, and we immediately got under way, exchanging a parting salute with the Consul General by a mutual dipping (slightly lowering and hoisting) of the ensigns. As we stood out to sea and left our flag waving among the trees on the shores of this sealed empire, it was a sight suggesting many speculations into the far future, and reaching even beyond a period when, as has been suggested, these isles of Japan may be to the nations of the Pacific what those of Great Britain are to Europe.

It is almost amusing to see the minute precision with which the Japanese carry out their treaty stipulations.

They agree to furnish us provisions, and hence the government itself undertakes the supply, and sent us fowls, which, by the way, were yellow and hard, as if lacquer was diffused through their substance.

They agree to furnish us coal, and there was the coal when we arrived all nicely done up in sacks on the wharf; and first-rate coal it was, the best we had used during the cruise. We were to be permitted to trade, and here was the government Goyosho, with its splendid collection of lacquered wares, kept ready for the arrival of our ships. They agreed to receive a consul, and although, when he came, they did not regard him as a very acceptable addition to the empire, yet we left him and his flag successfully planted on the beach at Simoda.

By some mistake or oversight in the Perry treaty, our money, in relation with that of Japan, was depreciated two thirds. As one of the good results of Mr. Harris's residence, this mistake has been corrected, and Count Pontiatine, the Russian envoy who visited there since this arrangement, told me that he had made contracts with them before the change of valuation in foreign silver, but this was effected before he made his payments. He offered to pay them at the valuation which existed when his contracts were made, but they insisted on receiving only the one third.

I am sorry to testify that their modesty is not equal to their honesty, as Simoda is provided with public bathing-houses in which both sexes meet freely, and in the public eye, without any incumberings of costume.

In most beautiful weather we steamed away from Simoda and down the green mountain shores of Japan, an object of great curiosity to the Japanese cruising off the land in their junks, and as the San Jacinto's dark body foamed through the waters without a sail set, and rolling forth volumes of black smoke, she presented a sight for many an evening's future gossip in the mountain villages.

XXVI.

SHANGHAE.

When we left the south of China, floods, we saw, were drowning out the people, overflowing their fields, and destroying their rice. In the north, in the vicinity of Shanghae, parching drought produced the same desolation, and as we passed through the Yellow Sea we had the evidence of this drought in the clouds of locusts which darkened the air—destruction born of destruction. We were surrounded by them. Although the breeze was not fresh, these insects seemed to have no control of themselves. Some were moving sideways in their struggle with the wind, and some with fluttering wings ridiculously moving backwards. They fell in great numbers upon our decks, and invaded our apartments below.

The drought had lasted all the summer, notwithstanding all the expedients resorted to by the people and the authorities to bring it to an end. Even the following were not of any avail:

"The military intendant (the *tau-tai*) and the chief magistrate of this district (the *chi-hien*) go daily in person, once in the morning and once in the afternoon, first to the temple of the Guardian Deity of the city within the walls, and then to the pavilion of the Three Magnates, situated outside the south gate of the city, to pray to the gods, to communicate to Heaven's court (these their petitions, so that the Heavenly Powers) shall speedily send down genial showers, and moisten the earth below. They have also issued orders, strictly forbidding the people to slaughter any living creatures, until after plentiful showers shall have fallen.

"Among the people resident in the city, each family now keeps erected at the front door of the house a tablet, on which is inscribed—

"TO THE DRAGON KING OF THE FIVE LAKES AND THE FOUR SEAS.

"Before this tablet, on an altar of incense, they lay out their sacrificial offerings to propitiate the gods. Close by their doors they also set up small yellow flags, on which they have had written sentences like the following:

"'With sincerity of the heart we pray that abundance of rain may descend.'"

A PROCLAMATION.

"This year a literary gentleman by the name of *Hu*, belonging to the department of *Tsing-chau* in Shantung, on the third day after he had died rose to life again, and said he had seen the holy sovereign Prince, *Kwan*, who delivered the following Mandatory Instructions, viz.,

"The judgments of Heaven are now going abroad, and this year, either by the sword and soldiers, or by disease and sickness, eight or nine tenths of the people are to perish. If, however, they will engage and depend on the Great Mistress of the Southern Sea and the Great White Star Prince, then these two divinities will interpose their strength to effect a deliverance, will scrutinize the good and evil deeds of the people, and if they find these nearly balanced, then the threatened judgments from Heaven shall in some degree be diminished.

"On the 9th, 19th, and 29th of each month, the people must burn incense toward the south; and kneeling and worshiping, they must swear that they will be true and faithful, dutiful to their parents and affectionate to their brothers; and likewise will abstain from the slaughter of all living creatures, and perform rightly every appropriate duty; then their petitions may be heard, and pardon and indulgence granted to them.

"If they will write out and circulate a single copy of these instructions, a single person shall have protection; if ten copies, then a whole family shall have protection; and if a hundred, then a whole neighborhood. On the other hand, if knowing these instructions they will not circulate them, then they shall perish, and so receive the punishments their sins deserve.

"Written and circulated on the 6th day of the 6th month of the 6th year of Hienfung (July 7th, 1856)."

The mode of one's introduction to person or place has ever much to do with our estimate of his or its character, so little is our judgment independent of circumstances imperceptibly influencing it. That large and influential portion of the body, which manages the business of our daily existence, is not disposed to yield the influence of its practical importance and coarse avocations to the aristocratic importance of the head and heart.

As good dinner tables make agreeable companions and give eloquence to diplomatic arguments, so an abundant and choice supply of provender wins one to speak kindly of the locality in which it is found. If any one who knows the place thinks my estimate of Shanghae enthusiastic and not sufficiently moderated by the evil I may speak of it, let him consider the circumstances under which I first made its acquaintance.

In October, 1856, we had, with the exception of a few days in Japan, been a year wilting, wearing and wearying amid tropical and summer heats—diluting our vapid existence with weak and insipid fruits. With the preparation of these experiences we came to the refreshing and invigorating coolness of the autumn atmosphere of Shanghae. Although the locust flight seemed unfavorable, that ended a day or two after our arrival, and rain came on. There was an eloquence which spoke of home, in the putting down of woolen carpets, and the putting up of stoves and winter curtains in the houses of our new but hospitable friends. The agreeable associations were continued in the streets, where we met long-cued Chinamen vending strings of wild pigeons, wild ducks, snipe and golden-necked pheasants. In such a relation the Chinamen looked picturesque, and in one's heart arose an argument for the unity of race, founded on the sympathy of "Foreign Devil" and "Celestial" for such respectable birds—the more respectable when introduced to us, as they were, assoiated with the hospitality of our resident countrymen; and continued in my acquaintance in the agreeable home to which I was welcomed by Mr. F. D. Williams.

Shanghae comes upon one as a magical creation—that is, upon one no better informed than I was in regard to it, and few can be familiar with it, for the place is just born. Most of us are accustomed to the rapidity with which cities spring up in our new West. But even in the genial and fertile atmosphere of "Young America," and with the stimulants of progression, they have the modesty to start with the infantile existence of villages; but Shanghae, as a city of foreigners, seems to have sprung at once into adult palatial strength and glory. Twelve years ago the place of which I am now writing was a swamp, dotted over with filthy bamboo-built Chinese hovels. Now, for a mile along the gentle curve of a broad river, by nearly the same extent in breadth, is a city of large, commodious and elegant residences. These houses are generally built in what is called a "compound," a wall-enclosed plat of garden and shubbery—the walls forming the boundaries of the streets, which are opened upon by carriage gates, guarded by porters' lodges. The streets themselves are of comfortable width, neat and clean, and bearing such significant, wholesome, intelligible names as "Mission Street," "Church Street," "Bridge Street," "Custom House Lane," painted on the corners. A sense of security is given by the appearance, in all parts of the town, of a uniformed foreign police.

The "Bund," a wide, pleasant promenade and carriage drive, curves along the river's bank in front of the city, and is active during the early hours of the day with business, and cheerful in the afternoon with equestrians, carriages and promenaders. The river itself, at each of our visits to Shanghae, was crowded with shipping, chiefly bearing the flags of England and America, but with a sprinkling of those of other nations—the elephant banner of Siam being among the more numerous, and indicating the growing trade between these countries. Ten of our own beautiful clippers, of over a thousand tons each, graced the harbor at the time of this our first visit.

The part of the foreign settlement of Shanghae at which we have now glanced, although made up of all nations, is called the "English Settlement." It extends from the Yan-kin-pang creek on the south, down the river to Su-chau creek, or Woosung river, on the north. Crossing Su-chau creek, the shore runs almost at right angles to its former direction, and here, with an indefinite limit of expansion in all directions, is what is called the "American Settlement," so called, I presume, because it is the location of the American Episcopal, and part of the American Presbyterian mission, being also, accidentally, the residence of the American consul. Again, above the "English," or central settlement, from the south shore of the Yan-kin-pang creek to the walls of the old

Chinese city of Shanghae, is a waste of sparsely settled territory, over which flies the French flag, called the "French Community," and particularly ticketed in its nationality by a sign-board, labeled "La Concession Française."

These national designations are instructive, as showing the narrow and exclusive spirit in which a little band of foreigners will attempt to perpetuate their peculiarities and divisions upon the little spot of the empire of China upon which they have planted themselves; instructive, also, as showing how such bigotry is swept away by the broad stream of a common necessity and a common prosperity. In the first settlement of this foreign community, the British authorities, somehow, from habit, perhaps, had the idea that the exclusive jurisdiction centered in them; and it was required that all the purchasers of property from the original Chinese owners should have their deeds made out and registered at the British consulate. These deeds contained a clause saying that the property was to be held subject to the regulations of the British consulate. No one paid much attention to the meaning of this provision, thinking it was all a matter of course; but one of these regulations was, that none but the English flag should fly upon this territory.

Messrs. Griswold and Cunningham, two members of the American house of Russell & Co., held, in succession, the office of United States consul, and had the firmness and spirit to resist these pretensions. The former gentleman planted a tall flag-staff, and from it he flew the flag of his consulate. The British consul ordered it to be hauled down, which was refused. Subsequently Mr. Cunningham, being consul, informed his countrymen that these deeds need not pass through the British consular office, but through that of the United States. This controversy, as far as I could learn, was carried on in no improper or captious spirit, but that of functionaries who gave each other credit for convictions of right. It was referred by the British consul to his home government for decision, and that government, in a just and expedient view of the case, assented to the claims of the United States consuls. The result is the elegant and prosperous city which has so rapidly sprung into existence, and over which, since that contest, fly the flags of many nations.

It was said that the French consul, at this day, insists upon some such exclusive jurisdiction over "La Concession Française." With the teaching of this past experience before him, one can hardly credit such a statement. If any demand for occupying the French Concession arises, of course such pretension must yield to it; and unless French commerce increases beyond its now two or three ships a year, that exclusive territory must remain a waste. One patriotic French house has now sate itself down in the "Concession," and, notwithstanding all its attractions of French importations, one may live, as many do, a long time in Shanghae, and not hear of its existence.

There are only about four hundred foreigners in this whole settlement; but there are more than twenty thousand Chinese, who have built or rented European houses in this foreign settlement, and come under the government of the foreigners, who, by a mixed council, control the whole place. Natives guilty of offenses are sent in to the rulers of the native city for punishment, and there is nothing they dread so much, preferring to trust themselves to foreign retribution.

We have had this chat about Shanghae, if near the Bund, amid bustling scenes and noisy cries—cries from the boats, cargo-boats, and others on the river—cries from the vendors of fruits, cakes, and confectionery, on shore; but, above all, on every hand, turning every corner, up and down every street, there comes upon our ears the wail, "A-hoo!—a-hoo!—a-hoo!"—the cry of the laboring coolies, who, with the bowed staff on their shoulders, and a burden on each end, are hurrying along with tottering steps, and an expression in this cry as though the breath was being pressed from their bodies at every step. And, from the weight of their burdens, this might well be the case, for all cargoes are transported to and from the wharves and warehouses by men. The locomotion of foreigners, and of most Chinese above the rank of laborers, is done in sedan-chairs upon men's shoulders. No burden vehicles or horses are seen, those of the Bund being mere displays of luxury. Human labor is cheaper than that of horses or machinery. A striking illustration of this fact was seen in the docking of ships. Instead of shutting the water out by gates, when a ship had entered the dock and the tide has passed out, from seventy-five to a hundred Chinamen, passing balls of clay from hand to hand, keep ahead of the coming tide, banking out the river and shutting in the dock. All of this, of course, must be dug out again, to permit the exit of the ship.

Adjoining this foreign settlement of Shanghae, shut in by dark, gloomy granite walls, thirty feet high, is the old, or Chinese city. The approaches and the entrance to it are most repulsive. On each side of the streets leading to the gates are grouped most disgusting, deformed, wailing and howling beggars. The details of the condition and appearance of these wretches would be too repulsive for narration. I have known persons deterred from entering the city by the horror of encountering these sights. I will merely mention that a common deformity, and one of the least offensive, is that of persons who have lost their feet at the ankle joint, by the attempt to bandage them into littleness. The common impression among foreigners is, that Chinese have no sympathy with each other's sufferings; but these congregations of beggars, placed in the thoroughfare of this Chinese city, must get their assistance from their countrymen; indeed, some of them have appeals, written in Chinese characters, spread out before them.

The gates are low arched channels, passing through the thickness of the city wall and embankment about thirty feet, and looking like the entrance to sewers. The streets are the sewers themselves, being about eight feet wide, and thronged with opposing currents of the people, whilst before and behind you are heard the shouts of burden or sedan-chair coolies, calling upon you to clear the track, to press close into the houses while they pass. In all this the humble coolie is authoritative, and sure to be submissively obeyed, as, unless you are prompt in getting out of his way, a chair-pole may knock you down, or you may be bespattered from buckets of filth, which would associate you most offensively with Chinese.

It is difficult to give an idea of the filth of this city. The sublimity of the spectacle of the decapitation at one time of hundreds of human beings, as frequently happens in China, will attract those whose sensibilities would shrink from a single execution, so there is almost an attraction in the exaggeration of the foulness of this place. It is dramatic—a spectacle to be looked on in wonder. It goes beyond the scope of an uneducated imagination, and fascinates one by daring their senses and powers of endurance, leaving a feeling of heroism after having successfully encountered the ordeal, as though a hydra had been overcome. Among the peculiarly disagreeable sights are the criminals exposed lying on the ground, in corners of the streets, with their necks in the cangue—a heavy wooden square, about three feet broad, with a hole in the centre, through which the head is placed, the cangue resting on the shoulders like a collar. Thus confined, the criminal lies in the surrounding filth on the ground, exposed to swarms of flies and insects, to the hot sun of the hot weather, and to the eyes of the public.

Among the attractions of Shanghae are the tea-gardens, a collection of artificial lakes, ponds, walks, grottoes, mountains, temples, pleasure-houses, with small picturesque bridges thrown over the streams connecting the lakes and ponds. It would naturally be supposed that the taste which could demand such a place of recreation and resort, would be sufficiently refined to make some approach to neatness and decency. It may, however, have seen more decent days; at present it is dirty, dark and decayed. Its waters are stagnant green pools. It seems given up to fortune-tellers, conjurors, quack doctors, obscene showmen, lazzaroni, loafers and rowdies. There, are, however, several attractive curio and painted fan stores in the tea-gardens; and on a festive day, when the people are in their more showy garb, the crowds in this place, the clanging of gongs and exploding of crackers, amid which the showmen, the tumblers, and the conjurors are busy, make it a characteristic scene of Chinese animation. I once visited this place when it was thronged with people upon the occasion of an eclipse of the sun. The authorities were assembled in the great temple, and the gods of the temple were placed out in its front. The din of gongs was terrific, the purpose being to frighten away the dragon who was devouring the sun. So far as the authorities were engaged in the affair, I presume it was merely a concession to popular superstition, as the astronomical knowledge of those of sufficient literary attainments to be in authority, would forbid any such delusion. Indeed, this very eclipse had been calculated with much accuracy by a native.

About two hundred thousand is supposed to be the present native population of Shanghae. A large trade is carried on with the interior, and junks from distant provinces are moored in front of the city, with water avenues between them, their masts looking like a thicket stripped of its leaves. It is the sea-port of the large manufacturing city of Suchow, distant about eighty miles; and the heavy silks, satins, embroideries, lacquer ware, and inlaid work of Suchow, give richness and elegance to the native stores of Shanghae. In the fall and winter seasons the fur stores are also attractive from the variety and richness of their wares, brought in from the Russian settlements. By a sumptuary law certain furs are only permitted to be worn by mandarins of a high rank; and what is called a robe, sufficient to cover the body back and front to the knees, sells for from one to five hundred dollars, according to genuineness and quality. A respectable Chinese citizen's winter wardrobe is very expensive, costing from one to two thousand dollars.

The great commercial prosperity of Shanghae, and the legitimate relations which the western nations have with it, are dependent upon its tea and silk trade. The following tables taken from the *North China Herald*, will exhibit the extent, nature and prospects of the trade of Shanghae.

Comparative Statement of the Export of Tea and Silk from the Port of Shanghae, during the Years 1854–55, 1855–56, and 1856–57.

TEA.

	1854–55.		1855–56.		1856–57.	
	Black. *lbs.*	Green. *lbs.*	Black. *lbs.*	Green. *lbs.*	Black. *lbs.*	Green. *lbs.*
To G. Britain.	39,586,059	10,428,036	24,668,430	8,543,424	10,607,084	10,794,487
" Australia...	2,798,548	1,250,431	3,197,172	543,340	286,144	184,576
" N. A. Colon.	814,852	419,659	—	375,680	—	275,026
" Continent..	1,031,784	152,995	960,229	71,712	1,195,905	303,043
" U. States..	1,154,573	22,584,308	289,442	20,650,537	381,553	16,886,572
	45,385,816	34,835,429	29,115,273	30,184,693	12,470,686	28,443,704

SILK.

	1854-55.					1855-56.					1856-57.				
	Raw.	*Thrown.*	*Coarse.*	*Refuse.*	*Cocoons.*	*Raw.*	*Thrown.*	*Coarse.*	*Refuse.*	*Cocoons.*	*Raw.*	*Thrown.*	*Coarse.*	*Refuse.*	*Cocoons.*
To G.B'n, *dir't*	38,287	5,293	755	368	53	36,300	4,961	903	42	18	50,304	2,418	1,598	405	93
" Hong Kong	5,424	3,838	—	—	—	9,206	4,835	26	2	-	27,255	8,261	262	20	209
" U. States...	—	—	—	—	—	1,188	—	—	-	-	1,632	—	—	5	-
Bales.......	43,711	9,131	755	368	53	46,694	9,796	929	44	18	79,191	10,679	1,860	430	302

In 1855, the money value of exports from Shanghae was £12,603,540, and of the imports from all sources £7,193,023, of which £2,335,017 was specie, and £3,174,949 was opium, leaving only £1,683,057 worth of manufactures and other products.

The principal green tea district finds its market and port of export at Shanghae, as do also the silk districts. It is sufficiently convenient to the black tea districts; though at present these find their chief market at Foo Chow.

Shanghae maintains its present commercial prosperity against great disadvantages. The first and principal difficulty is in the currency. It forms a substantial answer to the question, " What 's in a name?" According to the name covering the same value of silver, there was a very large percentage of value, at the time of our visit. A good, honest, respectable Mexican dollar, in shopping transactions, would only buy seventy-five cents' worth of goods; a " Carolus," or full-dressed "Ferdinand," would buy double as much; and in exchanging "Carolus" dollars for bills on London, each one was worth one dollar and seventy-five cents—the fictitious value of the " Carolus" being added to the difference of exchange caused by the above stated disproportion between exports and imports.

When teas and silks have to be paid for at such a rate of exchange, and, in every other portion of the empire at which we trade—at each of the five ports—there is only the difference of exchange, the discrimination against Shanghae may be estimated, and is evidently very great. There have been many efforts made by Chinese authorities, and by the foreign merchants, to arrange this difficulty, but they have all gone to prove the power of a national prejudice over a national policy. The interior men—the tea and silk cultivators—will take nothing but the "Carolus," and add to the evil by hoarding them, and thus withdrawing them from circulation. I have heard it supposed there were as many "Carolus" dollars buried under the ground as there were in circulation above it. Attempts have been made to imitate this dollar, giving equal weight and purity of silver, but as yet no such attempts have been successful. Of course, such an artificial and unnatural state of affairs could not be permanent. At my visit to Shanghae in the fall of 1857, the Carolus dollar had almost disappeared, and the currency was sycee—bar silver—the tael of sycee being worth the dollar of one hundred cents; values and prices were all estimated in taels, though generally paid for, except in large transactions, in Mexicans at seventy-five cents.

The other fact adverse to the fullest prosperity of Shanghae is, that it is a port of compelled honesty, while in the other ports that virtue is left to the discretion and interest of the parties concerned. The Chinese authorities, when they discovered that a large and growing commerce was to be carried on between their people and foreigners, at this port, with a sagacious regard for their own interests, and, at the same time, in a spirit of liberality and justice, authorized the establishment of a foreign inspectorate of customs; each treaty power was to appoint one of its citizens an inspector, and jointly they were to arrange all matters of duties and fees between foreigners and the Chinese authorities, were to advise and direct the

Chinese in all these matters to which they were so unaccustomed. To carry out this arrangement the native authorities gave the inspectors liberal salaries, commodious accommodations, and an ample corps of native and foreign assistants, with a revenue-cutter, armed, manned and officered according to agreement.

Chinese custom-houses are said to be peculiarly administered in bribery and corruption, so that a small portion of the just duties are paid, and of this small portion, a very limited sum passes the pockets of the officials who receive it, to the government treasury. If such be the fact where Chinese are concerned with Chinese, over all of whom the authorities have such despotic control, it is easy to see that should foreigners unworthily enter into such arrangements for defrauding the revenue, there would be still less chance of redress; hence committing these foreign revenue interests to a corps of well-paid and competent foreigners having no interests in trade, and responsible both to their own consuls and to the Chinese authorities, was, on the part of those authorities, a wise measure; but of course it puts Shanghae to the disadvantage of being in the bonds of official honesty, while the sister ports are left to the largest liberty of licentious freedom, and the measure naturally encounters the opposition of those who would like to avail themselves of that freedom. It also encounters the jealousy of the consulates which, not being those of treaty powers, are excluded from a nomination of the inspectors. The only reason why such an arrangement exists exclusively at Shanghae, is because of its greater necessity from the extent of its commerce; but if a useful system, it should be applied to the other ports.

Notwithstanding these drawbacks, the trade of Shanghae seems to go on most prosperously. I have known twenty-two vessels to arrive in one day, and have counted a list of over eighty in port at one time.

The following is a list of vessels, of heavy tonnage, which arrived in this port in the months set opposite their names of the years 1856–57:

NAME.	FROM.	CARGO.	MONTH.	TONS.
Neptune's Favorite	San Francisco	Ballast	October	1846
Eagle	London	Heavy	November	1296
Eureka	do	do	do	1041
Endeavor	San Francisco	Ballast	December	1187
Nor' Wester	do	do	do	1267
Don Quixote	Siam	Rice	do	1429
Romance	San Francisco	Ballast	January	1781
Eagle Wing	Hong Kong	Rice	do	1174
Contest	New York	Heavy	February	1098
Golden West	Hong Kong	Rice	do	1441
White Swallow	London	Heavy	September	1198
Swallow	do	do	do	1435
Alboni	San Francisco	Ballast	February	1000
J. Bell	Hong Kong	Rice	April	1381
North Wind	do	do	May	1045
Spitfire	do	do	June	1549
Sky-lark	do	do	do	1481
Intrepid	Calcutta	do	July	1178

I am particular in giving this list, because an impression has been sent abroad by high authority, that the difficulties of the river are opposed to the prosperity of Shanghae, and I shall hereafter have occasion to refer to it in an argument upon certain measures which I regard as expedient for the interests of the United States government. It is true that, upon the occasion of our first visit, the San Jacinto, drawing eighteen feet water, grounded in the river. It is equally true she ought not to have grounded, there being plenty of water in the channel—there being, at full tides, twenty-three feet water on the bar.

At the time of our second visit to Shanghae, in the fall of 1857, a change of Taou Tais occurred. Lan, who occupied the place, for some reason was appointed to another and less desirable position, not perhaps as any punishment or disgrace, but because the very profitable position was wanted by some more influential politician. Lan was removed, and Teue appointed to his place. Very soon after arriving at Shanghae, the ex and the new Taou

Tai notified the consuls of the three treaty powers that they would make an official call. The United States consul asked me to be present at the interview. A mixed entertainment, partly in our own fashion, and partly Chinese, was gotten up for the occasion. The Chinese part ot the tiffin consisted of various neat and incomprehensible articles of ornamental cakes, jellies and confectionery—the American part, of champagne wine. The day and hour had been appointed some days before; and nearly an hour before the arrival of the officials, a messenger came with three cards. These were those of the old Taou Tai, the new Taou Tai, and the prefect or district magistrate. To each pertained two cards—slips of pink paper about ten inches long and three wide. On one was the name of the individual, and on the others his titles of honor. With sounding gong and cries of their attendants, they came with a crowded retinue on foot. First, there entered our inclosure two lads in official caps, bearing, suspended from a stick on their shoulders, a crimson trunk, in which was a suit of criminal's clothes. These are borne before the Taou Tai on such occasions, to indicate to him his entire dependence upon the emperor's authority; that whenever an order from the emperor may reach him, in the house, or on the way, he must descend from his state, and, if commanded, appear as a criminal before his judges.

The officials were in full mandarin costume, with the respective buttons of their rank, their peacock-tail plume, and armorial bearings embroidered on the backs and breasts of their robes.

Having descended from the sedan chairs, they were met by us at the door, when they chin-chinned by folding their hands together in a fist form, and shaking them two or three times in front of their breasts, bowing their heads slightly at the same time, which motions we imitated.

After a few minutes' prefatory and ceremonial conversation in the dining-room, we adjourned to that where the table was spread, and our visitors partook of the refreshments at least with the courtesy of appearing to like them, taking wine with us as asked, and in return for such things as we helped them to, placing others on our plates.

They had, very prudently, not depended upon our providing them with the luxury of napkins soaked in hot water, but their servants had come provided with them, and, obtaining from ours the hot water, handed the smoking cloths to their masters at the close of the repast. Conversation as abrupt and rugged as ours is in its most courteous refinement, must appear harsh to people accustomed to language of such studied ceremony as theirs.

A Chinese gentleman with formal courtesy depreciates all that belongs to himself, and exalts all pertaining to him with whom he converses.

"How are the branches of your family tree?"

"My own little puppies are, etc."

"After the splendor of your own palace, I hope you can endure my little hut?"

"Your greatness of understanding is accumulating riches; my own stupidity condemns me to poverty."

"In your palace, how many ages have you remained?" or, "At your feet I inquire how many noble cycles?" *i. e.*, How old are you?

"How is he whose commands you receive and are obliged to obey?" *i. e.*, How is your father?

"How is the great, great person, who issues commands in the hall?" *i. e.*, your mother.

In the course of a few days, in return for the consul's entertainment, there came an invitation on a sheet of unfolded vermillion paper, in an envelope a foot long, written over with Chinese characters, and opening at one end. It may be supposed to read as follows:

"My house is thoroughly cleansed. On the twelfth day of the ninth moon, at ten o'clock in the morning, my table will be garnished; my wine-cups will be scoured and bright; and I will be waiting in an attitude of submission the light of your countenance." For such is the style of a Chinese invitation.

At the appointed time we went in sedan chairs with the dignity of four-bearers, wearing red-tasseled caps. Gongs and horns and guns saluted our entrance to the court-yard of the Taou Tai. His excellency met us, and we chin-chinned as before. He carefully inquired of the interpreter the respective rank of the individuals, and seated those of the highest on an elevated divan on his left.

This entertainment was similar to our own, with foreign wines, hot tea, and a pleasant drink of raw almond emulsion; and as we came away, the guns and the gongs saluted our departure as they had done our arrival.

XXVII.

SHANGHAE.

On the two or three last days of August of one of our visits to Shanghae, the boats in the river presented lines of bright lanterns, giving the appearance of an illuminated city, and the same were seen in the distant rural suburbs. It was the joyful offering of the people for the fruitfulness of the summer. Considering how unspiritual most of us are, there must be something very fascinating in this tangible acknowledgment made to unseen deities for visible benefits.

A few days after this an opportunity occurred of seeing the devotion of the Chinese mind to intellectual and moral superiority; still, however, manifesting the same reverential awe of dogmas which is expressed by the vulgar, in their imperfect English, "ola custom." Certain literary graduates were to receive a degree which put them in the line of political promotion, and upon this occasion they were to bow themselves before the shrine of Confucius. Through and through the tangled mazes and narrow lanes of the odorous city of Shanghae, under the escort of the Rev. Mr. Cunningham of the Methodist mission, we found our way to the Confucian temple in the suburbs. It is a simple structure, adorned with a little Chinese confused painting and some gilding—but no idols. The main altar, if it may be so called, contains an upright board, the tablet of Confucius, upon which, in gilded letters, are sentences from his philosophy.

Each side of the building contains a row of similar tablets of his principal disciples; and on either side of the main building are wings with the tablets of other distinguished Chinese sages and moralists.

The neighborhood of the temple, as upon all such occasions in our own country, was thronged with a curious crowd of spectators, most of them in their holiday clothes; and thrift-searching Chinamen had erected mat booths for supplying the demand for "refreshments." A large portion of this crowd consisted of neatly-dressed females.

We, who were in uniform, greatly attracted the attention of the crowd before the arrival of the distinguished individuals in honor of whom it had gathered together. They were more familiar with our missionary companions, and these, as was their habit, entered into conversation with the crowd. They always listen with great patience and attention to any view of religion which may be presented to them, however adverse to their own, and their only comment of dissent may be, "It is a very good religion for you, but will not answer for Chinamen."

An individual among them, from his attire, one of the people, was very voluble in his discourse, though in good temper, and a little as though inspirited by sam-shöo. Native courtesy, however, was conspicuous in this man. It was warm and tiresome standing, and he signed to us to seat ourselves on the stone sill of the adjoining porch. "Sit down yourself," said the gentleman with whom he was talking. "No, I am at home; you are a guest." The graduates, in rich costume, and all young men, came in sedan chairs, preceded by music. They were taking a degree equivalent to Bachelor of Arts. Preceded by the district magistrate, and following his motions, they bowed three times before the tablet of Confucius, not, however, entering the temple, and then they made obeisance in another part of the temple to the judge or chancellor.

The most curious part of the ceremonies was their conclusion. The instant the salutations were over, they rushed to their chairs, which the bearers had ready, and ran off in the wildest kind of hurry. This was to indicate their emulation in the race of life, and the speed with which they would reach the future literary and political honors which are now open to them. Literature is the Chinese road to political preferment; and hence at once a democratic practical principle is established, for brains have not their quantity and quality in birth. So general is the operation of this principle, that, as with ourselves, the stimulus and necessity of poverty is thought to be almost essential to success in China. The distinguished Key-ing, Governor General of Two-kwang, and Imperial Commissioner, was the son of a poor shoemaker.

I had an opportunity of seeing some of the influences which stimulate these young men to continued effort, and disseminate ambitious views among the youth of their villages and vicinage. Being on the side of the city opposite to, and some three miles from the temple of Confucius, I saw approaching me a crowd of laboring men and boys, hurrying along with bright-colored banners, and in the midst of the crowd, was one of these youths in his rich costume and decorated sedan chair. He was being thus honored and welcomed to his home by the people of his neighborhood. The examination for the Keu Jin, M. A., takes place in the principal city of each province once in three years, and also upon some special occasions. At the higher examination held at Nankin, the number of candidates is very large, the average being twenty thousand, and of these only an average of two hundred is successful.

"When the candidates enter, they are searched for books or scraps of writing which might assist them in writing their essays, and the strictest precautions are taken to prevent any communication between them while in the examination hall. Three sets of themes are given, each occupying two days and a night, and, until that time is expired, no one is permitted to leave his allotted apartment, and no attendants are allowed. This is to teach them that the disciples of the ancient sages must be self-denying, and not covet the good things of this life. The essays are scrutinized by officers appointed for that duty, to know if they conform to the regulations. They must not exceed seven hundred characters, nor contain any character which belongs to the name of Confucius, Mencius, or any emperor. Nor must there be any character written over the ruled red lines. No erasure or correction of any kind is allowed.

Essays of former examinations must not be copied, and any obvious fault in composition observed by the officers who superintend this department, would prevent the essay from being placed in the hands of the examiners. The eighteen assistant examiners then select the best essays, to the number of two or three hundred, and subject them to the examination of two commissioners from the Imperial Hanlin College, who decide which are the best, and arrange the names in the order of merit. The writer of the first is called Keae Yuen, the first to be recommended to the emperor. In granting offices, the emperor follows the order of names in this and the higher examinations.

"On the first two days the themes are taken from the four books with a line of poetry; on the next from the five classics, one from each; and lastly five papers of miscellaneous questions are given. To answer these questions, if the papers before us are to be taken as an average example, a most extensive reading in general literature must be expected from the candidates in addition to their study of the classical books.

"The first of these papers takes for its range the commentators on the classics; *e. g.*, 'Choo-foo-tze, in commenting on the Shoo King, made use of four authors—who sometimes say too much, at others too little; sometimes their explanations are forced, at others, too ornamental. What have you to observe on them?' 'In the Han dynasty there were three commentators on the Yile King, whose explanations and divisions into chapters and sentences were all different. Can you give an account of them?' 'Under our present sacred dynasty, literature and learning are in a most flourishing state. You, candidates, have been studying for several years. Let each of you make use of what he knows, and reply to these questions.'

"The second paper has for its subject histories, inviting a criticism from the candidate on the historical works of each dynasty in succession from Sze ma, the Herodotus of China, downwards to the Ming emperors. It is obvious that the examination can be no child's play when such comprehensive questions as these form a part of it :— 'Sze ma, in making his history, took the classical books and ancient records, and arranged the facts they detailed. Some have accused him of unduly exalting Taourists, and thinking too highly of wealth and power. Pan koo, a writer of the Han dynasty, is clear and comprehensive, but on astronomy and the five elements he has written more than enough. Can you give examples and proofs of these statements?' 'Ch'in-show had admirable abilities for historical writing. In his Three Kingdoms he has depreciated Choo-ko-leang, and made very light of E. and E., two other celebrated characters. What is it that he says of them?'

"The third paper questions the candidates on the ancient and modern divisions of the empire. They are required to state the authorities who record the earliest division into nine provinces, the changes which followed, and the discrepancies between the different authors in their accounts of them; then the changes that occurred under more recent dynasties, in the number, designations and mode of government of the provinces, are asked for. It is then added that the size of the empire having much increased beyond what it was in former times, diligent study ought to be bestowed on geography, and the candidates are invited, accordingly, not to conceal their knowledge, but state all they can.

"The next is on books. The candidates are required to relate where the existing accounts of certain lost books of high antiquity are found, and what emperors have made efforts to preserve books and to form libraries. It is asked: 'The Seuj dynasty collected books to the number of three hundred and seventy thousand. These were reduced by selection to thirty-seven thousand. Where was the library in which they were kept, and who performed the task of selection?' Questions are also asked on what catalogues of books have been made, and the method of classifying them that have been employed. The last paper is on the history of the water-courses and flood-gates in the eastern parts of this province (Keang Nan). It begins with the Emperor Ta Yu's hydraulic achievements, and asks for an account of the early names of this region. It then inquires why it is that the Woosung Keang is so beneficial to the neighboring departments by affording an outlet to the waters of the Tae Hoo. At the close it is added: 'Our emperor is always seeking to promote the people's good. You, who are inhabitants of this province, ought to be fully informed on the subject of its water communications. Now show your knowledge, that there may be proof of your fitness to be presented to the emperor.' "

Such being the rigid character of the literary acquirements which are essential to influence and political position in China, can the literary men of western nations wonder that they look with contempt upon nations whom, until recently, they have known chiefly through the acquaintanceship of commerce?

An elaborately-carved stone portal, which stands about the centre of the city of Shanghae, will be sought out by the seeker after celebrities and antiquities, for it is the monument of Seu-kwang-ke. He was born in this city about three hundred years ago, and the city may well pride herself upon being the birth-place of so distinguished a man.

Graduating as Keu-Jin (master of arts) in 1598, and being at the head of the list, he ran a successful literary and political career, receiving, seven years after the degree of M. A., that of Doctor, at the same time with his former preceptor.

He produced several works, with the following titles: "College Lessons for the year 1604;" "Seu's Chit-Chat;" "Six Memoirs on the Book of Odes," in fourteen volumes:

1. An Investigation of Objects.
2. An Elucidation of History.
3. An Exploration of Antiquities.
4. An Amplification of the Meaning.
5. A Selection of Beauties.
6. The Correct Sounds.

I give these subjects as a key to the character of Seu's mind. The appointment of "Honorary Member of the Institute" being offered to his preceptor, Hwang Te Jin, he declined, on account of advanced age, and recommended Seu, who received the honor. In succession he reached the places of "Examiner of the National Institute," "Minister of the Household," and "Assistant to the Board of Rites."

The Chinese scholar and statesman, Seu, became the Roman Catholic Paul, under the influence and teaching of the Jesuit missionary, Ricci, who reached Pekin in 1601, and attained to high influence and favor. Drawing from such sources of information as presented themselves to him, and enriching his facts by the fertility of his own mind, Seu brought forth, as the fruit of his intellectual intercourse with Ricci, works on "Military Tactics," "Agriculture by the Military," "The Salt Revenue," "Hydraulics," "A Disquisition on Canals and Rivers," "On European Hydraulics," "The Proper Rules for Tillage," "Miscellaneous Records on Husbandry," etc. Seu and Ricci jointly produced a translation of the first six books of the Elements of Euclid's Geometry.

The following are some of the remarks of Seu, which accompanied the issue of the work:

"This is a book of the most extensive utility, and, at the present time, it is one of the highest importance. As soon as I had finished the translation, I, together with a friend, got it printed and published. Mr. Ricci, who had written an introduction, was exceedingly delighted at the rapidity of the publication, and was sanguine in his hopes that it might be generally studied; but there are very few that give their attention to this subject. I conceive that a hundred years after this it will become a popular study, and then people will wonder how the subject has been so long neglected. There are some who, on first looking at this work, fancy it very abstruse and difficult to be understood, and say that I ought to have explained every paragraph and sentence. To which I reply: the principles of geometry and arithmetic are, in themselves, altogether free from mystery; and, as to the terms employed, if you duly exercise your minds upon them, you will soon find them become extremely clear and intelligible; but, if the thinking powers are not brought to bear on the subject, certainly it will appear mysteriously profound. Suppose a person finds himself surrounded on all sides by hills, not knowing in which direction to look for the road, he walks on till he comes to a foot-path, and, following it, finds the right course. So, let any one apply himself for ten days to the task, and he will be able to understand the whole from beginning to end; and every sentence and expression will appear extremely plain and clear."

One may be excused for quoting these sentiments of a Chinese scholar of three centuries ago, as well on account of their source as of their practical wisdom.

After this, Seu produced several other mathematical

works, correcting the errors of former works; and manifesting great intellectual activity and industry.

But a man so able and eminent maintaining and leading into influence a religion differing from that of those with whom he was associated, necessarily incurred the enmity of his rivals in literature, and his opponents in religion. These influences having free course by the removal of his imperial patron from life, Seu, and the foreign Christians whom he had protected, fell into discredit and under persecution. At this time, however, the Manchu power was threatening the native dynasty, and Seu, with the soul of true greatness, and the spirit of a patriot, brought his military science and his personal efforts to the support of the power which had been hostile to him. His value was too great to be neglected, and, once more, he reached a position of influence in the empire, carrying with him his foreign Christian associates. He was now appointed "High Chancellor of the Eastern Cabinet," and admitted to the private councils of his emperor, being also officially a member of the "Privy Council," and "Guardian to the Prince Royal."

His great work is, a "New System of Arithmetic," in one hundred volumes. Seu-kwang-ke closed his active life of more than seventy years, in October, 1633, and his remains now lie entombed near his native city of Shanghae.

He died rich in reputation and virtue, but poor in gold. It was represented to the emperor by one of the censors that, "In his zeal for the service of his country, Seu had omitted to make any provision for his family; and, having acted thus disinterestedly with regard to the emoluments of his office, if his imperial highness would now signalize his approbation by a display of his munificence towards the surviving members of the family, such an act would go far to discountenance and put to shame those who grasped at public office, merely for the opportunity of subserving their private views and interests"—a sentiment which it would be well for some more modern countries to apply to their official policy, instead of basing it upon the experiment of making "empty sacks stand upright."

The emperor approved of the request, and had it carried into effect, also conferring on Seu the posthumous titles of "Pillar of the State," and of "Secondary Guardian."

The edict appointing posthumous honor to the deceased, commences in the following language:

"The flowers (smoke) ascend from the gem-eared vase, while the goblets and dishes are replenished. In distinguishing you by the gift of this felicitous casket, I would diffuse the knowledge of your reverential and illustrious merit. I, having received your three-fold counsels, have rejoiced to behold thereby the people refreshed, as the earth with the showers of spring. Thus your meritorious aptitude for every department of government might be traced in the purity of your conduct while occupying the privy councillor's station. Looking upon the fidelity of your service towards me, I now grant you these honors."

The ancestral chapel stands on the site of the ancient residence of the Seu family, in the city of Shanghae. It contains the effigy of Seu, wearing the robes of the Ming dynasty. On the right is the inscription: "In the use of numbers, and the elucidation of husbandry, the teacher of a hundred generations could span the heavens and embrace the earth." On the left: "Abroad, a general—at home, a privy councillor; the same minister was a courageous warrior and a skillful politician."

The Chinese are by no means sparing of their honors to distinguished women. Among the carved granite portals which are seen through the country, are many to virtuous women, and among the virtues most entitling to such a distinction, is that of having lived faithful to the obligations of a first marriage. The family of the noble Seu, and that branch of it which belongs to the city of Shanghae, is rich in these virtuous women.

When, nearly three hundred years ago, Seu bowed before the baptismal font, joined with him in the holy rite was his grand-daughter, Candida. Being left a widow, and having set aside the matrimonial portions of her eight children, she devoted the remainder of her fortune to building churches, to the dissemination of Christianity. She built a foundling hospital, and a college for the education of a native ministry. The emperor conferred upon her a noble title, and presented her with a costly robe, which she sold for the purposes of charity. One great-grand-daughter earned celebrity by living a widow forty-one years from her fifteenth year. Another great-grand-daughter, Seusze, accomplished in arts and literature, upon the death of her husband, also devoted to literature, abandoned these pursuits, devoted herself to spinning, weaving, and frugality, dying after fifty-three years of widowhood. The wife of a great-grand-son of Seu-Kwang-ke, took a vow of widowhood, devoted herself to her son and her husband's mother, and lived a widow for more than forty years, earning for herself the title of "an inimitable pattern of constancy and filial piety."

Seven other ladies of this great family, coming down to the wife of the great-great-grand-son of the grand-son of Kwang-ke, were celebrated in the annals of Shanghae for the longevity of their widowhood, secondary wives joining with primary in earning this honor.

The facts of the foregoing short biography of the great privy councillor, embody many interesting points of Chinese history, and suggest many interesting reflections upon the fluctuating fate of Christianity in this empire. They present, too, an insight into the capacity of the Chinese mind for scientific investigation. That a higher national cultivation has not, in the course of so much time, resulted from the influence of such a man, may be, at least in part, attributed to the fatal union of knowledge and scientific truth with a false, a worldly and ambitious sectarianism. Had Seu been made an humble Christian, and devoted his capacities to the true mode of extending divine truth alone, Christianity might now have been the religion of the empire. Had he been solely scientific, and still a pagan, science, and foreign men of science, not having the hostility of opposing religion to contend with, might have been more progressive.

But more ancient than the associations of the privy councillor's gateway—more ancient than Christianity in China, than Christianity itself, are the records of God's ancient people in the Chinese empire.

" And behold these from the land of Sinim."* Who is it that is to come from the land of Sinim, and where is that land? Some learned investigators conclude that the vast territory of China is the land alluded to. If so, are there any of the chosen people—the ancient people with whom God held communion, in that land? Has the word spoken by His prophets been carried there save by Christian messengers? These interrogatories facts answer in the affirmative.

A people winning for themselves tablets of honor, and eminent Chinese mandarins and statesmen coming out from that people, are among the established marvels of the Chinese empire, and yet this people, and those statesmen and nobles, were Israelites—but an offshoot of the nation to whom the one God committed His word and law, so early in its history as to be ignorant of the Jewish title and of the history of Christ.

Soon after the establishment of Roman Catholic missionaries in China, more than two centuries ago, they

* Isaiah, xlix. 12.

were surprised by the fact, that in the interior of that country there had been existing, from a very early period, a sect, which, having heard of the new comers, claimed identity of religion with them. It was known as the sect "Teaou Kin Keaou," "the sect that plucks out the sinew."

Such investigation as these missionaries made at the time, though it was very imperfect, ascertained the existence of several Hebrew synagogues—one at Hang-chow-foo, one at Nankin, and one at Kae-fung-foo. None of these are now known to exist, except that at Kae-fung-foo, in the province of Honan, two hundred miles from Pekin. The difficulties of penetrating to this place, by those competent to correct observation and investigation, have been so great that our information is not proportioned to the interest of the subject.

Some of the modern Protestant missions have sent out Christian Chinese to collect information respecting these Israelites. Many obstacles lay in their path, but they succeeded in reaching Kae-fung-foo, keeping a detailed account of their journey.

They represent the community as consisting of but a few families, and these in a very decayed condition, though the evidence of the past honorable position of the community, and the distinguished character of some of its members still remained. No sufficient data have yet been reached to determine at what period these Jews entered China, but enough to establish that it must have been long before the Christian era; and the supposition is that the high tone and the pure morality of the Confucian philosophy is but a gleam from the burning bush on Mount Sinai. But at Kae-fung-foo was found in the noble old Hebrew character, word for word, and letter for letter, book for book, the same divine record and law which is the foundation of our national existence and prosperity. In the synagogue, over a tablet containing the name of the Emperor of China, is written, in Hebrew letters of gold,

"Hear, O Israel:
The Lord our God is one Lord;
Blessed be the Name
Of the Glory of His Kingdom,
For ever and ever."

After this, on a triple arch, was the following inscription in Hebrew:

"Blessed be the Lord our God;
The Lord is God of Gods, and the Lord
A great God, strong and terrible."

In separate tents, in the "House of Heaven," each enclosed by silken curtains, were twelve rolls of the law, and a central tent, in honor of Moses. On the extreme western walls, in golden Hebrew letters, were the tables of the Ten Commandments.

The new treaty may, perhaps, afford greater facilities for investigating this interesting subject.

XXVIII.

MARRIAGE AND FUNERAL DEBATE.

On a certain Monday evening, by the thoughtful womanly kindness of my friend, Miss Fay, I received an invitation to attend a missionary meeting, at which was to be discussed the duty of Christian ministers in relation to the established customs of the Chinese in their marriage and funeral ceremonies; that is, how far a conformity to the usages was to be permitted or countenanced in Chinese converts—a most interesting subject. When I entered the room, I found there, English, Scotch and American missionaries, with their families, and the ladies of their respective missions. There were English Episcopalians, and American Episcopalians, Presbyterians, Congregationalists, Methodists, and Sabbatarians. With several of these it had been my honor and my happiness to mingle in the Christian refinement and unostentatious hospitality of their own families. Here I was, face to face, with the whole body of men whom some of the silk and tea buyers, and opium smugglers, had described to me as an ignorant set of adventurers who came out on the missionary business because they could not earn their bread at home; and who were so miserably poor, they were glad to wear the cast-off clothes of these same silk and tea traders, and opium smugglers. Consistency did not forbid that the next speaker should add to this contempt a severe censure of the wealth, and ease and luxury in which these same missionaries lived. In other lands I had met missionaries, and I had found them generally a sincere, earnest band, faithfully trusting in the Lord, in His own time to do His own work, provided they obeyed His commands, not discouraged by the little apparent progress they made. I had found many of these men learned contributors to scientific, ethnological and philological researches; and displaying in their vocation a physical and moral courage which placed them in the rank of the noblest heroism. In all foreign lands I had heretofore found them, with very few exceptions, the best specimens of their respective countries, in education, in genuine refinement, and in all the amenities which grow out of cultivation.

'Tis true, and ought to be admitted, their dress is sometimes ungainly—their shirt-collars not of the most fashionable cut; and few of the commercial lordlings who despise them would be willing to admit they had ever honored by their persons the particular style of garment with which the missionary thinks himself sufficiently well clad. Representations will have their effect upon the mind, and I have felt a painful regret, in hearing missionaries spoken of with contempt, that the Lord should have permitted such unworthy men to go forth as the ambassadors of the Bible. I could not reconcile it with His purposes. At this time I had met but two or three of the missionary band, and upon venturing to suggest that these gentlemen seemed superior to the opinions expressed of their class, it was admitted they were exceptions; and those who were not exceptions I found were mainly known to their judges by their gait, their garb, and the contemptible fact of being wanting in wealth, which, however, was a common crime in the set. Here I was face to face with all of them—a thoughtful, earnest, sensible-looking body of men, and withal clothed like decent gentlemen. Notwithstanding my acquaintance with, and respect for a few of the body, I confess I was astonished by the dignity of the meeting, and the respectability of the audience. Several distinguished British officers were present as auditors. There were other conversational charges brought against these missionaries, such as spending the money contributed by widows and orphans for their own private use and enjoyment. "Judge not, lest ye be judged," may be interpreted, Judge not, lest ye judge yourselves. I ventured to suggest that as missionary boards and the sources of financial means were generally, if not invariably, composed of shrewd, intelligent, practical business men, who had established a close system of accountability, and whose interests were opposed to the extravagance of their foreign servants, such a latitude as those charges implied seemed scarcely possible. I must, however, say that the very detractors of missionaries would sometimes, in the chances of conversation, speak of the self-denial and disinterestedness of individual cases; but the prejudices of class, and the misconceptions of ignorance and prejudice, were too strong for any compassing cloud of witnesses to remove.

The evening discussion was opened by a most able essay upon Chinese marriage and funeral ceremonies, read by the author, the Rev. Mr. Syle, of the American Episcopal mission. The essay took the ground, if I remember correctly, that their Chinese converts might be permitted to retain their national customs, so far as they were not associated with idolatry, astrology and superstition. The discussion took a wide range, involving expediency, duty, practicability and taste. It was generally participated in by all the sects, with much difference of opinion maintained with Christian forbearance, and enlivened by wit and humor which shook the stiffness out of the most rigid features. Whatever view of the subject was taken, every debater admitted that it was surrounded with great difficulties, and no one, whatever his tendencies, seemed disposed to a positive and dogmatic opinion. In brief, the essential incidents of a Chinese marriage seemed to be, in many cases, if not in most, 1st, the betrothal of the parties by their parents and guardians in their infancy, and sometimes before birth, and the obligation of the young people to fulfill this engagement; 2d, the essential employment of systematic negotiators or go-betweens, mei-jin, whose office seems to have a wider range than that which is apparent, and may be connected with some superstitious association; 3d, the "Pasil," or giving of eight characters indicating the exact hour of the bride's birth, day, month, etc., this being for the use of the astrologer to determine whether the marriage is to be a lucky or unlucky one. If the magician determines the latter, no further proceedings are entered upon; 4th, exchange of presents, the decorated bridal chair, the vailing of the bride in a crimson vail, pledging each other in a wine cup, worshiping each other, and the bride worshiping the shades of the ancestors of her husband.

The great difficulty, and that upon which there was the greatest discussion, was the nature and obligation of the betrothal contract—how far were the Christian ministry justified in insisting upon their converts dissolving such contracts made for them without their consent, especially when the fulfillment of the contract united the new Christian by such influential ties to an unconverted heathen? It was generally admitted, but not by all, that there was no question as to the impropriety of all such contracts made after a profession of Christianity. Some contended that even this liberty should be allowed, as in Christian lands the professing Christian is united to one who is not such.

The precept, "Be ye not unequally yoked," was taken as the ground of those who opposed all consent to the union of Christians and heathens. Then arose the question how far the betrothal contract is a soluble one; was it not, according to Chinese law and Chinese usage, a virtual marriage, and only to be set aside by divorce? or was it, as such engagements with us, open to the caprice of either party, under the penalty of fine?

That the betrothal contract could not be violated without penalty, and that authority could restrict the parties from other contracts, was admitted. Still, the questions presented themselves, were there not usages and moral obligations stronger than law which required the Chinese Christian to fulfill his contract? Were there not obligations, under Chinese usage, to parents, which could not be set aside? Several cases were narrated, which showed the great difficulties surrounding this subject. Dr. Hobson, of Canton, when Canton was, related the case of a Christian daughter of a Christian Chinaman, who had been betrothed to a heathen—I presume, before the conversion of her parents. The young man claimed the fulfillment of the contract. The parents were distressed by the obligation of fulfilling the contract, and knew that their daughter could not be happy in her inconsistent relation. Their friends, among the missionaries, were also anxious upon the subject, and were willing to contribute any amount of money to have her released from the necessity. All the parties were poor, but the father said that, fearful as it was to him, the thing must go on—no amount of money could release them from the obligation.

The Rev. Mr. Yates, of the Methodist Church, who seemed to be very familiar with Chinese usages, stated that if the husband, when he first saw the bride to whom he had been betrothed in her infancy and his own, found her blind, or deformed, still he was not at liberty to end the contract. He must live single while she lives, and, I think he said, must support her.

Dr. Wentworth, also of the Methodist Church, of Suchau, narrated a case now giving them some anxiety. A young man who had professed Christianity, who had been in the United States, who was living a reputable and prosperous life, had made recently a marriage contract with an unconverted woman, and for this, the Church with which he had been in connection had cut him off. He had brought his certificate of baptism and of church membership to the Methodists, and asked them to receive him. He assured them that when married, and his wife came under his influence, he would place her in preparation for becoming a Christian.

These cases show the great difficulty attending this subject; and to appreciate its extent one has only to think for a moment of the power of national usages and customs. A Chinese family would not so much object to any of its members becoming Christians, for they rather appreciate the purity and spirituality of the religion, if the fact did not involve a departure from national usages.

The next part of the ceremonies which elicited a remark, was the "pasil," the giving the exact hour of birth. The objection to this was its astrological use—the fact in itself having no significance; and hence some saw no objection to the fact, unless improperly used. All the ceremonies of worshiping each other, ancestry, gods of the household, were, of course, to be rejected as idolatries. But there was a difference of opinion upon these subjects, some contending that there was really no act of worship, but only a conventional courtesy.

It was curious to observe the wide range of opinion upon the latitude which should be given to the association between the sexes. While some seemed to think that one of the great elements of western civilization lay in the privilege of "courting," and the right of "private judgment" in matrimonial matters, one of the most strong-minded and clear-headed participants of the discussion contended for all the reserve of the East in regard to females, from the hour of birth to the red vail of the bridal; and advanced the doctrine, that a judicious selection of all the circumstances which should determine a marriage, would be as conducive to happiness, would be as likely to be followed by a permanent and abiding love between parties heretofore unknown to each other, as though the union had been the result of a preëxisting and impulsive passion. When the many unhappy love-matches which mar the matrimonial relation are compared with the sober satisfaction of those which have been arranged for the parties, this gentleman's opinion would not seem to be so heterodox. It may be significant that the advocate of the largest freedom of courtship was an American, and that he who contended for reserve and arrangement was a Scot.

The subject, involved the usual conflict between duty and expediency. I do not feel justified in asking any assent to my own uninstructed opinion upon this complicate question; but it seemed to me that the whole of it might be very simply solved, as far as missionary duty was concerned. Teach heart, not formal Christianity, and its duties and responsibilities; and let conformity to all national customs be at the judgment of the individual. Let him fulfill his betrothal contract, and if it leads his companion to the Christian communion, it is well; if she leads him into paganism, then let him abide the consequences of his error. Let him receive the pasil as a ceremony; but if he makes a superstitious and astrological use of it, then he has failed in his Christianity, and he must be cut off. Many of the necessary employments and avocations of life tend to tempt the Christian from his duties, and to heathenize him; a sea-faring life, a military one—trade itself—indeed all external life, has a deteriorating tendency, and much of the argument against engaging in Chinese marriage may be brought against engaging in these pursuits; and if not armed against these temptations, the Christian is not properly armed.

Very few remarks were made upon the subject of funerals, as it was generally admitted the Chinese did not object to our external mode of burial; and as most that was connected with theirs was wholly and out-and-out idolatrous, the participation of a Christian in such ceremonies could not be sanctioned.

XXIX.

SIK-A-WA.

On Thursday, August 26th, 1857, a very great change took place in the weather at Shanghae. From being very hot, the weather changed to heavy rain, and so cool, that some more delicate individuals found a little fire comfortable. The wind was quite fresh.

On Friday, starting about eleven in the morning, I rode on horseback, with a heavy cloth cap on my head, and without any umbrella, out to Sik-a-Wa, a Roman Catholic college, about seven miles from our residence, and did not find the heat the least oppressive.

The roads are mere narrow bridle paths passing along the banks of ditches, and between fields of cotton, rice and beans. The cotton was now in bloom, and men with white aprons, like bags, before them, were gathering the bolls. The green rice fields were waving and nodding their heavy heads, almost ready for the harvest. Some fields were being hoed with pronged hoes, or should I rather say spots than fields, for every little side nook or elevation raked from a creek's bottom, was appropriated to use. The narrow line upon which we rode was so narrow, because no more could be spared to it. The whole green fresh country was a plain. The highest elevation we mounted in our seven miles' ride could not have been over ten feet. Once there had been groves of ancient trees inhabiting—yes, inhabiting, giving the idea of a higher and more enduring life—this plain; and occasionally, in the distance, some few of the solitary "oldest inhabitants" might be seen flinging wide their spreading branches, as if discoursing on the past, and preaching a funeral sermon over their departed umbrageous fellows.

There is a delicious eloquent communion to be held with one of these single old trees standing in a vast plain, and you and he entirely alone—no fellows of his kind, and none of yours. I have enjoyed it as I did on the evening of this day in other regions. Just as the sun is setting, and you are, hurrying on your way to escape the shadows and wanderings of the night, the old fellow, beckons to you with a long and gaunt arm. Your heart turns to him, but your eyes are on the big falling sun, and you think you will push on; but there is so much of beseeching in his moving arms, he is so lonely, you rein up your horse to have a talk. He tells you then of his chronology—of the vast and wavy sapling horde which stood around him in his green youth; how man and storm and disease had taken all but himself; how he had looked down upon race changed for race—plain for city, and city again for field. While you are thus absorbed by his eloquence, the shades of night are around you both, and he grows more animated as they fall around him. You bid him good-bye, and he waves you such a farewell, as his arms pass into the night-shadows, as seems to dismiss you into eternity, while he promises to wait there and tell the same story, and yours, too, to some traveler of a future age, who may stand in your place. There are few places where an old tree could tell more than one of these standing on the plains of China, on the banks of the Yang Tse Kiang, and near the walls of Shanghae.

An old map, of near a thousand years ago, of Shanghae and its vicinity, now before me, bears record to the old tree's evidence. It shows that near nine hundred years ago there flowed, but a few hundred yards from where I now write, a river over five miles wide. Two hundred years later it was but three miles wide, and now I cross it daily, a small stream, not one fourth of a mile in width. In the meantime the river in front of the city has grown to its present dimensions from a small creek, swallowing up a rampart built in Tsin dynasty fifteen hundred years ago. The paved streets of ancient cities are found in the rice fields. The site of the capital of the Leang dynasty has passed away, and the waters of Wild Mulberry and other neighboring lakes flow over cities founded from two to five hundred years B. C.

The old tree with which I had now most to do, had a very melancholy story to make up his most recent recollections. It was of the many of his fellows, most ancient worthies, whole grave communities, which had been destroyed by the Imperialist army, when it encamped on their plain, besieging the rebels in Shanghae, and then only succeeded at last by the impertinent aid of the French. I shall never forgive either French or Chinese Imperialists; not so much from sympathy with the rebels, as from sympathy with the trees—but, "let the dead past bury its dead." All around is now fat fertility, and busy industry. With their peaked sugar-loafed hats, some of the Chinamen are hoeing their fields, some are gathering their cotton. The women are sitting in the yards ginning it, by a gin which has probably been in use for centuries among these people, and is precisely the same as that which gave fame to Whitney, established a new element of western civilization, made our wealth in the South, and ties monarchical, oligarchical, *old* England to young, rampant, democratic America. Old and wrinkled China women, turning those two little cylinders, and dropping out cotton seed, how little do you dream, how little can you comprehend the great social, political, and religious machine, over which you are now getting so tired. It controls a world, makes noblemen, and does not clothe you much more than fig leaves would, and nothing like so neatly.

There in the shade sits another China woman, busily whirring round a spinning-wheel of the rudest and most simple construction, but carrying three spindles. It is kept in motion by a treadle, which is nothing more than a stick like a barrel stave, sharpened at one end, and that end resting in a socket upon one side of the plane of the wheel, while the other rests upon a little bridge, lifting it from the ground.

Just rising above the line of a high hedge or live fence, are seen the tiled roofs, with peaked and carved gables, of one story cottages—the dwellings of the Chinese farmers. There are various conveniences for the necessities of man provided by the authorities along the wayside, and here we have now come to one of them, a small, tiled-roofed shed, supported on four brick columns, and covering stone seats, upon which several wearied wayfarers are now resting themselves. Such is the purpose of these public resting-places. They are placed at the distance of every six miles or eighteen li.

In our short ride we have passed two low, squat monuments, or towers, with a hole in the upper part of one side. These are public baby-houses, to receive the bodies of those infants who are dead by chance or their parents' will. They are pitched into these baby-houses, and female children, being of but little value, make up the mass of the filling in of these towers. Just on the outside of the city we noticed a large building, covering much ground. This was a provincial Wei Kwei, or council hall of the men, who, from some neighboring province, were resident for the time being in Shanghae. It was also the place of deposit for their dead until an opportunity occurred of bearing them to their native place. Every province has such an establishment in these foreign cities in which those absent from their native province are in sufficient numbers to justify it. A few miles from the city, amid the farms and fields, another extensive and strongly-walled establishment attracted the attention. It was as carefully defended by its close walls as a fortress. This was a pawnbroker's establishment. It is well stored with goods at the eventful New Year when debts are to be paid, and being, upon other necessities, the depot of much valuable property, there is much care needed to guard the building from the assaults of banditti. I noticed that the walls of a similar establishment in the city of Shanghae are much higher than those of the city. In many places the farmers were still busy irrigating their rice fields. An exceedingly simple, but effectual chain pump, such as any person could make, and worked either by hand or buffalo power, drew the water from either the natural water courses, or from artificial ponds, and cast it over the fields. Most of the grain, however, was beyond this necessity.

At Sik-a-Wa, we were, as is the habit, very cordially received by the French and Italian priests, and conducted over their establishment, which was in most excellent order. The boys were then at their various amusements. They are generally the children of Christian (Roman) parents. The institution—indeed, China—has recently sustained a great loss in the death of one of the priests, who had great skill in modeling and sculpture. Some of the Chinese now work from the instructions received from this person; but his own models and work in the museum of the workshop, win the highest commendation of connoisseurs.

The poor people in the neighborhood of Shanghae lighted their thankful lamps too soon. When we first made their acquaintance last year, we found them parched and perishing with drought, and devoured by clouds of hungry locusts. This year all has gone on prosperously, and the lamp-lighted earth and waters bless the stars by imitating their brilliancy.

The first week in September came in with a light atmosphere and a frightfully falling barometer. The big ships lying in port began to look sensibly prudent and ugly—down came all their dandy work. The light tracery of their delicate spars and yards, which stood so proudly in the calm and sunshine, "hauled in its horns," just as the judicious snail does when a suspicion of danger to his house and home reaches his foresight. The rain and wind now came in all the power and quantity of a terrific gale, and when the flood tide came in, it rose above the river banks and spread out over the city. The next flood tide was yet more beyond all bounds and bonds. It floated two dead Chinamen, and one dead foreigner, into the yard of the French consulate. One could visit their friends and go to church in a boat. The tide had not been known so high in nine years.

Except that the light-ship anchored off the mouth of the river is said to have disappeared with all on board of her, we hear of no other loss of life. The Chinese steamer Confucius has gone in search of her; but the probability is, she went down at her anchors.

The country around Shanghae has been desolated. A few days ago, the fields were snowy with the ungathered cotton, and the full-headed rice was just putting on the rich color of maturity. Now they are all prostrate and mud-washed.

Ships which had recently left port returned after the subsidence of the gale, entirely dismasted, and many disasters told of the violence of the cyclone; at the same time a great deal of information was collected from the logs of different vessels, illustrating the law of rotary storms. The Buenos Ayrean schooner Antonita had the gale from N. E. to E. N. E., moderating round to E. and E. S. E. Another vessel, the Lanrick, had it at the same time from W. N. W. to W. S. W., moderating to S. W. These two vessels were, therefore, in opposite semicircles of the typhoon with its centre between them.

The Water Witch happened to be in that. The hurricane blowing from the north, fell to a dead calm for a a quarter of an hour. "The sky is bright overhead, and the stars are seen shining brightly, while all around is in gloom and darkness. Birds and even fishes are dropping and tumbling about the decks in great numbers. The tumultuous sea breaks in all directions, sweeping over the ship from end to end." * The storm then came furiously from the south, all showing that the Water Witch was in the centre of the cyclone. Captain Baker of this vessel, places her at midnight, on September 13th, in latitude 26° 12′ N., longitude 122° 18′ E., which makes its position one hundred sixty miles N. E. by E. from that of the Lanrick, and one hundred fifty miles S. E. by S. from that of the Antonita. The light-ship, after sundry narrow escapes, was found all safe, though much injured, down the coast.

XXX.

SEDAN CHAIRS.

These chairs are of two kinds. One an oblong, upright box, closed in with curtains and Venetian blinds, and having a heavy wooden top. This chair must weigh something like eighty pounds. Another chair, more chair-shaped, of light bamboo, open and uncovered, is a much more merciful burden upon the shoulders of the chair coolies. It is remarkable to observe what a degenerating and demoralizing institution these chairs are, and how rapidly the degenerating process goes on.

When a foreigner, especially an American, arrives in China, he is disgusted and pained to see comfortable-looking men sitting in their shady chairs, smoking their cigars, reading books, or being carried side by side with

* North China Herald.

a lady, who in another chair is thus *taking her evening walk*, while the chair coolies are reeking with perspiration, panting under their burden, and many of them marked with tumors produced by the pressure of the sticks upon their shoulders, while the same burning sun whose lightest ray the chair lounger shuns as a pestilence, is beating in ardent fury upon the often uncovered heads of his bearers. There seems something humiliating and unmanly in the admission that these two miserable, light "cash"-supported, rice-fed, contemptible, despised Chinamen should have the physical vigor to walk off with these ponderous vehicles upon their shoulders, and the dead weight of a beef-fed foreigner's carcase in addition, while the foreigner is unable to locomote his sole self.

On a slave plantation, or in any city of a southern State, the most delicate and fragile lady would be ashamed to make a beast of burden of the negro slaves, whilst it is not at all improbable that the two heavy old or new Englishmen now promenading upon the backs of these sweating Chinamen, are denouncing the horrors of American slavery.

So far as my own limited observation goes, it teaches that gentlemen from the slave States of our South are more repugnant in China to making beasts of burden of human beings than are any other foreigners.

Two reasons are urged in defense of this painful indolence. One is, that the coolies like it—that is, they want the employment; and the other is, the sun. There is a most fanatical horror of the sun among the foreign residents of China which does not seem to be at all justified by facts. As soon as a stranger arrives in China, every one who has the privilege of speaking to him at once warns him of the horrors of the sun. He must not move in it, must not show himself to it, nor by any means allow it to paint one bronzing touch upon his skin. It is fever, dysentery, liver complaint, though, strange enough, you never hear it is *coup de soleil*, and the stranger feels pestilence in every warming ray. Nothing, however, is said to the new-comer against sundry brandies and water—brandies and soda may pop harmlessly through every sweltering hour of the day—porter and port, sherry by the quart. Tiffins at one, of hot meats and strong drink; dinners commencing at 8 P. M., and floated along two or three hours on rosy wine, are only named as genial appliances of the climate. For exercise to work up all this material a drowsy stroll in the evening damps and chills of the ferns and rice marshes, or the violent evening exertion of a bowling alley or racket court or billiard-room is thought sufficient.

Although the sun is everywhere, in warm weather, uncomfortable, and too great an exposure to it dangerous, yet it may be a question whether this Chinese celery blanching of the surface, and the atony thus induced in the skin, and through it in the whole of the internal organs so extensively sympathizing with it, is not a greater source of disease than would be that degree of exposure to the open air and sun which would indurate and bronze the surface.

It is a well established principle that exposure in a malarious country is more safe in the middle and heat of the day than in the morning or evening chills; and topographically as well as endemically, as respects foreigners, China is a malarious country, and especially the neighborhood of Shanghae. It is my conviction, though, I admit, a merely theoretical one, that the sun of Shanghae, the solar heat, is not so influential for evil as it is in New York or Philadelphia, simply because it is not so great. The summer climate of Shanghae is more moderate than that of either of the above-named places. The general exposure of the loaded, laboring coolies of Shanghae to the midday sun—the burden coolies, chair coolies, and boatmen—could not take place in New York without more instances of *coup de soleil* than I ever heard of here. In fact, I never heard of any, though they may have occurred, although the streets were crowded with the bare, semi-shaven heads of these men tottering under heavy burdens at the fiery hours of the day. And I doubt if the cloistered, sedan and umbrella-blanched residents of Shanghae could compare in health with the sun-bronzed seamen, the officers of the national and mercantile vessels which visited the port. Of course the drunken and licentious ships' crews are not to be taken as a standard. I know it may be answered me, "These strangers are more healthy, because they are but temporarily exposed to the deleterious influence of the climate." True, but not being acclimated, they are more amenable to climatic and any special solar influence that may be existing.

It is my duty to say that these opinions are advanced contrary to the testimony of preceding writers, and contrary to the alleged and supposed experience of long resident lay and professional men. But a prevalent opinion is not always a correct one, and one that will stand the test of facts and principles. The most apparent sensible cause, particularly if it is one of physical annoyance, is often concluded to be the true cause of any immediate or simultaneous morbid effect. In our own agueish districts, when the thin, chilled, sallow victims stand in the genial sun's rays, they are warned not to do so, because the sun gives them the "ager." The sun is a seen and felt influence; the mysterious, invisible, nerve-shaking, and paralyzing malaria, which steals upon them in the shades of night, is not seen.

I throw out these suggestions for the consideration of those who are most interested in testing their truth, and have the best opportunities for doing so. The truth is important, not only in a hygienic but in a moral and religious point of view. I have heard those who were disposed to seek every flaw in the missionaries' character, and to censure them for human infirmity, say: "I saw so and so to-day (Sunday) in his sedan chair, on the shoulders of his coolies, going to church, to preach, and I did not go to hear him, because I remembered the command, 'Keep holy the Sabbath day, thou and thy servants.'" And although these same missionaries honestly believed they were the victims of a law of necessity, they are certainly open to the comments of those who find no necessity sufficiently urgent to prevent them from trudging about on foot. And when we see ladies seat themselves in a sedan chair, and mount the backs of two coolies, we are very apt to think of our own wives and daughters, and even of these same ladies who, without horses or carriages, or coolies, in the more intemperate climate of home, have to do all their visiting and shopping on foot.

My heretical tendency of opinion has the disadvantage of being opposed to the innate sensuality and indolence of men who find it much more agreeable to move about in the shade of a sedan chair upon the backs of coolies, than in the open air upon their own feet.

I did find some few obstinate men, who, in practice and opinion, conformed to my views, and who volunteered to me their gratification that I had denounced the popular luxury, but these were hard, healthy, brown, and somewhat rough-looking individuals. I was also sustained by the opinion of some non-resident professional gentlemen, and that of one who accumulated a retiring fortune in the south of China. He thought much infirmity was incident to the panic flight from the sun's rays, especially with children. Indeed, it has grown into a maxim that children, at five or six years of age, must be sent to their European or American homes to be saved.

This gentleman had for years acted upon this opinion,

16*

and spent many enthusiastic, laborious hours, in all the heat of a southern Chinese sun; but he could not do so if he took any stimulants. He left China in good health. One case is no conclusive testimony, but it helps to reach the truth.

Although, during nearly two years of my residence in China, I suffered from one of the debilitating diseases of the climate, contracted, originally, in Siam; yet, I walked much and freely through the sun, at all hours of the day, both in Hong Kong and Shanghae. I did this at times when, in prudence, I ought not to have done so in any climate, and at the cost of many lectures, protests, and threatening warnings from my kind friends. However, my repugnance to the chairs and to riding my fellow-men, not "booted and spurred," but chaired and cigarred, was very great, and, then, I owed the allegiance of a martyr to my heresy of opinion. My health was gradually but perceptibly improved. I do not, of course, attribute the result to the exposure—indeed, am willing to admit it may have retarded my recovery—and, yet, there may be a question whether my ultra and imprudent running about in the sun, with its toning and tanning, its indurating effect and that of the accompanying exercise, did not do me good, at least proportionate to the injury. However, I do not advise it as a general practice; I merely mean to suggest that an exposure to the sun of China is no more mysteriously dangerous than the same amount of exposure in Baltimore, Philadelphia, New York, or Boston; but, in the latter places, there are no chair coolies to make the sun such a pestilence. The most healthy foreign children I saw in China were those of missionaries—children who ran out of doors freely as they do at home.

These chairs are a part of the moral and social system of the Chinese, and hence there are reasons for their use, which foreigners have not. A chair of a certain kind and decoration is necessary to a marriage—a bridal-chair. The jealousy of their women, and the spirit of female seclusion, renders necessary some such means of shutting them up when they go out. The rank of a Chinese is indicated by the number of men who bear his chair, as well as by its color, only important men being entitled to a green chair. They are the traveling conveyances, about twenty-four miles being the day's journey with four bearers, each pair relieving at suitable distances.

XXXI.

THE AMERICAN EAGLE IN SHANGHAE.

There is, I am sorry to admit, too much reason for Americans in China becoming, as the old mandarin is said to have said, "second class Englishmen."

The United States in its collective personality holds its head very high at home. It professes to be very rich, very independent, very liberal, very elegant, very commiserating of other nationalities, and very superlatively good and great in all things.

> "But it shall come to pass
> That every braggart shall be found an ass."

In China this great boaster, with so much to boast of, this propagandist of the most modern and improved doctrines of political progress, is superlatively insignificant. The ostrich hides its head and thinks its great lumbering body is concealed. The American eagle looks so much and so proudly upon its own broad bosom that it does not see its distant tail plumage dragging in the mud. But drag it does, and so wretchedly that the eagle's best friends are ashamed of it. In China, instead of holding its head erect and spreading its pinions to a free air, it is a sneaking, mean, dependent beggar, maintaining its official existence by charity and all kinds of wretched shifts. All this will be very distressing to the loyalty of juvenile patriotism, and those who get their blood warmed with the fire of Fourth of July orations. Come on to the stage of life, then, as quick as possible, and change it all.

This round world over, there is no place dotting its surface—none—where it is more incumbent upon the United States to give the outward signs and symbols of its power and its intelligence, than in Shanghae. Here, of all other places, the bushel should be kicked off the light, and its candle set upon the highest hill. It is due to commerce, to morality, and to religion—to say nothing about the great obligations to Buncombe and to the Fourth of July.

We are admitted by treaty to five ports: Canton, Amoy, Fuchau, Ningpo, Shanghae. The extension by the recent treaty does not alter the argument. As Troja, Canton fuit, as far as foreigners are concerned, and before this salt-sowing of Yeh on the ground our feet had desecrated, all we had of Canton, as we have seen, were two close-built city blocks in a suburb outside the wall, and those who ventured out of their prison bounds did so at the risk of their lives.

Much tea is shipped at Fuchau, but this also has an inimical population. The others are but minor points, and afford no facilities for impressing the Chinese.

Now what is Shanghae? It is a large and growing European or American city, with all the comforts and conveniences of our civilization. It is the only city of the kind in China, except the English city of Hong Kong, in the far south, and that is isolated. The foreign Shanghae stands side by side with the murky wall of the Chinese Shanghae, and the freest intercourse exists between the two. Already the wide streets, lofty and large houses with their grounds and shrubbery in the foreign settlement, contrasted with the dirty narrow lanes, the low cramped houses of the Chinese city, have won so upon the natives that much of the foreign city is tenanted or owned by them.

Again, Shanghae belongs to no separate nationality. It is neither American, English nor French, but all—principally the two former in importance and influence; and gentlemen of these nations constitute its municipal government. It has nominal limits, it is true; but only nominal, the facilities for extension are indefinite, and Americans may here spread themselves and widen the area of their national institutions. This mingled nationality is an especial reason why the United States should put on a garb and costume befitting its dignity and importance.

Shanghae is the great silk and tea-shipping port. There are at the moment of this writing, eighty-two vessels in port, and some of them the largest sized American clippers.

Where American commerce can go, the American government can and ought to go with its ships; and for real service we ought not to have on the coast of China any ships drawing more water than such as are in the table, given in a former chapter, but we ought to have several much smaller.

Shanghae is not only the port of the silk district, of the green tea district; but is sufficiently convenient, for all practical purposes, to the best black tea. This, however, finds its egress chiefly at Fuchau. Its close proximity to the opening empire of Japan must greatly add to its future importance, and it is the port from which China chin-chins the United States at San Francisco. They nod and shake hands at each other.

So long as we get our news and information by the English overland mail, there is four or five days' advantage in being down at Hong Kong, but even now a favored merchant ship brings us sometimes as late news by way of California, and when we get steam communication from San Francisco to Shanghae, we shall have the advantage, at this latter port, of fifteen to twenty days over the English overland mail.

Shanghae is that part of China, and that only, in which natives and foreigners come into free contact with each other. Among its fleets of junks the skilled eye can point out those belonging to different provinces, hundreds of miles distant. Country people come into Shanghae to see the foreigners and their beautiful city. Learned men come from Pekin, and are found engaged in literary labors among the foreigners; and the latter travel without molestation, into the interior, although there is a treaty prohibition against it; indeed, some live there with their families, even renting of a mandarin. At this moment two young men are absent as emissaries of the American Episcopal mission, choosing a permanent location in some distant city. This was before the late treaty.

Such being this city of twelve years' growth, it is worth our while to look closely at our national official position in it.

At the point where the Chinese and the foreign cities of Shanghae rest upon its banks, the Wong Po, about a mile broad, makes a horse-shoe curve of from two to three miles from north-east to south-west. A low, green point lies in the hollow of this bend, but leaving the river to curve around it of uniform width.

We will not commence at the upper extremity of the curve upon which lies the Chinese city, but just below the east gate, where commences the foreign settlement. There is not much foreign population here yet; some Chinese houses; and recently built, a French Catholic educational institution upon the back part of the settlement. There are, however, a few large and commodious foreign houses. All this ground is what the French call

"La Concession Française," and we saw that the French consul's aim is to nationalize it, claiming that the people of his great nation shall live there, and I infer, on the contrary, that no other people shall, unless under French jurisdiction. The natural consequence is, there are large tracts of waste, unoccupied land, as, where there are so few Frenchmen, and these have their living to get, they will go where the most favorable site for business is found. As we walk down the "Bund," on the river bank, we come to a very large walled-in lot, with a very high flag-staff, from which flies the tri-color. This is the well-chosen location of the future imperial French consulate. At present M. de Montigny occupies a respectable residence near this inclosure.

We now cross a bridge over the Yang-kin-pang creek, and are in what really is the foreign city of Shanghae. This, as before stated, used to be called the English settlement, from the claim set up by the English consul for exclusive jurisdiction, and that none but the English flag should fly there. A claim firmly resisted by our countrymen, Messrs. Griswold and Cunningham, and set aside by the justice of the English government. Since then, it prospers under amalgamated flags and nationalities, and such will be the fate of "La Concession Française," when there is inducement enough to resist the pretensions of the French consul.

Amid the crowd of boats and the cries of boatmen and laborers, with the river and shipping on the one hand, and stately buildings on the other, we proceed for a mile along this busy way, until we come to where the broad Su-chau creek forms its junction with the Wong Po. Here, at this, the most beautiful of all the locations in Shanghae, looking down the reach of the river, up the waters of the creek, and over the whole settlement, surrounded by large grounds and brick wall, are the showy buildings of the British consulate. The consular residence and court-house, the post office, and the English jail are all here, with the union jack flying in their front.

Leaving this, we cross Su-chau creek on the new tile-paved drawbridge, and we are now in a swampy addition to the original settlement. Mud flats, rice fields, a few new European houses occupied by Chinese, and a village of the aborigine, constitute most of the settlement, excepting that here are the houses and the church of the American Episcopal mission. On this account it is called, I suppose, the American settlement. The "Bund," however, has recently been carried along the river on this side, and following it around, we pass the church and come to another small bridge, and over this we come plump up to a sailor boarding-house. The road, it is true, lies straight before us, marked out, but not made, and leading away into swampy rice fields. We, however, turn around the corner of the sailor boarding-house garden fence, and find our selves in a narrow, muddy alley, back of a row of coal-sheds, and turning into a gate from this alley, we are in the little yard of the United States consulate, a shackling two-story building, of seven small rooms, with a tremendous tall flag-staff flying the United States flag in front of this house which has no front approach to it. Taou Tai, Commissioner, Consul, Governor General, must all visit the United States consul by the muddy alley, unless they come in a boat. Here it stands, the very last house down the river planted in the swamp. Close up to its fence, under its windows, is a hole dug in the mud-bank for a dock-yard, and Shanghae, down the river, ends.

When all these remote and wonder-seeking Chinamen come in to see the foreigners at home, what must be the impressions they carry home respecting the nations whose consulates are in such contrast with each other? Is it any wonder that they regard Americans as second class Englishmen? It is scarce a wonder that Americans regard themselves as such.

But even this wretched place is to some extent a charity. It has been built by the wealthy American house of Russell & Co., as a refuge for the American consul, because there is none other for him, on any terms, and if there were any vacancies, they could not be had upon any rent the United States consul could pay. This place would cost in the United States about twelve or fifteen hundred dollars to build it, and it rents moderately at eight hundred dollars. Its cost here I do not know.

There is one great advantage in the United States consulate. Being the last house down the river, on the lower arm of the horse-shoe, it offers a beautiful view of the river and the city above it. It is said people go down into deep and dark wells to look, at noon-day, upon the stars in the high heavens. We take our stars down into the lowest depths, that we may look up at the flashing tri-color and the fiery cross of St. George. As we are down here, we may as well make the best of it. The place is a little damp, and dismal, and soggy, but what a bright, cloudless October day spreads a golden flood of light around us and over the scene. In front of us flows the river and over it lies the green lowland point with its groves, sailors' cemetery, and a few buildings. It hides most of the Chinese city, but beyond this point we see what looks like a sapling forest, stripped of its leaves by autumnal frosts. These are the up and down slender masts of the junks lying in front of the Chinese town. Just below them, seen over the point, commences the massing together of the tall masts and cross-spars of the foreign shipping, a curving crowd down the course of the river, thinning out a little as they approach us, until there are only about twenty-four opposite our position to the lowest limit about half a mile below us — forty-eight British flags, thirteen American, five Siamese, four Dutch, three Spanish, two Hamburg, two French, one Danish, one Bremen. These foreigners, though, except when they are busy with the cargo-boats, loading or unloading, present but the still or sleeping life of the river. They are resting from their long journey. Its life and animation are in the native junks. It is now flood-tide and a fair wind, and they glide by us in such numbers, with all their brown, tan-colored sails set, generally four narrow, oblong sails, the two longest on the two middle masts, one shorter on the bow, and one on the stern—it will puzzle you to count them. They glide by with the rapidity of railroad cars. The numerous little sampans, with their various and fanciful flags, red streaks, and arched mat roofs, gliding in every direction, with the tide, against it, across the stream, give animation to the scene. Everybody who has any thing to do upon the water has his own sampan; every ship in the harbor employs its own, and each of these private boats is distinguished by some private flag, and the number taxes the invention to find variety. In addition to these private boats, numbers lie at each wharf for chance hire.

Whilst these river scenes are passing before us, the sun has sank to his setting, and we have four nationalities celebrating the close of the day. Crack go two muskets, and these, followed by the notes of a bugle, tell that the Frenchman has made it sundown. A roll of the drum salutes the descent of the English and American ensigns, and then the band of the San Jacinto harmoniously carries the day into night, when the Russians raise their voices from the deck of the America in a Christian anthem to the God of all. But we have not done with our own eagle's doings in Shanghae. The consul is a judge, a sheriff. He daily makes arrests, holds courts, and is sustained with great physical ability by a stout marshal. The theatre of all these dignified doings is a little out-building just ten feet square, and alongside the door the eagle, with outstretched wings, is painted on a sign in the most ferocious attitude. But when the consul has tried his culprits and condemned them, what is he to do with them to meet the ends of justice? The consul's culprits are not much incumbered with scrip, lands or houses, and having probably been, at the last event, kicked out of some loafing refuge, for want of financial resources, they are not amenable to fine, and what is he to do with them? He has no jail; the British consul has. If the British consul were a crusty official, and not disposed to extend the hospitalities of the jail, there would be an end to the matter; but at the time of my observation, a courteous and gentlemanly person, Mr. Robertson, was in the office, and was very liberal of his jail facilities; still it was not proper to ride a free horse to death—and this consideration very often brought terms of justice down to terms of mercy. We may suppose some such sentence as the following:

"Your crime entitles you to three months' confinement, but inasmuch as I can not trespass so long as that on the hospitality of the British government, I send you over for three weeks;" or maybe the United States consul writes over to his British colleague:

U. S. CONSULATE.

MY DEAR MR. ROBERTSON:

I have six rascals who have been committing outrages in the country, and I want to shut them up for a month. I know that your accommodations are limited, and you have many claimants of your own. I am so often indebted to your courteous hospitality that I dislike much to be a trespasser, but would be glad to know the extent to which you can accommodate me, and if not to the whole number, they can draw lots for the chance.

Yours, with thanks for past favors,

—— ———. *U. S. Consul.*

H. M. CONSULATE, SHANGHAE.

MY DEAR COLLEAGUE:

I am a little crowded, but to accommodate you, and to secure the peace of the community, I will let out four of my mitigated rascals and take in six of yours.

I have the honor to be,

Your friend in official need.

—— ———, *H. M. Consul.*

The United States consulate was a good theatre for observing the ascendency of the Japhetic over the Shemitic race. I have seen the lowest puddle of our noble blood asserting its superiority in this wise: a fellow with a stout cudgel, felt hat pressed down over his reddened eyes and face, rings in his ears, dragging in two crying Chinamen by their long queues, to have them adjudged by his consul for some offense against this noble American; and when he found the consul was not there, and thought none saw him, King Demos wanted to know why the d—l the consul was not there, and with curses in English, and curses in Chinese, with an occasional kick, would, if permitted to go on, have been his own judge and executioner.

Without any exaggeration, indeed, feeling that I have failed to reach the force of truth, I have made an effort to show by facts and observation the nature of the United States consulate in Shanghae. Any one could attend to the stereotyped affairs of merchant ships and sailors; but the constantly arising questions to be determined without precedent, in such a chaotic jurisdiction require a man of the first order in character, ability, and legal attainments. I offer now the testimony of one of the most able United States consuls in China. His remark was, "We have never had a consul in China equal to the requirements of his position. He should be in character and acquirements all that an able judge is at home." There is often a good deal of cant about the poor pay of our officials abroad, because they can not compete with the representatives of other nations in dinner parties and other splendid entertainments.

I have never been able to recognize the force of this kind of argument; because the simplicity and honesty of our government have repudiated the falsity, the intrigue, and deception of the old diplomatic art, and asking nothing but what is right, submitting to nothing that is wrong, it needs no dinner-table diplomacy to attain its ends, and ought to be above using it; and as a principle to be reflected back upon its own people, I think that our foreign representatives should set forth the simplicity and economy of our government, rather than imitate the luxury and extravagance of those whose institutions we have set aside.

Further, I think that the whole system of permanent or resident ministers, and of permanent squadrons among civilized western nations, only relics of the necessities of a past age, and now productive of more evil and difficulty than good. In our country the diplomatic path is one of those which leads to political elevation, and all who have the opportunity are anxious to tread it. Hence, when a minister or naval commander finds himself upon a station where things are quiet, and gliding along peaceably, he feels that he is stagnating, and rather than do this he is tempted to raise a breeze of his own; to cultivate a crop of noxious weeds that he may show his skill in felling them beneath his diplomatic scythe. Flying squadrons; and foreign ministers only as occasions arose for their need, would take much from the motives to discord, and tend to the world's peace; but, as an unhappy result, there would be fewer places for office-seekers.

Notwithstanding such views of the manner in which our pacific and military relations with civilized nations should be maintained, I make China an exception. I now advocate that the United States be materially represented in China by an imposing official residence and squadron; that here, unless we are to be admitted to Pekin, should be the residence of the United States minister or commissioner, and not down in the Portuguese settlement at Macao, as far from the Emperor of China as he can well get. The consul should be fitted for the complicated duties we have seen to be continually pressing upon him, and should have a court-house and jail on the official grounds. These external displays of power are necessary to impress a people who can not read about us, can not comprehend our political position, and who regard an absence of state and display as the confession of imbecility and humility.

I have recently heard an anecdote related, I am not sure of its truth, that the French consul was expatiating to the Taou Tai upon the greatness and power of the French nation—pointed to its territorial extent, and spoke of its great navy. The Taou Tai replied: "It was strange the representative of so great a nation should reside in Shanghae, in so small a house;" yet the French consulate was a palace to that of the United States.

To facilitate our diplomatic relations with the Chinese, we should have properly trained interpreters of our own, and not be dependent upon the Chinese, who will never translate an unwelcome truth to a superior among themselves. Our interpreters also ought to be acquainted, not only with the colloquial dialect, but with the philosophy and literature of the Chinese mandarin language. So far, we have found our interpreters only among the missionaries.

On the morning following the night upon which I had written the foregoing, I witnessed a large group of Chinamen in the yard in much commotion, two of their commoner sort of sedan chairs, and two wretched, rowdy-looking foreigners in charge of the marshal of the consulate.

A most barbarous murder had been committed on the preceding evening upon a respectable, unoffending Chinese mechanic. Upon resisting some insult offered his family, these fellows had gone off, collected a band, and, returning, murdered the man, and mutilated him in the most savage manner. Such are the incidents by which we are to preserve the kindly feeling of the Chinese.

XXXII.

SOO-CHAU, THE PARIS OF CHINA.

On Sunday night, September 29th, after attending service at the American Episcopal mission, I went with Mr. Jenkins, the interpreter to the United States consulate, on board of his boat for a hap-hazard trip into the interior for a few days.

The neighborhood of Tzang Hai, above the ocean, or, as we call it, Shanghae, is that part of China which foreigners can visit with most impunity, and here they do so constantly, extending their journeys to hundreds of miles. Indeed, some have rented houses at a distance of seventy miles from the city, and reside there with their families.

There are certain points which are so habitually resorted to by foreigners that no difficulty occurs in regard to them. Our object, however, was to reach the great city of Soo-chau, about eighty-two miles from Shanghae. It is distinguished for its fine and rich work in art, and for the extent, variety, and elegance of its dissipation.

Our friendly relations with the authorities at Shanghae would seem to warrant the expectation that we might go under their sanction; but this had been tried before, and failed from their unwillingness to take the responsibility of any unknown and mystical vagaries of which foreigners might be guilty, or ignorant trouble in which they might involve themselves.

They are simply very well dispesed, very obliging, disposed to be courteous personally, but do not like to give an official endorsement upon a venture, the extent and risks of which they do not comprehend. "Never mind any permission, you go—maybe they will not interrupt you, or send you back; and if they do, that's all." It was one of those things to be winked at, not permitted.

"Our boat," the style of conveyance in which this kind of traveling is generally done, merits singling out, by a description, from the many-shaped and purposed boats which course the Chinese waters. In the first place, it was of a bright, pale, clear, inviting color, being that of the natural wood, varnished. Its general shape was that of a double triangle—an apex of four feet broad making the bow, and widening for two thirds of the length, and then narrowing to six feet from the stern. It was nearly forty feet long, by eleven wide, and drew six inches of water. About twenty feet of the body, or centre of the boat, was inclosed and roofed over with an arching roof, like a canal boat, and this was divided into three apartments—that nearest the bow, a miniature dining-room with a miniature table, all leaves, to drop and be out of the way, and the two side seats could be made two roughing, picnic berths for any extra passengers. But the main sleeping apartment was the central division, with two roomy berths resting on capacious sets of drawers, and with provisions for making the whole breadth of the apartment one field bed. Astern of this was a wash-room, pantry, china closet, and servants' sleeping apartment. It seemed that with Chinese condensation of storage, every plank in the floor, and around the seats of the apartments, covered some snug stowhole. The bow and stern, about five feet forward, and ten or twelve aft, were decked over, the former making a place for comfortable dry stowage, and the latter giving all the accommodations above and below, for the four crew, the cook and the kitchen; and for working the wonderful scull, or propeller, which is the great motive power in all these boats, large and small. The flat, arching roof of our apartments was made water-tight by a covering of black tarred matting.

The whole arrangement was so commodious, snug and comfortable, that it hardly allowed room for the excitement of privation and adventure. There was no chance to show one's make-shift abilities or cheerful endurance of discomfort.

We slept on board, so as to be able to take advantage of the first flood tide of the morning; and we did so on the morning of the 27th, at five o'clock. A mizzling, gray morning. We had slept our sleep among the crowd of junks off the cathedral of Tonkadoo, and the matin bells were calling the worshipers as we loosed our sail to the morning fair wind, and gave our hull to the flood tide. We had a sail and a mast on our light roof, and queer affairs they were. Two side stanchions ascended from the lower and more substantial part of the vessel, and rose six inches above the roof; upon these was fastened, across the roof, a strong piece of timber, and resting on a pivot, on this beam, so as to be elevated or depressed as occasion required, was a triangle of two legs, which formed our mast. When raised, a stay from the apex, hooked into the bow, kept it from falling aft, and a piece of wood, leading from each leg of the mast to the stay, kept it from pitching forward.

We were amid a crowd as we glided up the river. It seemed to be a thronged highway of junks, with their brown, tan-colored sails. In one group ahead, I counted seventy, and there were other groups on every side of us. Sometimes we would be among a crowd of them, and I feared that one or two heavy fellows bearing down upon us must crush us, but just as the crash was coming, these boats would glide by each other as if by a magic touch, or, at most, there would be but a slight brush. Loud and apparently confused shouts of the Chinamen in each boat seemed to be a necessary part of the movement, though, as they stood with poles in their hands, to ward off the impending shock, and without anger in their expression, I concluded that the cries were only part of the system. They are wonderful boatmen, these Chinese, but why should they not be? Why should not the bird fly, or the fish swim?—born in a boat, live in a boat, die in a boat. One of those which came rushing down upon us, had no one it, visible, but an old man at the helm, and a child standing amidships. I thought they must certainly come into collision with us, but neither the old man nor little boy seemed in the least embarrassed. Just as she seemed about to strike, the boy loosened a string, a lee-board dropped down the side of the boat, her lee-way was at once arrested, and she ranged up alongside of us, just failing to touch.

The banks of the river were as animated with life and the struggle for food, as the river itself. Hunger feeding hunger; the hunger of man guiding his intellect into conflict with hunger and instinct. All along both banks, rising and falling, were the great balloon-looking fishermen's nets. These nets are from twenty to thirty feet square, and suspended from the four extremities of two immense bamboo bows, crossing each other at right angles. A platform is built out on a frame a little way into the river; the junction of the bows is suspended from the apex of a triangle of two bamboos, which, passing horizontally to the platform, is pivoted to a roller on its end; from this roller another similar triangle rises into the air and has a weight at its upper end to counterbalance that of the net and its fixtures. A rope passes from the point of the triangle which supports the net, up over that which rises from the roller, and so down to a little mat shed on the platform, in which sits the fisherman. A child by this rope, and the intervening levers, can raise the net from beneath the water where it has been waiting its finny prey. The business this morning did not appear to be a profitable one. For miles and hours I watched the rising and falling of these nets, and saw but one tiny fish taken. The fishermen, however, do not lead a lazy, fruitless life, as, while waiting for their prey, they are busy in some other handicraft, net-weaving, or some kindred pursuit. But as the life is favorable to contemplation, and Chinese democracy takes its great men from all ranks, it may be hoped that these mat sheds are ripening some future Chinese philosopher and reformer. As the day advanced we met many boats laden with rice straw, neatly stacked and thatched. The shores, too, had a pleasant, rural look—snug, one-storied farm-houses, and many neat-looking, thatched-roof barracks standing through the fields. About noon we passed the town of Ming Hong, a neat-looking village of about thirty thousand inhabitants, and quite an extensive rice depot.

At dark we came to the large town on Pine river, of Soong Kong, a place of more than half a million of inhabitants. Our way lay by canal through a portion cf the city. We were now thirty-four miles from Shanghae. An hour was passed at Soong Kong while our men purchased and ate their supper.

It was still misty and rainy on the morning of the 28th. We were in a clean creek, or canal, of about one hundred feet width, passing through broad and heavily-grown rice fields, with comfortable-looking farm-houses and their accompanying graves. Everywhere on our journey were seen those constant dots on Chinese scenery, graves. The naked coffin, the matted grave, the bricked-up and tile-covered coffin, with a small grove around it—there they lie, through the field and on the banks.

The wind was now ahead, and two of the crew, with a long cord about the size of the little finger, made fast to the apex of our triangular mast, were on shore tracking the boat. We were approaching an old and crumbling arched stone bridge, just by a large, yellow-washed temple and a village. Some six or eight miles behind us were the hills, a series of small mountains about forty miles from Shanghae, and ahead arose a pagoda, that of the city of Ching-poo. At this place we arrived at a little before eight o'clock, and remained there two hours, to market and breakfast. The clear, creek-like canal we were traveling formed the broad moat of the city; and on one side of us, with a few feet of greensward and canal track intervening, rose the dark city wall, here and there hanging out a green banner of clinging shrub and climbing vine. The wall was of the black brick of China, laid upon a granite foundation, all smoothly laid, and the regular line of its upper edge was a succession of loop-holes. There were land gates and water gates, the latter passing under arches into the city. The narrow ledge of land intervening between the wall and the water was here and there stolen by some pious Chinaman, too poor to buy elsewhere the ground upon which to place the coffin of his father.

Our boatmen brought our boat up alongside the bank, just where a drawbridge, opposite a city gate, crossed the stream. We came here to eat our breakfast; but in the angle between the bridge and the wall, there was a lot of dead squatters, rich in corruption, if they were never rich in any thing before, and sovereigns of the soil by the right of occupation, and the grace of antique usages, but as a crowd of courtier flies buzzed around some of the fresher-looking coffins, I insisted upon our boatmen changing to a clearer spot of the green bank.

If a man had no other inducement to travel among a strange people, his vanity ought to be a sufficient incentive; I mean by "ought," would in general have sufficient power. It may be very disagreeably so, but a man under such circumstances is individualized and great for the moment. This momentary distinction is often the only pleasure of the kind which most of us know, and therefore we have a natural right to make the most of it. How often at home and abroad do we figure in "fuss and feather" parades and processions, attracting the eyes of the gaping crowd by our decorations, and carrying ourselves more proudly because of this popular gaze, although those who thus tickle our vanity never saw us before—see us only for a moment—never will see us again—would not know us if they did, and that which attracted them is no essential part of ourselves, and would have the same effect upon any other man. An Indian without the adventitious aid of paint and feathers must feel himself by and of himself something when he is the centre of a following crowd in a civilized city. Thus as the various boat laborers and boat households came along in their indifferent, listless, every-day manner, it certainly was a tribute to one's importance to see the whole change of expression which came over the tenants of these boats when they saw us standing in the bow of ours, or with our heads through its windows. The men would light up to a grin, break from silence into speech, and the women and children crowd the openings of the boat and peep timidly forth.

Upon leaving Ching-poo we turned suddenly from the wall into a narrow canal, on each side of which was a thickly built village. Here we were "distinguished strangers." The people in the front line of houses came out into the street, abandoning all occupations; the children looked at us with an appalled fascination, but clung to their mothers' garments. Most families were at their breakfasts—true enthusiasts rushed away from all, careful and prudent people brought their bowl of rice and chop-sticks in their hands, but suspended operations while they studied us. The mere sensualist and gourmand, who had no taste for the sublimity of novelty, was content to come only to the door, and with bowl and sticks to his mouth, toss the snowy grain down his cavernous throat while he took an indifferent look at us. Such people preferred food for their stomachs to that for their imaginations—the humble comforts of home to any foreign wonders. They wounded our egotism, and we have a reason for prophesying evil of them; we read their characters and careers in a single glance—"very slow bellies." Those benevolent individuals who delight in sharing their blessings with others, by a shout or a message called out their friends in the back settlements, who came down the side lanes to look and wonder. We had the general distinction of being foreigners, and in the sight of these shaven-crown, smooth-haired, long-queued, smooth-chinned Celestials, we had the specific attractions of bushy, frizzled heads, and bushy, grizzled beards.

Just after passing through this village several small boats sculled rapidly by us, one man in the stern, and along both sides and the bow sat grave and dignified rows of long hooked-beak, dirty, dark-looking birds, about the size of well-sized ducks, longer and narrower in the bodies. This was an illustration of the further encroachments of intellect, making a trained servant of the appetite and instinct of an inferior animal. These were the fishing cormorants, going out with their masters for a day's work and sport. Arrived upon the fishing ground, the unfeathered biped strikes the water with his bamboo wand, and over go his plumed associates, down under the water and up again with the struggling silver-scaled prey in their beaks, that is, if they were lucky or skillful enough to find it. No matter how many boats there may be present, or how great the intermingling of cormorants, each one returns without mistake to his owner's craft, and deposits his prize.

Various ingeniously contrived devices, wares, labyrinthine avenues of bamboo, with bamboo stakes across the stream, over which our boat scraped and cleaned her bottom, presented modes of fishing adapted to the tastes of the fisherman, and the habits of the fished for. Not only was Chinese energy at work upon the animal life of the water, but some small families, a young man and his wife, for instance, who had just set up in love and matrimony, with little other capital, were busy in their small boat in transferring the vegetation from beneath the waters to the surface of the soil. These boats, in the distance, seemed to be laden with heaps of fresh-cut green grass. It was the weed from the bottom of the stream. Two slender bamboos are fastened together as a pair of long-handled, straight forceps, and being passed to the bottom, grasps a few fibres, and then by twisting round and round, a mass of the long green hair is torn from the heads of the river gods, or whatever else it grows upon in the damp depths of the stream.

All this day would be called a cheerless one by those who measure cheer by the presence of sunshine and the absence of moisture in the atmosphere. But I could not get up any kind of gloom myself. These broad rice fields seemed to be laughing with fatness, and nodding wavy welcomes as we passed their borders; the people seemed to think us such funny fellows—they grinned so cheerily; we were such a cause of mirth to others, that how could we be less than merry ourselves? True, it was very perseveringly rainy, very head-windy, and very muddy, so that there was no getting out of the boat for a walk, and then our poor boatmen had to track—track—track on the tow path all the day through the rain and through the black mud; but if there had been no external novelties to attract our attention, we had, among our small number of Chinamen, two originals. Ayouk was our personal coolie, cook, chambermaid, valet de chambre, comprador, etc. He wore an old pair of what had been thick white-soled, embossed black velvet shoes, now down at the heel, and only used for out on deck, being reverently put off when he entered our apartment. He then came in his stocking, or rather legging, feet—cotton leggings which had a trace and tradition of once having been white; these met and overlapped at the knees, with their gaping, boot-like tops, a pair of short Nankeen trowsers, likewise of a traditional color, but most likely yellow, and leggings and trowsers were banded together with a pair of frayed black velvet garters, with embroidered white satin centres. Overhanging all these was a loose, large sleeved, toga-throated, faded blue Nankeen jacket, or compromise between shirt and jacket, fastening with loops over the remaining few dingy brass bell buttons which, in its days of freshness, had brightened it. His head was shaven a breadth of two inches all around, and the remainder of his long hair was plaited into a queue mingled with the white cotton threads of mourning, showing that he had lost some friend. This black and white plait of cotton and hair he wore as a coronal around his head. Ayouk was a philosopher and a student of human nature, and seemed so satisfied with himself that he was generally good-humored and quite fond of pithy remarks. In his many offices he had much to do, and got through it all by that great lever, an adhesion to plan and system. He had clearly come to the conclusion that we foreigners were a very impatient people, that our impatience was a gusty wind that should not turn him from his course, that we had certain periodic wants recurring with each hour of the day, and, therefore, however long and loudly we might call "Ayouk," "Ayouk," he only hallooed back in louder tones until he had got ready that thing which he supposed was fitted to that hour, when in he came with a smile of satisfaction, and was generally so correct as to divert the rising want and anger, or get plenty of time to meet the former. Thus by having his own way he did best for himself and for us. Such was "Ayouk," a man worthy in his vocation, and the cause of mirth on a gloomy day, or of vexation on a bright one, according as he was viewed.

Our other original was Ang, or son Number Five, such being the way in which some parents arithmetically name their children. This man was an illustration of the power of fashion. An umbrella at all times, and a lantern even on moonlight nights, is essential to Chinese respectability. Ang was the head man on our track, that is, the leading man at the rope. When the two men jumped ashore to take the tow line, the other one would do so in his bare feet, and with no useless protectors against mud and rain. But Ang must first lash on a pair of straw sandals; these, however, might have been of some use as a protection to his feet, but under his arm always was an umbrella, an old umbrella made of paper, but split in two or three places so that one third of it was gone, and son Number Five, as he bowed himself forward and pulled at the tow rope, had little protection from the driving rain; but still he had his umbrella, and the ludicrous combination could but be an amusement to the folk inside.

The night came on so gusty and adverse that we tied up alongside of a cotton field, and lay snugly there, all hands sound asleep, until the break of the following day.

September 30th.—When I first went out of the cabin my morning salutation was *qua, qua* from a crow. Upon looking up I saw a very respectable and portly looking individual in glossy black velvet, with a broad white cravat around his neck, and I saw, too, that he spoke to me from the heights of a grove of lofty trees, and therefore had two beautiful sightsin one look. I had more; with my vision thus elevated, and looking beyond the present, it rested in the misty distance upon a mountain, at least a rocky, forest-grown hill six hundred feet high, with a terraced pagoda springing out of its summit.

This was the hill and pagoda of Kwan Shan, and the hill is not only the distinguishing feature, but gives the title Shan. This is a city of nearly half a million of inhabitants, and we passed through its suburbs, again running the gauntlet of gaze and wondering excitement, about ten o'clock in the morning. As usual, a great many complimentary remarks were made upon us—of course complimentary, as they attributed to. us supernatural attributes, the only one translated to me being "White Devils," and modesty shrunk from any further attempt to get at the hidden meaning of the comments we elicited.

Gray as this drizzly morning, gloomy as the old graves around, and crumbling like this vast empire beneath the hand of Time and the influences of Heaven, three granite monuments, statues, sprung upon my sight from amid the tall grass and rice fields, just before we reached Kwan Shan. One was that of a horse, saddled and bridled. He stood erect and perfect; and, turning him from his original pagan interpretation, he may stand as the emblem of the coming man. A second was a colossal, robed priest—colossal it was, but the head was gone; a fit emblem of the future as of the past—a colossal paganism decapitated by an unseen power; and the third monument was overthrown, and lay mingling its elements with the earth from which sprung the green vegetation. It was a bearded goat, still embleming the animal existence and hoary sensuality which is to fall with decapitated paganism, and give birth to a newer and fresher and purer life. We provisioned at Kwan Shan.

Before getting to this city we had the creek pretty much to ourselves. Only here and there a boat disputed it with us; but now, of various forms and sizes and purposes, they crowded the way. About twelve, one of the beautiful but light, lofty-arched stone bridges was in the distance before us, and at one we were up with it, borne by a fresh breeze, and to the small city of Eding—about twenty thousand inhabitants. In the channel way we saw for the first time the beautifully-carved decorative gilded flower or pleasure-boats of Soo-chau, showing that we were approaching this point of luxury and dissipation. Several very fair, genteel and handsomely dressed females were on board these boats.

I omitted to mention among the incidents of the morning, that while we were lying at Kwan Shan, a large boat similar to our own, but handsomely decorated with gilding and lanterns, came tracking down the tow path. It bore a mandarin's flag, and as we lay just in her way, I supposed we would be cleared out; but, on the contrary, the boatmen took in their line, entered into friendly conversation with ours, and sculled around us. The inmates of the boat, chiefly females, showed the usual curiosity in regard to us. One of them, who stood boldly outside on the open stern of the boat, I at first took, from her handsome appearance and neat dress, with jeweled coronal, to be one of the ladies of the family. But as she laid, though sportively, hold of the sculling oar, and talked familiarly with an old woman who sat by knitting, I infer she was only a servant girl. We supposed from the flag that it was the family of the new Taou Tai going to Shanghae.

Every one who knows any thing about us at Shanghae, knows that we drink the waters of an opaque muddy stream, a solution of all imaginable filth and dead Chinamen. It was therefore refreshing, on the second day out, to see the water assuming a clean, clear green appearance. It was new and refreshing to look upon. But at three o'clock on the afternoon of the last day of September, we entered upon a beautiful lake. It was about two miles wide where we crossed it, and the road, or tow path, in its whole length, passed over a granite causeway. How long the lake is I do not know, but its clear waters were liquid emerald.

At half past five in the evening we came to alongside of the bank in a suburb of Soo-chau.

Soo-chau—the Paris, as it is called, of China—with ten miles in circumference of the walls, like London, is as nothing to the Soo-chau without the walls. One of these extra mural addenda is said to extend ten miles in every direction. Situated on the waters of the Great Lake, it is throughout intersected and traversed by broad and thronged water avenues, arched over with lofty stone bridges. Two millions of people, at the very least, are here gathered together, engaged in the turmoil of Chinese thrift, and the splendid excesses of Chinese dissipation.

Whenever, in Shanghae, I have been attracted by any beautiful piece of embroidery, of carved or lacquered work, of silk or satin, I was told it came from Soo-chau; and if by any chance I happened to see a fair, gracefully-formed, pleasant-expressioned girl, she too came from

Soo-chau. There was one in Shanghae for whom her husband paid three thousand dollars, as his evidence of his appreciation of her beauty; and there were several others of the Soo-chau chizeling. Even their local dialect is said to flow in softened tones, and to be that chosen for songs and tales of love.

All these excellences and attractions were sustained by our experience as far as it went. A Chinese maxim says, that earthly happiness consists in being born in Soo-chau, living in Canton, and dying in Lian-chau; the first giving physical beauty, the second a life of luxury, and the third the best coffin for the final repose of the body. The topography of Soo-chau is written in forty volumes. My stay at the place was from the evening of the last of September to noon of October 1st, and my view of it extended over seven industrious hours. But as an inch of honest sample enables one to judge the whole bale, and the truth of the character asserted for it, so my readers must put up, as I did, with my inch of observation of Soo-chau.

As we were now two or three days beyond any bounds prescribed by treaty for foreign travel, it became necessary that we should not provoke any idle curiosity, or make it the duty of any zealous mandarin to send us back in charge of a file of soldiers. We therefore concluded the most prudent plan would be to shut up our windows, and not expose ourselves until after dark. I will here remark, for the benefit of all who may be interested in the result, that I found this lying hid from my fellow-men, with an ordinarily fair human conscience, and for only two hours, so irksome a business, that I can not recommend any one to do so with an oppressive crime as the motive.

Whilst we were thus concealed, we sent for the proprietor of one of the small-sized decorated pleasure or flower-boats, which are common in this city of luxury, and negotiated with him to take us in his boat on the morrow to "Tiger Hill Mound," a celebrated temple and pleasure resort near the city; and also a turn through the city within the walls, for which we were to pay him three Mexican dollars, and were to bind ourselves not to land or show ourselves after we got within the city proper; and we were to transfer ourselves at an early hour in the morning, before observers were about, from our boat to his.

During this negotiation, which, like all Chinese bargains, required a great deal of talk, we had the proof of softened tone of voice and amenity of expression. In commenting upon us to our own Chinamen, this individual, instead of calling us "White Devils," spoke of us respectfully as the "gentlemen from afar."

At six o'clock in the morning his boat was alongside of us, and quite a fancy affair it was. Divided into three apartments like our own, but much smaller—a short uncovered bow, an ante-room open in front, and with two ornamental stools and tables; our own central apartment, or parlor, with a small mat-covered settee, two rose-wood mat-covered stools, and rose-wood little table, with blue-figured cloth cotton cover, and under it a brass pan of coals for the convenience of smokers. Back of this was the open deck, for the occupancy of the crew and scullers. The sides of our apartment were of ornamental panel-work of fanciful divisions filled in with three layers of transparent shell, like ground glass, with the exception of small glass panes, four inches square, in the centre of each panel—an eye for the world without and all its doings, while nothing but its softened light came through our shells. A fringed crimson satin curtain ornamented the front of our parlor, while sliding doors shut it out from both back and front.

Our ship's company consisted of a voluble, bland-tongued old gentleman, who, with a long pipe, occupied the bow, a young man, two ladies and two babies, who filled the platform in the rear, and did the sculling; one lady and the man at the oar at a time. And so we started to glance at Soo-chau.

Soon after getting under way I noticed that the man on the after platform was neatly arranging, one on top of another, some clean blue and white cotton napkins, and in a few minutes he opened the door and passed in a steaming roll wrapped in a white towel, and opening it, he handed each of us one of the napkins smoking with hot water. This was the courteous offer of the means of the morning toilet, the napkin being intended to bathe the face. This courtesy was immediately followed by covered porcelain cups of hot tea without milk or sugar, and the leaves floating in the infusion. These were attentively replenished during the whole of our journey.

For several miles our way lay along the city wall, black brick, or brown granite, where it could be seen, but most of it was draped, from bottom to top, in close-clinging creepers and running vines. We were approaching what, in the distance, appeared a thicket of junk masts. But we were among the marts for meeting the substantial wants and necessities of this great gathering of men. These were the signs of bamboo yards in which lay horizontal forests of this valuable and universally useful gigantic grass, which on shore and on the water, in labor and in literature, meets almost every necessity of a Chinaman. From these bamboo marts, or hongs, we passed to those of the more solid timber of the forest, which lay in quiet rafts, or being picked and moved and transferred from one owner to the other by the hands and pikes of busy gangs of men. A gentleman curious in such matters, calculated that the rafted timber lying at one time at Soo-chau, laid end for end, would extend from Shanghae to San Francisco. Lime hongs, buffalo hongs, and shrieks, yells, with ear-crushing grunts, tell us of pig hongs. From this avenue of cumbrous and miscellaneous utilities, we entered upon one of elegant luxuries and superfluities. Along the water lay splendid flower-boats, gay with carving, gilding, paint and silk hangings, tasteful with vases of flowers, and with skillful arrangements for shutting their inmates to privacy without gloom. Many of these boats were occupied by elegantly and handsomely, not tawdrily, dressed girls, who fully vindicated the claim of Soo-chau for the beauty of its women. There was nothing immodest or bold in their appearance, and yet, with their soft, fair complexions, they were but as whited sepulchres, those whose floating houses were the gates of death.

The stores along this avenue were alternations of gay lacquered ware, toy, picture, porcelain, fan and flower shops. These last were very numerous, and with their green plants and bright flowers, in fanciful vases, arranged on both sides on shelves, gave a very refreshing and gay character to the street. These flower shops seemed to be avenues to garden grounds back of them.

Gliding for some miles through such scenes, our water avenue led out into the country some little distance to a hill surmounted by a pagoda—Tiger Hill Mound, Heutsheu-Shan. This hill can specially be called classic and historic ground. I had also a family interest and connection with this place, a family connection not quite so ancient and honorable as that with Noah and Adam, but still sufficiently remote to hide original rascality in antique mistiness, which I take to be one of the secrets of value in the oldest families. It appears that when the Shemitic branch of the Wood family were tongue-divided from their Japhetic cousins at the Babel mutiny, their "confounded" tongues could not pronounce the final letter of their name, and they called it Woo. Now most of my journey had been through the kingdom of my Chinese cousins, this Woo family, of which, brilliant Soo-chau was their capital.

I am, of course, bound to give the most authentie account of such relatives. It appears, then, that some six centuries before the Christian era one of the kings of Woo died, and was buried on this hill where we are now standing; and, what was of more importance, three thousand two-edged swords were buried with him. Three days after this burial a white tiger was seen standing on the grave of this ancient worthy, and hence we have the name of "Tiger Hill Mound." Some three hundred years after this event, Tsing-sz-wang—he who built the great wall—wanted these swords, and like a prudent man who looks after his own business, he came here and had the ground dug over in search of them, but he did not find them. Of course not. There can be no doubt the swords had been there, but had passed away beneath the rust of two hundred and ninety-two years, the exact period which had elapsed before the wall-building Tsing-sz-wang came to look for them, which he did two hundred and twenty years before our era.

He, such a determined soldier, was of course very much irritated by the disappointment, and seeing a tiger standing in front of the grave, drew his sword and made a death-intended blow at-him. The tiger vanished, and the blow fell on Thousand Men's Rock; and as I stood upon the rock where the mark of the sword is still pointed out, all this must be true. Time rolled on, and other and different associations clustered around this remarkable place. About a thousand years after the sword digging, a Buddhist priest used this rock for a pulpit, and a thousand men, hence its name, sate on it to listen to his doctrine. More obdurate than stocks and stones, they listened unmoved and incredulous, but a sensible and sensitive stone standing near nodded assent and approval, being immediately received as the first disciple, and in the pool at the foot of the rock a water-lily sprung up and bloomed forth its testimony.

Such are some of the authentic facts in the old history of Tiger Hill Mound, as given by most veracious Chinese historians.

There have undoubtedly been many other important events associated with this locality; but the most recent, perhaps, will be the impression left upon those who fled from our bearded visages, that in the seventh moon of the Hien Fung dynasty, two of the ancient white tigers appeared and flitted a brief space over their old haunted hill.

We landed at a clean paved street of toy, fan, and picture shops, upon which opened the entrance to a Buddhist temple. Passing through a wayside of miserable beggars and a portal guard of dirty priests, we passed through the temple into a maze of neat and picturesque gardens and grottos, rock-work, lake and pleasure house, all fragrant with the odor of the golden mandarin flower, and, what was most wonderful, all was clean and neat—the white was snowy. Almost every step was a succession of pleasant surprises. From a common-place paved and walled alley, which seemed to be leading into some chamber, we would come suddenly upon a darkly-shaded rock-work garden, looking as though it were buried in a mountain, so solemnly secluded and quiet. On a rock, and reached by rugged steps, would be a neat little tea-house, and on one side of this quiet place would be a more capacious tea-room, looking from one terrace to another. We had scarcely entered this before some one placed two cups of tea on a table before us. A circular hole in the brick wall, large enough for a man to pass, would conduct from some alley or room to such a piece of rock-work. All of Tiger Hill Mound was made of these temples and gardens, its naturally picturesque rocks made use of in the designs of art. At one point, a narrow, time-worn, blue marble bridge, with well-like openings through its slabs, spans and looks down a narrow gorge of moss-grown rocky walls, to a stream below. This gorge is said to be the effect of the sword of the indignant sword-digger.

Having reached an open temple, in which were sold refreshments, on the summit of the hill, and on its perpendicular side, we had spread before us a magnificent and far-reaching view of field, lake, grove, and village, with Soo-chau some miles distant, with, however, nothing to make it conspicuous but three pagodas—the great defect, from the low character of the buildings, of all Chinese cities. A blue range of mountains, about thirty miles distant, were a prominent feature.

Most of the people, who manifested so much surprise at our appearance on our way, undoubtedly saw, for the first time, those wonderful barbarians of whom they hear so much. But when we stepped ashore in the streets, around Tiger Hill Mound, the first effect of surprise in those whose eyes lighted upon us, was startling to ourselves. Any one coming suddenly to a door as we passed, would start back in wonder; and, if a woman or a child, run in terror, as though a monster had risen before them. I wore our usual dark cloth costume, and heavy leather boots, with my undress uniform cap, but a light blue silk Chinese frock instead of a coat. As the English failed to find Soo-chau during the war of 1842, I think I may make the boast, so far as it is worth any thing, of being the first foreign naval officer ever seen in that city—certainly the first of the United States service.

I wish now to present to ethnographical and psychological people, to the controllers of costume fashions, and to boards for the getting up military uniforms, a fact for their study. On our way, the first effect, apparent to us, of our burst upon the Chinese vision, was mirthfulness. The sleepy sombre boatmen enlivened to a grin; young females laughed without mercy, as did all the children who were old enough not to be frightened; and one old lady, whose

> "———— Nose was thin,
> And rested on her chin
> Like a staff,"

laughed as she, most likely, had not laughed for many years. I felt a practical benevolence in giving her sides this merry shake upon the edge of the grave. Even the surprised people upon "Tiger Hill Mound," passed from surprise to mirthfulness. Now, the questions are, whether we were, as individuals, ridiculous specimens of our race? —whether there is any thing, which, not being familiarized to the native taste by use, is essentially ridiculous in our costume?—or, whether the Chinese mental organization is such that a sudden novelty startles it into merriment? I am inclined to attribute it partly to the essentially ridiculous character of western costume, and partly to the mental characteristics of the Chinese, which none of the many students of that people have yet developed. We know there is the ridiculous in nature and art. The gravest of us will laugh at a caricature costume; and a monkey will move us to mirth, while a rhinoceros will raise our wonder; and yet, if all the tribes of North American Indians were gathered together, and two full-dressed Chinese were paraded before them, I doubt if there would be as much laughing as we two sober, quiet citizens got up in our less than one hundred miles' journey between Shanghae and Soo-chau.

Sociable as our venerable boatman was, when he had us stowed away behind his translucent shells, I observed that, as soon as our acquaintance might be discreditable and dangerous, he very prudently dropped us. We expected him to show us the sights, and take the lead in our wanderings, but, upon looking around for him, we found that he had mingled with the thickening throng of spectators which pressed around us, and was looking at us with as much wonder as though he never laid eyes on us before. He had landed us in a retired corner where there were none to see our relations. Notwithstanding that he cut us so dead, he managed to prompt some of the spectators, generously, to lead us where he wanted us to go; thus often are the impulses of the multitude directed, by such cunning fellows as our boatman, to their own ends, Messrs. Masses thinking all the while their movements to be of their own spontaneous volition. Our old boatman was a model politician. He was, however, a timid one. Upon one occasion, when the crowd grew noisy and turbulent—not, however, from any mischievous purposes, but only from the excitement natural to a crowd—he vanished entirely, and only reappeared when we were so near his boat as to promise a safe arrival at it without any chivalric exertions of his own, verifying the Chinese proverb, setting forth the insecurity of politicians—"the horse's back is not so safe as the buffalo's"—and ours was an old horse trained in tricks. He had, early in our journey, declined taking us to the city within the wall, even by a water gate. He explained that nothing was to be seen inside equal to what was outside, and that, though he had no great apprehension for us, if detected, he would lose his boat, and, what he regarded as nearly as valuable, his head. I offered to treble his price if he would take us in, and as he declined this, or any compensation short of the value of his boat, I felt that it would scarcely be just to urge him to the fulfillment of his contract.

On our return, he conducted us through one of the business canals; and the crowd of boats of all kinds, lying along both sides, or moving as they could through the busy and thronged channel; the collision and the crashing; the cargo-boats, laden with bales and packages of manufactured articles and raw materials, and an occasional pleasure-boat picking its way, like our own, daintily and timidly, as a full-dressed lady might, caught in the business streets of New York—all this entanglement of boats, with consequent shouts and cries of boatmen—Chinese cries, too, though with Soo-chau softening—presenting an exciting scene of confusion, especially when we met at the arch of a bridge. A locking of Broadway omnibuses is as nothing to it. Among the varied boats lying in this canal, we passed, in several places, groups of post or post-office boats, for carrying the mail.

The first of these I saw in the open river, long, sharp, low, round, and black, was gliding over the water like a snake, and with almost as much rapidity. The *only* seen moving power was a broad oar or paddle, near the after end of the boat, dashing into the water with great quickness. As the boat rushed past us, a man was seen sitting, almost reclining, low in the stern, with the handle of this oar grasped between his feet, and giving it the rapid motion with his legs, while he as rapidly plied and guided the boat by another paddle with his arms. The boat was a sharp canoe, rounded over, and securing the mail from the weather by black painted matting.

By half past one o'clock we were back at our own home-like boat, and Soo-chau, so far as we were concerned, was done and done for.

As there was now, thanks to an accomplished purpose, no further need of concealment, we showed ourselves freely in and about our boat. A crowd of the neighboring population, of all ages and both sexes, gathered on the bank to look and laugh at us, and it occurred to me I would do a good work for posterity. I had no further interest myself in Soo-chau or its vicinage; but other foreigners may visit there, and might not be the worse for a pleasant impression of foreign visitors left upon these humble villagers; indeed, who shall say that it may not be the means of opening the Chinese empire to intercourse with the world? I could not say a kind parting word to them, but I had a small bag of ship biscuit; I brought it to the window, and commenced throwing fragments of the biscuit among them, especially to the women who had babies in their arms. I had, however, no idea of the excitement I was to get up. They all lost their timidity, and rushed down to the edge of the water, some of them into it, to collect the bread. One rather good-looking young woman, happening to get quite a large piece at the beginning of the scramble, seemed to think it made us old acquaintances, as she came forward with an air which said, "Of course you will give me as much more as I wish," as she quietly held out her hands. Seeing what was going on, the whole village came flocking like crows, and scrambled, with much merriment, for the handfulls of biscuit I cast among them. I had nearly got through with my stock, when I saw an old lady come waddling along with outstretched hand, and uttering ludicrous cries of distress, lest she should be too late. As I saw her coming, I reserved a whole biscuit, which, as she plumped down through the crowd to the water's edge, I put in her hand, to her great joy; and then, as the boat shoved off, I cast among them the remainder of my fragments, and we left, amid a parting salute of cheerful faces and kind looks—I hope of good wishes.

We tracked our boat against a high head wind all that

day; and at night, when it came the turn of the "fifth son of his father" to go ashore, although there was the light of a thin clouded moon, he had, in addition to the skeleton umbrella, and the tow-line, a lighted paper lantern in his hand, asserting his strict observance of the rules of Chinese respectability. Our head boatman was desirous of stopping at ten o'clock at night, although we had then a fair wind which would have relieved them all of much labor. He made many objections to proceeding, and at length said we were coming to a part of the river infested by pirates. We, however, loaded our single fowling piece, and ordered him to go on. He did so until midnight, when he again made fast alongside the bank, and as the day's work had been hard, we let him have his way.

On the 2d of October, in the morning, we found that we had passed through Kwang Shan, although we had towed most of the way. We had made about thirty miles in twelve hours. For a little distance, this morning, we had a fair wind, which was a refreshing novelty, and the day was comparatively clear; but we got into terrible bad company, and an awful amount of it.

During our stay about Shanghae this summer and fall, we have watched, with pleasure and interest, the progress of these ripening fields; we have seen them, not from the beginning when the ground was laboriously prepared, and each spear of rice set out by hand; but we have seen them carefully irrigated with water drawn from the streams, much of it by hand; and as yet, excepting the limited destruction by the gale of September, within the limits of tide-water, nothing has impeded the happy progress to a full and fat harvest. Much of our pleasure in the present excursion has been derived from the broad expanse of green and golden fields through which we have passed; regular beds of green vegetables being interspersed with the fields of rice.

As we stood at our cabin-door, after breakfast, enjoying the day and the prospect, we noticed, at first only a few black objects flying over the surface of the grain-fields, and at once suspected their terrible character. A very little further progress confirmed our suspicions. We were in an atmosphere of locusts—they filled the air like, as we noticed last year, the driving flakes of a heavy snow storm, far as the eye could see, upward and around in every direction. The green grass was rusty brown with them, layers deep; and also the green gardens and every spire of rice was fixed upon, and darkened by several at once, disgusting as plague spots upon the healthy body, and yet the air was darkened by coming myriads of the unportioned voracious host. In this one day, all this season's labor and hopes, all these fair fields, are to be laid waste; the people have labored to find one day's meal for these locusts—in every sense of the word, beastly insects. It was pitiable to see these poor farmers, men, women and children—it was disease, death and starvation to them. Vainly as sweeping out the ocean, they were with gongs, cries, cloths tied to poles, endeavoring to frighten them away; even the sport which the poor children made of this work was melancholy in its ignorance of the coming misery.

Once our boat glided close into the bank near an old woman who had been laboring hard at the fruitless labor, and was standing in an attitude of despair. I suppose she may have read in our countenance our sympathy in their wretchedness, for she threw up her hands as she looked at us, and spoke in a tone of hopelessness. Her words, as translated by my companion, were few, but significant —"We shall all starve." All day long we passed through this consuming plague. In the afternoon there were men, women and children, busy with sacks and baskets, gathering up these insects—I at first thought for food; but

18

upon inquiry, learned that they received two cash (the five hundredth part of a dollar) for every catty (one and one third pounds). The cash may be useful to the people, but the impression upon the locusts may be appreciated from the fact that while the fields were abandoned to the locusts, and the air was filled with them, these people were getting all their supplies from the water's edge without making the least perceptible impression upon the mass. Towards night our persevering head wind increased to a gale, but our boatmen tugged against it, as we were anxious to reach tide-water, and to pass the triple-arched stone bridge of Woodang before its gates should be closed at eleven at night, so as to go down with the first ebb. We reached the bridge at ten, when the wind was blowing terrifically, with heavy hail and rain, so that we just passed the bridge and came to, rejoicing that a storm so annoying to us was death to locusts, and life to Chinamen.

We were now twenty-four miles from Shanghae, and the gale still continuing, my companion being obliged to be in Shanghae before the outgoing mail, started through mud and rain, on foot. I at first thought of accompanying him, but as much of these Chinese roads are a muddy, slippery, narrow ridge through fields, I concluded to wait alone the chances of the weather, and get along with our Chinamen by my signs and their sagacity. I had the proof, very soon, that I was safe in that of Ayouk. Indeed, language seemed of no use in the honest, straight forward wants of life, and silence quite a luxury. Nothing was wanting. At dinner time, Ayouk, walking peremptorily up to the table where I was writing, was sufficiently expressive. The dinner was put on without a word; but wishing an absent bottle of pickles, I merely closed my left hand as if holding the bottle obliquely, and picking up a fork, I thrust it two or three times at my hand—the pickles were immediately brought. I next wanted a small plate—that was easy enough. I pointed to a large one, and rapidly drew the circumference of a smaller in the air—the plate came. I next held my hands four inches apart, and drew a circle in the air two inches in diameter—that meant a can of preserved strawberries. A point to a crumb of bread, and another circle in the air, meant biscuit. They all came at the first sign, and never a word spoken.

By two in the afternoon the wind had hauled a little more favorably, and although the tide was against us, we got under way. I was now alone with my friend's boatmen, and if before this I have felt in any way ungrateful to him or to them, I wish now to acknowledge my fault, and to thank them for one of the merriest rides I ever had in all my wanderings. These boatmen were essentially the children of still life. They had been brought up to the perils of tracking and poling a boat through some stagnant canal. Said the great canal engineer—"Rivers have been made to feed canals." Said my boatmen—"Flowing tides and fair winds are necessary to show the skill of poling in dead water through reed swamps and over mud banks."

At first the tide was against us, and we ventured to spread a little sail to the following breeze, and got along according to all rule, and as stupidly right as all the other boats which, with sail spread, were accompanying us down stream. But there came a change in the tide; instead of being conservatively in opposition, it became a rushing torrent of progress. My boatmen shrank from the power of favoring wind and tide, and struck the sail. Now, with her bulging roof and mat-shedded quarter, our boat had the head and stern proportion of what is called a bottle-fly or spider; and consequently the sail being off the bows, the wind took us on the balloon quarter, and away she went, stern foremost, down stream; fortunately we were in a long reach which gave us a stern run of a mile clear of every thing. The thing was so ludicrous I could not make up my mind to stop it. But unfortunately there was a bend in the river, a promontory, and with a crash, crashing our rudder, we came up stern foremost on that. The mud held the stern long enough to let the wind bring the bow round, where, for some distance, we regularly whirled and waltzed down the stream, cushioning, like a billiard ball, from one bank to the other.

The poor boatmen seemed to think it was only necessary to keep busy with the long bamboo poles over the bow, trying to push this tail-strong boat into a proper course, but as there was only room for two to push on the narrow bow, and since the loss of the rudder the helmsman steered by the sculling-oar, there was one still unemployed; it was the umbrella, lantern-bearing "fifth son of his father;" and as he seemed to think it necessary to be doing something, whenever the boat got into embarrassment he plunged a rag mop, with a long handle, into the water, and, with nervous rapidity, washed off the bow of the boat. While engaged in this laudable pursuit, the boat rushed madly on to a bank, and the "fifth son of his father," swab, mop and all, went overboard. After this catastrophe, at which time the boat glided high up the bank, and all hands jumped overboard to push her off, it was concluded to take the mat covering off the stern, so that less wind would be held there. Still, this did not answer; the boat was stern-heavy, and beyond pole management in the central wind and tide. I now tried to suggest that a little sail on the forward part of the boat would balance this heavy stern, but they either did not understand me, or could not understand a principle contrary to the "ola custom" of their fluvial training, and insisted upon keeping the boat close in to the dead water of the bank, where mud and grass would moderate its speed to the control of the poles. It was no discouragement to them that an occasional fix upon a mud-flat required all hands to jump overboard and shove her off.

In this laborious manner we worked our way down stream, while boat after boat, with sail set, rushed by us down the tide. We had reached within four miles of Shanghae at eleven o'clock at night, and the tide was still flowing down, when all at once a rushing sound came up the river, and with it the flood-tide in a swelling tidal wave or bore; it swelled furiously under our boat, foaming along the banks. The anchor was cast overboard; the chain straightened out rapidly, and we were fixed to a flood-tide for the next six hours. I went ashore with Ayouk as a guide, and wading through puddle and mud, reached the settlement, my room and my bed, about one in the morning—and slept.

Soon after my return from this trip, we left once more for the south of China. In my wanderings through the streets of old Shanghae, I picked up many interesting remains of a long-buried antiquity. I caught the disease of "old crackle."

A very certain kind of disease to which strangers are subject in China, North China especially, is "old crackle;" rather it is the third and last stages of a disease, and is apt to be severe according to one's susceptibility in taste, and fertility of imagination of the subject. It is caught in old curiosity shops, and, indeed, the tendency to visit them is a predisposition to the malady. The first stage manifests itself in a desire for curious bronzes, the second for antique vases of rare colors, and in the third, "old crackle" comes upon us with tremendous and exhausting power.

At first, when you are in the bronze and bright-color stage, you look with contempt upon the lined and marred and scarred bowls, vases and cups, which here and there are seen in the curiosity shops. You are not yet out of the fresh greenness of your own soil. You are under the untutored fondness for garish brightness, unworn perfection; and if you take to antiquity at all, it must be that antiquity which, in bronze and vase, keeps its form and its color perfect.

Perchance, you listlessly point to one of these old cracked affairs and ask its price. The answer strikes you with amazement. You now look a little more at old crackle. By degrees your vision brightens, strengthens; the delicious disease is upon you; in those cracks and lines you see the beautiful wrinkles of an old age; but such old age! Coarse features, skins, and complexions are early marred by the lines of age, but when they are drawn over fine textures and symmetrical forms, you admire the beauty which wins time's touch so gracefully, and at once you fall in love with "old crackle," as did the lovers of Ninon d'Enclos, despite her sixty years.

In purchasing the specimens of the porcelain art, lost to modern times, you buy the association of centuries—the tastes, the social characteristics of an age artistic and refined, when forests grew where the cities of the great republic stand, and even where those of old mother England stand. The nobleman whose drawing-room it decorated, has passed away; his palace has passed away; soil and vegetation have accumulated over the old vase which has cracked beneath the heats and frosts of centuries, but retaining its complexion and its polish more perfectly than the enamel of a shell. When all this comes up, you are smitten; money has no value; and eighty per cent. exchange will not save you.

I had an opportunity, by care and perseverance, of adding some fine specimens to my collection.

XXXIII.

BATTLE AND BLOOD.

When we left the south of China, the waters of Pearl River, and the vicinity of the "City of Rams," we had indications of the growing animosity of the Cantonese toward all foreigners. The strong Anglo-Saxon current of arrogance crossing and ruffling that of the Chinese, the persistent and lawless manner in which the Chinese gave expression to their animosity, rendered it evident that ere long a national rupture must occur, as we tolerate no lawlessness but our own.

From the more extended relations of the English and Americans, the chances were that the task would devolve upon one or the other of these powers. But the authorized murder of a French missionary, Chapdelaine, in the province of Kwang-se, rendered hostility from the French government a prompt possibility; inasmuch as that government has so much less responsibility to the nation, in declaring war, than either the English or ourselves.

As the French have no commerce in China, the war on their part would be one of religious propagandism; on the part of English and Americans, one of expected commercial extension.

Within a recent period the English had to complain of various outrages, which they were unlikely to tolerate, even though, if the Chinaman's story were heard, they arose from provocation.

The American complaints were of the attack, by a half-piratical Chinese fort, upon the American steamer Kum Fa, out upon a pleasure excursion with a party of gentlemen, ladies and children. Several shot were fired at her, and one struck her, if I remember correctly.

There were several classes of Chinese extenuators; 1st, those who recognized the wrongs done them, and yet admitted their faults—advocates of justice; 2d, those who, engaged in some petty underhand Chinese commerce in collusion with subordinate Chinese authorities, dreaded a rupture; and 3d, those who, from animosity, jealousy, and hatred of their own authorities, were anxious always to put them in the wrong, and the Chinese in the right—a small but violent faction—who worked in China, and with the press in the United States and England. The two latter said the Kum Fa was fired into because she was in a branch of the river where she had no right to be. But such a ferocious and savage assault, for a thoughtless indiscretion, admitting it to be such, was the exponent of a feeling which would not long tolerate peaceful relations.

Then again came the firing upon the American steamer Willamette, and, upon these sources of irritation, the shock of the murder of an American gentleman, Mr. Cunningham, of Fu-chau, by a party of Cantonese, in the streets of that city. Whether accidental, or provoked by imprudence, it added to the general feeling of insecurity and animosity.

Added to these specific incidents were the general insulting language, the dangerous and offensive missiles with which all foreigners were likely to be assailed if out of the narrow precincts of the factories at Canton. The posting of the inflammatory handbills before we left the neighborhood of Canton, showed that on the part of the Chinese the hostility was assuming some form. In this general hostility to "Barbarians" there seemed to be no disposition or ability on the part of the authorities to prevent or punish the outrages of lawless bands.

Even though the outrages were committed by what was apparently a government fortress, most likely it would be said the offenders are not agents of the government, but pirates and marauders, who had temporarily occupied an abandoned fortification. Thus the people felt no restraint in their aggressions upon foreigners, either from the fear of their own or other powers. From the haughty exclusiveness of the court of Pekin, it deprived itself of all means of gaining correct information in relation to foreigners, and was open to any deception or imposition which it suited the interest or designs of the Cantonese authorities to impose upon it; and one of the most prominent of these was to create the impression that the foreigners were easily managed, controlled, and subdued by the great skill and vigilance of those authorities. Morbid and infuriated Canton was the eye and ear through which the Chinese empire saw the world. In this state of affairs the Imperial Commissioner at Canton, Yeh-Min-Ching, was of all persons the one most fitted to precipitate the coming collision. One of the highest rank in the empire, he added to all the arrogance of his race that of his position; of large ability and unscrupulous character, he could produce a political paper flowing with sentiments of justice, morality and humanity, whilst coolly, in support of his tyranny, he floated his sovereignty upon rivers of blood—it being his boast that he had cut off the heads of one hundred thousand rebels, seventy thousand, it is said, in one year. He had acquired much reputation by his successful dealings with rebels, and, in his ignorance, seemed to think he might culminate his glory by expelling all foreigners from his jurisdiction.

Under such circumstances, only an ostensible cause of collision was wanting, and it would be a limited and unreasonable view of the subject to suppose that the merits of the particular difficulty would at all be an expression of the real cause of hostility. It was only the break in the barrier which held the flood, but not the flood itself.

It was therefore scarcely a surprise when, at Shanghae,

in October, 1856, we heard that a collision had occurred between the British and Chinese authorities at Canton. The account of the difficulty reached us with much perversion and exaggeration. It has since been so fully and so critically examined, to answer the ends of various parties, that a mere statement of its nature is all that is necessary here. A lorcha, the Arrow, licensed by the authorities of the British colony of Hong Kong to fly the British flag, had been seized at Canton, accused of or detected in smuggling. This proceeding was resisted on the part of the British authorities, the controversy being carried on across the walls of Canton by documentary communication, with all its delays and difficulties, although the parties were within a few hundred yards of each other. In the course of this correspondence the British demanded that the discussion should be carried on and the matter decided by a personal interview with the Cantonese authorities within the walls of Canton, a privilege which had been yielded by treaty, but never conceded in fact. In making this demand, the British asked it not only for themselves, but for all other nations. If there had been any disposition on the part of the Chinese to avoid a difficulty, this would have been a natural means of doing so. Such a concession, however, accorded but illy with the arrogance of Yeh, or the animosity of the fierce democracy of Canton. The proposition and all concession were refused. To enforce the demand, and, under the erroneous impression that a few shot and shells would bring the Cantonese to terms, a limited district of the city, including the government buildings and the Yamun, or residence of the Imperial Commissioner, were shelled, and the wall breached by the naval forces under the command of Rear Admiral Sir Michael Seymour.

Whatever may be the view taken of these events, by interest, policy, or honest judgment, as to the policy and expediency of this course, all acquainted with the character of this distinguished officer know that his action must be viewed with the respect due to abilities and experience directed by the principles of the Christian gentleman. Although he might execute the severest measures from a sense of duty, the glory of military achievement was no compensation to him for the inhumanities of war. Among the more reckless and impulsive, his efforts to spare bloodshed and desolation were made a reproach to him.

With exaggeration and perversion, rumors of these events reached us upon the "Bund," the gossip exchange at Shanghae; and also that our newly-arrived sloop-of-war, the Portsmouth, was mingling in the fight.

Commodore Armstrong, therefore, hurried with the San Jacinto down to the scene of hostilities, and arrived in Hong Kong on the 8th of November, 1856.

The Chinese, in return for the attack made upon Canton, had retaliated with some spirit and energy. They had made a bold attempt to blow up H. M. S. Barracouta by means of fire rafts. Four of these were at great risk towed out of the way, and she only avoided the fifth by slipping her cables. They had also nearly succeeded in blowing up the English club-house in which were quartered at the time several hundred English soldiers.

Yeh had put forth a proclamation offering a hundred taels apiece for the heads of all foreigners, or "barbarians," as the paper read. It was said, by some, that the reward was only for the heads of English barbarians. If this distinction were made, it took nothing from the practical effect of this savage measure of war, as the head of a Yankee in the bag of the fortunate Chinaman who succeeded in getting it would be worth as much as that of an Englishman; so literally, in this case, were the sins of the fathers visited upon their children.

Most fortunately the United States ship Portsmouth,

Commander A. H. Foote, was at Hong Kong when these troubles opened, and the Levant, Commander Smith, arrived there in their early stage. With all these threatenings to our countrymen and interests, under the judicious management of Captain Foote these ships were moved up the river to the anchorage at Whampoa, and their crews quartered on shore for the protection of the lives and property of our citizens penned up in the limited locality of the Canton factories, and threatened with destruction by an infuriated Chinese soldiery and mob. There being no French force present, Captain Foote detailed a part of his force for the protection of the French consulate, which, upon the arrival of the Virginie, was relieved by a detachment from that ship.

In view of the threatening state of affairs—the events which had already occurred—the known hostility and ferocious animosity of the Cantonese to all foreigners—the blood-thirsty proclamation for heads put forth by the chief, who openly avowed and represented this hostility as a political principle—it is to be presumed that Captain Foote, or any officer of prudence and discretion, would have spontaneously taken these steps. But, in addition, Yeh had given official notice that he could not be responsible for the safety of those who remained in the factories; and Captain Foote received the following dispatch from the only civil representative of the United States then in Canton:

UNITED STATES CONSULATE,
CANTON, *October* 21, 1856.

SIR,—

I inclose you herewith a copy of an official communication I received this morning from Harry S. Parkes, Esq., Her British Majesty's consul.

From the tenor of Consul Parke's dispatch you will perceive that a collision may possibly arise within twenty-four hours between Her British Majesty's forces and the Chinese, and as the lives and property of American citizens may thereby be placed in jeopardy, I have taken the earliest opportunity to notify you of the danger, in order that you may timely place a proper and sufficient force here to protect American lives and property.

I am, sir,

Your most obedient servant,

OLIVER H. PERRY,
United States Consul.

COMMANDER ANDREW H. FOOTE, ESQ.,
Commanding United States Steamer Portsmouth,
Whampoa.

It is a discouraging picture of human nature, that notwithstanding so clear an indication of the proper and humane duty of Captain Foote, his course has been severely censured, not only by a low, mercenary, commercial interest in China, but by an unhappy faction in our own squadron.

Such unjust censures spread through the press of the United States, came to the knowledge of the leading American citizens in Canton and Macao, who addressed Captain Foote the following letter:

MACAO, 9th February, 1858.

DEAR SIR,—

We have been informed that in some of the American newspapers, it has been stated in a communication from China, that the force taken by you to the factories at Canton in the month of October, 1856, while difficulties existed between the English and Chinese authorities, was not only not necessary there, but that you were requested to withdraw it.

In justice to yourself, we beg to say, that of the necessity for the force there at the period in question, we are fully satisfied, and that it imparted great confidence and security to the Americans generally in Canton; we, of course, can not know if you were requested to remove it, but are convinced, that had you done so, the danger to life and property would have been greatly increased.

We are very happy also to avail ourselves of this opportunity to express to you our acknowledgment for the prompt and willing manner in which you had given your assistance and support to your countrymen in this part of China whenever it seemed to you that you could be of any possible service, or that circumstances required them. With our best wishes,

We remain,

Your friends and countrymen,

James Purdon, Jr., of Canton.
S. Wells Williams,
Gideon Nye, Esq.,
John B. French,
C. F. Preston,
W. C. Hunter,
J. B. Endicott,
James Napier,
Henry Devins,
C. F. Harding.

To Captain A. H. Foote,
U. S. S. Portsmouth, Hong Kong.

Upon the arrival of Commodore Armstrong in the flagship, all was in a state of turmoil and feverish excitement. The wrongs and injuries, real and imaginary, of the English residents of Canton, were also those of our countrymen, accumulating year by year, and nursed in remembered wrath for future settlement. The conflict of diverse and equally arrogant races had commenced, and the age-built mountains of national exclusiveness and bigotry were about being torn from their foundation, to open a future of cheerful and humanizing national communion.

It is not strange that many of our countrymen in China felt the English war to be equally our war, especially as the right of admission of officials into Canton had been demanded by the English for us, as well as for themselves, and, if granted them by treaty, it must, by implication, be conceded to us; and in itself the demand seemed only just and expedient.

It was opposed to the chivalry of our countrymen that the English should be left alone to redress common wrongs, and to secure common rights. Besides, there was an impatient feeling to have a helping hand in opening the tempting glories of the future.

Such considerations and impulses caused most of our countrymen to fraternize with the English—to assume the conclusion that we must be side by side with them —to feel some shame that we had not taken the initiative upon our past grievances, and to be querulous of any steps of our authorities, keeping our forces from the conflict.

There were others, with cooler hearts and more calculating heads, who by long-established usage assimilating to Chinese principles of monopoly, had the streams of commerce flowing by time-grown channels in fixed reservoirs, out of which none dipped but themselves. Such were of course averse from any measures which might change the existing state of things, and promise a future in any way different from the stationary past.

There was also a lower class, who filled their coffers by a small smuggling trade, sneaking along the river coasts in collusion with petty mandarins. These were also in the interests of peace at any humiliation, and could go all lengths for its preservation without any sacrifice of their honor.

It was reasonable that the English, not understanding the principles of our foreign policy, or the responsibility of our public agents, should have expected our material support in the present difficulty, and believing that the course to be pursued would depend solely upon the individual views and feelings of the commander-in-chief of our naval forces, they only acted out a natural policy, and did but their duty in directing toward him every honorable effort to win him to alliance and concert of action.

By all these various influences, interests and opinions was Commodore Armstrong assailed upon his arrival at Hong Kong. Old and settled residents claimed to exercise an influence upon the ground of experience, and it would have been presumptuous not to receive such experience, and then try it by common sense and true principle. It might have been equally injudicious to permit these men to construe their own experience. Sometimes the greater the experience the greater the perversion, when a man has been walking by his prejudices and interests. It is experience, time, and the constant pressure of the same circumstances which make the "golden lily" foot of the Chinese lady, but it cramps five toes into one, and unfits her for locomotion. Such was the kind of experience authoritatively asserted by the Commodore's Chinese counselors; and as he did not accept it, he exposed himself to all the hostility of the machinery which wealth could place at the disposal of wounded vanity and an intolerant selfishness.

It was determined to give every proper protection to our countrymen and their legitimate interests; to redress every wrong done them; but to abstain from entering upon any war of our own, or entering into any alliance with that of the English.

To be near the scene of action, Commodore Armstrong ran up in the San Jacinto to Whampoa, the nearest anchorage to Canton; and not knowing the extent to which American interests in that city might be endangered, or whether the present force was adequate to the emergency, he sent an addition to that force from the flag-ship; two boat-howitzers, with Lieutenant Bowen, the marines under command of Captain Simms; Assistant Surgeon Semple accompanying the party.

In the course of the same day, however, finding that the difficulties between the English and Chinese had settled into form, and that the latter were taking regular measures for resistance and attack, he determined, much against the views of the belligerent interest, to withdraw all our force from the city of Canton, lest we should be compromising our neutrality. But, for the security of such of our citizens as chose to exercise the right of remaining in Canton, he determined to anchor one of the sloops-of-war off the factories, as a defense and refuge for our consul and citizens in case those buildings were assaulted, as they were liable to be at any moment.

The propriety of these steps was confirmed by Captain Foote, who came down from Canton to report to and advise with Commodore Armstrong; and on Saturday, November 15th, Captain Foote was on his return to Canton, in a small, unarmed ship's boat, when an unhappy incident occurred, which changed all our relations, gave the most exultant hopes to the belligerent party, and gave to the English the promise of our alliance, and did, to a limited extent, give them our efficient aid.

In the boat with Captain Foote were the Rev. Mr. Macy, seamen's chaplain at Whampoa, Lieutenant Macomb, United States ship Portsmouth, Assistant Surgeon Gihon, of the United States ship Levant, and Robert Sturgiss, Esq., of the house of Russell & Co. As they approached a point in the river, defended by four very strong and heavily-armed granite fortresses, these opened a fire upon the boat with round and grape shot. Mr. Sturgiss snatched the boat flag and waved it conspicuously; but the firing still continued, the shot falling thick around the boat, which was compelled to return to the San Jacinto. Indignation now became very general in the ship, even among those who most regretted the unfortunate event. It was fire to a magazine.

The cause of the assault could only be a matter of conjecture. At the commencement of the English difficulty these forts had been taken without resistance by the English, and at once abandoned by them. Some supposed that the attack upon our boat was the result of accident from not recognizing her flag; one conjecture was, that the forts, after being abandoned by the English, had been occupied by Chinese pirates and junk men; another, that our having a force in Canton had provoked the hostility of Yeh; and, again, it was conjectured that Yeh, in accordance with his character, had determined to make war upon all foreigners.

That evening, in an interview with Commodore Armstrong, he said to me, he had been very desirous of preserving our neutral relations, but circumstances seemed to render it impossible; that this outrage required a prompt lesson, and that to-morrow he should transfer his flag to the Portsmouth, and with that ship, and the Levant, attack the forts.

Very early on the morning of Sunday, November 16, Lieutenant James C. Williamson, of the San Jacinto, and Mr. Ayres, the pilot, were sent, in our fourth cutter, to sound the channel toward the forts; and at the same time an order was sent, by a branch of the river, around the forts, for the return of the detachment sent the day before to Canton. The busy note of warlike preparation, the getting up and passing ammunition, the transfer of men to the two ships, were in strong contrast with the sacred character and habitual usages of the day, and our Chaplain, the Rev. Robert Given, who had joined us, for the first time, the day before, found that his first message of the glad tidings of great joy, and of peace and good will amongst men, must silence its soothing sound before the clatter of arms and death dealing-arrangements.

As with these occupations the morning wore on, some anxiety began to be felt for the return of Lieutenant Williamson, in the fourth cutter, which seemed unusually delayed. At last, however, she was seen approaching, and as she neared, the form of a dead, or wounded, man lying in her. It was that of Edward Mullen, the coxswain, who, while standing in the bows of the boat sounding, had his head carried away by a round shot from one of these same forts; as the mangled trunk was passed over the ship's side, the indignation and spirit of vengeance were roused to the highest degree of excitement, and was eloquently manifested by looks and fierce murmurs, although discipline prevented its violent expression. There was now only one course left.

Captain Bell, of the San Jacinto, with the returned detachment from Canton, Lieutenants Lewis and Carter, went on board the Levant, of which ship Captain Bell took command, Captain Smith being left in command at Canton. He subsequently left there and with Captain Simms of the marines participated in their respective positions in the capture of the forts.

Commodore Armstrong, with his secretary, Mr. Van Den Heuvel, Lieutenant Rutledge, of the San Jacinto, Assistant Surgeon Daniel, who requested to accompany me, and I, went on board the Portsmouth. Here, now, we experienced one of those embarrassments which arise from the exceedingly injudicious nature of our squadron on the coast of China. In the rapid tide currents of the river, our sailing vessels were comparatively unmanageable, and the steamer San Jacinto was too heavy to ascend to the barrier. It could hardly be expected that peaceful merchant steamers could be induced to tow ships-of-war under the guns of hostile fortresses. However, we did employ the steamer Willamette, commanded by an American citizen, of Savannah, Georgia, Captain Curry, and the little American steamer Kum Fa, of which one of her owners, Mr. Cooke, also an American, took charge.

It was fortunate that we could procure two vessels under the American flag, for that of Portugal could not compromise its neutrality by coming into our employ, and that of England would have identified us with the English quarrel, and these were all the flags covering the steamers of these waters.

About two o'clock in the afternoon, the Portsmouth in tow of the Willamette, the Levant in that of the Kum Fa, we started for the scene of action, which we reached in about an hour, when the Willamette cast us off, within five hundred yards of the fort, one of the largest, lowest down the river, on its left bank.

It was a beautiful, soft afternoon, like those of our Indian summer; not a breath was stirring, and the river flowed without a ripple. All nature seemed to rest in sleepy repose, and tune the heart to peace. At one moment the long granite walls and dark embrasures of the forts, without sound or stir, gave effect by their unnatural repose to the prevailing stillness and quiet—the next, the whole scene shook with noisy animation; the belching of fire from these embrasures, the roar of the guns, and the hurtling of the grape and round shot around the Portsmouth before her anchor had been let go, were mingled with the loud and clear orders, and the preparations on our deck for bringing the ship into action. The Chinese had boldly begun the war.

There was a significance in the crack of these guns and the whistling of the shot, beyond that of their destructive association. There was no waiting for explanation, no delay to see our purpose; but, on the contrary, no choice left us. Here was stern, defiant and unmistakable war. I felt my respect for our enemy rise with this reception of us, and, at the same time, I confess to an indignant wish to see it returned with vigor.

I have no wish to give a dramatic exaggeration of the scenes of our conflict with the Chinese; but I feel that there is a difficulty in giving a truthful representation of them to those who are accustomed to the mistake of regarding the Chinese as destitute of courage or military art. It is true that the resulting loss of life would seem to indicate a contest of no great difficulty, but all agree that the little loss of life, under the circumstances, is mysterious and inexplicable. There can be no mistake about the Chinese standing to their guns and fighting their forts well against the more destructive machinery of their enemies. In some of their recent conflicts with the English, as I was told by a British officer present, they stood to their guns on board the junks until they were cut down at them. There can be no mistake about the hazard of a small body of foreigners pulling on shore in boats right in the face of the fire of these heavy fortresses, and marching up to them, still in the face of that fire of grape, gingals and rockets, over muddy swamps and ditches. That they were not all swept away can only be accounted for, by the fact that the Chinese, having fixed the elevation of their guns, had no ready means of altering it, and this elevation was generally too great. Their great disadvantage was the want of explosive shell. Finding that their fire from the walls did not annihilate the small body of men approaching them, they generally fled from a hand-to-hand conflict. I do not regard this as a want of ordinary personal courage. Had their assailants been Chinese, the parties would have met, as they often do, to the great loss of life. But they have not yet got rid of that mystical exaggeration of the prowess of the bearded barbarian which strikes them with a panic dread of personal contact. This, however, they are getting rid of. Again, the small effect of the fire from the walls, so inexplicable, and so cheering to the assailing party, was equally mysterious and proportionably discouraging to those defending the walls.

When the fire first opened from the forts, Commodore Armstrong, with his staff, and the Rev. Mr. Macy and Purser Dobbin of the Portsmouth, were standing on the poop, and so thickly came the grape, that a little greater depression of the guns must have swept it.

Without steam, without wind, in a narrow and unknown channel, it was sometime before the Portsmouth could bring her guns to bear and open her fire, being all the time exposed to that of the fort, but when she did, at about half past three, the roar of her heavy, and effective battery, and its quiver through the ship, was cheering and consolatory. Although Captain Foote fought his ship himself, the Commodore remained on deck, a spectator of the engagement; and to those who had nothing to do but look on, it was a great satisfaction to observe the collected coolness and the perfect discipline of both officers and men, the more remarkable as the officers and crews of two ships, who now met for the first time, were working together, and many, if not most of them, for the first time in their lives under fire; this, too, in a service which had abolished the lash, as a means of discipline, five years before.

One earnest and enthusiastic captain of a gun, most anxious for accuracy of aim, would ask any officer who passed him just as he finished training, "Will you please tell me, sir, how that shot falls?" and Peter Gam, the captain of the San Jacinto's band, who had no quarters on board the Portsmouth, occupied himself with a musket on the poop-ladder firing at any Chinaman he could see about the fort.

The Levant, most unfortunately, had run on some rocks, about a mile below, and could not come into the action, much to the annoyance of all on board, whose only consolation was in marking the efficiency of our shells. They were also gratified by seeing how wonderfully we escaped the hostile shower, for, as one of her officers subsequently remarked to me, "the water about you was tossed like snow." In the subsequent engagements, the Levant, by her prominent position and efficiency, made up for this afternoon's misfortune.

The Portsmouth kept her broadside upon the nearest fort, by means of a spring upon her cable, but this, in the course of the action, unfortunately came up, and she tailed round with her stern upon the fort, thus losing, in some degree, the efficiency of her fire, and exposed to the raking of that of the fort. It therefore became necessary to tear away the cabin, to run a gun out of the stern ports. Whilst this was going on, a thirty-two pound shot came directly into the centre of the cabin, carrying away the right arm and dreadfully crushing the right hip of Patrick Melvin, a marine.

He was at once carried down to the sick bay, where the Surgeon of the Portsmouth amputated the arm and made such surgical appliances as the case demanded. From the cabin to the sick bay was an immediate transition from the excitement to the horrors of war. Its gloom was more shown than dispelled by candles. The blood from the wounded man damped his pallet and the deck, while his groans mingled with the crash of the guns directly overhead, the more impressive from being so near and yet unseen.

About dusk, the Commodore feeling anxious about the Levant, had a boat manned and pulled down to her, accompanied by his secretary and myself. As we left the ship, it being dark enough to make the flashes of the guns quite bright, the cross-fire between the ship and fort had a very good effect. That of the fort was very much slackened, and before we reached the Levant ceased entirely.

It was the Commodore's purpose to have the Levant kedged up against the ebb tide, but before we reached her we met, through the gloom of the night, a long line of boats towing her up. Upon getting on board we found her presenting all the discomforts of a man-of-war ready for action, and very much crowded with men and officers, the cabin torn away, and the ward-room all aslop from wetting down the decks while passing powder.

It had been originally intended, after the nearest fort had been silenced, to land and assault it; but as the night came on dark and rainy, and we had no guides, nor any one acquainted with the plan of the fort or the nature of the surrounding ground; as we were entirely ignorant of the extent of the Chinese force, or their facilities for assailing our necessarily small landing party from ambuscades, Commodore Armstrong, gave orders that no landing should be attempted that night.

We all, Commodore, Captains and officers, sat down to supper in the Levant's ward-room, and upon this occasion I could but remark how the conventionalities of rank, which separate, in peace, classes of officers into messes, were all swept away by the first exigencies of war—the very emergency for which it is all intended as a means and a preparation.

The Portsmouth was still out of position, and it was of course expected that with the coming day the forts would reopen their attack upon her; and at a little after one o'clock on Monday morning we returned to her, and as we drew near could see, by the gray light of a clouded moon, the little steamer Kum Fa, Golden Flower, busily at work endeavoring to get the ship into an effective position. The crews of the two ships had now been steadily at work, from Saturday afternoon until this Monday morning, in the preparations for the attack and in working the ships; and those of the Portsmouth, all of Sunday afternoon in fighting the guns. All Sunday night both crews were at work, and no murmur or objection came from them. When I got down on the berth deck of the Portsmouth it was pitiably picturesque to see the groups who, temporarily relieved from labor, seemed to have fallen asleep in the air, and then to have sunk in a heap upon the deck. And yet these men received no further encouragement or thanks from their government than the mere approval of the general order which Commodore Armstrong issued to them. With so little personal encouragement how can we expect to have an enthusiastic Navy? Once we treated our men as devils, now we assume them to have the pure and disinterested motives of saints. Whatever the merits of the contest, the men who display subordination and bravery should have some testimonies of it—a scrip of paper, or a cheap medal. Officers may be trusted to other considerations.

I rolled up my coat for a pillow, and got an hour's sleep on a mess-chest among the men. With daylight came a mizzling rain, but still the forts did not reopen their fire; fortunately for us, for with the strong tide ebbing and flowing, it seemed impossible to get the ships into position and keep them so. Nearly all day the Portsmouth lay aground, and entirely at the mercy of the forts; an officer of a division remarked to me, they could rip our three masts out and we could not bring a gun to bear. Still, as Monday wore on, they remained passive and silent. This course upon the part of the enemy seemed to call for a change of action on ours. It will be remembered that we came up to the attack to redress our injury and insult, but ignorant of the motives and authorities which caused it.

The present silence of the forts might arise from their inability to continue further hostilities, and that nearest us was seen to be very much broken down and dilapidated, in which case sufficient correction had been inflicted. Or else, having made the first assault in a mistake, the authorities had determined to refrain from further contest. In either case the cessation of hostilities during Monday, afforded a favorable opportunity for opening a correspondence with the Chinese authorities, to ascertain whether we were to be at continued war, or our difficulty was to terminate with this correction of the insult to our flag.

For the purpose of opening such a correspondence with the Chinese Imperial Commissioner, Commodore Armstrong returned with his staff to the San Jacinto, at Whampoa, leaving Captain Foote in command, and with orders to get and keep the ships in efficient position, but to make no attack upon the forts unless provoked to do so.

The following extract from the report of Commander Foote, refers to the opening action of this contest:

"I can not help believing that the heavy and prolonged cannonading of the Portsmouth, on the 16th inst., was most important in preparing the way for the operations which succeeded. The powerful battery of this ship, consisting of sixteen eight-inch guns, each of sixty-three hundred weight, so paralyzed the nearest fort, which was within a range of four hundred and eighty yards, that it was never afterward able to do the injury which it might otherwise have inflicted. I am disposed to think, too, that a ship of a smaller calibre could not have sustained alone the hot fire to which this vessel was that day exposed, from the four forts combined, much less could have silenced the two nearest forts, as she did, under a brisk fire of between two and three hours' duration."

XXXIV.

PEN, PENCIL* AND POWDER.

HE who stands upon the elevated bank at the river's mouth, and looks down upon the sea into which it empties, will see clearly the narrow channel winding its way among the foaming breakers, and offering the only safe entrance to the harbor; but those who, down upon the ocean surface, upon a level with those breakers, are struggling in a small boat to pass them, see no such clear channel. The line of foam, upon the one hand, overlaps that upon the other, so that all looks a continuous whirl of ingulfing surf. Carefully must the helmsman watch the cresting wave on the starboard, and then on his port bow, as with prompt decision he avoids first the one and then the other, picking his dangerous way by coolness and skill. A fault in his eye, a mistake in his hand, the failure of an oar, and boat and crew are swallowed up and lost.

In like manner, he who now undertakes to judge the events of the East India squadron, at the time we are considering them, is in the position of him on the river's overlooking banks, with the whole scene spread out before him, but safely removed from its agitation, its responsibilities, and its dangers. In a like favorable and secure position was the government which coolly deliberated up-

* Chinese Writing Pencil.

on these events, and gave to Commodore Armstrong its approbation, after he had securely guided his country's interests and his own reputation, through the new and unchanneled sea which threatened his destruction.

The conflict in which we were now involved gave a fixed form and greater activity to the various and conflicting interests which, honorably and dishonorably, attempted to influence the commander-in-chief of the squadron to their own ends. The voice of most was for war.

When it is considered that we had received repeated wrongs and insults from the Chinese; that there was not the least probability of these wrongs being redressed, except under compulsion; that there was no security for the future; that the Chinese not only permitted us no representative at their court, but would not allow face to face interviews between our highest representatives and their own inferior officials; that they were adepts in a tortuous, evasive, and interminable correspondence, and returning with contempt our communications in English, threw upon us the burden of translation. When all these things are considered, it might be difficult for an officer to determine whether, in a progressive age, public opinion and that of his government might not require him to avail himself of the present rupture to break down this exclusive arrogance. Also, it must be considered that the instructions of the government are, upon many points, necessarily of a vague character, admitting of different opinions; and the course which might win the approbation of one administration, might, upon the same instructions, be disapproved by another, or, indeed, by the same administration at a different time.

However, Commodore Armstrong had determined, as his policy, to limit, if possible, our present hostilities to the event which called them forth, and, great as were the motives, enticing as the opportunity, to avoid all acts which could, by the Chinese, be construed into an English alliance. When two people, as the English and ourselves, alike in all respects, were at war at the same time with a people so ignorant of us both as the Chinese, one fighting them in one part of the river and one in another, the difficulty of keeping up distinct action was great—the difficulty of impressing the Chinese with a conviction that we were not in alliance, greater.

For suspending hostilities and entering into correspondence with the imperial commission, a storm of opposition assailed the commander-in-chief. Had he not done so, where and when would the affair have terminated? What so many desired would have been effected, for good or for evil—a permanent war with China, and English alliance.

On Monday afternoon, we proceeded down the river in an oared boat, belonging to Mr. Sturgiss, and manned by Chinamen. We kept a sharp look-out upon the river's bank, when our course lay close to it, and also upon the Chinese boats in the river. It is at all times infested with pirates, but, under present circumstances, we should have been an honorable and profitable prize. The movements of one boat were very suspicious; from the earnestness with which it was watched by our Chinese boat's crew, they must have thought so, as well as ourselves. However, we reached Whampoa without interruption.

So much of the force had been drawn from the San Jacinto, she was almost defenseless in case of an attack. Boys, servants, and all, there were not more than sixty persons on board. With the same boldness with which they had attacked the English ships with fire rafts, they might, by dropping one or two junks, or lorchas, alongside, in the dark, have thrown two or three hundred men on board, and overwhelmed our small number—true, they must make up their minds to much loss. The Commodore ordered forty of the San Jacinto's crew to return to her. On board the San Jacinto we found Dr. Peter Parker, United States Commissioner to China—and I here take the opportunity to do this gentleman justice. The indignation which was caused by the suspension of hostilities craved some object of personal attack, and hence jumped to the conclusion that it had been instigated by the commissioner; and he was assailed by violent language and intemperate newspaper comments. One gentleman went so far as to protest, on the part of himself and other American residents of Canton and Hong Kong, verbally and in writing, against this assumed action of Dr. Parker. The truth was, Dr. Parker had nothing to do with the matter. The course of action was determined on, and the following letter drawn up, before he reached the San Jacinto. I allude to these things here, as illustrative of the conflict of opinion, and because the opportunity occurs of exonerating the United States Commissioner from any blame in the matter. He fully sustained the action which Commodore Armstrong had decided on, but was not responsible for it.

COPY.

UNITED STATES FLAG-SHIP SAN JACINTO,
WHAMPOA, *November* 17*th*, 1856.

SIR:—

I regret to have to notify your Excellency that it became my duty, on the 16th instant, to assault and silence the works known as the "Barrier forts," on the river between Whampoa and Canton. The following are the unpleasant circumstances which imposed this duty upon me.

On the 15th instant, a boat of the United States ship Portsmouth, in which were Commander Foote of the

Portsmouth, with other officers of my command, and citizens of the United States, in passing peacefully to Canton, was repeatedly fired upon by both round and grape shot from these forts, and impeded in their course upon waters in which she had a right to be, and to expect protection rather than assault. No possible mistake could exist as to the nationality of the boat, as she bore not only the flag of her country, but it was waved distinctly toward the forts by Mr. Sturgiss of Canton.

This outrage is the more unjustifiable, because, during the hostilities existing between your government and the English authorities in China, it has been the endeavor, both of myself and the officers under my command, carefully to preserve that neutral position proper to the friendly relations existing between the governments of the United States and of the Chinese empire. The officer, Commander Foote, who was the subject of this hostile assault, has been especially cautious and prudent in maintaining the neutrality, and prompt in checking any measure which might infringe it. At the very time he was fired upon, he was on his way to Canton to withdraw the American force which had been landed to protect the lives and property of American citizens during the unsettled state of affairs in Canton at the commencement of the difficulty before alluded to. It was my wish to trust the security of neutrals and their interests to the obligations and the sense of justice of your Excellency's government.

Having taken the means now communicated to you to redress the outrage upon, and the insults to, the flag of the United States, I now ask of your Excellency an explanation of the attack made upon that flag, and a proper guaranty for its future security.

Unless a satisfactory reply of your Excellency to this communication shall be returned within twenty-four hours from the delivery of this note, I shall take such further steps as I may deem the gravity of the occasion to require.

Very respectfully, etc., etc., etc.,

(*Signed*) JAS. ARMSTRONG,

Commander-in-Chief of the United States Naval Forces in the East India and China Seas.

HIS EXCELLENCY,

The Imperial Commissioner YEH, *etc., etc., etc.*, CANTON.

True copy. A. VAN DEN HEUVEL,

Commodore's Secretary.

A feeling of annoyance at the substitution of negotiation for continued hostility was naturally felt by the officers and crews of the two ships left lying off the forts, and they were impatient to have the cessation of hostilities terminated.

The night of the day on which the Commodore had commenced the correspondence, the little steamer Kum Fa, which had been kept as busy, as bustling, and as buzzing as a bee, during all these operations, came down from the forts with a delegation of officers from those ships, and a leading merchant of Canton, to urge the Commodore to go on with the assault. He, however, adhered to his determination to make inquiry into the state of affairs. The officers returned to their ships, and the gentleman, unwilling to give up his views, remained with us over night.

At an early hour on the following morning, I was called from my bed by a message from the Commodore. Upon entering the cabin, I found the United States Commissioner, the commander-in-chief, and the commercial representative of American opinion, in earnest consultation.

The Commodore did me the honor to say, that in the existing emergency he wished to act with the greatest prudence, and they were now holding a council upon the course to be pursued, which he wished me to join.

The result was a conclusion to send the above letter, and know definitely and justly where we stood. It should be particularly noticed that the whole ground of the letter is upon the assumption that the forts were silenced, or had ceased from the disposition to be aggressive.

The gentleman protested against the couclusion of the council, and it is only just to say, he assigned as a reason that negotiation would lead to war with China, rather than prevent it. Yet this same gentleman had said, upon the authority of Howqua, a prominent Canton merchant in the confidence of the Chinese authorities, that the firing upon our boats was the result of accident and not intention. Such a rumor was, in itself, a sufficient reason to induce a just man to refrain from the further destruction of life. We had, probably, by the bombardment of November 16, destroyed many hundred Chinamen, and yet, a member of the same firm as the gentleman now alluded to remarked to Commodore Armstrong, "he hoped soon to hear the booming of his guns around the walls of Canton!"

Almost every communication which came down from the forts manifested the existing impatience at their inactivity under the circumstances expressed by one of them, "The game is ours if we are permitted to start it."

On the afternoon of the 18th, Lieutenant Bowen, with forty men, rejoined the San Jacinto, leaving the force of the forts about five hundred strong. A new condition of things was presented by the report of Lieutenant Bowen.

He said the enemy was no longer quiet and inactive, but was renewing and strengthening his works, erecting a temporary battery near the ships, on which was mounted a gun of large calibre, trained directly upon the Levant's quarter.

This was a condition of things the reverse of that upon which the cessation of hostilities had rested. It was renewed aggression, and therefore Commodore Armstrong at once said to Commander Foote, "that, pending negotiations he was unwilling to take any aggressive steps without sufficient cause," but these hostile movements on the part of the Chinese, Commander Foote was directed to prevent by such measures as his judgment might direct, even if they led to the occupation of the forts.

Before he was aware that such instructions had been sent him, Captain Foote wrote for authority to take these very steps, and saying that his force was sufficient for any orders the Commodore might give. These instructions were sent him on the 19th November.

The want of a proper steamer was felt more and more, and repeated applications came from the forts for one. The Commodore endeavored to engage the American armed steamer Antelope, belonging to the house of Russell & Co., but she was dismantled at Hong Kong undergoing repairs; the Lily, belonging to an American house, was under the Portuguese flag, and the Governor of Macao refused to let her be so employed. Our only resource was continuing the litte Kum Fa, which was therefore chartered and placed under the command of Mr. Sheppard, the Sailing Master of the Portsmouth.

At this juncture Dr. Parker addressed a circular to the American residents at Canton, advising their removal, as the extent of hostilities could not be foreseen, and no force could now be spared from the United States squadron for their protection. The clouds of war were settling about us.

Early on the morning of the 20th, our ships were at work; we could distinctly hear the report of the guns and see the smoke rising over the tree tops. At eleven A.M. the look-out at the mast-head reported that the boats were landing to attack the forts, while one of the ships was shelling; in half an hour more all firing had ceased. About two in the afternoon the Kum Fa was seen approaching from the scene of conflict, and, we feared, to bring some killed or wounded ship or messmate. Fortunately our apprehensions were unfounded—she came for a supply of shot and shell. The largest and nearest fort, that which sustained the bombardment of the Portsmouth on the 16th, had been for three hours in our possession, and was then undergoing the work of demolition. The crew of the Kum Fa were quite worn out with their continued labors, and being Chinese, objected to doing such duty as towing our ships under the fire of the forts, not upon any grounds of patriotism, but, very sensibly, because they did not ship for such hazards. Volunteers were therefore called upon from our own ship's company, and the crew, mistaking the extent to which they were wanting, made a general rush to the mast, each one urging particular reasons why he should have preference. Those who had been at the forts and brought down before the recommencement of hostilities, thought that a reason why they should be sent back again. As, however, only six firemen were actually wanting, these were selected. The engineers also all volunteered, but settled their claims by drawing lots, which fell upon Mr. Biles and Mr. Victor.

At seven in the evening the steamer again came down with Lieutenant Simpson, of the Portsmouth, to report the day's proceedings to the Commodore.

The fort taken had forty-seven guns mounted. Its walls were twelve feet thick below, supporting a projecting platform from which rose a granite wall four feet thick. The killed had all been removed from within the fort, but outside were about fifty dead soldiers and a mandarin. After taking possession of the work a hostile demonstration was made by from four to five thousand men from a neighboring village. A small party was dispatched to disperse them, and succeeded, one of our men being wounded in the leg.

Two of our boys were accidentally killed by the discharge of a Minnie rifle in landing. One man was wounded by the bursting of a gun in the fort, and another was shot in the thigh. So far our loss has been three killed and four wounded. Most probably, in the shelling of Sunday and that of to-day, there have been four or five hundred Chinese killed in all the forts, so that Mullen's spirit is likely to have a large attendance in the "world of the hereafter."

At the same time that Lieutenant Simpson came to report the occupation of the fort, the following reply was received from Yeh:—

COPY.—TRANSLATION.

YEH, *Imperial Commissioner, Governor General of the Two Kwang, etc., etc., hereby replies on business.*

On the 19th inst. I received your Excellency's communication, and have made myself acquainted with its contents. The American Consul, Perry, previously informed me that in consequence of the difficulties between the Chinese and English, he desired that protection might be given [to Americans,] to which I replied on the 24th ult. After the English cannonaded the city of Canton, the people were all in a state of unmanageable excitement, and I was afraid that I might have no leisure to look after their protection, of which I informed him on the 27th ult. Subsequent to that day, the gentry and people came to me, representing that American men-of-war were stealthily coming to the place, and that it was not proper, having regard to the constant good will and intercourse between China and the United States, for them thus to be helping the English attack the city, and this I stated to Mr. Perry, that he might make inquiry and inform me.

Furthermore, seeing that the people of Canton are now engaged in a struggle with the English, in which one of the parties must succumb, and being afraid lest I might not be able to extend protection to the Americans, I deemed the best course would be for their merchants and people to withdraw, for then all risk of becoming involved would be avoided, and learning also that men-of-war were off Canton to protect, it might be difficult to distinguish to what country they belonged in the event of an engagement with troops. If, however, the merchants and citizens would move away, the men-of-war being uncalled for would follow them, all risk of a chance wound or becoming involved would be taken away, and all apprehension and doubt [of their intentions] on the minds of the natives would also be removed. These important considerations I communicated to Mr. Perry on the 4th and 10th insts. for his information. Knowing the amicable relations which have long existed with the United States, I spared no trouble in repeating these things often to him, supposing that he would make them known in detail to your Excellency.

Why, then, did American vessels again pass these forts, and that, too, at a time when our troops were on the alert and very watchful? An American man-of-war can be distinguished from an English one, or from her troops, only by her flag; but from a long distance the two can not instantly be discriminated. It should be remembered, too, that the minds of the people are now much excited and confused, and it is not surprising if it be difficult to prevent mistakes and [false unauthorized] acts among them. I have already said so and repeated my remarks, but they were all taken as if no one heard or paid attention to them. Your declarations in this letter now received, therefore, respecting so inexcusably firing upon and insulting the flag, is what I request may be carefully noted, for I, the Governor General, really fearful that just such an occurrence might take place, thought of it beforehand, and with the best intentions on my part so informed Mr. Perry. Why, I ask, did he not let your Excellency know it?

Hereafter, if American vessels, large or small, do not pass these forts, then all will be harmonious and properly arranged. For this end I send this reply, wishing your Excellency the greatest happiness and good will.

True copy. A. VAN DEN HEUVEL,
Commodore's Secretary.

COMMODORE ARMSTRONG,
Commander-in-Chief of the United States Naval Forces in East India and China Seas.

CANTON, November 20, 1856.

True translation. (*Signed*) S. WELLS WILLIAMS,
Secretary and Interpreter to U. S. Legation to China.

Although it did not alter the necessities under which the naval commander-in-chief had acted, this letter of Yeh showed that he had reasonable grounds for misapprehending our position. Unfortunately, now that he had received an official assurance of our neutral position, he did not disavow the act of his forts, make any apology for it, or promise our flag that respect in the future to which it was entitled. It should be noted, too, that although the French had, equally with ourselves, garrisoned Canton, the French flag was freely passing with impunity those very forts with which we were at war. It was very apparent the hostile action of the forts had been authorised by Yeh. His dispatch was replied to as folowls:

COPY.

UNITED STATES FLAG-SHIP SAN JACINTO,
WHAMPOA, *November* 20, 1856.

SIR,

On the 17th instant I had the honor to address your Excellency a communication informing your Excellency that I had attacked and silenced the "Barrier forts" for an unprovoked outrage upon one of the boats of this squadron. Not wishing to carry measures of redress into those of aggression, I suspended the fire upon the offending forts until I could receive an explanation from your Excellency. Availing himself of this forbearance, the officer in charge of the forts was observed renewing and strengthening his means of assault. I, therefore, was compelled to order this hostile movement to be stopped, and the result (the occupation of one of your forts by a part of my force, and destruction) has, I presume, been communicated to your Excellency by the officer in command.

Your reply to my communication has this moment, seven o'clock, P. M., reached me, and considering the desire expressed by your Excellency to preserve friendly relations with the United States, and the means I was taking to preserve those relations and strict neutrality at the time of the assault upon my boat, it is very much to be regretted that the reply of your Excellency, just received, is not more satisfactory. You do not give me any guarantee that the flag of the United States shall have that safety upon the waters under your Excellency's jurisdiction to which the amicable relations of the countries would entitle it. Upon the contrary, you intimate that if it attempts to pass those forts it must expect insult and hostility. Whatever may be your Excellency's purpose in this declaration, and I trust you have not considered its extent, it amounts to a declaration of war upon the flag of the United States, which has the same right as that of any other nation holding peaceable relations with the Chinese empire to free and peaceable passage on its waters. And it now becomes my duty to take such steps as I may deem proper to secure it that right. But I assure your Excellency there has not been the least intention, nor is there the least wish on my part to engage in unprovoked hostilities against the Chinese empire.

I therefore shall be most happy to learn from your Excellency that you have removed the necessity of continued hostile action, by providing for the flag and for the citizens of the United States that security under your Excellency's government to which they are entitled, and which will result in the happy restoration of peaceful relations.

Very respectfully, etc., etc., etc.,

(*Signed*) JAMES ARMSTRONG,
Commander-in-Chief of the United States
Naval Forces in the East India and China Seas.

HIS EXCELLENCY YEH,
Imperial Commissioner, etc., etc., etc.,
Canton.

True copy. A. VAN DEN HEUVEL,
Commodore's Secretary.

On the same day, November 20th, H. M. S. Coromandel came down to Whampoa from Canton, bringing Dr. Parker a letter from Sir John Bowring, earnestly asking an interview for himself and Admiral Seymour with the commissioner and Commodore Armstrong; and proposing that if these gentlemen could not come up to Canton, Sir John and the Admiral would on the morrow visit the San Jacinto. Sir John went on to say they had been actively shelling the residence of Yeh and other parts of Canton, and yet the Chinese commissioner continued unyielding; and concluded by the wish that the political atmosphere was as beautiful as the physical one of to-day.

The commissioner and Commodore concluded to go up to Canton in the morning in the steamer Lily, which had been placed at their disposition for this purpose by her owner, Captain Endicott, and to meet the British functionaries there. I was directed by the Commodore to accompany him. We were off at an early hour, by seven o'clock in the morning. The weather continued its soft brightness, and we made the run by the picturesque passage of Blenheim Reach; back of the forts. The Chinese peasants and fishermen were quietly harvesting their rice fields or spreading their nets in the river. These peaceful occupations contrasted with the din of war which two powerful nations were making on their country. For at the same moment over these fields and in another reach of the river, could be heard the roar of our guns, and could be seen the white smoke of the bursting shells in a space of landscape framed in like a picture between two tall pagodas.

> "Not war if possible,
> Lest from the abuse of war
> The desecrated shrine, the trampled year,
> The moldering homestead and the household flower
> Torn from the lintel."

We reached Canton about ten o'clock, but not the Canton of my last summer's visit. The crowd of Chinese population living along the river had gone. The country and the canal boats, the busy sampan, the gilded flower-boats, had all gone, and the river, once busy with life and occupation, now flowed between desolate borders. Forts in ruin, houses torn and being torn down, junks extemporized into guard-boats watched over by red-coated sentries, grim men-of-war lying in the channel, with a net-work of booms ahead to keep off fire rafts, were now the river scenes.

The once clean and quiet garden-walks were now littered with rubbish. Bullock pens, shanties and tents now occupied the grass plots, and soldiers were drilling around the square. The club-house and library were turned into quarters for the soldiers and sailors.

The house of the United States Consul, to which he accompanied us, had been shut up for some days. It had last been occupied by a part of our forces. The hall was lumbered with their various stores, and the rooms above were in the forlorn desolation to which they had been abandoned by the sudden departure of our garrison. A few gold-fish moving languidly in the vase added to the dreariness of the scene. Before locking up the house again we gave them another lease of life in a fresh supply of water. We walked through the long aisles which led through the factories to the various residences. At my last visit it was lively with compradors, shroffs, and Chinese clerks, and ringing with the clatter of the piles and masses of dollars being weighed. Now, every door was closed, and I and my companion were the only human beings present. At the end we came out upon a mass of bricks and rubbish into which some houses back of the hongs had been tumbled. The Chinese streets in which we had been accustomed to buy elegant wares were of course deserted, the stores were empty, and the doors standing open. At the end of one of these streets two ragged Chinese children, a small girl and smaller boy, seeing us approach, fell on their knees and put up their hands for charity. But the sentry on post at the opposite end warned them off, and they fled to their hiding-place and starvation.

Upon my return from this view of war's desolation, we proceeded to meet the British functionaries at their residence in the British consulate. At the opening of the interview, Sir John remarked that every thing there said, must be strictly confidential. As the result has since been given the English public, by official communication, my obligation of secrecy is, of course, at an end.

Sir John said that Yeh had shown an obstinacy and determination not anticipated, and that it could only be accounted for by supposing that he had entered upon a course which, unless crowned by success, would lead to his decapitation. The difficulty now turned upon the right of foreign officials to meet the Chinese authorities in the city of Canton. For the support of the narrow exclusiveness which prohibited such interviews he was bringing upon himself and people all this trouble. In the name of the three treaty powers they had demanded the right, and were determined to maintain it; and the object of the present interview was to ask the coöperation of the United States. He said, further, we had a common cause, and his instructions were to confer with the representatives of the United States and France. To this, Doctor Parker replied, that we admitted the common interest, but that it was the purpose of our government to negotiate this right in the renewal of our treaty, but that we had no warrant for demanding it by force, and that we could not complicate our present trouble with the city question. Commodore Armstrong said that his authority extended only to redressing the injuries offered our flag and countrymen, and what steps this might lead him to take he could not foresee. Admiral Seymour said he had no specific instructions upon the subject; but in redressing the injuries done his flag, the necessity for negotiation and explanation followed, and upon that arose the question of the place where and the persons with whom such negotiation should be held. The focus of opposition to general usage upon this subject, was Canton, and the exclusiveness broken here, it would be easy to remove it from every other portion of the empire.

Doctor Parker remarked, that they were somewhat differently circumstanced to us. The specific right they contended for had once been conceded them by treaty. We could not claim this.

The gentlemen then hoped that our flag would not be withdrawn from Canton, as it would in so much weaken the moral force of their demand; and, moreover, it would be represented at Pekin that we, one of the present contending parties, had been expelled from Canton. There was no hesitation in giving the assurance that our flag should be maintained in Canton. Admiral Seymour said that if we could not spare a force from our present business to maintain our flag in Canton, he would look out for that himself. In the preliminary conversation of the interview, Sir John Bowring had made an allusion to a proposition of his made previously to Dr. Parker in writing, to detach a small steamer from the British squadron, at once, and go to the Gulf of Pe-che-Le, and both powers communicate with the court of Pekin. Dr. Parker had, for various reasons, discountenanced it. Sir John, now resuming the subject, said he also did not think it expedient; that it was not well to detach any force from the squadron, that there was little likelihood of success, and that instead of one Yeh they would have hundreds to contend with.

Individually, I think that this has been the radical error of all foreign negotiations with the Chinese. That instead of treating with subordinates two thousand miles away from the central government, we should have treated with that, or not at all. If the distant locality has a special interest to maintain, the remote court looks upon it as a distant and trifling matter in which it has no direct responsibility—a question among the servants in the kitchen, beneath the notice of the drawing-room. It has no motive to come out of the ignorance and misrepresentation in which it rests, and can say to its subordinates, "Do as you please, it matters nothing to us." Our minister to China is a minister to the viceroy of Canton.

In the course of some general conversation after the interview had closed, Admiral Seymour said he would be glad to let us have the services of an experienced engineer officer to aid in mining the forts in case we should determine to blow them up; and also the use of one of his steamers. I am not sure that he made these offers then to Commodore Armstrong, but he stated his readiness in general conversation. However desirable, of course their acceptance was out of the question.

During our visit to Canton we learned that five thousand "braves" were said to be assembled near the factories, immediately inside the walls.

At noon we started on our return to the ship. The firing at the forts had ceased for some time, but an occasional explosion showed that the work of demolition was going on. We found no more recent intelligence upon our reaching the ship, but sometime after, a hurried note was received, calling for more ammunition, and saying that four bodies would be sent to us for burial.

At daylight, on the morning of the 22d, I received the following note from the Surgeon of the Levant:

UNITED STATES SHIP LEVANT,
November 21st, 1856.

MY DEAR DOCTOR,—

We have had a very hot day's work. The Kum Fa took us into capital position, and in about an hour the fort on the left slacked firing, and just after eight the boats shoved off in tow of the little steamer, and occupied the fort. Two men were killed and one was wounded by a single cannon ball, while in the boats. The Levant was struck and shaken by large shot, a good many times, but fortunately no one was hurt. One gun was struck and disabled. The Round fort is occupied by us, and the only remaining one is so completely commanded that it must fall, though it is now keeping up an ineffectual fire at long range, which we do not answer.

I send by the comprador, who has to-day visited us, my papers, etc., which I believe are all right.

In haste, J. H. Wright.

Dr. Wood, Fleet Surgeon.

At eleven o'clock the Kum Fa came down, bringing Captain Foote and five bodies. Three of them had been killed by a round shot striking the San Jacinto's launch, in charge of Lieutenant Lewis. It is somewhat singular, that every man killed by the enemy belonged to the San Jacinto, which ship was not engaged. Captain Foote reported all the forts in our possession, mounting one hundred and seventy-six guns—one of them a monster brass piece:

Extreme length,....	22	feet	5	inches.
Greatest circumference,	8	"	8	"
Least do	4	"	5¾	"
Circumference of trunnion,	3	"	3½	"
Diameter of bore,		"	8½	"

Probable weight, say about fifteen tons.

The gun was burst in the following ingenious manner:*

Ten one and one-eighth inch holes were drilled in a line about half way round, some ten inches forward of the vent; after which the piece was loaded with twenty-five pounds of fine powder, on which was rammed a wet wad, then a large ball, and afterward clay and sand up to the muzzle. The gun was exploded by means of a slow match, and burst thoroughly, the fissures extending nearly the whole length. The time occupied for this labor was a day

* By Assistant Engineer C. Victor.

and three quarters; and by its destruction gave general satisfaction.

Among the weapons used by the Chinese most effectively against us in this contest was one which probably represents the "fiery darts" of the Bible, and, if so, establishes that early knowledge of gunpowder. It is a heavy, metal rocket, with a sharp dart or spear-pointed head, and a feathered bamboo shaft six or eight feet long. One of these passed through the leg of a marine, carrying straw and dirt with it as though in its course it had passed over a paddy field, and struck the ground. It shattered one of the bones of his leg, and the man subsequently died of the effects of the wound in the hospital under my charge. Indeed, my unpleasant relations with this contest were carried over more than a year's charge of men in hospital wounded in the fight.

One of our great difficulties was to get some one acquainted with the intricacies of the channel to pilot the Kum Fa while towing the boats to the assault of the forts—a most exposed and dangerous duty for all in this egg-shell of a little steamer. It was, however, undertaken by W. M. Robinet, Esq., a naturalized citizen of the United States, and a merchant of Hong Kong. The ready abandonment of the comforts and luxuries of his hospitable mansion in Hong Kong for the exposure of this dangerous duty in the service of his adopted country, has, I believe, received no official recognition by the government, although its attention was officially called to the fact. Mr. Robinet also landed with the assaulting parties where his better knowledge of the ground enabled him to facilitate their movements. His gallantry and skill upon these trying occasions, cause all who were witness of them to regret the misfortunes which have subsequently been associated with his name. The services he then rendered can not be denied, even if he has since fallen into error.

XXXV.

RUINED CASTLES.

THE final attack on the four Barrier forts commenced on Thursday morning, November 20th, the guns saluting the gray dawn, and by Saturday, the 22d, although the Chinese had fought fort after fort, they were in our possession.

Those who have followed this narrative have seen there was no intermission, and no rest, day or night, until the capture was accomplished. The efficient coolness which characterized the most fiery hours of the combat, has already been commented upon.

Men and officers worked with the earnest enthusiasm of those doing their duty, to many a painful duty, with a wish to perform it efficiently, but with none of the wild excitement of deeds to be gloried in; and there was no exultation of success claiming commendations for what had been accomplished, or expectancy of the reward of popular approbation. In fact, I do remember, that when some young and hopeful hero suggested that the events might do the service good, by showing the country that the Navy had not lost its efficiency, he was met by the general sentiment, that when the events reached our distant homes, they would fall flat upon the public attention, and scarce attract a day's notice. They did. I do not think a single letter was written by any officer of the squadron to vaunt its achievements and attract popular admiration. None of the quacking arts by which reputations are made, not won, were resorted to; but the duty done, the forts taken, the honor of the American flag and name vindicated, the dead buried on the hill-side at Whampoa, and the whole reported to the Department, the matter ended.

Those who had not been killed might be thankful for their escape, but certainly had no temptations to desire a different result, or any compensation to hope for beyond the consciousness of dying "in the love of duty." When those trained in a life of military aspiration had, with a philosophical appreciation of the real worth of military deeds, reconciled themselves to this chilling indifference, it might have been hoped that a fair human nature, admitting the general depravity of the article, would not have gone out of its way to depreciate the extent of the performance and the merit of those engaged in it.

But as such envy, malice and uncharitableness were found among Americans, it becomes my right to assert the true claims of the duty done. It is consolatory that our English rivals were emphatic in their commendation of the deed itself, and the manner of its performance. As the Portsmouth descended the river, after all was over, the British fleet manned their rigging, and saluted her with hearty cheers; and the officers engaged were congratulated by those of the English service for the honorable testimonials *they would necessarily receive from the United States government*, and could not understand why nothing was expected.

Those who, upon the spot, undertook to insinuate opinions of depreciation, did not underrate the unexpected strength of the fortresses, nor in any one instance dare they intimate a want of skill and courage among the assailants. The false impression is conveyed in a few words of truth. "Yes, they did take the forts, but were a long time about it; they were three days in doing what the English did in a few hours."

All true. All false. The English have a business interest in making the most of every successful achievement, and will press its importance upon their authorities as an honorable ware which has a value of specific compensation. Their true courage, which exaggerates no dangers, will often laugh at the business language in which their deeds are reported. The government, or its military policy, would rather err by the exaggerated acknowledgment of a small achievement, than by overlooking one which should be acknowledged. Promotion attends not seniority, but skill and success. "He was made for so and so," is the expression, setting forth the cause of an officer's promotion.

Notwithstanding this official temptation to make the fullest claim for every deed, warranting such a claim, there was too much English honesty and English pride to make any merit of their capture of the Barrier forts. Because these forts were taken at the very commencement of the troubles, when the Chinese were expecting no attack, and were, consequently, defenseless; the small garrison abandoning them without resistance.

When attacked by the United States naval forces, these forts had been actively preparing themselves for war with us all, mounting heavy guns, and increasing their forces to the utmost extent inside and out. The contemptuous insinuation, while loaded heavily with the meanness of its purpose, breaks its back by carrying the refutation of that purpose. If the forts were a long time in being taken by the United States forces, as there is no charge that there was any shrinking from duty, and as there was no cessation of the attack from its recommencement on the 20th of November, until the final success, the longer the time, the greater the proof that it was an undertaking of real difficulty, and no child's play.

Making no reference whatever to the reports of those engaged in the work, I will refute the whole imputation by the reports of the English themselves; and we can but respect them for that justice which some of our own countrymen have denied.

Extracts from Admiral Seymour's report to the Admiralty, dated on board the Niger, at Canton, November 29th, 1856. Blue Book:

"Since our operations against the Barrier forts on the 23d ult., they have been rearmed, and were at this period garrisoned by a strong force, with troops in the neighborhood. The corvette* commenced firing at four P. M., and continued until seven o'clock, the Chinese returning it with spirit. On the following morning the whole of the American force was withdrawn from the factory to man the ships.

"At seven, A. M., on the 20th, the American ships reopened a very heavy fire on the forts, as the Chinese had commenced the construction of batteries in their rear, which was continued during the whole of that day, and at intervals during the next two days. On the evening of the 22d, Commander Foote called on me to report the capture of the four forts, and the partial destruction of the works, the guns also having been burst and their carriages burned. During these protracted and arduous services, the American officers and men displayed their accustomed gallantry and energy. Their loss amounted to five killed and six wounded. That of the Chinese, I am given to understand, was very heavy, as they made a most determined defense."

From the same, December 14, 1856:

"The American ships-of-war completed the destruction of the Barrier forts on the 6th, and dropped down to Whampoa. These forts were of enormous strength and solidity, being entirely built of large blocks of granite, with walls nine or ten feet thick. They were heavily armed, many of the guns being of seven or eight tons weight, with a bore of thirteen inches; one brass eight-and-a-half inch gun was over twenty-one feet long."

* Portsmouth, Captain Foote.

With such testimony, all disparaging insinuations may be left alongside the unworthy motive in which they originated.

We now had the forts, but their possession was very like that of the undisposable elephant. What was to be done with them?

To turn them over to the English would put us in the position of having captured them in the English interest. If we abandoned them as they were, so long as only the bare walls were left standing, the whole effect of the capture upon the Chinese government would be lost; not only so, but an impression directly the reverse of the truth be produced. The instant we left the spot, the Chinese masses would rush in and occupy the works, hoist their dragon banners, and report to the imperial court at Pekin that, by their courage and skill, they had expelled us, thereby increasing the arrogance of the imperial court, its contempt for us, and adding to the difficulties of future negotiation. Indeed, in one of the forts a flag was found, bearing this inscription:

"THIS FORT ATTACKED, BUT NOT TAKEN."

The following extract from a letter of Assistant Surgeon Daniel, received by me on the day following the final capture, shows what would have been the result, had the forts been left standing:

"* * * None of the commanders are here. The Chinese appear to be occupying one or two of the forts again, and Mr. Lewis has gone up with some of the launches and marines. No order was left for him to do so, but he was, most assuredly, right, for in twenty-four hours the rascals will get some of the guns to bear, and the consequence will be more loss of life. For, if we are to destroy the forts, they must be held until it is done.

We have lost enough, and too many, of our people already."

The destruction of the forts seemed the only safe course, but it was a tremendous labor, and very distasteful to officers and men, now worn out with the constant occupation of the capture. But this course was, after some delay and discussion, determined on, and a corps of laborers, with necessary implements, were hired from the throng of unemployed merchant seamen, now crowding the streets of Hong Kong.

While this discussion was going on, the following tempting proposition was received from Admiral Seymour:

COPY.

Her Majesty's Ship Niger,
Canton, *November* 24, 1856.

My Dear Commodore:

If you are disposed to hold possession of one of the Barrier forts—say that on Kuper Island—I will, on learning your wishes, act against the French Folly fort. This combined movement will give us the command of the Whampoa channel. We should then be in possession of the two river communications between the city of Canton and the sea, a circumstance well calculated to make a deep impression on the Canton authorities.

I am, my dear sir,
Faithfully yours,
(*Signed*) M. Seymour,
Rear Admiral and Commander-in-Chief.

His Excellency Commodore Armstrong,
Commander-in-Chief of the United States Naval Forces.

To which proposition Commodore Armstrong felt it his duty to reply as follows:

UNITED STATES FLAG-SHIP SAN JACINTO,
WHAMPOA, *November* 24, 1856.

MY DEAR ADMIRAL:

I regret that I can not enter into the arrangement you propose, because the moment I receive a satisfactory communication from the imperial commissioner, my business with him is at an end, and I must necessarily return to the pacific relations the United States held before the insult to its flag. But, until the communication does come, I shall hold the forts and go on with their demolition.

I remain, my dear sir,
Most truly yours,
(*Signed*) JAS. ARMSTRONG,
Commander-in-Chief of the United States
Naval Forces in the East India and China Seas.

His Excellency, Rear Admiral
SIR MICHAEL SEYMOUR, K. C. B.,
Commander-in-Chief of her Majesty's Naval
Forces, China.

The demolition of the forts became also very convenient upon another policy. The Imperial Commissioner, Yeh, had evidently determined upon an indefinitely protracted controversy, unless it were carried on with the strong hand upon his throat.

So far we had received from him no regret or disavowal of the past aggression, and no security against its repetition. If he continued in this spirit, we must in all consistency follow up our demand in such a manner as would initiate new and more permanent war measures. But while we were day by day tumbling his costly castles into ruins, he had motives to come more speedily to juster views.

Such are the difficulties of the Chinese language, that

even learned foreigners do not enter upon the translation of an important document without the aid of native linguists and teachers. All these had been ordered by Yeh to leave the factories, and any aid they might give would be at the risk of decapitation. Commodore Armstrong's letter was, therefore, sent Yeh in English. He returned it. It was again sent by Dr. Wells Williams, the Secretary of Legation, accompanied by the 81st article of the treaty, which gives us the right of communicating in our own language.

But this had no influence upon the imperial commissioner. He seemed rather to desire in this way to rid himself of any necessity for accounting for his proceedings, by cutting off all medium of communication. It was shorter than continued evasive and tortuous documents.

Such are the difficulties and dangers of the Chinese non-intercourse policy; showing the propriety and the necessity of the demand made by the British authorities, for personal negotiation. Finally a translation of the document was sent in, and five days after its date a reply was received. This only repeats his first letter, and says that no commerce exists now; that the French and Portuguese consuls had retired from Canton, and says, "I also think that your Excellency will act in the same manner. To maintain amicable relations between our two countries in all respects, there is no better way than to move elsewhere. Henceforth, lest American ships, while passing here and there on the rivers, during this time of hostilities, should not be distinguished, and should by mistake be fired at and injured, I request that you will order merchants and ships for the time to cease going about." Commodore Armstrong reiterated his demand, that the treaty rights of the American flag and of American citizens should be respected, and received, in due time, a reply, the nature of which is shown by the following answer to it:

UNITED STATES FLAG-SHIP SAN JACINTO,
WHAMPOA, *November* 29th, 1856.

SIR:

Your Excellency's communication of the 28th inst. is now, 7 o'clock, P. M., for the first time before me, and as I have distinctly and repeatedly informed your Excellency that the rights and privileges of the flag and citizens of the United States would be defended by me against all aggressions, it would be useless to consume the time of your Excellency and of myself in repeating this determination. But there are a few points in your Excellency's letter which show so much misapprehension of the rights of friendly nations, and the duties of one to another, that I must call your Excellency's attention to the errors under which your Excellency is laboring.

In the first place you demand that the citizens and the flag of the United States shall retire from your Excellency's jurisdiction, because there are hostilities existing between the English and your Excellency, and because the French and Portuguese have done so.

The United States has, as your Excellency must know, by treaty, entered into friendly relations with the imperial government of China, which give its citizens the right to a residence, to trade and to protection in certain portions of the Chinese empire, one of which happens to be under your Excellency's government. The demand of your Excellency is in violation of that treaty, and will call forth the surprise and indignation of my government, and can not be acceded to by any of its officers.

With the course of the French and Portuguese, the authorities of the United States have nothing to do.

These authorities, while most desirous of acting according to right and justice, must form their judgment irrespective of that of other nations, and under the present circumstances they only claim that to which the faith of the imperial government of China is pledged, and which your Excellency can not refuse without taking upon yourself the responsibility of violating that faith.

Your Excellency further says, "When the English opened their fire, on the 29th ult., upon the city, men of other countries scrambled over the walls with them, and when they attacked the French Folly, on the 6th inst., the citizens and villagers repeatedly saw all that was done, and reported to me that there were Americans mixed up among their forces. Moreover, I am told that the English consul, Parkes, has spread abroad the report, that the Americans have encouraged them to maintain their parts bravely in these hostilities. When these things came to my knowledge, knowing the long continued good feelings that your country had shown to us for so many years, I put not credence in them, notwithstanding all the declarations of the people, but in consequence repeatedly informed Consul Perry that he might enjoin it on his countrymen and the American men-of-war, to move elsewhere, and thereby to take away all cause of fear and suspicion. This advice was certainly given with friendly feelings, and he ought to have acted in accordance therewith." For what "the men of other countries" have done, your Excellency must know the United States are not responsible.

In all the correspondence I have had the honor to hold with your Excellency, this is the first communication in which your Excellency has complained of the interference of Americans in your difficulty with the English, and even now, you make that complaint upon the vague reports of "citizens and villagers," whom your Excellency, in former communications, stated to be in so excited a condition they could not distinguish the American flag from the English. Can your Excellency consider such uncertain reports as these a sufficient cause to make war upon a friendly power? to fire, without warning, from your forts upon a small boat, which, relying upon the faith and honor of your government, was, on a friendly and peaceful errand, passing under their guns? It must need very little reflection to convince your Excellency that any reports spread by the officer of another government, not under my control, are not a sufficient cause for such hostile proceedings, even though the reports were strictly true. Americans have a right to hold and to express whatever opinions they please in relation to their own or any other government, and so long as they refrain from any improper action upon those opinions, they are not responsible to any power. It may be supposed, and probably is the case, that some Americans sympathize with the Cantonese, but this would not be claimed by the English as sufficient reason for making war upon the country of such persons.

If any citizens of the United States were so indiscreet as to engage in the hostilities between your Excellency and the English, it would certainly be a just subject of complaint on the part of your Excellency to the United States authorities to which these citizens are responsible, and your Excellency might have every confidence, as you have the evidence, that such a course on the part of American citizens would have been reproved and put an end to.

The following extract from the circular issued by the senior naval commanding officer in my absence, is proof that you can have no complaint against the government whose flag you have assaulted:

"The United States naval forces are here for the special

protection of American interests; and the display of the American flag in any other connection is hereby forbidden.

(*Signed*) "ANDREW H. FOOTE,
"Commander United States Navy,
"Senior Officer present, commanding United States Naval Forces, Canton.
"CANTON, CHINA, *October* 29*th*, 1856.

With so clear and proper means of redress before you, neither his Excellency, the Commissioner of the United States to China, nor myself, received any intimation from your Excellency of any cause of complaints, until after you had fired upon the boat of my squadron, and thus made war upon a power at peace with your government.

From the nature of your Excellency's communication, I am reluctantly led to the conclusion that the assault upon the flag of the United States was by your Excellency's authority. I have shown that the complaints under which your Excellency endeavors to excuse that injury are too vague and undefined to justify any hostility; that, even if true to the fullest extent, your Excellency's course was a reference to the representative of the United States in China. It is plain that your demand to retire the United States flag from the country under your jurisdiction, is a violation of the treaty obligations of the imperial government of China, which can not be acceded to.

If your Excellency, upon considering the subject, shall see the impropriety of this demand, and shall give orders that in future the flag of the United States shall be treated with respect and friendship, the present difficulty will be at an end, and from the friendly feelings you express, and which I both feel and will act upon when all provocation is removed, there ought to be no obstacles to this happy result.

Unless your Excellency sees the justice of the views I

have endeavored to set forth, and acts accordingly, with your Excellency must rest the responsibility for all the evils attending the difficulties you are creating between the governments of the United States and of the Chinese empire.

Returning your Excellency's expressions of good will,

I am, very respectfully, etc., etc., etc.,

(*Signed*) JAS. ARMSTRONG,

Commander-in-Chief of the United States Naval Forces in the East India and China Seas.

HIS EXCELLENCY YEH,

Imperial Commissioner, etc., etc., etc., Canton.

True copy. A. VAN DEN HEUVEL,

Commodore's Secretary.

This communication was answered by another, in which the imperial commissioner concludes as follows:

"You remark in the present letter, 'your Excellency must certainly know on reflection, that the United States has no concern with the acts of other nations;' and further you say, 'if you see that it is contrary to the rights of friendly nations for the Americans to withdraw, if you will issue orders to all your officers henceforth to treat them with respect and friendliness, the present difficulties will be at an end.' From this I see fully that your Excellency has a clear knowledge of affairs. There is no matter of strife between our two nations. Henceforth let the fashion of flag which American ships employ be clearly defined (or made known), and inform me what it is beforehand. This will be a verification (or proof) of the friendly relations between our countries. For this reply, availing of the opportunity to hope that peace may be yours."

Simultaneously with the receipt of this satisfactory letter, the last granite wall of the forts was blown into ruins, and peace restored.

The Levant was ordered to lie off Canton for the refuge of such of our citizens as chose to remain at the factories.

She had only been there two days when, from Whampoa, we saw the evidence of a large conflagration in the direction of the city. The Chinese had burnt all the factories, and expelled the barbarian from the little foothold he had so long held. Our interests there were at an end for the present, and the Levant was recalled.

XXXVI.

THE REIGN OF TERROR.

"Every person lawfully acting as a sentry or patrol at any time between the hour of eight in the evening and sunrise, is hereby authorized, whilst so acting, to fire upon, with intent or effect to kill, any Chinaman whom he shall meet with or discover abroad, and whom he shall have reasonable ground to suspect of being so abroad for an improper purpose, and who being challenged by him shall neglect or refuse to make proper answer to his challenge.

"If any Chinaman, not being the holder of a night pass, shall carry abroad with him, whether night or day, any deadly weapon whatsoever, he shall be guilty of a misdemeanor.

"No act done or attempted in pursuance of this ordinance shall be questioned in any court."

Our own immediate war might be supposed to be over, but we could not pass to the rejoicings of peace. Heads were still worth money, and the lawless Chinese population about us knew nothing of treaties and paper obligations.

Besides, the English war was still in progress, and a fleet of rebels, or pirates calling themselves rebels, lay anchored in the river near Whampoa, ready to pounce upon any prey which passed them; and in the meantime they amused themselves by robbing and burning the neighboring villages, the smoke rising to our sight over the hill tops.

We lay still and stagnant amid the river "chops," or floating shops and residences of Whampoa, but nevertheless, surrounded by war's alarms. Commerce was dead, except that a few small craft, buzzards on the battle-field, were carrying on some surreptitious traffic with dishonest mandarins—Yankee and Chinaman alike out of the pale of God and man.

There was one valuable American interest on shore—a fine stone dry-dock, belonging to the house of Hunt & Co., which was worth our protection, but it seemed, in the present state of affairs, to be a necessary convenience to the English, and the British frigate Sybille, lay off the dock.

The Chinese were very bold in their attempts at injury. Near us lay the chop of an Englishman by the name of Cooper. On the evening of December 20th, a boat of Chinese ran alongside of it, under the pretense of delivering a letter, seized Mr. Cooper's father from the midst of his family, and hurried him off in their boat. Nothing satisfactory was ever again heard of him. He was either decapitated and his head sold, or died a prisoner in Canton. The British arrested some of the principal men of the village, and threatened to burn the place unless the old man were returned, but no knowledge of the transaction could be fixed upon them.

How much of the trouble of the world arises from men and people misunderstanding each other! The Chinese view of their civilized and Christian enemies may be learned from the following

Public Declaration of the Gentry and People of the City and Hamlets of Canton.

Until the parricide* be cut off, there will be no peace in (men's) dwellings. When blood-thirstiness and vicious

* The word is compounded of the name of a bird that devours its mother, and a beast that eats its father; and is used here to signify, *par excellence*, an atrocious monstrosity.

perversity rebel with violence, (against the rule of right) a virtuous indignation should be manifested by all in common.

The English barbarians having commenced a quarrel without a cause, imputing to us their own offense against what is proper (or decorous), have destroyed our forts, have assaulted our city, have burned the lowly dwellings of the people, have sacked their villages; merchant* vessels and passage boats have been plundered; the wayfarer and the traveling merchant have been assassinated.† At the village of Lieh-teh (by the Barrier forts), three women were ravished,‡ and for shame have destroyed themselves. Such is their brigand soul, such their wolfish nature; wo be to the city of Canton, if they be suffered to dwell there long!

It behoves us to raise a force of sons and brothers,§ to exterminate them, ere we eat our morning meal; to gather together the population of the villages and the city, and sweep away this fiendish pestilence. It is now determined that, on a day to be appointed, there shall be a meeting at Fat-ling Shi (north-east of the city), for purposes of general deliberation. Every inhabitant of the villages near the city, from sixteen years of age to sixty, shall take his place in the ranks; a rate shall be levied on lands for their subsistence; the more remote districts shall aid to swell the cry. These barbarians must be ex-

* *Lit.* Silk vessels.

† Have suddenly suffered wounds and death.

‡ There was an idle rumor that some women were violated near the Barrier forts, when they were taken by the Americans. The circumstances of that capture considered, there is very small ground indeed for crediting a report which has been for years past the inseparable companion of every narrative of barbarian misdoings.

§ The proverb says, "that of such should be formed the force that hunts the tiger, or that goes to battle."

terminated, and the port* closed to them; nor must they ever again be allowed to trade at Canton, that men's hearts may be satisfied, and the calamities of after time be prevented.

Even were the high authorities resolved to be gentle and considerate, and in this spirit mercifully tolerant of these dogs and mice, they could not go against the resolution of the rural population, hundreds of thousands in number; they could not thrust aside the common feelings of the people. Yet there has been of late a rumor to this effect; while these barbarians have been destroying the Lien-hing and other streets, acts which it was as much to be assumed would have roused the virtuous indignation of the inhabitants of the western suburb, as it was not to be assumed that they would have tacitly assented to them, allowing the silk-worm thus to eat (its way), a report has been, notwithstanding, current in the street and on the highway, which goes the length of asserting that the substantial and wealthy merchants of the western suburb, who have so many years traded with the rebellious barbarians, some because they have business establishments abroad, some because they have shares in foreign vessels, are tenderly regarding their personal interests, while they ignore the sentiment of patriotism; that they have some time since made a secret compact (with the barbarian) that neither party shall molest the other; and that this is the reason why they are composedly looking on, as if nothing extraordinary were taking place.

A tale like this, told in public places,† were doubtless not to be greatly trusted; but with such noise and frequency is it passing from man to man, that it has, indeed, astounded those who hear it; and it is but too probable that the western suburb will, in the end, find to its sor-

* *Lit.* The wharf must be destroyed.

† *Lit.* In the markets and by the wells.

row that it is become the point on which popular indignation has concentrated itself.

If duly mindful of their duty to their homes, of the abundant bounty in which they have been steeped by dynasty after dynasty, they will pillow them on their arms, determined and united with us in our patriotic movement; let them, sharing with us our animosity, and treating as foes those whom we hate, grasp, one and all, the ear of the ox,* and join our confederacy.— *China Mail, December* 18th, 1856.

Perhaps we make as disparaging errors in our judgment of the Chinese.

On the evening of December 23d, I retired early, with the hope and prospect of a quiet night's rest. But truly no man knows what an hour may bring forth, especially at a time when you do not know whether you are at war or not, and if at war, whether it may be with a regular government, regular rebels, or irregular pirates.

There had been a rumor for some days past that one heavy fleet of armed junks was to descend the river, and another to ascend, and between them both, the British frigate and ourselves were to be overwhelmed.

Soon after lying down, the repeated concussion of heavy guns shook the air about us. But almost every night there has been some heavy firing in the direction of Canton, and a small business is going on day and night in our vicinity, and, though these heavy guns seemed much nearer than Canton, concluding that it was no business of mine, I went to sleep, but in a few hours was waked by a terrible confusion on deck, with the noise of a steamer near by. The British steamer Queen, on her way from

* In the time of the Fighting States—the Confucian era—when a league was to be formed, an ox was sacrificed to Heaven, and his ear being cut off by the senior of the confederacy, the blood from it was drunk in wine by the members of the alliance.

Canton to Hong Kong, about seven miles below us, had encountered a fleet, said to be of one hundred armed junks, coming up the river, who had fired upon her, and driven her back.

This midnight intelligence came upon our ship with startling effect, and the noise on deck was that of tearing the cabin to pieces, and running a gun out of the stern port. Presently all hands were called—steam was got up, with a general dispersion of all sleeping facilities. With the better information of the next day, we ascertained that the firing had been of a serious character. The iron steamer Thistle had preceded the Queen down the river, having in tow a lorcha of valuable goods, worth from forty to fifty thousand dollars, and first encountered these hostile junks. The attack was a very vigorous one, and the commander of the Thistle, a Dane, by the name of Weslein, behaved in a most gallant manner. He took the helm himself under the fire, and endeavored to run through the fleet with the lorcha, but finding he could not do this, he brought her alongside, removed every one from her, and cut her adrift, and passed the fleet with his steamer, having several of his men killed by the fire of the Chinese. It was in contemplation to give Captain Weslein a complimentary testimonial for his conduct upon this occasion, but before this was done a more unhappy day came, when his steamer was captured and burnt, he, and all on board, being massacred. Armed Chinese, in disguise, went on board of her as passengers, and at a favorable moment rose upon the ship's company, and destroyed it.

During this state of affairs our communication with the shore is very much cut off, but it has developed a curious feature of Chinese character, in the attachment to our ship of a small fleet of native boats. There is our "fast boat," or general carriage of all work, for ship visiting and gadding about the harbor; one or two bum-boats, equivalent, the reader now knows, to the "corner grocery," without, however, the liquor. From these the crew buy pies, cakes, cooked fish, eggs and meats, fruits, and fancy articles. These boats, all of them, hoist small American flags at their mast-heads, and identify themselves with our nationality. They are a great convenience to us in many ways, and especially in the laundry department, as our clothes are washed and ironed by the families of these small boats. All of them are tenanted by families, and old Assing, the pilot, has a wife and five children, the youngest six months old. Mrs. Assing is not at all satisfied with the state of affairs, and is very anxious that we should all get out of this locality, and worries the old man a good deal about it, urging him to leave us, if we will not go into safer regions. When making neighborhood trips in her boat, the old lady tells me piteously, in pigeon English, of the "too much fear" she has; and upon one occasion Assing asked me when we would go down the river, as "my very much fear." I told him he need have no fear while with us, as we could protect him.

"Byme-by," he replied, "you go New York side—'Merrikey side; my stay China side—mandarin cutee off my head, all my catchee, now forty-five dollar one moons; no, enough."

Having heard that criminals condemned to death will sometimes buy persons, who have distressed families, to suffer in their stead, the money being paid their families, it occurred to me to ascertain Assing's price for his head, as he evidently put a money-value upon it. When I asked the question he hesitated some moments, and then said: "Pay five hundred dollar my wife—my children—can take Assing's head," and I have no doubt that the article could have been had on the terms.

In addition to our regular suite of boats, we have,

almost constantly, just under the quarter, a group of mendicant boats—miserable little floating troughs, with some wretched looking old man, old woman, or little child, who, by means of a sculling oar, constantly in motion, keeps in a position to pick up the scraps and offal of the ship; no matter what—potato-parings or orange-peel—it is dexterously gathered up by a small hand net.

Among these dependants is an intelligent, but distressed-looking, child, with whom I have got up such a friendship as prisoners do with the mice or spiders in their cell. He solitarily and patiently plies his oar all day. One wonders, in looking at his thin, ribby body, where the strength comes from. In my visits of relaxation to the poop-deck, I have made him the recipient of my small charities, sometimes going to the extravagance of pitching him a whole ship's biscuit or an orange. I am fully paid by seeing his eye brighten as I come, and to hear him say, in clear English, "Thank you." No other word has ever passed between us.

From twelve till two o'clock we have much entertainment in an animated bazaar on board. However studiously or churlishly we may have shut ourselves up in our rooms, this daily trade brings us out. Venders of lacquer ware, of ivory, sandal-wood boxes, shawls, fans, camphor-wood desks, dressing cases, and chests, come off at this time, spread out their wares on the decks, or the tables of our apartments, and get up quite a lively scene in the competition of purchasing, or of amusement in the various applications of "pigeon English."

"My talkee true—propa price—plum cash;" which last expression means prime cost.

One hard-faced, grim and rascally old gentleman none of us will ever forget, as, with a sing-song voice, he constantly reminded us that his wares were "number one qualanty—good ting no cheap—cheap ting no good."

Some stupid, starch-laced Navy officers might have thought these scenes an invasion of disciplinary propriety, but in our position they were a moral good, and medicine for the mixed anxiety and monotony of our existence.

As there was but one American trading house at Whampoa—the floating one of Cook's chop, of which the resident proprietor was the United States Vice Consul—and as our relations with the Chinese were nominally pacific, there did not seem to be sufficient reasons for keeping the squadron at Whampoa, and there were many requiring our presence in Hong Kong, where an immense amount of American shipping had gathered, and where much alarm and anxiety existed. Commodore Armstrong, therefore, sent notice to the United States Vice Consul that he intended to leave that place, and tendering any facilities of convoy to those who did not feel willing to remain.

Considering our friendly relations, and the understood disposition of some of the Chinese on shore, they all felt safe in remaining, merely requesting that the little steamer Kum Fa, which had been so active in our hostilities, might be taken with us. Engineers from our ship were put on board of her for that purpose, and on Christmas day we got under way to descend the river. It was a most beautiful day. As we passed the Boca Tigris, the Calcutta and Nánkin were lying there. The extensive forts, with the exception of two on the islands in the river, were in ruins. These two were occupied by the English.

Soon after passing this very picturesque point, and entering upon an expanse in the river which spreads away like a lake between its distant mountain shores, we came upon a most agreeable surprise. A steamer was on her way up from Hong Kong, and seeing our approach she stopped; a boat was sent her and we received our home letters by the last overland mail. Getting them so suddenly, and in such an unexpected place, made them the greater prize, and our second Christmas from home quite a home festival.

Arrived in Hong Kong, we found the place in great anxiety; most of the British force was up the river. There had been rumors of a general massacre and burning of the city by the Chinese, who, even in that English town, were in overwhelming masses. The hundred-dollar value for foreign heads still existed; the Thistle, too, had been captured and burnt; and the opportunity for plundering the city alone invited to conflagration, so that each day closed in apprehension as to what might happen before morning, and every day seemed to bring news of some unexpected tragedy. The inhabitants felt more unsafe than if upon a savage frontier, because to treachery and ferocity were added the resources of a great empire and the devices of a partial civilization.

In this disturbed condition of things I was compelled, on account of the sick and wounded—the shattered and amputated limbs—to take a hospital on shore, and was fortunate enough to engage one in charge of an Italian priest, the worthy Father Geronimo. It was in a remote part of the city, and surrounded above and below, for it stood on a hillside, by a dense Chinese population.

In the existing state of things, the always foolish contempt with which John Chinaman had been viewed, now gave place to an exaggerated estimate of his prowess.

It was a morning of congratulation when the night had passed without any realization of the existing apprehensions. Our situation was so exposed at the hospital, and our wounded, our one-armed and one-legged men, so defenseless, that a part of the marine guard was stationed there, and another at the naval storehouse in the neighborhood—all under command of Captain John D. Simms

Arrangements were also made for the landing of boats in case of any night attack. Every private house had its guard of foreigners and its private armory.

So far, every success had been with the Chinese. They had expelled us all from Canton, burnt the factories, captured a valuable cargo, and destroyed the steamer Thistle, and soon after, in like manner, destroyed the Queen. Each report was of some new disaster. On the 5th of January all Hong Kong was excited by a report coming from among the Chinese themselves that the British armed steamer Coromandel had been taken and all hands destroyed. On the 6th, however, war-worn, but safe, she came into the harbor. Her account of the action in which she had been engaged, gives some idea of the increasing boldness of the Chinese, and corrects the error of despising their prowess and courage. Located in the hospital, I became now a settled Fankwei, and will give the reader a look at my home and its surroundings, in which, too, we are to have some incidents. Although removed from the heart of Victoria by some distance, we are in the midst of busy scenes. Perched like a cage on the mountain side, which rises bold and craggy behind us, we look down upon the main thoroughfare, and over the bay to the hills and villages of the mainland of China, two miles distant.

Directly under, and a little in front of our building is a large Chinese-owned rice-mill, worked by human foot-power, treading on the ends of levers which alternately raise and let fall a heavy pestle in a stone basin in which is contained the grain. Day and night this place is going. To me, and to most persons who come into my room, it is like the shaking of the machinery of a noisy steamboat, jarring the wood-work as this does my room. Some liken it to the tramp of horses, and others to the pounding of an industrious gang of caulkers.

Having become accustomed to it myself, I now never notice it unless my attention is called to it. It is the sound of the whole day until one o'clock in the morning, and then I believe there is an intermission until daylight. If, however, it stops at any other time, my attention is called and I awake from my sleep. During the height of the apprehension here respecting Chinese hostilities, the apprehension of blowing up, and conflagration, I was awoke one night by the sudden stillness of the rice-mill. It at once occurred to me that possibly the Chinese engaged in the establishment had made all their arrangements for blowing us up, as had those of the adjoining baking establishments for poisoning us. I mentioned my suspicions to the officer associated with me on duty. We determined, however, that we must take our chance for that night, but to-morrow we would see what was under us. We were glad to find it all the solid earth of the hill. The bakery from which all Hong Kong was poisoned is just above the rice-mill, and another opposition bakery drives its smoke into my windows from the opposite side.

Nearly opposite to us is a busy ship-yard, the more busy now that the shipping is driven from the docks at Whampoa; and one side of us a gang of Chinese are actively employed in blasting and quarrying the granite from the hill. On one tumbling-down space of the hill are the remains of an old grave-yard, and to me it is a melancholy association, for the grave nearest my window, on the tumbling verge of the clayey hill, is that of a brother officer whom last I saw in life, in another hemisphere, eighteen years ago, and then at a gay dinner party, giving his fine voice expression in one of the most beautiful songs of our language. What a contrast!—there lie his bones.

In front, we look out and down upon the bay, with its shipping, and the villages of sampans, or small boats, which, at the close of the day, gather to their rendezvous, and cast their joss-fires upon the waters.

Opposite, about two miles away, are the hills and mountains of the mainland of China, and the white beach upon which we see people walking, is that of the Kowloon shore. On a calm evening, it looks a pleasant and inviting pull in a boat over there, but, neighborly as the two shores seem, and placid as all looks, the white man who should try such an evening excursion would, probably, leave his body there, while his head traveled in a sack to Canton.

On the opposite side of the street, and a little below us, in a street made up of Chinese fruit shops, brokers' offices, cook-shops, tinmen, brass-founders, and the varied industry of these Celestials, rises a neat granite chapel, and next it is the residence of the Sisters of St. Paul, seven worthy, and, so far as my observation goes, agreeable women, who have charge of the "Asile de Sainte Enfance," an institution which receives and takes care of children abandoned by their parents. Many of these unhappy cases arise from the horror the Chinese have of having a death in the house, and hence they send a dying child to this institution, or abandon it to its fate by the road-side. A melancholy instance of this came under my own observation.

The mountain, as before said, rises abrupt, rugged, and rocky, immediately back of the hospital. About twilight, on a Sunday evening, one of the men, who had been out walking in the day, came to me, and told me there was a little Chinese girl, about ten years of age, lying behind some rocks on the mountain side, in a dying condition. I immediately sent out to have the child brought in. The messengers returned, after dark, without her, and said there was a savage-looking Chinaman with the child, who refused to permit her to be taken away.

The Chinese belonging to our establishment told me that the parents of the child had hired this man to stay with her until she died, not wishing her to die in the house. Taking two of the men, I now went myself in search of the sufferer. By the light of a lantern, we clambered the mountain, but, after some difficult wandering among boulders, failed to find the place. The light of the lantern confused the guide. Leaving the lantern with me, he continued the search in the dark. After an absence of ten or fifteen minutes, we saw him descending from above us, followed by the Chinaman, with the child in his arms. They said it was dead. However, upon lifting the lantern to its face, this was found to be a mistake. It was rather a handsome child, with full face and large black eyes, which it turned inquiringly upon our strange features, but with an expression more of hope than fear. It slowly stretched its hands towards us, but could not speak. The pulse was very feeble, and the whole body chill with the damp night air. A very little more exposure would have put an end to its existence, or the ruffian who now held it in his arms would probably have aided the matter by laying his hand over its mouth and nose. With some trouble and delay, I found two old Chinawomen, who washed and clothed the child, and remained with it over night. By the administration of a little warm cunjee, or rice-water, and a little wine, the warmth returned to its skin, the pulse rose, and the brightness of its eyes seemed to give some promise of recovery. On the following morning it was kindly received into the asylum of the Sisters of St. Paul, where it lived several days.

Being immediately on one end of the Queen's road, I am called frequently to look over the front railing, by the sounds of music—if music it may be called—bagpipes, gongs, tom-toms, loud and rapid; and, as we look down into the street, we see a rabble approaching us almost at a trot, they walk so fast.

First, we have the musicians, and then, resting in a square box, suspended from handles, resting on men's shoulders, is a pig—a full-grown hog, roasted whole and done brown. What is it—a wedding or a funeral? Slung on poles, resting on men's shoulders, there next comes part of a trunk of a tree, hewn smooth—a very cumbrous-looking affair. It is a funeral; that is the coffin. Some have nothing but the plain wood, others are covered with red cloth. Then follow five or six fancifully-ornamented sedan chairs, or rather small-sized temples, in each of which is some flower-dressed article of food. After these come half a dozen persons, in white sugar loafed caps, and three or four dressed in long white dresses. Behind all comes a solitary sedan chair, perhaps conveying some real mourner. The same music, the same provision for feasting, with a gayly-dressed sedan chair conveying the bride, substituted for the log-like coffin, makes the funeral a wedding.

From our terrace look-out, we have a view of much of the economy of out-of-door Chinese life. In front of the ship-builder's residence is a long and comfortable verandah, projecting over the pavement, and sheltering it from sun or rain. I have made a very pleasant acquaintance of the eye (I mean they are among the familiar objects of my daily range of vision) with two respectable, matronly Chinese ladies, who daily come with their low stools and baskets of sewing, and take their seats under this verandah, and there remain quietly and industriously at work, until the hour of returning to the evening meal. These are pleasant objects, because they are so neat and tidy in their appearance, so industrious in their vocation, and their location is so suggestive of economy and good management.

There they are, with plenty of air and light, well protected from the weather, and immediately on the main thoroughfare, where they see every thing that is going on; all so much more comfortable than staying all day in the, perhaps, crowded den which makes their home; and then, I infer, they pay the ship-builder no rent for sitting under his porch. Sometimes, a Chinese cobbler, with his kit, joins the old ladies for a day or two, and they have quite a chat. He is not, however, a permanent tenant, but, I presume, travels round under all the porches and loafer-havens of Hong Kong, and brings to the more fixed occupants budgets of travelers' tales. Such are the economical uses made of all the sheltering appurtenances of Chinese towns.

At the end of the short lane which led from the main street directly up to the hospital was a small porch in front of the Chinese shop. I got up quite an interest in the sitter under this porch. She evidently now belonged to one of the most humble walks of coolie life, as indicated by her position as worker in the street—and by her poor attire. But she had been born to much more aristocratic position and with higher expectations, for she had the smallest of small female Chinese feet. Her ankles terminated in points smaller than the hoof of a new-born colt, and with all the poverty of her attire the boastful feet were clothed in neat crimson slippers. Although haggard and care-worn, her countenance was more intelligent, animated and refined than was characteristic of the class to which she now belonged; her complexion, too, was more fair. Playing around her on the ground were two little sickly-looking children, with their mother's thin, pale features. One of them more often lay languid and listless on the mother's knee. I necessarily had to pass this family group every time I went upon the street, and I got into the habit of giving a few copper cash to the children, who, when they saw me approaching, would run toward me, when they were well enough to do so, holding out their hands and crying, "Chin! chin!" The mother made what I believed to be an affected effort to stop them, but would look pleased and thankful on account of the pittance given her children. I was even surprised at the delicacy which induced her to affect any objection to the "cum shau," as taking what they can get seems a proud Chinese virtue. However, I soon missed her and the children from the porch, and next noticed they had taken refuge with the elderly matrons on the opposite side, a position I less often passed. I once called the attention of a friend to her, remarking, "There is a Chinawoman whose delicacy is so great, I have driven her from her former locality by giving small sums of money to her children." He said that he would, therefore, as he passed that way, give them some money as a reward for her delicacy. He did so two or three times, and she again disappeared.

There is, however, another possible theory of this mysterious and uncharacteristic flitting. It is that, perhaps, in her fall from the aristocratic position of her birth, she may have dropped into the hands of some uncouth coolie of the neighboring workshops, and placing a mysterious value upon a gem which had unexpectedly fallen into his hands, he feared that all who approached it might equally value and desire it, and therefore by his lordly orders these movements—the pale woman with the little crimson-slippered feet and the two pale children were taken from the incidents of our every-day Hong Kong existence. One little melancholy star which glimmered in the gloom had set, and the shade of darkness around us was more shadowy.

Other of our neighborhood associations were suggestive of urbanity and kindly feeling. Down below us, far between our upper-air elevation and the street, there seemed to be descending terraces of habitations, besides the mill which beat and pounded at the base. Some of these rooms Father Geronimo had let out to Portuguese, and even in this little and exceedingly limited and obscure part of a remote colony, I found there were distinct unassimilating and exclusive ranks. First, I say first, perhaps, because nearest to me—perhaps, because what is in nature first will rise above all conventionalities, and present itself first to the mind. In my professional capacity I came into intimate communion with all these classes, and marked their peculiarities. First, there was the family of a Portuguese mechanic, a baker. His children, boys and girls, all worked hard, following the example of their mother and himself. They rose early, fed the pigs and the poultry. My bedroom window overlooked these morning avocations. They dressed and went to school and chapel—learned English, wrote it well, spoke it well. They drudged in the laborious road of life, but hedged it with courtesies and graces. Having rendered them some little professional assistance, almost daily, ever afterward, there came to my room a varied bouquet, or a glass dish of jasmins, banana flowers, etc.; occasionally cake and confectionery, or the more substantial acknowledgment of a roast sucking pig bedded in roses and other bright flowers. And when I was about to leave their neighborhood, father and son came in their best attire with a final bouquet of gratitude.

My neighbors were not confined to the shore. China is celebrated for the amount of its population which has no foot-hold upon the shore—families living in small boats as their only homes, and living, too, a healthy, cleanly and independent existence. No ground rent to pay, certainly, and surrounded in abundance with two of the essential elements of comfort and health—air and water.

In the day-time one can scarcely realize the extent of this water population. The boats are then scattered, each family following its avocation. Upon landing from a ship visit on a very dark night, I fell in a quarter of a mile or more above the point I intended to strike, and I found myself almost lost in a floating city of small boats, and upon a part of the bay which I was accustomed to see every day as a piece of open water. The boat's crew were compelled to lay in their oars, and pull from boat to boat through such lanes as we could find, amid the clattering tongues of the women, the cries of disturbed children, and the perhaps alarmed patience of the men, who did not know what kind of an invasion was upon them.

On the following evening I noticed these boats gradually gathering in—gathering in as birds to their nest; and beside this spectacle, interesting in itself, I had presented to me a most beautiful religious ceremonial. As each boat took up its anchorage, a member of the floating family, I presume the head, appeared suddenly with a bright torch of burning paper, which flashed brightly on the water, as it was waved two or three times toward some invisible deity, like the gleam of a meteor, and then, being cast upon the water, left the family to the repose of the consciousness of a fulfilled religious obligation. One after one, sometimes two or three at a time, of these fire offerings gleamed over the water as the boats came in to their rest, and in some of them the clanging of a gong accompanied the offering. This noisy tribute or demand upon the deity may have been peculiar to Chinese pharisees who wished to be heard of men. But the offering itself shows how deeply implanted is the religious sentiment, and this evening worship only needs to be directed to the one God, with equal sincerity, to elevate and purify the national character.

On the morning of April 3d, we had the shock of one of those tragic occurrences which seem to be incident to the state of affairs in which we are living. Directly in the heart of the main street, an old gentleman was found strangled in his bed, the marks of the suffocating fingers upon his throat, and his Chinese coolie had fled—a thing easy enough: a short pull of a boat would land him upon the Kowloon shore. It certainly seems most extraordinary that the English do not occupy that point. It is the basis of all hostility against Hong Kong, and the refuge of all who are guilty of crimes against the community.

On the night of this same day, as I was returning to my home, on one of the long, uninhabited reaches or commons below the town, I met three Chinamen in charge of a policeman, who had them, as is usual, tied together by their tails. Such an unhappy grouping was so common in these times that I was passing without giving more than a glance at the group, when, to my surprise, I heard my name, or rather title, called, almost in a tone of shrieking agony, by the tallest and most conspicuous person of the group of prisoners. He was a very tall man and threw his arms high in the air as he called upon me. I found it a professional brother in distress, a tall Chinese leech vender, whose profession had brought us into acquaintance and sympathy. He had been caught out, after the fatal curfew hour, without a pass, and thus ingloriously tied by the queue to two other delinquents, was on his way to the lock-up. I could do no more for him than recommend him to the best treatment of his rough custodian.

The Chinese have no Sabbaths. From day to day, without intermission, the toil and the noise of labor are seen and heard throughout the land. But as the year draws to a close, and the new year approaches, for weeks and months the enjoyments, the rest, the social meeting, the gathering of families together from long distances, are a constant subject of talk and happy anticipation. Then debts are to be paid, then the year's profits are to be estimated, and the costly wardrobes of Chinese gentlemen and ladies to be displayed—silks, satins and furs, decorations and jewelry. The wardrobe of any respectable Chinese gentleman we know to be a costly affair, worth an occasional display.

Money must be had at this time for the purposes of pleasure and to fulfill obligations, for the Chinaman who goes into the new year with debts unpaid, goes into it with disgrace. About this time it might be written in the Chinese almanacs, "expect dishonest servants,"

> "For those steal now who never stole before,
> And those who always stole now steal the more."

The shops begin to look gay—confectionery is more abundant and more brilliant, fire crackers more constant in their confused and confusing detonations.

"Must catchee now for two, tree day!" says your Chinese servant as he steps into the room, and unwinding the tail wrapped around his head lets it fall to the floor; to come into the presence of a superior without this mark of deference would be a discourtesy of which no well-bred Chinese would be, and no subordinate dare be, guilty. Courtesy and politeness is a Chinaman's religion.

"What for must catchee?"

"Chinaman no makee pigeon now for two, tree day—no can buy every ting."

This year the English ordinances prohibited Chinese festivities, and they had to confine themselves to walking about in their gay dresses, and this alone was a brilliant scene, or to leaving their crimson visiting cards with their friends and acquaintances. I called upon some of my shop-keeping friends, left my card, and partook of their neat little tables of confectionery and other refreshments.

Even our sectional new year's calls are a Celestial inheritance.

My Chinese acquaintanceship was neither numerous nor aristocratic; neither was my English. I belonged to a profession which was socially of low caste with both people.

Among my earliest acquaintance with the natives was that of a genteel-looking, well-dressed man, in whose store I made a purchase, directing it to be sent on board ship. With my mind then imbued with the prevalent vulgar notions of Chinese trickery and dishonesty, I was annoyed upon finding the article delivered did not hold out in quantity, and went to the man and stated the deficiency. He replied with some dignity, shaming my irritation—"Of course what you say is correct, you need pay for only that you received."

A more careful examination showed the mistake to be that of my servant—all had been delivered. I again went to the man and confessed my error; he said it was of no consequence, and politely invited me to take a glass of soda water with him.

As the 15th of January, 1857, approached, all hands on board the San Jacinto were in a state of hopeful exultation. Then she was to leave the disheartening scenes and life of Hong Kong for the pleasures and beauties of Manilla. But, alas, on the morning of the 15th there came a sickening disappointment. The breakfast in the hospital wards was an hour or two before my own, and soon after it had been served the hospital steward rushed into my room saying all the men in the hospital were poisoned. I hurried in and found it true. On both sides of the long ward the men were suffering violent and distressing illness, and all naturally in a great state of alarm. There was only one exception to the general sickness, and that man was suffering from lock-jaw in consequence of a rocket wound.

I supposed the cause of illness was local, confined to our own establishment—the Chinese coolies were suffering as well as our own men. The cook, a Chinaman, was very much frightened and agitated. In the course of two hours, by the use of appropriate remedies, the men were all relieved and quiet, and Captain Simms and I went to our breakfast, taking the precaution to make our own tea. By a most trivial and accidental occurrence neither of us ate any bread. This was supplied us from an outside bakery; and it was only after our own breakfast my attention was called to the fact that the lock-jawed man had escaped; and he alone had eaten no bread. By this time, however, most of Hong Kong had breakfasted, and I received a hurried call from the ship-builder's establishment on the opposide side of the street. They were all, European workmen and Chinese laborers, as my hospital had been two hours before. I had scarcely prescribed for them when a sedan chair came for me to hurry up to a friend's commercial establishment a mile or two up town. I found them in the like condition, including the commander of a Russian man-of-war staying with them. But other medical gentlemen were in attendance.

All Hong Kong was poisoned, from the governor and family down, and my honest friend, the gentlemanly grocer, Essing or Alum, with all his establishment, was arrested for the crime.

The supposed plan was to poison all they could, and then take the city. Essing was the proprietor of the largest baking establishment in town, worked by expensive machinery. He supplied the city, the shipping, the troops. In the first indignation it was proposed to execute him summarily, but law and order prevailed, and he was committed for trial. I carefully studied the trial, and came to the conclusion that he had no knowledge of the matter or participation in it. The poison, arsenic in large quantities, was introduced into the bread by two of his workmen, who made their escape; and it is creditable to an English jury that in the conviction of Essing's guilt resting on the public mind, they had the clearness of judgment and honesty of purpose to acquit him. He was, however, detained in prison after his acquittal, and ruined in name and fortune.

The following extraordinary sentences are from the speech of the attorney general of the colony:

"Would any one have disapproved if a different course had been pursued towards the prisoners, and instead of allowing them a trial, which such monsters do not deserve, they had been dealt with in a summary manner, and had suffered those short and sharp pangs of death which they had intended we should suffer? Their crime deserved the fate of a drum-head court martial; but much, gentlemen, as I may regret that they are before a jury at all, still they are now before one, and I am bound to tell you, that if any reasonable doubt of their guilt rests upon your minds, you are bound to acquit them. But, gentlemen, it will not be your duty to stretch the points set up for their defense to too great a length; and in this opinion I feel certain the Bench will concur."

A poetical narrator of the transaction seems to accord in the views of the attorney general, as did most of the foreign inhabitants of Hong Kong—

"It has been inferred,
By the historians of our present time,

That in the long, elaborate summing up,
In which his lordship was most fair and clear,
There sometimes would peep out a word or two,
As if conviction in that good man's mind
Were somewhat certain of the prisoners' guilt.
Howe'er it be, the gentlemen with whom
The fiat rested, or for death or life,
Chose, no doubt wisely, to accord the last.
The chief raised high his most celestial cap,
And bowed his gratitude—both for himself
And martyr-comrades. He could be polite—
(So too can cut-throats).—But, 't was not polite
For one unfeeling rascal to roar out,
As he, *the freed conspirator*, passed down
The court-house steps—'O, ye Gods! I wish
That we could know, but for one single hour,
The Vigilance Committee, or Judge Lynch.'"

Altogether the state of things was very uncomfortable, and it was thought hardly in accordance with duty to our own countrymen and with comity towards the English, for the San Jacinto to leave the colony at this time, especially as Commodore Armstrong had received the following request from Sir John Bowring:

No. 14. GOVERNMENT OFFICES,
VICTORIA, HONG KONG, *January* 6, 1857.

SIR,—

A number of masters of American merchant vessels now lying at anchor in this port, have suggested to Captain Watkins, the harbor master, the expediency of my making application to your Excellency for assistance in securing the protection of the shipping at night.

In the present state of affairs I do not hesitate to accede to this suggestion, and shall feel greatly obliged if your Excellency can make arrangements for rowing guard during dark.

The scantiness of the British naval force permanently in harbor, and the large amount of mercantile shipping now berthed here, induce me to trouble your Excellency with this request.

I have the honor to be,
Your Excellency's most obedient servant,
JOHN BOWRING,
Governor, etc.

HIS EXCELLENCY COMMODORE ARMSTRONG, etc., etc., etc.,
United States Steam Frigate San Jacinto.

But, as before said, the times were very uncomfortable. The Chinese authorities had issued a proclamation for all Chinese to leave the employ of foreigners. The English had passed an ordinance that authorized any foreigner to shoot any Chinaman who might be found in the streets after 8 P. M., unless he answered a hail, and no court or authority was to inquire into the act. Two English policemen were found in the streets shorter their heads. One of our marines was missed from roll-call, and his dead body came ashore; his cries of murder and for assistance having been heard two or three nights before.

After 8 o'clock at night the streets, which last summer were thronged, are deserted—every house was a fortress. Solitary passers about are belted with sword and pistol. Drum-beatings, armed patrols, guard-mountings, hails of sentries, meet you in the once peaceful streets. Before night sets in you may meet the musters of special police, composed of Malays, Lascars, humble citizens out of employ, drunken sailors, and even Chinese, with muskets, pistols, pikes, and all sorts of outré costumes.

Take us Fankwei altogether, we are, gentlemen, soldiers, rough-scuff and all, drunk and sober, about two thousand on the island of Hong Kong. The Chinese are seventy thousand.

Whilst this state of things was wearing out time and men, I was sitting quietly in my room one evening, removed, by a charming page, to other scenes, when I smelt strongly the odor of burning pine. I thought my room must be on fire close to me, and even fancied I saw smoke in the air; but upon a careful examination, discovering nothing of the kind, I resumed my book, although the odor continued and increased. In about half an hour I was aroused by a confused noise in the streets, and looking out, saw a dense column of smoke ascending from behind the residence of the "Sisters of St. Paul," and immediately it burst into flame.

Upon hurrying to the spot I found it was the flour warehouse of an Englishman by the name of Duddell, who had taken the unfortunate Essing's establishment. While fire engines were hurrying to the conflagration, troops were mustering in the defenseless parts of the city, so that all purpose of greater evil than the destruction of the flour was prevented. But the enemy's incendiaries were evidently among us.

Sometime after this, Commodore Elliott captured some Mandarin junks, and on board were found certain papers which made developments respecting the fire, the poisoning, and other pleasant demonstrations in which we were interested, telling us of some which had failed, but of which we had no knowledge. The following are the revelations of these interesting documents:

"Man-hing—the nephew of Man Tsap-shin, a gentleman, the author of an unsuccessful attempt to burn or blow up the city of Victoria, and the probable agent in the destruction of Duddell's store, of which his nephew gives notice two days before." They kept a close eye upon us.

On the 21st of January, Ch'an Tsz'-tin informs his brother that his braves are so planted at Sha-tin and Tai-wei, in rear of Kowloon, as to command all the approaches to the latter place, which is separated from the others by the steep range of hills facing Hong Kong. Victoria, he hears, is in great perplexity. "A proclamation is issued once a day, and three sets of regulations every two days. People abroad at night are taken up in haste, and discharged with equal precipitation." No one is allowed out after eight o'clock; the shops are forced to take out tickets (passes?) and to pay sixteen dollars a ticket, and these have to be changed every few days. Boats passing to and fro between Kowloon and Victoria are not searched, but a bakery (it is not here stated whose) had been closed, and some forty people imprisoned for poisoning a number of English devils.

On the 24th of January, he reports an improvement in the working of the interdict to the eastward, in the region overlooked by his pickets. Two of his braves have visited Victoria, and counted one hundred and ten foreign vessels in harbor, but declare that there is not one tenth of the usual quota of native craft belonging to the province. There are some from other provinces, viz., north and east coasters. The west end of the city is quite deserted, and the English, by the unanimous declaration of the Chinese, thoroughly dispirited. All mat and wooden buildings had been demolished toward East Point. He also reports a great burglary in the centre of Victoria; the burglars had escaped with several thousand dollars, over the hills.

On the 5th of February, Ch'an Tsz'-tin writes to his elder brother Ch'an Kwei-tsih, that an intended expedition of the braves across the water (to Hong Kong) had failed. The English were too well on their guard. Cannon are fired by night at intervals, to keep their spirits up. Cruisers constantly sweep the harbor. The black troops who have come on, drill incessantly. "Such being the doubt and alarm of the English rebels, we must wait until they tire a little; a blow will then be sure." This was the first notice we had of such a hostile movement.

Ch'an Tsz'-tin has further news from Victoria. After admitting his misgivings above-mentioned, he thinks we are "so utterly broken" that we shall not venture to disturb Kowloon. The Americans, at Hong Kong, look on the present state of things as full of danger, and are sending their ships away.

He is sanguine about the safety of Kowloon, and his confidence is strengthened on the 21st of February, when an English steamer brought over seventy-two pirates and surrendered them to the fort. Kowloon was in great alarm, and the garrison stood to their arms. The English went away, however, without doing any mischief. "What their purpose (or intention) may be, it is indeed difficult for any man to divine."

This vigilant Chinaman is not the only one mystified by this transaction. It refers to a capture, made in the vicinity of Hong Kong, of some Chinese junks. It was doubtful whether they were pirates or rebels. Instead of trying the question in Hong Kong, the English authorities sent them over to Kowloon, where, if rebels, their fate was certain. The leader claiming to be a rebel chief, protested against this surrender, in the following language:

He said, "Had I been found guilty of any thing against the laws of Hong Kong I would cheerfully have given up my life, but with no such charge against me, to be handed over to the men against whom I have been so long engaged in upholding what I consider a good cause, the act is infamous."

The following are two verses of reference to the matter, by a poet of Hong Kong:

THE KOWLOON DISPATCH.

Sir John presents his compliments
To his friends on the Kowloon shore,
And begs to submit to their tender care
Some seventy subjects or more.

The prisons are full, and the *den* is unfit,
At least so the *public* say;
So he trusts that his Kowloon friends can dispose
Of the dogs in some quieter way.

The captured dispatches contained this other pleasant information:

On the 21st of February, Ch'an man-sin, nephew of Ch'an Sz'-tin, writes to his uncle to inform him that the San-on committee had forwarded to Canton an English head taken from an English cruising boat (it is believed he means to say near Aberdeen on the south side of the island). The rest of the crew escaped to land. "The Canton committee are giving now only thirty taels for devils taken, dead or alive." (It will be remembered that Yeh's earlier proclamations promised one hundred taels reward for Englishmen taken alive. He then interlines.) "For a devil's head they may possibly give but thirty dollars; the San-on committee (consequently) do not now much prize devil's heads." He goes on to mention, that some days had elapsed before the braves consented to receive the reward lately sent; requests his uncle, if he is going to employ his own braves in the getting of heads, to tell them plainly the state of the case; and, finally, recommends him not to be keen in the head-hunting, as it is unremunerative.

These Chinese documents give an outside view of our settlement and the designs upon it. For the security our squadron gave to Hong Kong in this reign of terror, the United States received through Lord Napier the thanks of the British government, conveyed as follows:

COPY.

NAVY DEPARTMENT, *April* 22d, 1857.

SIR,—

I take much pleasure in forwarding to you the inclosed copy of a note of the 17th instant, addressed to the Department of State by the British minister, expressing the thanks of his government for assistance rendered by you in protecting the property and commercial interests concentrated at Hong Kong.

I am, very respectfully, your obedient servant,

(*Signed*) I. TOUCEY.

COMMODORE JAMES ARMSTRONG,
Commanding U. S. Squadron,
East India and China Seas.

True copy. A. VAN DEN HEUVEL,
Commodore's Secretary.

COPY.

HER MAJESTY'S LEGATION,
WASHINGTON, *April* 17th, 1857.

SIR,—

Her Majesty's government have learned, with much gratification, from Sir John Bowring, that the officer in command of the United States naval forces at Hong Kong has afforded his coöperation to the British authorities for the protection of the valuable property and commercial interests concentrated at that port. I am directed by the Earl of Clarendon to tender his thanks to the United States government for the assistance and good offices so obligingly granted by Commodore Armstrong.

I have the honor to be, with the highest consideration,
Sir, your most obedient, humble servant,

(*Signed*) NAPIER.

THE HONORABLE LEWIS CASS, etc., etc., etc.

True copy. A. VAN DEN HEUVEL,
Commodore's Secretary.

As the year 1857 passed along, all foreign residents in China had learned to respect the prowess of the once despised Chinese. The following language of a Hong Kong paper shows the changed judgment:

"That the Chinese have abandoned all hope of meeting us with great guns is not to be wondered at, but that they are confident of their ability to repel us in the field, the little affair of the 'Bantam' (a recent action in which the British were driven off), we submit, fully illustrates. Indeed they seem anxious to fight, and their courage against such desperate odds shows matter for congratulation that we have commanders who do not despise the enemy."

But troops, black and white, ships and gun-boats, French and English, thickened as the year advanced, and on its last days, the contest was relinquished; a slight resistance, and the City of Rams fell into the hands of the allied barbarians, who, at last, though excluded for a thousand years, trod its streets as masters.

Everybody expected the capture of Canton, and therefore this was no surprise; but none looked for the taking of that great living mystery, Yeh-ming-ching, or, as he is generally called by the Chinese, Yeep. The hereditary baron, the fourth prince of the empire, he who had chopped off one hundred thousand rebel heads; the hyena dragging his enemies from their graves; the wolf tearing them down amid the faintings of famine; the tiger springing upon them in the moment of security; the lion roaring a bold and gallant defiance to all the world; the wily fox writing diplomatic essays upon morality, and deceiving all who trusted his virtue—for all this was Yeh—was taken in his den.

At one time it was reported he had died the "golden death," the honorable end of a defeated Chinese statesman. As explained to me, it is effected by swallowing some destructive fluid, cupped in golden leaf. Our friend

Lan, the Tautai, whom we met at Shanghae, did die this death, but Yeh became a prisoner on board an English man-of-war. He attempted to escape in the dress of a laborer, and one of his friends made a chivalric attempt to pass himself off for his master; but he was as wonderful looking as he is wonderful, and was recognized; being about fifty, nearly six feet high, of great corporeal volume and with an enormous brain. Physically and mentally he is great.

Taken with him was Moh, the Tartar general, and Pehkwei, the Governor proper of Canton. This last, a native of Pekin, had filled several important offices in different parts of the empire. Some years ago he visited Sir John Davis at Hong Kong. Subsequent to this visit, in 1849, he had a conversation with the late Emperor Taoukwang. It is given in Meadows's "Chinese and their Rebellions," and is worth repeating, as showing how they regard this city of Hong Kong; how they look upon foreigners and that commerce which we regard as the ultimate end of war and diplomacy.

He said to the emperor:

"The English barbarians have gone to great expense in building houses, with the view of permanently residing there (Hong Kong) and living in quiet. The people of Hong Kong and its neighborhood took, at an early period, an aversion to these barbarians; and local bandits have long been waiting, with mouths watering, for the place. The barbarians are therefore constantly in dread, fearing they may lose it."

Emperor. So they have added to their troubles by giving themselves another internal care. However, notwithstanding this, they have always got their own country for a haunt (literally, nest and den, expressions frequently applied to the capitals of foreign sovereigns).

Answer. Yes, Sire.

Emperor. Do you think, from the appearance of things in Kwang tung, that the English barbarians or any other people will cause trouble again?

Answer. No. England itself has got nothing, and when the English barbarians rebelled in 1841, they depended entirely on the power of the other nations, who, with a view to open trade, supported them with funds. In the present year the (here follow two words which do not make sense with the context, "teen te," literally, "laws and territory;" probably, "subject territories" were the words used) of England yield her no willing obedience.

Emperor. It is plain from this that these barbarians always look on trade as their chief occupation, and are wanting in any high purpose of striving for territorial acquisitions.

Answer. At bottom they belong to the class of brutes (dogs and horses); it is impossible they should have any high purpose.

Emperor. Hence in their country they have, now a woman, now a man as their prince (wang). It is plain they are not worth attending to. Have they got, like us, any fixed time of service for their soldiers' head, Bonham?

Answer. Some are changed once in two years, some once in three years. Although it is the prince of these barbarians who sends them, they are, in reality, recommended by the body of their merchants.

Emperor. What goods do the French trade in?

Answer. The wares of these barbarians are only camlets, woolen cloth, clocks, watches, cottons and the like. All the countries have got them, good or bad.

Emperor. What country's goods are dearest?

Answer. They have all got both dear and cheap. There is no great difference in their prices (of similar articles); only, with respect to the camlets, the French are said to be the best.

Emperor. It appears to me that the barbarians depend entirely on Kwang tung for gaining their livelihood.

Answer. The people of Kwang tung thoroughly see that the barbarians can not do without that province.

Emperor. Have the English barbarians of late been reduced in power or not?

Answer. They appear to be somewhat reduced.

Emperor. Do the soldiers at Hong Kong amount to three or four thousand?

Answer. Not more than two or three thousand, the greater half of whom are really but nominal. The greater half of the green-clothed soldiers (Ceylon Rifles?) have dispersed on account of the insufficiency of the funds for the troops. Trade does not flourish at Ningpo and those ports.

Emperor. I have heard that it is not good at Ningpo and Amoy, and at Shanghae too. From this we see that prosperity is always followed by decay.

Answer. The English barbarians were in a bad state last year in their own country, where they were visited by an epidemic; and in Hong Kong, last year, upwards of a thousand people died from the hot exhalations.

Emperor. In all affairs prosperity is followed by decay. What avails the power of man?

Answer. Your Majesty's divine fortune is the cause (of the decay of the English power).

Amid these unhappy conditions of Fankwei and Celestial, information reached Commodore Armstrong that possibly some of our countrymen were in slavery among the savages of the island of Formosa. It was also very uncertain what might be our ultimate relations with the Chinese, and hence all attainable information respecting this island was desirable. The Commodore, therefore, dispatched Captain Simms, of the marine corps, to Formosa, where an American merchant had an independent settlement, to make inquiries respecting our reputed enslaved people, and to acquire such other information as might be useful.

In taking this step, Commodore Armstrong anticipated the subsequent orders of the government. Captain Simms, after a residence of some months, made the following report of his mission. It presents an interesting glance at a part of Formosa, and goes far to allay the unhappy anxiety of those who have had friends in ships which have been lost in those wild and desolate regions.

SHANGHAE, *December* 17th, 1857.

SIR:

I wrote you on the 25th ultimo, informing you of my arrival here from Formosa. My letter was a very hurried one, as I only heard, a very short time before I wrote, that an opportunity was afforded me to do so. I will now endeavor to give you a fuller account of my mission to Formosa. A few weeks after my arrival at Takow—my designated station—I forwarded your dispatch, accompanied with a Chinese translation of it, to the Teen Tae.

I sent it through the mandarin who commands the department of Cocksicon, who promised to have it safely delivered. After a long delay I received a document, which was delivered to me by the Chinese shroff of Messrs. W. M. Robinet & Co., who informed me that it was for you, and was written by the official through whom I had sent your letter. The shroff also informed me that the mandarin directed him to say to me, that the Teen Tae would not receive the dispatch I had sent him, assigning as a reason for his refusing to do so, that the authorities of the island could hold no diplomatic correspondence with foreigners without permission of the Emperor of China.

Previous to my sending your letter to the Teen Tae, I had an interview with the mandarin through whom I transmitted it, and explained to him that my visit to Formosa was of a friendly nature, and that your letter was an amicable one. He appeared to be very desirous to give me every facility in his power to accomplish the object of my visit, and promised to use every effort to acquire the information I wished. He was in charge of the district of Cocksicon at the time I sent my dispatch, but has now charge of the department of Tamsui, situated on the northern part of the island. I frequently visited him before his departure for Tamsui, and urged him to use every endeavor to discover if any foreigners were prisoners on the island. He always assured me that he had done all in his power, and, from the information he obtained, he was convinced there were no white persons held in captivity by the Chinese inhabitants. In regard to their being any prisoners among the aborigines of the island, he could give no information, as there is constant war between the two nations, and no Chinaman dares to enter their territory. These aborigines live generally in the mountains, and I have not been able to see any of them; some few have been met with in the northern end of the island by the masters of trading vessels, who describe them as resembling the Malays, and as being a savage race. During my stay at Takow a report was in circulation that some white persons were prisoners with these natives. I made the most particular inquiries to discover if such was the case, but could learn nothing to make me think there was truth in the report. I have not allowed myself to be influenced by the statements of the Chinese officials, but have mixed a great deal with the people, for the purpose of getting all the information possible, but could never hear of any foreigners being prisoners on the island. I have had no opportunity until now to forward you the mandarin's letter to yourself.

In relation to the outrage alleged to have been committed by the Chinese inhabitants of Takow upon the officers of the American brig Progressive Age, I have been unable to learn any thing from the Chinese authorities, as they pretend not to know any thing about the affair. I inclose you a statement from Mr. Marcus L. Woodard, who was one of the parties ill treated, and from all I could learn at Takow, I think his account of the affair is a correct one.

During my stay in Formosa, I made several trips into the country, and was always kindly treated. On the 13th of August last, in company with M. Markwald, Esq., the agent of Messrs. Robinet & Co., I visited a Chinese town named Pitow, which is seven miles in the interior from Keow. Our road took us through a very beautiful country. On all sides were to be seen luxuriant fields of rice and sugar cane; indigo and hemp were also to be seen amongst the numerous productions of the fertile soil. I never tired admiring the beautiful scenery, and regretted exceedingly that I had not artistical skill sufficient to sketch the picturesque landscape that was presented to my view. We traveled in sedan chairs, carried by Chinese coolies, and were nearly three hours in reaching our place of destination. Pitow is a walled town, and contains about seven thousand inhabitants. We went all through it, and were kindly treated. The people crowded around us, and regarded us with a great deal of wonder, but their curiosity never led them to be rude. They are very timid, much more so than any Chinese I have yet met with.

After spending a few hours looking about the city, we took up our lodgings at the house of one of the officials, who treated us very hospitably, and gave us a Chinese dinner. Having seen all that was interesting in Pitow, we returned to Takow. This last-named town is also called Keow by some, and is only a place of residence of fishermen and their families. Its harbor is considered the best in Formosa. There is a bar at the entrance, on which, at the highest tides, there are twelve feet of water, and at the lowest, nine feet.

The entrance to the port is very narrow, being only about two hundred feet in width. On the 10th of September, Captain Bovey, of the English bark New Margaret, very kindly invited Mr. Markwald and myself to take passage in his ship up to Ungpong, the sea-port of Tayman-Ho, the capital of Formosa. We accepted his invitation, and as he sailed the same day he gave us his kind offer, we immediately went on board, and arrived the next day off our destined port, but, owing to very rough weather, we did not land until five days after our arrival.

We had to pass through a very heavy surf while crossing the bar, upon which there is about four feet of water. In crossing the bar we narrowly escaped capsizing, being struck with a heavy roller. After getting out of the breakers, we found ourselves in a small bay, with very little water, the whale-boat in which we were frequently touching the ground. After a pull of about an hour, we entered a large canal, which leads up to the city of Tayman-Ho. At this point, we exchanged our European boat for a Chinese sampan, and in two hours we were in the capital of Formosa. At the entrance of the canal to which I have alluded, there are the ruins of a very large fortification, which was built by the Dutch during the time they were settled on the island. This fortification must have been of immense strength, as those walls which are now standing are of great thickness, and a deep and wide ditch surrounds it. Below the fort there is now a water battery, upon which fifty guns might be mounted, but at present it has only about fifteen. From what I could see of them, they were only fit to frighten Chinese pirates, but against Europeans they would not be very efficient. We lived in the suburbs of Tayman-Ho, as no foreigners are permitted to reside in the city proper, which is a walled town, but its walls are in a very dilapidated condition, and would be of very little use in case the city was attacked by any civilized nation. We remained four days at our hong, and were always treated with politeness. During our stay, I made all the inquiries in my power in relation to persons being confined on the island, but learned nothing. After fruitless efforts to enter the walled portion of the town, and having seen all that was to be seen in that part of the town in which we had taken up our quarters, we took our departure on the 18th of September for Keow, which place we reached the same night, at nine o'clock. Our mode of traveling was in sedan chairs, which was by no means so pleasant or expeditious as our railroads at home. We passed through a country very much like that I have described in my visit to Pitow. The population is very dense, as the Chinese only occupy the plains, while the aborigines inhabit the mountainous parts of the island. Coal, camphor, and sulphur are to be found in Formosa, and I was informed that gold was also to be obtained. Camphor appears to be very abundant, and large quantities are exported from the island. I have not been able to visit the coal mines, but have been informed by those who have visited them, that, with proper machinery, they could be worked with great success.

In my communication to you of the 25th ultimo, I informed you I would remain here until further orders from yourself, but, as the schooner Carbon leaves here in a few days for Takow, and wishing not to be too long absent from my post, I have determined to return in her, and await your further instructions.

I am, sir, very respectfully,

Your obedient servant,

(*Signed*) JOHN D. SIMMS,

Brevet Captain United States Marines.

COMMODORE JAMES ARMSTRONG,

Commanding United States Naval Forces,

East India and China Seas,

United States Steam Frigate San Jacinto,

Hong Kong.

True copy. A. VAN DEN HEUVEL,

Commodore's Secretary.

XXXVII.

THE HEAVENLY PRINCE.

ONE Sunday, upon returning to the hospital, I was informed that the Rev. Mr. Roberts, a Baptist missionary, was in the ward among the sick, where he had been upon a former occasion during my absence.

This most worthy man has an association with the great rebellion which is now shaking the Chinese empire, from having been the theological instructor of Hung-Sew-Tseuen, the founder of this rebellion.

Mr. Roberts did me the favor to stay and dine with me. In the course of our conversation, I learned that he was a native of Tennessee, but brought up in Kentucky. There seemed a fitness in these States having a relationship to the wonderful movement of progress and reform in the Chinese empire.

The following account of Hung-Sew-Tseuen is condensed from Meadows's "Chinese and their Rebellions." In a note the author remarks,

"At Nankin, the most active of the more military

leaders—the Northern Prince, who had never seen any foreigner until I found him there, spoke to me about Mr. Roberts with much interest and respect, merely in consequence of the account which had been given him by the then 'Heavenly Prince,' Hung-Sew-Tseuen."

Hung-Sew-Tseuen was born in 1813, thirty miles northeast of Canton. His father being a poor peasant, he early exhibited such intellectual capacity, that his family exerted themselves to educate him; and as he advanced toward manhood, he was relieved from hard manual labor by being appointed the village schoolmaster. In 1833 and 1837 he made unsuccessful examinations in a competition for literary degrees in the city of Canton, or, as it is properly called, Knang-Chow-Foo. At the last of these visits, his attention was attracted by a Protestant missionary, preaching by the aid of an interpreter in the streets of Canton. At the same time he received from Leang-a-fah, a Chinese friend, who had been converted to Christianity, a number of tracts which had been composed by himself, consisting of essays and sermons, with chapters from the Old and New Testaments, and called "Good Words for Exhorting the Age."

The mental and physical exhaustion consequent upon the competition at the literary examinations is very great, and sometimes terminates in death. Hung-Sew-Tseuen was very ill for forty days after his failure in 1837, and during this illness he had some wonderful dreams or visions, compounded of Buddhistic and Confucian superstitions, modified by the twenty-first chapter of Revelation, one of those contained in Leang-a-fah's tracts, and which Hung-Sew-Tseuen, it is inferred, had glanced at previous to this illness. After his recovery he returned to his duties as village schoolmaster. During six following years, till 1843, Leang-a-fah's books lay unnoticed in Hung-Sew-Tseuen's book-case, when circumstances brought them to the notice of Le, a friend of his. They both studied the tracts, and Hung-Sew-Tseuen saw in them the key to his former vision, which now he believed to have revealed to him God—Jesus Christ—idols as demons, and the people of the world as brothers and sisters. He and Le were converted, administering the rite of baptism to themselves, and commenced preaching.

Hung-Sew-Tseuen took the high ground that he was appointed by God in his vision, and by these books, to the conversion of his country to the worship of the true God—the God of the early ages of China for the Manchoo subjugation.

His first converts were among his own family and relatives and village schoolmasters. One of these, Fung-Yun-Sau, was the most zealous and important. Finding themselves abandoned by their pupils, Hung-Sew-Tseuen and Fung-Yun-Sau traveled as peddlers of ink and writing brushes, preaching the new faith. They made many converts; but after a few months' absence, they started at separate periods of time to return to their native province; but Fung-Yun-Sau on the way engaged himself among a gang of earth carriers, converted some of them, with their employer, who employed him as a teacher. He remained several years in the neighborhood, converting families and tribes, who organized themselves under the name of the "Society of God-worshipers." "It," says Mr. Meadows, "was this society which subsequently formed the strength of the religious political rebellion that now shakes the imperial throne, though in its founder, the earth carrier, Fung-Yun-Sau, I believe we have at once the most zealous and the most disinterested preacher of the new faith in its soberest form."

In 1847 Hung-Sew-Tseuen, who had been engaged in various religious writings, entered himself with Mr. Roberts, as a student of the Bible. Mr. Roberts says, that though able and studious, he saw nothing in him indicating his subsequent remarkable career. After two months' study he left Mr. Roberts's establishment, this gentleman having refused to receive him by baptism, because he at the same time applied for a monthly support, being induced to this by the persuasion of a countryman in the same establishment. He, however, saw the reasonableness of Mr. Roberts's course, and has since spoken of him in terms of respect and gratitude.

Hung-Sew-Tseuen declared, "Too much patience and humility do not suit our present times, for therewith it would be impossible to manage this perverted generation." In the execution of this sentiment he and his followers proceeded to the violent demolition of idols, and were first brought into conflict with the civil power. Fung-Yun-Sau was imprisoned; but the Chinese government had granted freedom of Christian worship to Chinese as well as to foreigners, and upon this plea Hung Sew-Tseuen intended to apply for the liberation of his friend and colleague. Fung-Yun-Sau, however, being sent in charge of two policemen to his native province, converted them on the way, and they followed him to the rendezvous of the new sect. In the autumn of 1850 the society of God-worshipers came into conflict with the local authorities, and at once assumed the attitude of political rebellion.

Events transpiring about this period, tended to bring about this wide and hostile relation to the Chinese empire. In 1849 the British squadron on the coast of China broke up a large number of pirates. These united themselves with bands of bandit rebels in the province of Kwang-se, in which were concentrated the society of God-worshipers. Hung-Sew-Tseuen, being compelled to defend himself against an attempt of the Mandarin government to capture him, organized all these robber rebels under his standard, and placed himself in open rebellion to the empire, with the avowed purpose of expelling the Manchoo dynasty and establishing that of Tai-Ping, or universal peace. It is not our object in this book to follow the various and wild fortunes of the rebels. The end, none, according to the means of human judgment, can see. But those who see in the singular circumstances of its origin and success so far, and in the leaven of good principles it carries, the finger of Providence, have no doubt as to the final result, and the advantages it is in time to bring to China and the world. Having made a triumphant progress and captured many imperial cities, with several million of inhabitants, in March, 1853, they got possession of Nankin. This was the imperial city under the Ming dynasty, and was now again made so by the insurgents. At the time of its capture it was held by the hereditary garrison of Tartar banner-men, which, with their families, numbered twenty thousand. All these, men, women and children, were destroyed; not more than one hundred escaping.

The view which will be taken of this rebellion, will depend very much upon the political and religious tendencies of those to whom it is submitted for judgment.

The favorers of monarchical governments, and the opponents of progress, are naturally disposed to censure and condemn any popular movement opposed to an existing government, and to put the worst construction upon all institutions favoring a popular element. The subjects of the Queen of England and of the Emperor of France, in China, are, by political prejudice, opposed to the rebel movement, but I doubt if their worst ideas of the Chinese rebellion are excelled by the opinions entertained by much of Europe, and proclaimed in its most respectable press, as to the disorganization, the irreligion, the fanaticism, the ruffianism of the great American democracy. I have read in the most influential English journals as degrading things said of us as can possibly be said of the Tai-Ping-Wang movement.

It would at first be supposed that representatives of the great American democracy in China would entertain counter views. But it is not so. These gentlemen zealously represent their country and their flag, and patriotically stand forth in their defense, in all circumstances of rivalry and competition with other powers. But they do not sympathize with the masses of their own country. It would be very strange if they did. They early leave a class of society which is, in social position, something above the popular mass; and they are not apt to appreciate the worth and political intelligence it contains, especially as they are here in contact with what they consider an inferior and degraded race. The tone of society, the social influences among which they here reside, and to which they naturally conform, are given by Europeans, and are, of course, far removed from any popular considerations whatever; hence their views of a popular movement would coincide with the very men with whom they would quarrel upon an abstract question of political principle.

In all the remote regions it has been my lot to visit, I have noticed much feeling of opposition of sentiment on the part both of the respectable merchants and the adventurers, who compose the American and European residents, towards the missionary establishments—growing, with some, out of the opposition of the latter to the license and indulgence of the former, and to their interference with profitable vices. So far, therefore, as the Tai-Ping-Wang rebellion is supposed to have any connection with missionary influence, it comes under the disparagement of all under these adverse influences.

Finally—as the rebels denounce opium-smoking, they fall under the condemnation of all who find profit in opium-smuggling; and this is the source of much of the European and American Chinese fortunes.

With, therefore, almost all testimony against one, it seems very presumptuous to say any thing in favor of the rebels, and the more so, that I believe the body of them to be made up of wild, daring, adventurous scoundrels, and of fanatical blasphemers; but there are good, honest, and intelligent men among them. I think the difference between them and the regular imperial government of China is, that the latter is an indurated system of routine, corruption and rascality, crystallized into form, from which no good can come, save by its destruction. The former, while tending to chaos and confusion, has within it the divine spark which shall light up the way of progress and civilization and the harmonious institutions of Christianity.

The pure truths of Christianity themselves, among the most intellectual nations, and in the most enlightened ages, have been used to vitalize absurdity, fanaticism and blasphemy. How, then, can any such truth be expected to be found unadulterated among a nation of hundreds of millions of arrogant pagans? More especially, how can it be looked for in the wild scenes of political commotion in which races are warring against each other, and throughout so vast an empire ambitious and unscrupulous chiefs are striving for the ascendency over an ignorant and superstitious people?

For but a limited period the foreign teachers of Christianity have been laboring at a few points on the remotest edge of such a vast empire. If, then, when it is heaving in political convulsion, and threatening to shake down its age-fixed throne and institutions, one spark, however clouded, of Christian truth, is found in the movement of disorganization, I think it should be viewed as the leaven that is to leaven the whole lump, as at least a reason for hope that Providence is directing it to wise ends.

There are, certainly, avowed principles in the following formula of the rebels, which must, at some time, separate the true from the false.

Among the rebel articles of belief are: There is but one God. Idolatry and image-worship condemned. The Ten Commandments are enjoined, and the salvation of sinners by the death of Jesus proclaimed. Eternal damnation to the wicked, and salvation to the righteous. The influence of the Holy Spirit, and the doctrine of the Trinity are recognized.

PRAYER FOR THE PENITENT.

I, thine unworthy ——, kneeling down upon the ground, with a true heart repent of my sins, and pray thee, the great God, our heavenly Father, of thine infinite goodness and mercy, to forgive my former ignorance and frequent transgressions of the divine commands, and earnestly beseech thee of thy great favor to pardon all my former sins, and enable me to repent and lead a new life, so that my soul may ascend to heaven; may I from henceforth sincerely repent and forsake my evil ways, not worshiping corrupt spirits, nor practicing perverse things, but obeying the divine commands. I also earnestly pray thee, the great God, our heavenly Father, constantly to bestow on me thy Holy Spirit, and change my wicked heart; never more allow me to be deceived by wicked demons, but perpetually regarding me with favor, forever deliver me from the evil one; and every day bestowing upon me food and clothing, exempt me from calamity and woe, granting me tranquillity in the present world and the enjoyment of endless happiness in heaven, through the merits of our Saviour and heavenly brother, the Lord Jesus, who redeemed us from sin. I also pray the great God, our Father who is in heaven, that His will may be done on earth as it is done in heaven. That thou wouldst look down and grant this my request is my heart's sincere desire.

Ten Important Rules to be observed in a Regular Camp.

1. Carefully to observe the celestial regulations.

2. Make yourselves thoroughly acquainted with the commands of heaven, and the forms of worship, with praise and thanksgiving, to be used every morning and evening, as well as the orders issued by the sovereign.

3. Cultivate good morals; avoid the smoking of tobacco and the drinking of wine; be just and mild; do not conceal offenses nor indulge partialities, nor comply with inferiors at the risk of disobeying superiors.

4. With united heart and effort obey the requisitions of officers; do not conceal the number of military weapons, nor hide gold and silver ornaments.

5. Observe the distinction between the camp of the males and that of the females; let not men or women give or take from each other's hands.

6. Make yourselves familiar with the signals given for the assembling of troops, by means of the gong, horn or drum, whether by day or night.

7. Do not, without necessity, go from one camp or legion to another, lest you should throw into confusion public arrangements.

8. Learn correctly the proper title of officers and the terms to be used in addressing them.

9. Let your arms and accoutrements be always in order, and ready for immediate service.

10. Do not falsify the laws of the state nor the regulations of the sovereign; do not communicate the military signals or the regimental order.

Shorter and better than our articles of war.

The rebels can scarcely make things worse than they are. A writer, interested in maintaining the prestige of monarchical and despotic governments, while condemning the rebellion, says, "Yet that China needs reform in every shape, particularly in her government of the people, can not admit of a doubt. Her monarchical authority is trembling; her executive is everywhere corrupt; her army weak and imbecile, and her administrative boards throughout the country thoroughly rotten."*

XXXVIII.

COMMERCE, CHRISTIANITY AND OPIUM.

"COMMERCE" is one of those kind of words which appear in dinner-table speeches and popular orations, as a sort of term which gives nobility to any kind of trash which may be uttered—and bold must the man be then who would for a moment think, or utter the sentiment, that Commerce might be a suspicious character, ought to be examined into. Commerce has gold in his pocket, and is above suspicion so long as he has it. He is truly a national benefactor, and it would not be expedient to inquire whether sometimes he was a rascally fellow or not, for we mean to have his benefit whether he is respectable or otherwise. Christianity sometimes comes in along with Commerce on these festive occasions, and Commerce knowing that Christianity stands pretty well in public opinion, is very willing, for form's sake, to have the association for the time being.

There must, however, be something radically wrong in one or the other of these interests and facts, for when they get out to China they become antagonistic, and it may not be altogether profitless to look at the matter and see which is to blame.

* Edinburgh Review, October, 1858.

...an opium smoker!" "I
...e, get rid of him, you
...moment; he'll rob you,

...lish, and only a few days
...upon the subject. He
...sting into tears, said he
...his father, who died of
...And yet this boy did
...by thieving and running
...quaintance with English
...him valuable, and always
...yment. As another illus-
...knowledge, a respectable
...several times, or rather
...upon other subjects, asked
...smoking, for a friend of
...the Chinese remedies in
...maciated and haggard ap-
...the victim. I told him I
...finally he came to me in
...was the man, and must have
...as, to use his homely but
...made such a bobbery he
...nothing for him, and have

...ghae I have been in those
...hops—I doubt if the opium
...e go—and shall never forget

...illustration or two, but as these
...ous, just as groggeries in our own
..., my lifting a single curtain affords
...extent of the vice.
...and dirty blue curtain which swings

termination to our national connection with opium smuggling, for he believed not a few members of his flock, and personal friends in China, men of benevolent disposition and of the highest respectability in the private intercourse of social life, were implicated in this system, against their better convictions, and were almost involuntary participators in the contraband traffic. He desired to see a termination to the temptation in the way of English merchants."

It would certainly be well to remove the temptation from the way of English merchants, if not for their sakes, for that of the people they poison. True, the English merchant should not let his interest lead him into the sin. Let him give up the dollars and he gives up the crime. There may be English merchants who do so; there are American houses which do, and some which do not.

Here then we have certainly a practical exemplification of "good for evil." We see Commerce repudiating Christianity, and Christianity kindly mitigating the rascality of Commerce; asking that temptation may be taken out of its way, that it may be more honest and upright.

It may well be doubted whether the conscience that can accumulate money and build palaces upon the opium trade, has support enough of principle to resist any advantageous money transaction. It certainly owns no subjection to, or deference for, the laws of God or man. It's a terrible trade. Only a dim speck of the dark cloud has passed before my eyes, only the outer shore ripple of an ocean of wretchedness; and God forbid I should ever see out on its broad surface.

Let us hearken a moment to those murmurings of agony which do reach us.

An old Chinese resident dining with me fixed his eyes intently upon the very intelligent boy who was waiting at my table, and as soon as the boy left the room he remarked earnestly, "That boy is an opium smoker!" "I fear it." "You must, of course, get rid of him, you do n't know how to trust him a moment; he'll rob you, sooner or later."

The boy spoke very good English, and only a few days before this I had talked to him upon the subject. He denied it out and out, and bursting into tears, said he had too unhappy a warning in his father, who died of opium smoking at an early age. And yet this boy did smoke opium nightly; he ended by thieving and running away. His intelligence, his acquaintance with English and accounts, would have made him valuable, and always have secured him good employment. As another illustration coming under my own knowledge, a respectable Chinese mechanic came to me several times, or rather incidentally, in conversation upon other subjects, asked me for some remedy for opium smoking, for a friend of his. His friend had tried all the Chinese remedies in vain. I suspected, from his emaciated and haggard appearance, that he was himself the victim. I told him I could give him no remedy, and finally he came to me in the greatest distress, said he was the man, and must have some medicine to cure him, as, to use his homely but expressive language, "his wife made such a bobbery he could not live." I could do nothing for him, and have not seen him since.

From Singapore to Shanghae I have been in those wretched dens, the opium shops—I doubt if the opium merchants have been or dare go—and shall never forget the scenes presented to me.

I will present only an illustration or two, but as these shops were so numerous, just as groggeries in our own degraded city localities, my lifting a single curtain affords a view of the broad extent of the vice.

You lift the dark and dirty blue curtain which swings

at the door, and enter a gloomy, dingy room, along which are soiled mat-covered couches. On these couches are lying the victims, often two on a couch, with the smoky opium lamp between them. The black mass, like a paste, is dipped by a wire from its receptacle and pushed into the narrow tube of the pipe. This is now held over the lamp; it fumes and bubbles while the smoker draws two or three inhalations, passes his hand over his brow, and gazes intently upon some ecstatic vision in the dim air, often at the same time spreading his lips to a smile as ghastly as his gaze—the gaze and smile of a skeleton. The eyes are deep sunk in their sockets—the skin drawn tightly over the cheek bones, and the ribs stand out in bony curves. Emaciation in an old opium smoker seems to have reached the extreme tenuity compatible with existence. Such are the shop scenes. Shall we take them as the interpreters of unseen domestic woes—a daily path of horror which often ends in selling wife and daughter for the drug? Most of the opium smokers I saw in the shops, were in the physical condition I have attempted to describe, but upon one occasion I saw two youths, not over eighteen years of age, genteely dressed, and whose cheeks and forms had not lost the rotundity of their time of life. These, with hope and life before them, voluntarily entering a road of certain destruction, were a more melancholy spectacle than those who were at the close of their unhappy career.

In these dens we only saw the opium smoking of the lowest classes. The upper classes have their private smoking apartments and luxurious couches. There were few of the respectable tradesmen, artists, etc., with whom I had dealings in their houses, but had some one or more members of their establishment addicted to this terrible vice, the faint, sickening odor of the drug pervading the atmosphere of their houses; and often in a partitioned cell of some dark corner, the glimmer of an opium lamp just served to show the recumbent form of the victim beside it. Such, however, is the benumbing influence of the vice, that its essential nature—the question as to whether opium smoking is a vice or a virtue—in the reasonings of Chinese foreign commerce, seems to depend upon the extent to which it prevails. The advocates of the innocuous nature of opium smoking—who would almost elevate it to the rank of a virtue—contend that the largest number addicted to it is from two to three millions. Dr. Hobson, a medical missionary then at Canton, makes the following estimate:

"Allowing the consumption of 68,000 chests, at one mace a day (one mace is equal to fifty-eight grains), it will not exceed 2,500,000. Many take less than one mace a day, but others, again, consume two, four, six, and even eight mace a day (the latter quantity being equal to three hundred grains of the present opium). Native opium, obtained principally from the province of Yun-nan, in the south of China, is also used, and must add to the 2,500,000 named above."

As to the mortality arising from its use, the conclusions Dr. Hobson arrives at are as follows:

"1. That the mortality from opium is not so great as is generally supposed, and certainly not at the enormous rate of 1,000,000 a year, even supposing that 20,000,000 took it. He could not give the proportion of deaths, because there are no data or statistics on which to make the calculation.

"2. That opium is probably more seductive and tenacious in its grasp than alcohol; and he should certainly affirm that it was not so frequently fatal to life, nor so fruitful of disease and crime, as is the case with intoxicating drink in Great Britain."

Again, a Mr. Lay, who was at one time an agent of the

British and Foreign Bible Society, says, in regard to opium:

"In China, the spendthrift, the man of lewd habits, the drunkard, and a large assortment of bad characters, slide into the opium smoker; hence the drug seems to be chargeable with all the vices of the country. Opium, doubtless, has her victims in persons who, but for her fascinating lures, might have escaped their ruin; but, in the great majority of instances, she only adds one stain more to a character already polluted. Investigations and some statistics may throw light upon the subject, and show, in some measure, how far the use of the drug has been the principal, and not the accomplice only, in the undoing of individuals. Many use it '*in moderation*,' and are sufficiently masters of themselves to keep on the right side of slavery. But it is a subtle and traitorous inmate, and no one who has ever felt the exhilarating effects of it, is sure that he will not one day fall a prey to its delusions."

Speaking of the degraded appearance of a confirmed opium smoker, he says:

"Such sights, however, are not very common, for the miserable beings generally hide themselves from public view, so that, amidst many thousands of healthy and happy faces, *we only see here and there one* of these prodigies of evil habit."

Quoting the above, a newspaper exponent, of opium tone, in China, defends opium upon the ground that there may be worse vices, and reaches the conclusion that it is a necessity:

"Ten dollars a piece from two and a half millions will pay for about all the opium imported into China in a year. How many are there in the countries of the heaviest of the opium denouncers, who spend their ten dollars a *week* in that ten times worse than opium smoking—dram drinking. Such is the sluggish nature of their food, that, with many Chinese, opium is *a necessity* to stimulate digestion."*

All that seems to be positively known is, that opium smoking is a great evil, and an extending one, ruinous to the happiness and morals of a population, only small because measured by that of nearly a half of the population of the globe. It is equally evident that it is a profitable commercial vice, and hence an honorable one. It keeps up lines of expensive private steamers between India and China, supported by the difference of rise and fall in opium from day to day. It is not only a vice from its material, physical and moral effects upon the human frame, but it is a great gambling excitement. Opium commerce is but betting upon the change of price with each arrival from India, the chests never changing hands.

The importation of opium into China is but one element by which to measure the amount of it consumed. No one knows the extent of domestic cultivation. Most of the palatial English, American, and Parsee houses belonging to the same firms, in the five consular ports, are built upon this trade. No amount of percentage upon the regular silk and tea brokerage they profess to do, could keep up these magnificent establishments, and retire, as they do, a partner every three or four years, with an independent fortune. They all have, in defiance of Chinese law, their smuggling receiving ships, most of them, it is some consolation to know, under any flag but the American, but I am sorry to say, it flies over an opium receiving ship of our countrymen in China, although the owners, individually, are entitled to all the commendation bestowed by his lordship the Bishop of Victoria, upon his own respectable flock. Yet, the United States treaty

* As this writer contends for the small number of Chinese who use opium, what becomes of his argument of necessity for the hundreds of millions who get along with their digestion without opium?

with China says our flag shall have no connection with this traffic.

One curious argument of the friends of opium is, "It is no use for us to be so virtuous upon this subject, as the Chinese authorities themselves are so loose." The result of such reasoning in morals any one may estimate, if carried out in all the relations of life. I suspect that morality and religion in the Chinese trade are regarded, as Wellington is reported to have said of them in military life, very much out of place. Havelock and others have disproved the old chieftain's maxim, and there is hope for eastern commerce.

The fact is, the Chinese must wink instead of kick at the violation of their laws, if, according to the practical maxim of St. Paul, it is hard to kick against the pricks.

"On the 23d of August, 1844, Mr. Davis transmitted to Aberdeen another communication from the imperial commissioner, in which he declared his fear of the consequence to himself, should he propose to the emperor any measure involving the legalization of opium, and plainly intimating that the opium trade should be carried on by mutual connivance."*

Suppose for a moment the Chinese were to capture all those opium ships lying under European and American flags, in the Woosung and Canton rivers, what would be the result? History has already answered that question.

The Earl of Shaftesbury presented to the British authorities a memorial upon the Chinese import of opium, which contains the following charges:

"1st. That the opium trade on the coast of China is, with scarce an exception, carried on under English colors and by British subjects. 2dly. That it is attended with a more appalling mortality than in the case of the slave

* Papers relative to the opium trade in China, presented to the House of Lords.

trade. 3dly. That it is dishonoring to God and to the character of our nation. 4thly. That it is prejudicial to the commercial interests of Great Britain. And 5thly. That frightfully aggravated results must follow the great and somewhat recent extension of that traffic, together with the fact that her Majesty's plenipotentiary in China, only a short time since, induced the King of Siam to admit opium to be imported by British subjects into that country free of duty."

In reply to these charges it was answered:

"With respect to the last of these points, Sir J. Bowring stated that so far from having induced the King of Siam to admit the importation of opium free of duty, he stipulated for the exclusion of opium from the general operation of the free-trade system which his treaty established. British subjects are not allowed to import opium into Siam *free of duty*, the importation being placed under separate and severe restrictions by confining its introduction and sale to the Chinese farmers of the opium revenue. . . . It was a matter of general notoriety that many of the principal American houses dealt largely in opium, and that the flag of the United States was unfurled at the opium stations over American ships with American registers. . . . As to the religious bearings of the opium question, and the paralyzation of missionary efforts consequent upon the trade, Sir John Bowring's opinion was, that the small success of missionary efforts in China was traceable to other causes than the opium trade."

The opinions of Sir John Bowring upon that or any other subject are entitled to the respect due his ability and opportunities of observation, and at the same time are to be taken with that grain of allowance which must be made for all men who are interested in the matter submitted to their judgment. It must be remembered that Sir John is the governor of an opium-founded, opium-breathing, and opium-supported colony. The deadening, benumbing, sensual influence of the drug seems to have pervaded the moral atmosphere, and brought it to such a condition that nurtures expedient vices as the substitute for virtuous principles, as is seen in a recent ordinance of the colony legitimating licentiousness as an appropriate means of revenue.

"A new ordinance—the last specimen of legislation which we have been favored with—certainly caps all former attempts. The plain English of it is, that it is an ordinance for obtaining an increase of the colonial revenue by encouraging and protecting prostitution."—*Overland Register, December* 16, 1857.

Irrespective of its morality, of its infringement of the laws of China, its respectability must bear up the crime of smuggling to that level. "There is no article in the treaty with China prohibiting the importation of opium, or making its introduction an offense under British law. In the absence of any interdiction in the treaty, opium stands among the articles unenumerated in the tariff, on which articles a duty of five per cent. is leviable; that five per cent., under any circumstances, is due to the Chinese treasury, and inasmuch as this duty is not paid, there is a clear infraction of the treaty."*

The general commercial sentiment in China seems to be, not to get rid of the vice, but, as in the case of licentiousness, to legitimate and make it profitable. The honorable, philanthropic, just and Christian sentiment is, to aid the effort of the Chinese authorities to suppress the vice and to punish the opium smuggler, as the law does the poor wretch who by night steals brandy and tobacco

* Papers relating to the opium trade in China, presented to the House of Lords.

into England. But in China commerce and opium are supreme, and have their diseased, elephant-legged foot upon Christianity.

XXXIX.

GETTING ON.

"THAT 's the way we get on, you know," said Captain Forsyth, of her Majesty's ship Hornet, to me, as I met him on the Bund in Shanghae, just as we heard of the English troubles in Canton. "I am very anxious to be there, because that 's the way we get on."

And I am very glad to say he was there, and did get on, for most eminently had he earned and deserved it.

"The Gazette promotions for late affairs in China will be hailed by the service with unanimous approbation, and the Board of Admiralty will gain no small share of commendation for their speedy acknowledgment of the distinguished services rendered by Captains Forsyth, Corbett, Rolland, Turnour, etc. This reward, following so quickly upon an official report of services that deserve it, is trebly welcome to the recipients, whilst it offers a spur to emulation that is of incalculable value to the country.

"In the selection for these promotions Captain Forsyth's name stands most fairly at the head of the list, not only on account of his seniority, but in consideration of his repeated acts of daring gallantry. Of his services in former grades our columns have given frequent notices. He earned his lieutenant's rank by hard work at marine surveying, and he won his commander's commission by most important services in the same branch, and by his able, zealous, and skillful arrangements in supplying the British army with provisions during the Kaffir war. We may add that Captain Forsyth is a child of the service, and not an officer of interest. He has achieved his position solely by distinguished merit, the appreciation of which by the Board of Admiralty reflects credit on their lordships.

"Captain Corbett, of the Inflexible (6), steam sloop, has made short steps to that promotion which he richly deserved, had he not had an opportunity of again distinguishing himself. It is sufficient to say of him that he is the officer who performed one of the coolest acts of daring on record as a lieutenant. He was at the bloody fight at Lagos, under Admiral Bruce; and it was he who volunteered, under the most deadly fire, to unshackle the cable of the Teazer, we believe, and thus save those on board from severe suffering. He succeeded, but escaped almost certain destruction, with four or five musket-balls in his body and a broken arm. This deed of daring gave him his commandership and a pension for wounds. For his new claims upon the country he has received the most gratifying installment by advancement to that senior rank in which we trust he will have further opportunities of showing to the world that the young blood of the navy is not inferior to that of the heroes of old."*

And thus, during our whole year in China, from the time of our own short, sharp, decisive actions, to the capture by the English of Canton, we had the gratification of seeing our English friends "made," after the intelligence of these deeds reached home. Promotion to higher rank—promotion which carried some home, and gave their places to rejoicing new men, was a cheering, hopeful promotion; and not as with us a desponding look upon the coffins of our friends and companions. No matter though the whole British nation was in division as to

* London Morning Herald, 13th August, 1857.

whether the Chinese war was a just one, those who were maintaining the honor of their flag had the impulse of direct, personal, individual hope to cheer them on.

Chinese shot killed those it hit as dead as though they had been fired by Russian or Frenchman, and therefore those who ran the risk were entitled to their reward.

What a contrast with the expectation and hopes of the officers of our own squadron! In boats and ships we had been fired upon to death by Chinese forts, and had vindicated the honor of our flag, and yet avoided a continuous war. Although no other honorable or creditable course of duty was open to us, yet the first feeling was that of uncertainty as to whether the action of the squadron would be approved or disapproved. If the latter, the consolation was in the consciousness of having done a duty which could not be left undone; if the former, the best hope was that of a formal official approval, which came, was read, listened to, buried amid the records of the squadron and Department, and brought advantage to none.

It has been said that a Frenchman's motive of action is glory; an Englishman's, duty. The American must be yet further removed above the inferior impulses of humanity, and expected to do his best deeds under the chance of censure, and without the hope of reward.

Whatever may be the national characteristics in this respect, it would be only very human, though perhaps not angelic, that individual, as well as national glory, should be an incentive in the military service of any race. The abiding, enduring spirit, may be that of duty; the active, enthusiastic, "go in and win" spirit, must be that of glory, and if we are to have a military service, with all the incentives to active efficiency, it would seem to be only reasonable to present it with those which human nature acknowledges.

There are, it must be admitted, difficulties about the subject, as military reputations are sometimes, like patent medicines and slop-shop clothing, made prominent by quackery. Still, it does not appear impossible to devise a system by which those who clearly and definitely risk their lives in battles or exploits of unusual hazard, under orders to do so, shall win some special connmendation or reward independent of political influences, or the approval or disapproval by an existing administration of the orders under which they acted. I think it can be done. "A navy reputation is at best but a four years' reputation," sententiously said one of those who suffered by the decisions of the Retiring Board. This man remembered the days of his youth, when he felt impulses to have a good name with the Department, and thought he was laying up a capital of that kind. But he lived long enough to find there is no cumulative reputation. A young officer, when he first wins favor at the Department by meritorious deeds is stimulated to go on and increase his stock of reputation, but he becomes disheartened when he finds that every four years he must be successfully interpreting new dreams for new Pharaohs, and at last depends for the smallest rights upon court intrigues, and the good will of the chief butlers. The older he gets, and the less disposed to sit at the chief butler's table, the less consideration he meets. The distinguished gentlemen who are called to the honorable position of presiding over the Navy Department and the Navy, have a responsible, arduous and intricate charge. They have not only the control of governmental possessions and interests, but of an organized body of men—a state within itself—with its own internal usages and polity, and dissentient politics. Among these he is called to be lawgiver and judge, and is so circumstanced that he can not hear the voice of the Navy but as it is interpreted by few and interested parties. Principles lie latent and dormant around him, as they do in nature around all of us, but only the instructed art of the scientific hand can develop them into vitality and activity; and a life-time is necessary to acquire the art. Hence arises a discouraging supposition—perphaps a necessity, that the rights, interests, fortunes of the members of the naval body, are much at the control of the subordinate and more permanent residents of the Department.

An estimable friend and distinguished naval captain, whose merits and position should have secured him every right, once said to me, "I am entitled to so and so, and want it; I have never gone below the head of the Department for any claim; shall I do so now?"

"In my opinion, certainly not; rather go without it."

In the absence of any fixed system of duties and compensations, the action of the Department must necessarily be variable. One Secretary of the Navy, taking a large and liberal view of the law under which the Navy is paid, and considering that all pecuniary gain is limited by that law, will make allowances to the extent of legal authority; another, influenced by principles of rigid economy, will restrict all compensation to the narrowest limit which the law will permit. The small amount which can be saved to the government by any restrictions, annoying as it is to individuals, would be more cheerfully submitted to if it was not contrasted with the large amounts which are sometimes taken out of the Treasury for the advantage of a few fortunate individuals, and which extravagances the executive can not control.

In these unsettled conditions and uncertain competitions, a large amount of energy is lost to the government in the time and efforts expended in the protection and maintenance of what are thought rights—energies and abilities which might otherwise be expended in the performance of duties.

Even promotion by seniority has now become a palsying influence; the flow from behind is greater than the outlet, and the current, instead of being onward, rests in a pool of stagnation.

A sudden and rugged opening was recently made, and a temporary rush took place, bearing onward a crowd of fresh branches, yet in their verdure, and tearing up some of the old trunks which had long stood upon the bank, and overshadowed the waters of the stream. But the waters now stand again, a dead sea, and its influence reaches yet further back than before. Many of these young branches know that they have brought up on their final resting-place, and must wither without further progress; but they may rest.

In my own corps things are worse. When the law shut down and limited the number of officers in each corps, the surgeons were sixty-nine in number, accidentally, I believe, there being an unfilled vacancy at the time. All these are supposed to be on the active list. In the meantime duties, ships and stations have increased. There are seventy-six captains, and one hundred and six commanders on the active list; and whenever a captain or commander is wanting for duty, with but few exceptions, a surgeon is also required. Hence the chances for rest in the staff and line are very unequal. But besides these captains and commanders on the active list, there are, of both grades, forty-five on the reserved list; but of the small number of surgeons, none are reserved, although some have been in the service forty years and over, and nearly one fourth of the whole number are unfit for duty. Now it would seem that the most simple and practical mode of relief, both for line and staff, after the staff has been brought up to fair numbers, would be a limit of age, up to which, an officer should have done his full share of duty in every grade to which he is eligible, and whatever fortunate exceptions there may be, "by reason of strength." I have never seen the man over fifty years of age who was fit for ship-board life, especially for herding in mixed and forced association. His mental and physical faculties may be good, but he has lost the plasticity of adaptation and the buoyancy which float him over annoyances, or bear him onward to meet and overcome them. He fits the night-cap better than the cocked hat. To my friends and associates of the San Jacinto, there is left, to the only one older than myself, the commander-in-chief, rest, if he desires it in the honors of duties fulfilled; to the others, some slight hope of advancement to a certain degree; to myself, time-worn and weary, the same corduroy road which I have trod for twenty years (when I reached my present grade), through the plain of necessity, but more rugged and uneven from wear and neglect; and my case is that of all my brethren.

If any reader has had the perseverance to follow me thus far in my wanderings, he will see that at the close of 1857, and at the time of the capture of Canton, we had been two years and two months away from the United States.

When we left there a cheery idea drifted among us that our cruise was, at the extent, to be only two years from home. In the meantime the powers under which we left home had given place to new men whose purposes we could not divine. But some new encouragement was given to the hopeful prospect of a shortened exile. Stay as long as we might, we did but do an accepted duty and had no right to complain; but a duty under a kind and considerate master is more cheerily and more efficiently done than if performed under an exacting task-master. We had now been on the station over two years, and were then at least a quarter of a year's time and distance from home. Still there was no relief—disgust and despondency settled upon us as a cloud.

After the close of our war, the commander-in-chief, broken in health, made application for relief in his flag ship, stating that his health would permit no arduous over land journey. In the beginning of 1858, he was informed that he would be relieved by Flag-officer Josiah Tattnall, and might return to his home by the overland route. It was a hard journey for an old and disease-enfeebled man. Some thought it scarcely compensated for by the high encomiums two administrations had awarded him.

That of President Pierce had written him by the then head of the Navy Department, Mr. Dobbin:

"I approve, therefore, of the course pursued by you and those under your command. The brave and energetic manner in which the wrong was avenged, is worthy of all praise; the gallantry, good order and 'intelligent subordination' displayed by all engaged in the various conflicts with the enemy; the precision and admirable success with which the guns were managed, were highly creditable to the service. Be pleased, sir, to communicate to the officers, seamen, and marines, the Department's very high appreciation of their good conduct."

And the following appears in the report of the honorable Secretary of the Navy, now presiding in that Department. Alluding to the East India squadron, he says:

"The duties of this squadron have been arduous, and the officers and men attached to it distinguished themselves upon a memorable occasion. On the 15th of November, 1856, as one of the boats belonging to the squadron was passing up the river to Canton, with the American flag fully displayed, it was several times fired upon by the Barrier forts, endangering the lives of all on board.* This outrage was promptly resisted and redressed, by the capture and destruction of the forts and razing the walls to

*It may be added to this that another boat was fired upon and a man's head carried off.

the ground. These forts, four in number, commanding the approach to Canton, were among the strongest defenses of the empire, mounting one hundred and seventy-six guns. The prompt and decisive course pursued by Commodore Armstrong, his officers and men, has caused the flag of the United States to be respected by the Chinese, contributed largely to the security of our citizens in China, and, during the trouble which followed, has probably been the means of saving many lives and much property."

The sloop-of-war Levant, which sailed after the San Jacinto, had already been relieved and started for home, and the Portsmouth, which sailed months after the San Jacinto, followed the Levant in a few weeks; but the San Jacinto remained, with the cloud thickening about her. There were undoubtedly good reasons at Washington for these proceedings, but it was the misfortune of the tenants of the San Jacinto not to see them. The apathy of "hope deferred" settled upon the ship. It may be thought that the increase of one fourth pay, paid to men who are detained over their time of enlistment, is a compensation for that detention. Such is not the case. The sailor, as every other man, likes to have a word to say in the disposition of his rights and property, and not to have it taken from him at the arbitrary estimate of one party to the contract. He would rather have his discharge than pay for detention. He ships for three years from the time he signs his name, and although it is stipulated that if detained he shall be paid an additional rate, he looks upon that as a chance contingency; whereas the tail has been swallowing the body, the contingency becoming the whole law.

Officers have, of course, no rights of this kind, but must rest entirely upon the demands of service, and the justice and liberality of the Department.

The time now draws near for taking leave of the ship and station. The next overland mail was to leave Hong Kong on the 29th of January, 1858. Just before we started, an English naval captain said to me, "What a quiet set of men you have in your squadron." I was happy to reply, "A quiet, contented and subordinate set of men." The Commodore and Secretary of the Navy had complimented them upon their intelligent subordination."

The remark of the English captain reminded me of a duty I owed the men of the squadron from which I was about to part—the humble tribute of my testimony as to its character, and through that to the workings of the new system under which the Navy is governed, and which must be carried far higher and much wider before our service is properly regulated or governed, for governed by any thing but principle it never will be, and beneath principle all mere selfish, egotistical tyranny must fall. Not coming under this harsh designation, but as a part of the childish tom-foolery by which the relations of men are caricatured and their manly self-respect lowered, is what is called officers "getting permission from the first lieutenant to leave the ship." When this permission has a practical value, among the crew and youth, may be granted or denied, it is all right and proper enough; but it is absurd when men, lieutenants themselves, the associates, companions and mess-mates of the first lieutenant, all of the same grade, and other officers his seniors in years, and sometimes of higher rank, go like school-boys and say, "May I go out?" The officers who ask the permission are themselves the best, and sometimes the only judges as to whether their duties will permit them to leave the ship, and knowing this, the gentleman acting as first lieutenant never takes the responsibility of refusing. Some officers of true dignity of character feel the absurdity of this usage, and dispense with it in those cases in which it has no practical bearing; others are so much wanting in self-respect, and need so much support for their own opinion of themselves, as to receive it as a tribute to personal superiority, and reply, "Yes," or "Certainly, sir," with as much self-complacency as though they really were conferring a privilege. The reason alleged for continuing this usage is, that the first lieutenant knows when the ship is going to be in those circumstances which will admit of officers leaving her. He may or may not. But this reason has no existence when, as is generally done, the time in which the privilege of leaving a ship, when it will commence and when it will close, is announced, be it so many hours, days or weeks. The other lieutenants, and the staff-officers of a ship, are as trustworthy in the use of this privilege as their associate, who happens to be first lieutenant, is, and are more under responsibility and obligation when the privilege is used at their discretion, than by a formal permission.

Even the British service, if I am correctly informed, has made a progress, in the disuse of this nonsense, ahead of ours, it being the custom in some ships, at the discretion, I suppose, of some sensible commanding officer, to have a slate at the gangway, at such times as the ship can be left, upon which the officer going ashore registers his name, erasing it upon his return.

The old man loves the memory of even the annoyances of his youth, associated as they are with a hopeful and joyous period of his life. The "good old times" never are the present, and much of the trembling-toned lament over the "old discipline" of the service, must be put down to this lingering look-back of age upon its past youth. There may be some, who having had the rough hand of despotism upon them, think they are not even with the world until they too put it upon some one else;

and these are apt to decry the new system because it will not make tyranny a virtue.

What were the results of that "old discipline?" Some may say, "Our naval victories." They were associated with it, but I trust had their basis in a solid foundation of national courage, and were won despite of the "old discipline," which drove many a brave man from the national colors. In my service, of a generation's existence, I have done duty in one navy yard, cruised in one twelve-gun schooner, four corvettes, three steamers and two frigates. But those who object to my testimony, may say I am not an expert, not being an officer of the line. In all this time and service, I have lived under military authority, and exercised it, and have faithfully listened, on the first Sunday of every month, when in a sea-going ship, with uncovered head, to the solemn absurdities of the "articles of war." Under the "old discipline". the cry of "all hands to witness punishment," called us from any hour of the day-light day, to leave our rooms, avocations and studies, buckle on our swords, and assemble on deck to see some "man" stripped and flogged with cats until the blood burst from his livid back, while the crash of the colt was the before-breakfast settling up of the night's offenses.

During these times, men never went ashore but in charge of and watched by officers of boats—never trusted to their self-respect. Consequently drunken boats' crews and desertion were constant. On liberty, our crews were the terror of the cities in which they held their orgies and revels; on board ship, bottles, belaying pins and shot have been hurled at officers as they passed along the decks in the dark. Whole ships' companies have mutinied, and tricing up the ladders from one deck to another, cut off all approach of their officers until their grievances were redressed.

The heart and soul of the "old discipline" passed away with the "cats." A more cheery and genial atmosphere pervaded our men-of-war. It has influenced not only the government of the crew, but also that of the officers, just as a bad or good spirit will visit itself upon others than those who call it forth. The drum-head court-martial system died out early in our ship for want of material to constitute the courts. There were, it is true, the chief engineer, at the head of a large corps, the purser, who had been over ten years in the service, and myself, who had been in it more than half my life; but we were not eligible to courts martial as members—not even to be represented on them in cases in which we were ourselves parties, and the question one of principle, upon which those composing the court are committed by prejudice and interest against us. Just as though a jury of violent partisans were to decide the case of one whose principal offense had been opposition to them. Not because we are wanting in honor, judgment, familiarity with the laws and usages under which we live, and an equal respect with our brother officers for the obligation of an oath; not because of these are we excluded from the commonest principles of justice and the benefit of the maxim that every man should be tried by his peers. But because in those days when ignorance was the pride of the soldier, and armed chiefs, ignorant of penmanship and orthography, signed their names by pressing their ink-stained hands upon the parchment—then, when merchants, scribes, lawyers, mechanics and publicans, as well as doctors, were not permitted to sit upon courts alongside of these same mailed bandit chiefs; because of this usage of that respectable age, are we, in the middle of the nineteenth century, and in a republic made up of these same mechanics, farmers, scribes and publicans, and in a service composed of the sons, brothers and fathers of these useful members of the community, excluded from representation on the juries before which we are an equal party with those who do sit as both judges and jurors. So once said Attorney General Berrien: "If we look to the origin of courts martial in England (from whence we borrow them) it would be difficult to believe that a tribunal which has succeeded there to the ancient court of chivalry could be composed of other than military men."

That opinion, it is true, was given thirty years ago. Since then the world has made some progress, and the courts of these vulgar United States may be made better than courts of chivalry—courts of justice despite all precedents, even were it possible to show that any who live under and are amenable to military law are not military men.

Whilst our service has been holding on to the old Lion's tail, and being dragged through weed-grown bogs of old usage, he has taken a sudden leap over the ditch of selfish and stupid illiberality, as regards medical officers, and left us plump in it.

The queen, by a recent warrant, has divided medical army officers into seven grades of rank, as lieutenants, captains, majors, lieutenant colonels, colonels, brigadier generals and major generals; and the warrant further provides that such relative rank shall carry with it all precedents and advantages attaching to such rank with which it corresponds, except presidents of courts martial.

Commanding officers of a regiment or detachment, though junior in rank to medical officers, shall always be entitled to first choice of quarters. Medical officers are to be entitled to the same honors as those of equal rank, except guards. Pay and extra allowances are largely increased. All medical officers retire upon a liberal pay at fifty-five years of age, except deputy inspectors and inspectors; these retire at sixty-five.

So it appears that medical officers are members of those courts of honor, even in that England from which, according to Judge Berrien, we borrowed them.

But the courts having died out, the external display ot any visible controlling authority—any thing dramatic, like public executions, were never seen in the San Jacinto. There were quiet punishments, but they were all within the competency of the executive power of the ship, and yet I doubt if a more efficient, subordinate, well-disposed and happy crew, barring the protracted cruise, have ever been in a public vessel; and this is not only my own testimony now, but the frequent conversational tribute of the officers of the line who were in constant contact with the men; and both Sir John Bowring and Admiral Seymour expressed their admiration of the deportment of our ship's companies during the provisional occupation of Canton. It was all very natural. The "Damn your eyes, tie him up and flog him" system of the "old discipline" being done away with, much of the devil went out of the ship, fore and aft, with his traps and baggage, and gave place to agencies of a higher relation. Much, however, is to be attributed to the humane and just character of the commanding officer, Captain Bell.

Officers became more conciliatory and just in their action toward the men, and the men gave a higher respect and more cheerful obedience to their officers. Still, the old boy has not carried all the "old discipline" overboard with him, as we have seen, in the unnecessarily restricted right of visiting the shore.

At the time we left the United States, the supply of midshipmen had been exhausted, and neither the San Jacinto, Portsmouth, nor Levant had any, and the men were necessarily trusted to themselves in the boats, without any one to watch, to irritate and annoy them. The results were so favorable that it excited comment and remark among our English associates, and believing it to be a system of our service, they expressed a wish that it could be adopted in theirs.

At length came the 29th of January, 1858, and with it ended my relations with the San Jacinto and China. The fine steamer Ottawa, surrounded by boats, and pouring a volume of smoke from her pipe, was ready for her departure on the homeward trip at 2 P. M. At 11 A. M. the broad pennant of Cómmodore Armstrong came down with a parting salute, and when he took his departure, the ships manned their yards and cheered their late commander-in-chief.

As I stepped on board the Ottawa, there was a welcome of home in the very name. It spoke of my past wanderings around our great lakes. There it would have been in keeping, but what had our western, Indian, sonorous-sounding names to do with these Asiatic cruisings? The boat, like myself, was a Fankwei, a wanderer from the waters of the St. Lawrence. It seemed almost at once to transport me to the great interests of our new world, and the grand social and political problems there being worked out, dwarfing our man-of-war existence and interests, and reducing our stormy contests to tempests in tea-pots. One wonders that he has ever permitted squabbles and heart-burnings about class privileges, artificial distinctions and rival decorations, which have no relation to the noble institutions of his country, and only a shipboard importance, to lessen his true manliness, and make him almost false to the nobility of his American citizenship, and he sees then, with respect and esteem, the worthy, noble and good qualities of associates which may have been obscured in a mist of artificial and official relationship.

It may, perhaps, be well that we have so few incentives to "getting on" in the ways of war so many inducements to remember with pride that we are citizens of a country whose grandest influences are found in the ways of peace and humanity, and to which we return and cling with strengthened affection.

With the sailing of the Ottawa ended my career as a

FANKWEI.

CPSIA information can be obtained
at www.ICGtesting.com
Printed in the USA
LVHW041628060123
736479LV00001B/187

9 783375 128562